Praise for

AND THE SKY BLED

"*And the Sky Bled* is a book that grabs you by the shoulders, stares into your eyes, and does not let go until the end. It's set in a fascinating, deeply built world that explores extractive colonialism and the resultant environmental devastation, but does so through the very human experiences of its characters. It's an intricate tangle of histories and relationships—loss, guilt, regret, hope, survival, and the shifting balance of power. It's a book that asks "What now?" and then answers: "Now we find a way to move on." —Moniquill Blackgoose, author of national bestseller *To Shape a Dragon's Breath*, a *Washington Post* and *NPR* Best Book of the Year

"*And the Sky Bled* is a dazzlingly original, epic, and totally blood-soaked fantasy not for the faint of heart. The dying, dystopian city of Tejomaya and the three intersecting stories of its desperate antiheroes took my breath away. A fresh addition to the fantasy genre! Hati is certainly a writer to watch." —Esmie Jikiemi-Pearson, *Sunday Times* bestselling author of *The Principle of Moments*

"The desperation of the characters leaps off the page. A new addition to the genre, this book explores themes of survival and revolution in refreshingly new and interesting ways." —Marvellous Michael Anson, author of *Firstborn of the Sun*

"A remarkable debut! *And the Sky Bled* does what an excellent fantasy novel should: it forces readers to confront the powers, politics, and pitfalls of their own world by plunging them into a magical one." —Hannah Gordon (@hngisreading), BookTok influencer

"This dark tale of power, loyalty, and a world on the brink of destruction pulls you in, holds on tight, and refuses to let go." —Jaysen Headley (@ezeekat), global top 5 BookTok influencer

"*And the Sky Bled* is exactly what fantasy is meant to be: powerful and emblematic of the catastrophes we face globally. The characters' brutal and raw determination to survive pours off the page, and Hati's talent for world-building is undeniable. This was excellent!" —Azanta Thakur (@azantareads), book influencer

"*And the Sky Bled* is a powerful fantasy debut that sucks you in immediately to a devastating world filled to the brim with corruption and desperation. Hati weaves a captivating story of survival and power, and it leaves you raw yet still hopeful. Consider me obsessed!" —Basma (@bookishbasma), book influencer

"An intimate study of power and revolution in a magical, ferocious world. Hati's riveting prose and reimagining of South Asian culture form a thrilling climate fantasy that left me on the edge of my seat." —Ayushi (@bookwormbullet), book influencer

"An evocative and timely tale of climate and colonialism filled with high stakes and compelling characters. This searing debut immediately found a place on my favorites shelf." —Taz Hossain (@tazisbooked), book influencer

AND THE
SKY BLED

AND THE SKY BLED

S. HATI

Published by Fantasy & Frens, an imprint of
Bindery Books, Inc., San Francisco
www.binderybooks.com

Acquired by Zoranne Host

Edited and designed by Girl Friday Productions
www.girlfridayproductions.com

Cover illustration: Cat O'Neil
Cover design (paperback): Charlotte Strick and Paul Barrett
Cover design (hardcover): Charlotte Strick
Image credit (hardcover): Sea fan coral © Somdul Pienroj / Alamy Stock Photo

ISBN (paperback): 978-1-959411-68-0
ISBN (hardcover): 978-1-959411-90-1
ISBN (ebook): 978-1-959411-69-7

Library of Congress Cataloguing-in-Publication data has been applied for.

First edition

This is a work of fiction. Names, characters, places, and incidents are
either the product of the author's imagination or are used fictitiously and
not to be construed as real. Any resemblance to actual persons, living
or dead, organizations, events, or locales is entirely coincidental.

For my parents

CHAPTER ONE

Zain

The bloodstrippers were on a hunt.

Zain peered over the sodden brick wall, scowling as uniformed guards filled her vision. The coarse scarf wrapped around her mouth had grown pungent from sweat. Souls, it was hot, but the sheen of moisture coating her skin was as much a result of her bundled nerves as the oppressive heat.

Next to her, Bilal let out a low laugh as Zain shoved his head out of view. His rumpled gray shirt fit loosely now, but the recent sedentary months hadn't taken away from his considerable height. Zain wasn't certain the guards patrolling the town square would mistake the top of Bilal's unshorn head for the city's usual grime. She'd rather not risk it.

Bilal sank lower to the ground. "Been a while since we did this, huh?"

"Six months and twenty-seven days," she replied, flatly. That's how long it had been since the blood rains fell, and she had been naive enough to hope that everyone else would be as out of practice as she was. No such luck. The drought had lasted longer than anyone anticipated, and Zain might be the only person in the world who hated that it was about to end.

The drought meant she could stay indoors and avoid the monsters prowling her streets. It meant she could dream of a different life—taste it, touch it, see it. Just yesterday, she had been helping her guardians with Temple and housework, weaving clothes from plant stalks and coaxing a garden from their barren yard. Over half a year of the closest thing she had known to peace, only to be plunged back into the place she hated most.

No, not the place. It was this job she hated. The job, the people, the cold bite of the gun strapped to her trousers. And the Gehennese bloodstrippers patrolling the square, their inky livery like mold on the dull-brown hues of Tejomaya.

"We better get moving," Bilal said. "We're running late. Who knows when we'll get another chance? I say we ditch the harbor and move farther out to the corner turbines."

The rains hadn't fallen yet, but they were inevitable. Zain knew that as soon as she looked up at the ocher sky. The sight never ceased to chill her to the bone.

The entire sky was veined like a putrid corpse, spindly red lines stretching across its shadowy-gray flesh. The vessels convalesced into a grotesque fissure that stretched from above the Tejomayan harbor to the Isle of Vis, a long-lost piece of the city now a small island across the Soulless Sea. For six months and twenty-seven days, the rift had remained stagnant, but it turned out the sky had life in it still. She could swear it throbbed, the gaping wound preparing for release. Its serrated edges carved the rift clean from the rest of the heavens, its crimson maw the source of calor—the substance that fueled the world. And below the tear in the sky lay the bane of her existence, the Isle of Vis, with its jagged lines, like the teeth of a leech that sucked the sky dry.

Zain was a leech too.

She shuffled onto her knees, glancing over the top of the wall once more. Two bloodstrippers congregated by the giant brass city bells, right in the middle of the courtyard, between the town square and the sprawling harbor to the south. Gold filigree emblems were inscribed on the guards' breast pockets, indicative of rank and national affiliation. One she couldn't identify, but the other she could trace blindfolded: twin pillars entwined within a crown of nascent leaves. He was a member of the Gehennese force and, from the small size of his insignia, new to the battalion. Probably eager to make an arrest and drag her by her thick braid to earn his laurels.

"Fine, let's go," she said, reluctantly. The harbor was an easy spot for calor theft. There were so many turbine facilities that if the leeches got there early enough, they'd usually find at least one without its allotted number of guards. Today, they were too late.

"Cheer up, Zainy," Bilal said. He'd been calling her that since they'd become friends at the age of seven over a fierce game of hopscotch. The round had ended with their spit-covered palms clasped together, vowing to expel Zain's bully from the group. The nickname persisted despite her attempts at keeping Bilal, and everyone else from those days, at arm's length. "I promise this will be fun. On three?"

Zain shot him an exasperated look, which he returned with a mischievous smile. They'd never waited till three. Before either could start the count, they darted toward the nearest alley, Bilal chuckling as he rounded the first corner after her.

"One day, I'll beat you," he said, looping an arm through hers.

She cracked a smile despite the sick feeling brewing in her stomach. "Keep trying."

On either side of the narrow street were brick and sandstone buildings piled on top of each other, like a child had built them with blocks of clay. They ducked beneath scalloped archways, past chipped staircases and doors splashed with long-faded colors. The city's close quarters used to be their playground; when they were young, they would turn its labyrinth into a game, see who could make it across the street by hopping from stair to stair, who could scale the pair of minarets that guarded the entrance to the courtyard. Zain had skipped down this alley countless times, teeming with excitement when she spotted the uneven rows of ocean-blue tiling on the mechanic store's walls.

Now, as they entered through the shop's battened doors, she felt nothing but dread. A faint, exhausted bell jingled.

"We're here!" Bilal bellowed.

As he barged in, Zain lingered behind, tugging at the loose sleeves of her beige kurta. Nothing here had changed. The inside was warm and crowded; to Zain's right were a pair of hand-painted almirahs flung open to reveal shelves stocked with strange curios and trinkets. Across from them was a long cabinet scattered with tools. It smelled like metal shavings and damp wood, tinged with hints of a recent meal. An old man sat across the sal wood counter, already scrutinizing. Already judging.

"I was waiting to see if you lot would come in," he said, retrieving a burlap bag from below the table. "A little late, aren't you? Good to see you, Zain. I wasn't sure if you were still working with us."

Despite his gruff tone, Yadav smiled, and a wave of fondness came over Zain.

"What can I say, I love having my partner back," Bilal said, nudging her shoulder.

She rolled her eyes. "Someone needs to do it."

No, *she* needed to do it. Or she would have to answer to *him*.

The calor she stole from the Gehennese kept the people of Tejomaya afloat. Centuries ago, calor deposits were found all around the world, and the calor revolution saw rapid advancements in their ability to extract the sky's own ichor. The substance was civilization's lifeline; it powered their lights and transportation and helped manufacture everything from cosmetics and fragrances to the bullets in their guns. Its presence in soil fertilizer did miracles for their harvests. During the peak of calor research, over a hundred years ago, various groups demonstrated its healing properties, and calor's medical value ricocheted into the stratosphere.

Then, they realized calor could steal life just as quickly as it gave it. Extended physical contact proved lethal; Bilal once subjected her to weeks of nightmares from stories of people's brains exploding from touching calor for too long. But protective equipment was developed, and calor consumption continued with renewed fervor.

It was impossible to believe now, since the sky above most countries had been mined and depleted well before Zain's twenty-three years of existence. Today, no one could access the skies for calor; its flesh was dry as a prune, shriveled. For the last fifty years, calor had been found in one place and one place alone: the blood rains of Tejomaya.

Yadav nodded. "I hope this will help matters, the souls have been harsh to us these last six months. Bilal keeps complaining about food, and I'm this close to feeding him mud."

"It's true," Bilal agreed. "All this dry rice is not enough for my muscles. I've lost all my weight!"

Zain pursed her lips. People had fallen sick during the drought, and without rain to replenish their calor supplies, they could not be treated. Food rations were dwindling and homes were faced with depleted energy, worsening an already harrowing situation. Guilt festered within her.

Yadav pushed two waist bags toward them, his touch kinder than she deserved. She secured one to the other side of her adapted holster, fingers tracing the vials that lay within the jute bag. She wanted to put her head inside it and scream, smother her airways so she could capture her pain in the smallest of places, but nothing was capable of holding it.

"Be careful," Yadav said. "Too many new bloodstrippers recently. They'll have enough bodies to watch all the turbines. Can't count on many being left unguarded."

Bilal secured his supplies to his person. "I miss the days we didn't have turbines."

"You weren't alive," Zain deadpanned. The turbines were more of a recent invention, spurred by the blood rains, but she and Bilal had been born after they'd been devised.

"But I can imagine it," Bilal said, holding his hand out for dramatic effect. "Flying, sucking calor out of the sky, none of this battling over turbines. They're so damn loud too."

Now, most of the rains were funneled through pipes and into turbines in holding facilities. Some rains did inevitably fall on land, but not enough to make a difference, and ground-siphoning tools were less effective.

Yadav leveled a look of vexation at Zain, one she used to be quick to return. *Good luck with this guy,* he'd say, and she'd laugh. This time, though, she averted her gaze, shrinking away from the friendly exchange.

"Come on," she said, tugging at Bilal's arm. "Let's go."

Bilal's obnoxious farewell to Yadav—something about his being a hero sent off to war—faded as they stepped into a city caught in a hushed breath. Above them, the sky pulsed in warning. No black uniforms to be seen.

When everyone else hid, the leeches emerged.

"You go west, I go east?" she murmured

Bilal nodded. "Watch your back."

With that, they parted ways.

She slid between the narrow copper walls down the nearest pathway, cursing as her feet pounded the ground. No matter how hard she tried, she could never achieve the lynxlike grace of other leeches. Her body was too wide, her hair an unruly mass of curls that flew everywhere, and the rolls on her stomach fought against the holster belt. As she raced up the hilly streets of the merchant district, also known as the Hammer, the sharp smell of metal pierced the air. Zain clamped her lips together, trying to inhale through her nose as she continued her ascent.

The first time she smelled the rusty scent of the Tejomayan showers, felt the thickness of the blood rains coating her fingertips, she had rushed to the nearest dumpster and exorcised her lunch. The nausea hadn't improved once she became a leech to steal the rains. In her new role, she and Bilal devised a plan of attack, a continuing rotation of turbines to target. What she lacked in stealth, she made up for in speed and a near-perfect memory of every nook and cranny the Gehennese used to hoard each last bit of calor. She and Bilal would move long before the rains started and be gone before anyone arrived. But after six months and twenty-seven days of bone-dry turbines, they had been too late to execute their well-rehearsed routine. Not to mention the unexpected bloodstrippers in the courtyard.

Zain moved east, much farther than she would normally care to venture. She was dangerously close to the Sickle, a disputed territory between the slums and the Gehennese, but the area had been quieter since the drought. Hopefully, it stayed that way, because there was a set of old turbines tucked into a filthy corner, one of the few that hadn't been locked away. She was certain the Gehennese had forgotten about it when they last tightened security around the turbines a decade ago.

She scanned the main road. No guards. Her mouth curved in satisfaction as she spotted the tops of the turbines peeking out from the side of the building.

Then, the sky rumbled in warning.

Souls, she had mistimed it all. Zain looked desperately for shelter. All around her, the alleyways were bare. She faced the barren back of a building; any doors were on the other side, likely locked. She wouldn't make it in time.

Another thunderous sound, and then she heard it. A sonorous purge.

Zain threw her body under the broken eaves that skirted the building, heart pounding from the close call. Her back scraped against the wall in an attempt to avoid contact with the downpour, and she tried not to think of how the rains sounded like muted gunfire. The concrete before her turned red with its casualties.

Six months and twenty-seven days hadn't been long enough.

CHAPTER TWO

Zain

Zain's muscles cramped like a bitch by the time the air settled into its regular shade of sickly orange.

She let loose a breath, assessing the street in each direction before heading toward the turbines. There was no real chance of anyone outside at this time; no one walked in the rain. Not only was long-term exposure deadly, but it was also disrespectful, especially at this time of year. The Anniversary of the Carnage—the day Tejomaya had been conquered by the Gehennese, leaving a vicious rift in the sky—was only ten days away.

She succumbed to the spell of old and familiar routine. Zain hooked up the first glass vial to the turbine and cranked the lever, watching the machine groan to life and fill the tube with processed calor, pale yellow once separated from blood. Disgusting. All this ruin and war and misery over something that resembled piss. It was even warm as she slid the full vial into her pocket and hooked up a new one. To her despair, the flow sputtered.

Already? This was far less than she'd expected, less than he would want.

Surely the others would have just as much trouble at their collection points. Souls, this had better fill her quota. Zain's knuckles whitened as she thought of what he might do if it wasn't enough.

Panic fluttered in her throat. He wanted so much from Zain but he couldn't expect her to unlock the sky. For nine years, she had been under his thumb, bringing him his personal stash of calor without anyone knowing. The drought had gifted her freedom, a world without him, but suddenly she was back to square one. Her pathetic breakfast of stale bread threatened to make a reappearance. Maybe she could take some calor for herself, maybe she could trade it at the underground market, buy her guardians and herself a ticket out of here, maybe—

A hand clamped around her wrist, another over her mouth.

A low voice whispered, "I don't think you want to touch that."

She hadn't heard anyone come up behind her. But of course not. Who could hear over these ancient machines?

She had been overconfident, so desperate to get this over with so she could return home. Zain rolled in her captor's grip, surprised when he didn't resist, coming chest to chest with a man not much taller than she.

It was the Gehennese bloodstripper from the square.

Zain took in his olive skin and green eyes, the firm set of his jaw against his honey-brown hair. Venomous features she had spent her entire life avoiding. She had never been caught before, had foolishly lived the kind of existence that precluded her from imagining such a situation, since she had never been—despite all efforts to learn and train—a fighter. Zain wasn't particularly brave or reckless, but she was a master at crafting a reality that never involved being arrested.

"Stop it," he said. *Hit them with your head,* her guardian

Samiah would tell her, but Samiah and her nonexistent fighting experience clearly hadn't anticipated a time when Zain's head was also being restrained. She kicked out and fell backward, the bloodstripper landing on top of her as they let out identical shrieks. A loud clatter as her gun skid uselessly to the side, just out of reach.

Spectacular.

He didn't waste a second in pressing his advantage, pinning his knees around her chest.

"Please," she whispered, but Zain couldn't think beyond the weight of this man on her body, his hand on her mouth. She couldn't move, couldn't breathe. The world closed in on her, a world she couldn't see because of her tears distorting its edges. So damn foolish. She would never see her guardians again, never get to thank them for all they had done for her.

All because of one man, who had trapped her as a child, costing her everything. Fury burned through her veins.

The man let go of her mouth and she let out a strangled shout. He slapped her.

The sting shattered her mind. He was panting, his head haloed against the violet sky so his skin looked like it was on fire. It was hot, far too hot in Tejomaya, and even hotter underneath him.

"Listen to me!" he yelled, and the souls must have doomed her because she actually did. "The calor," the bloodstripper continued. "Do you have more of it?"

Zain shook her head, too afraid to speak. But then she remembered, she did have some. A vial tucked into her pocket. It pressed into her stomach, just above where the man's thigh cut across her body.

"One will do for now," he murmured, looking to the turbine

where her abandoned vial lay, its paltry contents a nauseating yellow. She realized he was *loosening* his grip on her, lost in thought. *Move, you idiot.* But her body wrestled against chains of fear. Her chance was slipping away, the end of the rope held between the tips of her fingers.

Just as the bloodstripper refocused on her, Zain yanked her arm out from under his leg and pulled out the vial of calor. Without taking a second to think, she smashed it against his ear.

He tilted off her with a cry of anguish, and she rushed to her feet quicker than the time the Temple bully had chased her with a vat of steaming water. She had been caught then and had the burns on her back to show for it. Zain refused to be caught again.

She didn't stop to see whether the glass shattered or what the raw calor did to his flesh. She was off, curving around the corner with the kind of speed only fear could fuel. The bloodstripper called after her, but her world had taken on the sharp focus of prey escaping imminent danger.

Zain dove deeper into the city. No matter how Tejomaya's hills squeezed her of air, it would be worse for him. Zain had grown up running through these streets, and with every turn and lift in its terrain, she knew he would not be able to follow. Each corner of her city held places to hide.

The Gehennese viewed Tejomaya as an opportunity, a place they could bend and mold with their oily palms while they stole calor from the sky. Maybe they had succeeded to a certain extent. After all, the island and the edges of the harbor were the only places that received the blood rains, and the Gehennese had claimed those parts, well and truly. But Tejomayans knew the city was as alive as the people in it. They knew the city's heart, with its intricate innards and throbbing vessels, was just as valuable, if not more, than the one etched across the sky.

Zain was a rat, a leech, a forgotten child; she belonged to the creatures who claimed the slums and its sprawling network as home, and the city returned her affection tenfold. It was a city that rewarded survival.

The streets molded her path, guiding her to the broader avenues that made up the Bow, home to the wealthy and privileged. As she approached a large granite home on an intersection, she caught no sign of the bloodstripper. And if the reliable echoes of the alley ways were any indication, no one was pursuing her. Still, she had to move out of sight, process the evening's occurrences somewhere safe.

She let out a low laugh. She had assaulted a Geng, as most locals crudely referred to the Gehennese. A bloodstripper at that. Safety no longer existed for her—at least, not out here. Zain squatted on the pavement to give her sore legs some reprieve.

If only she didn't have to show up to the slums to report on her lousy day, but she wasn't planning on making her miserable life even worse. Zain straightened to leave, then heard the unmistakable sound of footsteps.

CHAPTER THREE

Zain

Zain froze.

"... don't know where it is, okay? Now can we discuss the Anniversary? I want to make sure the package exchange happens before then."

It was pure atavistic instinct that she dove into the shadows in time. *Listen,* the walls hummed.

"I don't have much time left," someone replied. It was hard to make out what they were saying; their voice was scratchy, and she could detect a light accent. A Gehennese accent, but it wasn't the bloodstripper who'd caught her. The stranger added, "He said to expect a messenger at the harbor two days before the Anniversary. Here's some to tide you over until then—he'll throw in extra if you provide a location."

"This is sufficient," the man replied, and that's when she knew. Every hair on her body stood up. Zain didn't need to see his face to imagine what he looked like—jaw clenched, mouth curved into a perpetual sneer. She could practically see him tapping his ringed fingers against his gun, and there it was, that faint metal clicking. "And as I've told you before, I don't have a location. But you certainly don't look too well, Councilmember Dheera. The city's grown as allergic to you as you to it."

Zain scrambled to make sense of what she was hearing. *He was here, speaking with a councilmember.* This was brazen, even for him.

Slumlords did not meet with councilmembers in dark alleyways.

"It's you lot that are the disease," Dheera replied, indignantly, then coughed like it had cost her something. "But let's stay focused on what matters here. This deal is important—it would benefit both our people in the long run."

Zain placed her fingertips to the ground to steady herself.

"Oh, I haven't forgotten," he replied. She could hear him smile, the kind he reserved for moments of victory. "How unfortunate you won't live to see it through."

Their voices waned as they moved away from her hiding spot. Zain warred with the urge to follow them, but damn it, she had to get back to the slums, especially before he did. His dalliance with Councilmember Dheera was precious time, and time was a gift that came to her sparingly. She got to her feet and raced.

From up on the knolls, the slums looked like a sprawling anthill, a black mass on burnished land. It had been six months since Zain had been here and felt the crush of the heat from hundreds of thousands of people—nearly three-quarters of Tejomaya's population—crammed into what started as a thin slice of the city. In just that time, the perimeter had expanded, adding shanty homes made of wood and corrugated metal next to more permanent brick-and-mortar conglomerates. No calor meant more people without jobs, without homes, without anywhere else to go.

The slums would take them all. Many turned their noses up

at this last resort, complaining about the stench of sweat and leaking sewage and the way it was never quiet. Bilal used to say the din was the slums groaning with the weight of so many, its back depressed from each new inhabitant.

But Zain was accustomed to coming here and being consumed whole by a thriving community. Zain had seen children tear across the makeshift pathways, dodging shafts of bamboo sunk deep into the damp land. She'd heard the camaraderie as people helped a new family get settled in, smelled the food someone was cooking from spare ingredients to share with their neighbors. She wasn't sure why she'd imagined it had stayed the same, waiting steadfast for her return.

She could hardly see or hear a soul now. Like the slums had let out its final gasp.

A painful disorientation shook Zain as she followed the path to the meeting point. Here, past Mahini's timber hut with the chipped front door, where she'd be forced to eat jalebis or fried rice before finding the other leeches. She weaved past the famed row of entrepreneurs, who'd had to move and adapt their businesses when the Gengs bought out their homes from under their noses. Their jobs used to be in calor-heavy industries, but they were now potters, cooks, and textile makers, doing the best they could with clay, grass, and other materials available to them. Their ingenuity formed the backbone of an area discarded by the rest of the city.

As she drew closer to the center, sounds of life grew. No one was in their homes because they were here, and she'd arrived in the worst fashion possible: late and empty-handed.

All the leeches were there, mingling with other denizens, chatting about the downpour. Bilal and Yadav sat up front, engaged in a heated discussion next to two empty wooden stools, one tilting on a broken leg. Zain collapsed at the back, taking in the excited swirl. The rain had inspired hope. Everyone was talking about what it could mean for the new sewage recycling system the dons had been working on, or if they could finally muster enough power to cool the healer quarters. But there was an unmistakable tension too. Whispers about how much calor they'd gotten, if it would be enough.

Zain's empty hands were so cold.

"Zain?"

She fisted her bloodstained tunic as two figures fell to the seats on either side of her. To her left was Gayathri, Bilal's sister, her dark-brown hair cropped to her chin, much shorter than Zain had remembered it. With her was Laila, Mahini's fourteen-year-old daughter, who beamed at her like she was the sun come to shine at last.

"Bilal told me you were out there today," Gayathri said, dusting her hands on her wide-legged pants. "But I needed to see it for myself. Zain Jatav, in the flesh. It's been almost a year!"

While her tone was warm, possessing the compassion associated with the slum's most prominent healer, the accusation was just as noticeable. Zain hadn't seen anyone in the slums in the past half year. And it had been the best time of her life.

"It's felt like forever," Laila cried, wrapping her bony arms around Zain.

Zain shuddered as the pronounced edges of Laila's ribs dug into her belly.

"I didn't realize you'd missed me," Zain tried to joke, but her delivery was flat. She put a hairbreadth of distance between her and Laila. "I've been busy at home, helping with Temple work during the drought."

"How are Kanak and Samiah?" Gayathri asked, referring to Zain's guardians.

Something in Zain's chest warmed at their mention. She could tell Gayathri and Laila about the meager garden she and Kanak had managed to cultivate in their desolate backyard. About uncovering a new way of processing flax plant stalks without calor, to help Samiah weave her new line of kurtas. Or about the times the three of them had scouted sites for the new Temple, and Zain imagined the rough touch of its walls against her skin, cool and impossible to burn, unlike its wooden predecessor.

She could tell them it hadn't mattered that one yield was all they'd achieved, that there were no plants to harvest, and that rebuilding the Temple had been ruled out due to the prolonged calor shortage. It was the closest she had been to Kanak in a decade.

But it was too intimate, even with people she once considered friends. Her renewed relationship with Kanak had blossomed only because she had left the slums behind, and even though Gayathri and Laila were neither henchmen nor leeches, they were still part of that past.

"Good," Zain said.

Gayathri gave her a knowing look before taking in the blood on Zain's clothes and the tension in her fists. It was well known that Zain's guardians did not approve of the work she had been doing all these years. As if she'd had a choice.

"I miss Kanak's roti," Laila complained. "Can you bring me some like you used to?"

Zain gave Laila a noncommittal nod. She wasn't sure what was harder to face—Laila's hope or Gayathri's sharp appraisal. She asked, "How's Lufi?"

As predicted, Laila's face twisted at the mention of her four-year-old sister. "Annoying as always, she has this doll that needs to go *everywhere* with her. At least she's stopped asking for my pendant." Laila fiddled with the beautiful sapphire necklace around her neck, a precious heirloom from her grandmother, then perked up. "She asks about you all the time. You should come to dinner tomorrow!"

Zain's stomach heaved. "I don't know, I might be busy. I'm only here for work today."

Laila pouted. "But Mama got cardamom and mustard seeds! She spent the last week getting expiring vegetables from Thoro's stall. She's making vindaloo."

With proper spices? From where?

Gayathri added, "It's true. We just got spices, grains, lentils. Dev told us we would be shocked, but I hadn't believed the delivery would be so large. I thought I'd died and ascended."

Hearing his name was like being dunked in a frigid bath. "Is that so?"

Laila nodded proudly, smoothing out the creases of her frock. "It's been bad. I've had to eat old leaves for weeks. Do you know it makes my gums bleed?" She pulled a face, as though she was describing an ugly dress rather than the effects of starvation. "Mama said with no rain, no calor, there's no other food. But not with Dev around."

"I don't know who that man sells his soul to," Gayathri said, shaking her head.

Zain did. She had seen the devil herself.

They chattered on, telling her about how Mahini had gone to Dev worried about Laila coming down with a fever and shivering despite the insurmountable heat in their hut. How Gayathri had noticed malnutrition across the slums skyrocketing, had watched as their scant medical equipment broke down from a lack of calor. A bounty of food may be a temporary balm, but Dev had delivered it when they'd needed it most. Their eyes shone like stars, yet all Zain felt were the claws of dread sinking into her skin.

"That's wonderful," she managed to get out. This wasn't worth it, sitting here, nodding like a puppet. This was precisely why she didn't come here anymore. It was better to leave, better to face her punishment later, when she could at least wear an honest face—

"I thought I was going to see my workers, not a fucking classroom." The voice was thick and gritty, like nails on rock.

Two men emerged and stood next to Bilal. Iravan Khotar wore a loose blue shirt that stretched across his broad frame, sleeves rolled up to his elbows, and black trousers adorned with two shiny pistols. His dark hair was long and unkempt, like he had just awoken, but Zain knew he had likely been raking through it while stressing over calor. The man next to him who had spoken was slenderer, with black hair slicked back. Where Iravan wore a constant look of sorrow, Devraj Basu smirked like he was mocking the world beneath his feet. The black metal on Dev's fingers glistened from a distance.

A storm of emotions swept Zain away while everyone around her jumped into action, shouting about reports and supplies. Laila yelled something in Zain's ear before dashing off, but she couldn't recall what was said. She couldn't feel her extremities. She knew what she was supposed to do: join the other leeches in telling Dev that no, she did not have any calor for him that day, and not only that, she had been compromised. Seen by a guard.

Heard him dealing with a Geng councilmember.

An itch grew under her skin.

"Stop," Gayathri said, stilling her hand. Zain looked down to see she had scratched away a patch of her skin, seedlings of blood shooting up. Then, ever so subtly, the healer stretched an arm toward her, fingers closed in a fist. She pushed it into Zain's side and released something. A vial of calor.

"Bilal left one behind in our hut," Gayathri said, casually. "Take it."

Zain resisted the urge to snatch it up. "Won't he notice?"

Gayathri chuckled. "You know he can't count to save his life."

"How did he even get that much?" Zain asked. She'd barely gotten a vial's worth from her useless turbines.

Gayathri shrugged, "He broke into one of the advanced turbine holding cells. Said he got lucky, found two junior bloodstrippers on guard and was able to knock them out. Take it, he'll be fine."

Zain's throat thickened with emotion, but no words of gratitude came out. She wondered if the healer knew. If she understood why Zain had stopped visiting her, why it was still too difficult to be there. But Gayathri only patted Zain on the leg and declared that she had patients to see.

Despite the swarm of people, Zain felt more alone than she had in a long time.

"Not enough," Iravan said, gruffly, his head sinking into his hands after counting the last vials. A hush had fallen, punctured by the clink of glass as each drop of stolen calor was measured for its worth. Anyone who wasn't a leech had left or drifted to the periphery, united by an undercurrent of desperation.

The slums had been dangerously low on calor even before the drought, the intricate ecosystem Iravan and Dev had built a smidge away from falling apart. All eyes would be on these last dregs of calor. Would they choose whose kitchens to power?

Purify the water in communal areas? Or would it go to Gayathri and the healers to develop medicines?

Was survival possible when you were choosing between necessities?

Dev sucked his teeth. "Disappointing, but not surprising. Good thing I got my hands on nearly three times as much yesterday."

Silence, then an uproar.

"The ceiling is leaking, we need to upgrade the roofs before it rains again—"

"The *sewage* is leaking. It smells like shit outside our door—"

"At least sewage won't kill you, jackass, but lie in that toxic blood too long and your pretty little head might explode—"

"How the fuck did you *find* all that calor—"

Dev raised a hand, a demonic conductor, and the violent orchestra stopped as quickly as it had started. The energy of the silence metamorphized into a parasitic hope. Miraculous Dev to the rescue once more. Their issues absolved. His tainted calor would do nothing, Zain wanted to scream. It would only delay the inevitable.

"I cannot keep doing your jobs," Dev warned, his tone switching. The words were a steel blade running featherlight against her throat. "You're right. We need to fix the sewers and the roofs, find more food and water. People can't live in tents when it's raining. Calor toxicity will kill us before hunger does. We need more, and you're all going to have to pull your damn weight. This showing"—he spat at the meager pile of vials next to him—"is pathetic."

Iravan stood abruptly, as though to remind everyone of his presence. "Bilal, take two men and scout out the Sickle this evening. The rest of you, pick guards of your choice."

Dev continued. "The new squads are positioned by the harbor; they're tired from the journey. They'll be transporting their supplies by boat tomorrow night. Should be easy targets even for you lot, and you've got a day to prepare."

Zain's head snapped up at this piece of intel.

"And cover your heads. I don't need this shit coming back to bite us in the ass because they remember one of your ugly faces," Dev said. "I need double what we have now."

A murmur of unease went through the crowd. Maintaining the little peace they had with the bloodstrippers was a terrible but necessary curse; they would never have resorted to robbing the guards' boats before the drought, but that was the state of things.

Maybe the issue of the guard that had caught her would be resolved this way. She imagined his body floating in the waters, lifeless green eyes staring up at the torn sky.

"I knew we went too easy on you all during the drought," Dev said. "It stopped raining and you all became a bunch of cocksuckers. Are we making ourselves clear?"

This time, the response was an explicit yes. The air turned brittle as the group fractured into more familiar pieces: Gayathri over by her apprentices, discussing the status of their latest patients. One sobbing woman pulling Iravan by the arm, screaming about her sick son. Leeches huddling to decide how they were going to meet their quotas. Before, Zain had had her place with them, but then she'd been chosen to be special. Chosen to be different.

As he always did, Dev found her in the crowd. Instinctively, her shoulders curved forward, but there was nowhere to hide. He walked away from the slums, and Zain followed.

She already knew where they were going. He liked to twist the knife, see her face drop at the sight of the Temple of Many-Souls, burned to ashes. The city had darkened over time, but there was something about this area, tucked between the wealthy Bow and the slums, that made her stomach roll.

A dilapidated chawl hovered like a hung skeleton over a coffin of ruins, and a modestly sized hut sat beside it. An empty chair rocked outside the closed door, cigarette butts rolling under its legs. Iravan's home. But he wasn't there at the time. No one was.

"So, Z, what have you got for me?" Dev asked, as he came to a standstill.

Zain's hand trembled as she retrieved the vial. The initial relief of Gayathri's gift was overwhelmed by the heart-wrenching reality that this, as everything else she did, would be a disappointment.

As she held her hand out, a shadow darkened his face.

"I'm working on getting more," Zain hurried to say. Her kurta fought against her unsettled stomach. She flinched as Dev stepped forward, and his face flickered as though she had struck him.

He cupped her cheek, his rings icy on her flesh. "I wish you weren't so frightened all the time," he said, cocking his head. "You haven't disappointed me. I have other sources."

Oh, she knew all about his sources. His meeting with the councilmember was as fresh in her mind as the rains, but the accusations she wanted to levy caught in her throat. By the souls, she wished she were the kind of girl who could demand the truth from him, but that version of Zain lived only in her head. She wanted to push him off, walk away for good, but her rigid body was an insurmountable force. Zain hated the way she relaxed a little at his touch. She hated that the first thing she felt upon hearing the softness of his concern was a need to please.

That was the thing she still did not understand about herself. How her body and mind could war with one another and be positioned on both sides of the battle. The child who had met Dev, hungry to be seen and accepted, had at least been whole. Zain, at twenty-three, was a piece of every person she had been, except she hadn't grown the way people normally did, gradually. She had been turned violently, each facet broken and put together again, her insides hardwired against herself. She wanted to thank him, she wanted to vomit. Her skin burned at his touch, and she wished she could scream.

"I want five vials by the Anniversary," Dev said. "And you'll join the raids tomorrow night."

Zain's blood ran cold. Dev had never given her a deadline like this, but then . . .

Now can we discuss the Anniversary? I want to make sure the package exchange happens before then.

Did this have anything to do with his conversation from earlier? No, she couldn't worry about that, not when she had only ever been able to deliver two vials, maybe three after a healthy downpour. The Anniversary of the Carnage, commemorating the formation of the rift in the sky, was in a little over a week. Who knew when it would rain again?

"I thought you said you had enough," she said, pathetically.

His smile slid off his face, and his hand settled around her neck. He bent down until his lips brushed her ear. "Oh, but it's so much more fun when it comes from you. Our little secrets make you such an obedient pet."

His grip tightened, just enough for her breath to catch. This was his admission and his warning, that he held the strings to her life like a master puppeteer. If he pulled the curtain on her sins, he may as well sign her death sentence.

Suddenly, he let go. Someone had called her name.

Kanak approached from behind, dressed in a long olive-green kurta that cinched at their waist before flowing down to their ankles. Their favorite cotton-handled bag, embroidered by Samiah, was tucked into their side, clutched tightly as they drew closer to Dev and Zain.

"Out for a little walk, Kanak?" Dev asked, smiling at the aco-lyte who had adopted Zain when she was five.

"You know I like coming by the Temple, Devraj," Kanak said crisply, their hand interlacing with Zain's. "I wasn't expecting to see you here, so close to the Bow."

Dev dipped his head, but there was no semblance of respect in the gesture. "Why not? It's home to so many wonderful people, such as yourself. And I've always loved visiting the Temple. There is something . . . comforting about its ashes."

A phantom heat suffocated Zain. Fire lashed against her skin, then withered to gray. She scratched her palms, wanting to get the soot *off off off*.

Kanak squeezed Zain's hand three times, bringing her sharply back to reality. It was their code, Kanak's way of asking *Are you okay?* after noticing how Zain had turned to stone. Zain returned the gesture, but her grip was weak as she followed her guardian away from Dev, who was undoubtedly furious at the interruption. She would pay for it later, and despite Kanak's presence, Zain sensed the edges of her life distinctly.

That was the thing about men like Dev. They could make you feel unsafe in the safest of places. There was nowhere she could go where he could not follow.

While Zain braced for questions, Kanak, as always, surprised her.

"I traded some of our grains for these today," they said, holding out a hand. Green seeds rolled in their dry palm.

Zain hesitated before responding. "What are they?"

"Roses," Kanak replied.

It was an indulgence, and they both knew it. Coaxing anything to grow without expensive calor fertilizer was almost an impossibility. But Kanak had done it anyway, and the hope in their voice told Zain that their time together these past six months was as precious to them as it had been to her. Even now, when she walked back with her guardian, blood-soaked and ashamed, they created a space where she could do something beautiful.

Kanak's relentless gentleness in a cruel world was Zain's source of vexation and inspiration. It was why she knew she could never tell them the things she had done, the lives she had ruined. And while Devraj Basu still walked the streets of Tejomaya, his power as palpable as the rift above their heads, she would never be free to plant roses.

But an illicit desire kindled at the sight of those seeds, the promise of the life they could bring. The answer to her freedom was always there, but every time she came up with a plan to destroy Dev, it had always gone terribly wrong. His web extended across the city, and she was but one of the insects ensnared under his control.

But maybe she hadn't looked hard enough. Dev hadn't been as careful with his double-dealings as he'd thought. She had just heard him consorting with a councilmember right here in the city.

Devraj Basu was a traitor, and it would be his downfall. She would make sure of it.

CHAPTER FOUR

Anastasia

Anastasia Drakos smiled as the blood rains fell, and the Isle of Vis changed from gray to red.

Above her, the sky shuddered like a rotted pipe, spitting and coughing out its sickly contents. It had been a long time since the last rains, even longer since Anastasia had felt calor seep into her skin, dampening her gossamer dress. She loved this, the winding cord of energy that coursed through her body, filling her with potential.

It had been a long six months, and she had only seconds to enjoy it before it grew too much to bear.

Fragile stones cracked under her sandaled feet, sloppy crimson footprints marking her path. The island's rugged terrain sloped into fog-festooned waters that smelled of iron and salt. Ahead of her loomed the object of her warpath, a sprawling forest long turned to stone. It was a grotesque sight, an aberration. All rock and sedimentation, a never-ending ashen mass of minaret-shaped trees and gnarled branches so white they resembled knots of bone. She had hated looking upon it every single day of the drought, its interior Council chamber a glaring reminder of all that had gone wrong.

Her body grew leaden the moment she stepped under the chamber's veined roof. The calor withdrawal would pass, but she couldn't afford for her symptoms to show. Not when every inch of the alcove's concentric stone benches overflowed with people. The only areas clear of bodies were where blood dripped through the canopy and pooled on the floor, as though a freshly mutilated carcass hung above their heads. There, and on the eleven thrones perched atop the raised platform toward the back, each carved from petrified trees.

The thrones were ghastly. The armrests were knobby branches that twisted toward the ground, the backs made up of thick trunks, gutted by decay. The cavities looked like disfigured mouths, caught in curdling screams. Poised to swallow anyone that dared to sit in them, entombing them in cold, hard stone for eternity.

Anastasia took deliberate, slow steps toward the platform, and a hush followed her. She had worn white for this reason—knowing that even in the dim lighting they would see the evidence—the stained skirt clinging to her thighs, beads of blood hanging from her dark, waist-length hair—of what she continued to defy.

She swept her hair to the side, sending droplets flying. Someone fell to the ground behind her, digging after what she had discarded. Fools, the lot of them.

"Must you always send people to their knees as you pass by?"

Anastasia's mouth quirked. "Those who worship do so with eyes wide open," she said, coming to a stop just past the teeming heart of the crowd. "Those worshipped do not notice."

Charvi appeared, wrestling her hair into a tight bun. Unlike everyone else who gave Anastasia a wide berth, her oldest and only friend stepped close, the warmth of her body palpable.

"Always so dramatic," Charvi grumbled.

Charvi was dressed in her gatherer robes—the large brown ones that overwhelmed her lean frame, stained with years of sweat and grime. *Not one speck of blood,* Anastasia noted.

"Hamish asked me to be here instead of at the turbines," Charvi said, referring to the island's Council Head. "He wants me to be the gatherers' liaison with you and Councilmember Dheera once she's back from Tejomaya, which is obviously nonsense. I think he thinks I'll keep you in check."

"He's in for a treat," Anastasia replied. She'd been looking forward to this session, to meeting with Dheera afterward. Tejomaya had been falling apart over the past six months—they'd heard reports of sickness and hunger. The city's dons were rumored to be at their wits' end. It was the perfect time for her to strike.

"And just so you know, Matthieu will be here as well," Charvi added.

Anastasia grimaced. Matthieu Beaugene had made history as the first non-Gehennese head of the bloodstripper force, a mousy old man she had detested upon first sight. The only pleasant part of his existence was that he typically remained on Tejomaya, far on the other side of the waters.

"At least the drought ended," Anastasia said. "The souls know we need more calor for power. I haven't enjoyed a warm bath in weeks." She'd treat herself to one if today went as planned.

"The rains aren't always good," Charvi said. "Last time it rained, people in the slums got caught in it because of a lack of shelter. It killed them. Hopefully, they've improved their roofing."

Anastasia let out a hoarse laugh. "Their roofing will be the least of their problems soon."

"What's that supposed to mean?" Charvi asked. Around them, the crowd buzzed with anticipation. "You're going after them."

Her friend didn't even know the half of it.

"For what?" Charvi demanded, when Anastasia stayed silent. "For their calor? Not after everything that's happened—what are you thinking?"

Anastasia ignored the sharp pain in her chest every time she thought about Tejomaya. About the people in it. Once, she would have responded to such threats with protectiveness. But she and Charvi carried the events of the last decade very differently.

"It's him, isn't it?" Charvi asked, quietly, reading every rise and fall of Anastasia's expression. "You still haven't forgiven him."

It was an effort to keep her breathing steady. Anastasia enjoyed the highest tier of calor allocations; she lived in one of the largest houses on the island, could have portable coolers and silk gowns, a whole host of luxury goods not affordable to most. Yet forgiveness was a privilege she'd never grant, not when it came to the people who'd betrayed her, costing her everything she'd ever held dear. Her rapidly diminishing time in this world had only stoked the fires of her deepest grudge.

The calor withdrawals were staying a little bit longer after each rain, leaving her weak and trembling during long nights. She wasn't going to last much longer, which was entirely unacceptable given how much she had left to do. It was time to be aggressive, push the pieces on the game board she'd laid out in her head. With the Council's backing, she could fulfill the old promises she'd made to herself, vows of retribution sealed to the sound of her pathetic heartbeat.

A sudden wave of chatter rippled through the chamber. In

the dim yellow light, Anastasia made out the source of the rumble: one by one, the Council of the Isle of Vis filled the ten stone thrones. One empty in anticipation of Dheera's return.

"This conversation isn't over," Charvi said, as Head Councilmember Hamish raised his hand to quiet the muttering crowd. His face was impossibly long, eyes wide set and unsettlingly perceptive. His once jet-black hair was now the color of the stone forest. He towered over the rest of the councilmembers, exuding power. Next to him stood Matthieu, beady blue eyes calculating. Anastasia bit back her retort.

"The skies have graced us after a long while," Hamish said. It was impressive how his voice rose above the resounding cheers. "As the Council's expert on the turbine system, Councilmember Dheera will be meeting with our gatherer liaison to understand today's calor collections."

Charvi scoffed. "Next time, tell him you can be liaison on your own, like you normally are."

Her friend's scorn was no surprise. Rain had always been holy to Janmiris such as Charvi, a gift from the souls that had passed. Janmir and much of the Lower Tectonic used calor far more sparingly than Gehanna and the nations of the Upper Tectonic. Its use had grown after Gehanna had entered Janmir over fifty years ago, adapting the region's infrastructure to rely more heavily on the substance. To the Council, all they did to extract calor was an advancement benefiting the global community. To Janmiris like Charvi, it was a gross mollification of the truth—the blood that fell from the heavens after the Carnage was the blood that ran through the veins of her ancestors.

Anastasia remained unmoving when Hamish focused his glare on her. What he was really saying was, *I asked your little gatherer friend to be liaison so she would not be out there. You will remember this.* His first move in a contest they had both anticipated. The difference was while Hamish had the Council to run and the fate of the world's most precious resource in his hands, Anastasia had been preparing for this for years and had nothing left to lose.

She lifted her right hand, let Hamish survey the bloodstained sleeve of her chiffon dress.

He ignored her. "We wanted to spend today discussing mitigation strategies in the event the rains continue to be sporadic." As he prattled on, however, it became clear all eyes were on Anastasia.

"Questions already, Anastasia?" Hamish asked, dryly. Not interrupting Council proceedings was an unspoken rule. Anastasia didn't care much for rules. Matthieu in particular looked displeased, which only made her more eager. "We have much to cover today, and unless you provided notice of the matter you would like to discuss, I would ask that you wait until the end, like everyone else."

"Apologies," she said, her intent anything but. "I appreciate your carefully thought-out agenda, but I do not see the point in spending time discussing the same matters we bring up week after week. The calor shortage has grown dire, as you yourself have said, and so I must ask: What is our plan for reallocating calor quotas for personal reserves?" The chatter grew, interest piqued as she nailed the question on everyone's minds.

The councilmember seated to Hamish's right cleared her throat. "Anastasia may have a point," she said. "Exports back home in Finze have fallen drastically, even more than Gehanna, and there are growing concerns about riots over the new power curfew. Increasing caps on personal use may placate sentiments of sedition."

"Matters are similar in Nohri," a different councilmember said. "They are most unhappy about the youth we continue to draft into the bloodstripper force in Tejomaya."

Oh, Hamish would not like that. When the Council was first established, it had been made up entirely of Gehennese members. As global calor supplies dropped and interest in Janmir—and specifically Tejomaya, its capital—increased, a coalition was formed between the three nations of the Upper Tectonic: Gehanna, Finze, and Nohri. As an act of good faith, one Council seat each was granted to Finze and Nohri, but over the years they had pushed for more. Now, only seven of the eleven seats belonged to Gehanna, and the others were growing more daring.

"The Council cannot be so shortsighted," Hamish argued. Charvi flinched, but Anastasia's smile widened as the Head continued, just as she had intended him to. "This is but the first rain following a long drought. The extractors are studying the weather patterns to determine when and how much rain we can expect. We must wait for their report to ensure our communal safety before we prioritize personal use."

One of the Nohri councilmembers, Jezeme Cano, nodded thoughtfully. "But it may be time to consider alternate resources. How long can we depend on the skies for our lives and force our people to live and fight here? Retreating may—"

"You are welcome to retreat if you wish," Hamish said. Jezeme and their fellow Nohri councilmember bristled, but everyone knew better than to argue with Hamish Drakos when he was upset.

Everyone except his daughter.

"All valid concerns," Anastasia said. "But instead of entertaining such drastic measures, how about something simpler? The slums in Tejomaya have been collecting calor for years. Their leeches rob us of our vessels. Even now I can promise they are out there, moving in the shadows. They have reserves running their savage shacks, supplies we could have our bloodstrippers seize in moments if you give the command."

She was grossly exaggerating; the slums had never successfully acquired such vast amounts of calor, and it was hardly enough for them to stay afloat. It certainly would do nothing to support the advanced water filtration and cooling systems in the large marble homes on the Isle of Vis. Unfortunately, the Council wouldn't act upon her personal grudges; she needed to speak to their greed, and they trusted her insight into the city given the time she had spent there. Anastasia could feel heavy disappointment radiating off Charvi.

The Finzish councilmember, Petra Aguilar, spoke up again. "I like the idea of being more aggressive," she said. "Our parliament in Finze has been pushing for us to be more heavy-handed. Both Nohri and Finze have brought in more bloodstrippers, and since we're already asking them to be away from home, we may as well put our numbers to use."

"I can discuss with the platoon leads," Matthieu interrupted, bowing in deference as Petra nodded approvingly. Anastasia resisted the urge to itch at the spot where her blood-hardened sleeves chafed against her skin. She had to pacify all nonfamilial members of the Council if she were to have any chance of being elected, and on top of all the work she did to manage the gatherers, directly opposing her father was the most effective way to demonstrate she was her own person. And if everything else went according to plan, she'd be up there soon, cementing the Gehennese foothold in the Council.

She was too far to see, but Anastasia knew the vein on Hamish's right temple was pulsing with rage. All ten seated councilmembers looked as though they were on edge from the tension she had sown.

They all leaped from their thrones when a scream tore through the chamber.

Everyone turned to the northern entrance, where a figure rushed through the stone forest, their cries blistering passersby as they headed for the Council's stage. The crowd cleared a path, and Anastasia strode in the disruptor's direction. Maybe someone had dared to stand in the rains for too long, and now calor was shredding them from the inside out. Or maybe another boat had broken down, its last drops of calor burned through, leaving its occupants stranded on the Soulless Sea. Maybe someone had jumped.

It was a gatherer, dropping to their knees in hysterics. The councilmembers surrounded them, some attempting to soothe while others demanded answers. Only Hamish remained quiet. The island's bloodstrippers had already formed a barrier between the general population and the Council, Matthieu at its helm, but they parted reluctantly for Anastasia.

"She's dead," the gatherer said. Their brown skin was splotched with fear.

"Who?" Hamish demanded.

"Dheera," the gatherer choked out. "Councilmember Dheera is dead."

Horror rippled across the chamber, but Anastasia felt a deep, sickly sense of relief.

A throne was open for the taking.

Anastasia despised the sounds children made.

She drowned out the bickering, wishing desperately that she had parted ways with Charvi when the disastrous Council session had ended. But no, a councilmember was dead, the island was up in arms, and Charvi was going to subject her to her child's tantrum before continuing their conversation about Anastasia's plans.

She squinted through the window at the sparks appearing across the horizon. Strange. Her home did not face the mainland; she preferred a view of the Soulless Sea instead of the city that reminded her only of pain, so she didn't know if such a phenomenon was common these days. The sky played many tricks, though most were quite tame after it bathed you in blood.

"Anything interesting, or are you tapping your foot to that infernal bar song just to be annoying?" Charvi asked.

Anastasia held her toes down on the beige-and-rust-colored serapi carpet running across the granite floor. Charvi was sitting on the plush bed that took up most of her one-room cottage. There was little else here; to her right was an ornate dining table with cabriole legs and matching chairs, hand-carved by Charvi herself. The other bare wall had a small bookshelf filled to the brim with leather-bound books. Simple accommodations by Isle standards, but a luxury compared to the city.

Charvi yanked a wide-toothed comb against her daughter's knotted hair, who sat sobbing on the ground in front of her, clutching at the hem of her sleeveless cotton dress. Apparently, this was a matter of vast importance.

"Just watching," Anastasia replied, wondering why Charvi bothered. Her daughter would scamper off in a second, only to return with hair in equally abysmal condition.

"Ma, it hurts!" the child cried out, but even her glistening tears were no suitable bribe. Charvi was notoriously stubborn when she had a task at hand.

"If you stay still, Baruna, it won't hurt so much," Charvi scolded. Baruna's little shoulders trembled as her mother ran the comb through her hair again. Anastasia exhaled heavily, uncertain if it would be appropriate for her to ask for answers just yet.

"On my soul," Charvi muttered. "Between the two of you, all my hair is going to fall out. Baru, go play; Mama and Ana need to talk."

The girl didn't need to be told twice. She raked her little fingers through her hair in a desperate attempt to fix the damage before rushing to the door.

"Listen, you have to be home soon, okay?" Charvi said, following Baruna with a pair of dainty frilled socks. "And make sure you only play in the stone forest. If it rains again, I don't want you to be out in it."

Baruna sat on the floor to put on her socks, then her timeworn shoes. "Is it because the rain isn't safe anymore?"

Anastasia and Charvi went still.

"Where did you hear that?" Charvi asked.

Baruna shrugged. "That's what everyone's saying. Even Cole's mama, when we tried to play hopscotch near the port."

"First of all, do not go near the port," Charvi said, angrily, kneeling to help Baruna tie her shoelaces. Then, she proceeded to break a cardinal rule of their friendship and involved Anastasia in her parenting. "Look at Ana, all covered in blood. She is okay, just like you will be okay, but I do not want to have to wash your clothes because you got them all dirty."

Anastasia shot Charvi a glare. Her dress had long dried and stiffened, but the tactic worked to appease Baruna's fear. Born in the city but raised on the island, Baruna had never seen the blood rains as anything but what the Gehennese had taught her: a gift. A gift that she was to collect and present to the Council but never take for herself. Like her mother and others from Janmir, Urjan, and the other nations in the Lower Tectonic, she would be trained in gathering, to work the rain turbines across the island to ensure all the calor was properly extracted for island use.

"If it rains, you should come inside," Charvi said, quietly, helping Baruna to her feet. "Actually, I'm going to come with you, just to make sure everything looks okay." She shot Anastasia an apologetic look.

"But it will harm you?" Baruna asked, as Charvi took her hand.

"No," Charvi said. Baruna frowned at the lump in her mother's throat. "The rain is a blessing to us all."

Anastasia wondered if mothers always lied so easily and if children always pretended to believe them.

CHAPTER FIVE

Iravan

Iravan grabbed the girl by her collar and pulled her into the alleyway.

"Do you have any on you?" he asked. Just a few streets down, the leeches had disrupted the solemn night with raids on the bloodstrippers' boats. The girl nodded, face slick with sweat.

Iravan stepped back in surprise. It was Zain Jatav—he hadn't seen her around the slums in forever, but he didn't have time to wonder about her resurrection. She handed over the two cases of calor tucked under her arm.

"Good, get back to the slums," Iravan ordered, already scanning the scene behind her.

Zain hesitated. "I can take this to Yadav. You should go—"

"You let me decide what I do and don't do," Iravan said. This time, she took the hint and bolted. Iravan could hear screams and bullets, a familiar cacophony. He used to thrive in this discordance, but now he moved through it with little more than duty and routine; he couldn't wait to settle back into the quiet of his hut.

Iravan stuck to the shadows until he reached the back of Yadav's store, which also functioned as the mechanic's home. The unit had three rooms: a living space primarily used as a work area, a storefront, and a small bedroom. No one but family ever came through the back; while the doors were never locked, opening the latch from the outside required a finesse that only a few had been taught.

Inside, Yadav and Dev were huddled around the back room's centerpiece: a large, crowded table with strange vials rolling in the space between them. The ongoing conversation halted as soon as he entered.

Iravan eyed them suspiciously. He had long left them to their own devices when it came to strange inventions; he had neither the time nor the patience to listen to Yadav yammer on about calor density and stability and how its properties affected his latest tools' siphoning abilities. But he was getting damn tired of feeling like the third wheel in their disharmonious cog.

"How is it going out there?" Yadav asked, innocently.

"Bad," Iravan groused. "There's already chatter about what we're going to do with the calor. I had to break up a fight before the raids; there was some accusation about calor hoarding. Said the bathrooms in the back quadrant haven't received water in days."

Strife had only grown as the drought continued. Their supplies were largely communal, so it was inevitable that someone had a problem with how things were distributed. Suddenly, everyone was an expert on calor, but no one had answers for its scarcity.

Dev flicked the rings on his hand. "Was it Nitesh again? I'll have a word with him later. At least tell me we did good today."

Iravan set the cases down in front of them. "Most of the guards were called away to the island after the councilmember's death, so we had them outnumbered. I told the leeches to take the rest of the loot back to the slums. I'm sure the Geng pigs will be back soon enough."

"This is perfect," Dev said, gathering the stray vials on the table into a briefcase. He snapped it closed and slung the strap over his shoulder. "I can get started on the next step and think through allocations." Then, to Yadav, he added, "Don't forget to tell him about the meeting tomorrow."

"I'll take care of that," Yadav said, ushering Dev out the door. "Get out of here quickly, before they start coming around the Hammer."

"What meeting?" Iravan asked, irate at being left out.

"It's important, Ravi," Dev called. "Please. On Amu's ashes." They hadn't invoked Amu, their fictional mother, since they were teenagers. What had started as a morbid joke between orphans had turned into a promise, an ask for a leap of faith in their group of friends.

Iravan ground his teeth. "Fine. Get out of here."

With a mock wave, Dev slipped outside. The commotion was dying down, but Iravan didn't want to leave Yadav alone just yet. Besides, he needed to hear more about this meeting. Yadav busied himself tidying away the remaining sheets of metal and glass strewn across the table.

"The meeting tomorrow is at the underground market, with an Urjan merchant," Yadav said. In the dim light, his white hair and pigmented skin made him look ghostlike, but his movements were heavy and practiced. "It's about the soul-sickness."

The sickness. Iravan remembered the mother who'd come to him after the debrief with the leeches, begging him to look into the strange illness that had seized her child and so many others over the last few weeks. He was a don, not a fucking doctor, but he'd comforted her until she stopped crying, stupidly promising to find a solution.

The sickness was a grisly thing too. Skin that slid off the bone like it had been picked clean by sharp teeth, hair that resembled burned tufts of grass. The smell, fetid as the bowels of hell.

"I've been looking into the sickness myself," Iravan said, his hand finding a metal coin in his pocket. His thumb brushed against the engraving he knew so well, two mountains with the sun poking out between. Like the etching, the coin itself was worthless now. The sun—concealed by the sky's rot—hadn't been seen in Tejomaya since before Iravan was born, when calor became the currency of the world. Still, for a man with no patience for religion or superstition, he found its touch soothing, an anchor.

Iravan continued. "I went to see the acolytes and asked for records they had on any patients, anyone who came to see them with the same symptoms. Each and every person is from the slums; not one person from the other neighborhoods reported anything of the sort. It's targeted."

Yadav raised his eyebrows. "That doesn't mean anything. It could be infectious."

Iravan shook his head. "I thought of that. But it doesn't make sense given how much everyone in this city interacts with one another. The last three who died all had stalls at the underground market. And the councilmember who bit the bullet—guess where she and her people spent the most time?"

The delegation had been snooping around the slum borders, and Councilmember Dheera had attempted to engage Iravan and Dev in peace talks. Traitorous Janmiri bitch—her family had moved to the Northern Tectonic when she was young, and she'd spent her years sucking Geng cock and trying to win their goodwill.

"That's why I'm pushing for expansion of the slums into the Sickle," Iravan continued, although the thought of the disputed territory threatened to incite one of his migraines. "We're too densely populated right now, and our western face is wide open. With the Sickle, we can set up perimeters. The bottleneck entrance would make it harder for others to access, strengthen our security."

Yadav nodded. "You should talk to Dev about that. It makes sense to me. But I know what you're trying to do—and you should still take that meeting with the Urjan merchant tomorrow. See what she has to say about the plague."

"The last thing we need is another foreigner in our affairs," Iravan protested.

Yadav blinked in surprise. "She's not Anastasia Drakos."

It was like he had been dunked into a tub of calor. Iravan's skin grew hot, and he fought to school his expression. "It has been ten years, and I still don't care for that name."

"Just because you have chosen to forgive her does not mean the rest of us have forgotten. She ruined our lives and is probably planning our complete demise as we speak," Yadav grumbled. "If this sickness doesn't do so first."

Outside, something—or someone—crashed into the pavement. Cries of pain grew louder as the disarray they had planted at the harbor spread through the city like a disease. But all Iravan could think of was Anastasia Drakos. The last time she was in the city, Dev had orchestrated a meeting with Inas Shah—the Head Acolyte—and Anastasia at the Temple of Many-Souls to broker peace between the Gengs and the slums. It had ended with the monument in flames.

"I've neither forgiven nor forgotten," Iravan said, "but I don't choose to live in the past."

Yadav howled and slapped his knee. "Oh, that's a new one."

"Stop," Iravan warned.

The old man rubbed at imaginary tears, chortling away. "All those people out there might listen to what you say, but remember who got you here, eh? You might not tell *them* the truth, but don't try that bullshit with me."

At that, Iravan paused, taking Yadav in. In his early sixties, Yadav was one of the oldest people in Tejomaya; people were lucky if they made it past fifty these days. Fifty. That was only ten years away for Iravan. If Yadav left, and Iravan soon followed, then he would abandon his city without fulfilling the promises he had made to keep them and their land safe.

"All these years later, and she still winds you up like my best clockwork," Yadav continued, shaking his head.

Iravan groaned and said the only thing that would shut Yadav up.

"I'll take the meeting tomorrow."

The underground market was neither underground nor particularly secretive. It was held at the intersection of arguably the most popular and accessible part of the city where the slums, the Hammer, and the Bow met, along the main road that locals referred to as the artery of Tejomaya. Or in Dev's case, the asshole of Tejomaya.

As one of the few city traditions that predated Gehennese invasion, the market served as a pulse check on the health and wealth of its inhabitants. Janmir used to be a thriving agrarian economy, and its capital boasted artisan guilds that were renowned across the world for their fine textiles and craftsmanship.

The market was the fulcrum of Janmiri community, drawing visitors and merchants from diverse locales.

The area still bustled, but it was a piss-poor rendition of what it used to be. The crowd had thinned, as had the peddlers who set up week after week. Gone were the stalls with abundant legumes, exotic fabrics, and cutting-edge technology, both local and foreign, brought to and from cargo vessels. The products available now involved as little calor as possible: grass-based clothing, natural wood-carved ornaments, raw food ingredients like lentils and beans. It was all anyone could afford to buy or trade. Iravan doubted he'd see anything more alluring until the Anniversary, when the moribund city would fight tooth and nail to resuscitate its former glory.

The Urjan merchant was easy to find against such a stale backdrop.

She stood under a fluttering charcoal overhang beside the grain vendors, looking entirely out of place. Her pristine pearl blouse billowed around the waistband of a floor-length skirt, its bold red and traditional orange patchwork identifying her as Urjan. Her skin gleamed black, as dark as the tight ebony curls cascading down her back. Long gold earrings hung from her lobes, matching the accents on her thin-frame glasses, and delicate bracelets clattered around her wrists.

Iravan had spent the early hours of the morning tallying their loot from the previous night and sending out spies to determine if the bloodstrippers were planning any sort of retaliation. The Gengs were still reeling from their imbalanced Council—such a fragile little power hold they had—but it bought him time. Still, he was tired of people and made no effort to hide this as he approached the woman Dev claimed had vital information about the sickness.

Her expression was unreadable, but the way she tapped on her sleeves, twice on the wrist and a brief flick of her index and middle finger, suggested she was praying for goodwill from the Urjan Gods. An old, defunct tradition that no Urjan refugees in Tejomaya did anymore. Spiritual, then. Nervous even. He could work with that.

"Hello," he said in Urj, stopping a safe distance from her.

"Hello," she replied in accented but clear Janmiri. He relaxed, much preferring to hold business conversations in his native tongue.

"I'm Iravan Khotar," he said, extending a hand. "I work closely with Devraj Basu and Yadav Das."

She seemed distracted by something behind him. "Oh yes," she murmured, waiting a second too long before reaching out and wrapping her fingers around his palm for a brief shake.

"Mariam," she said. "It is so nice to meet you. I've been looking forward to asking you my questions."

Who did she think he was, a tour guide? Iravan attempted a conciliatory smile and said, "I thought you had information on the sickness."

"I may have something for you," Mariam replied, cocking her head thoughtfully. "But first, I wanted to ask you about Tejomaya's calor reserve."

Iravan laughed in her face. Did she think she could bargain with *him*? And about the reserve! Since the beginning of the drought, people had been drawn back to their favorite theory: that of the mythical calor reserve. Mentions of it had been recorded in a leaked acolyte journal or book—Iravan didn't know, he'd never cared to look—and despite the acolytes' definitive statement that its author was speculating, it had been enough flint for the city's easily flammable rumor mill. Why wouldn't they believe it, when a stupid fantasy could solve all their very real problems?

I heard the reserve has enough calor to replenish our soils. We could actually have enough food the next harvest, a passerby had said just earlier that day, giddy in a way that grated Iravan's nerves.

I heard there's enough to let us fly again, someone replied, and Iravan had damn near fallen over himself.

Aviation was a dream that Tejomaya had never woken from, a body they had never put to rest. And of course a fucking calor reserve would have the ability to resurrect what should be buried six feet under.

"There is no reserve," Iravan said, collecting himself. "Can you tell me about the sickness, or are you here to waste my time?"

The woman's cheeks flushed. "I am an official representative for Urjan. I was told to address the Council directly, but I came to you because I thought it would be more helpful, given your true command over the city. I understand the reserve is sacred here, but I'm not trying to steal it. I want to study it. It's important."

She was an official representative? Things in Urjan must be worse than in Tejomaya. "Everything is important," he said, gesturing around him. "And we don't need anyone's help."

She grabbed his arm. *No one* grabbed his arm.

"Look," she said, pointing behind him. Against his will, he obeyed, needing to know what inspired the wonder in her tone.

She was watching the rift above their heads. The sky was less violent after rain; it was recovering from the work it had just done. In fact, it looked normal, and disappointment flooded him. Then again, the rift and its rains existed only above Tejomaya. It was why the Gehennese and every other greedy paw wanted to be in his city. She simply hadn't gotten used to it yet.

"What about it?" he asked, impatiently. "It's the sky."

"Look closer, do you see the vapor?" she said, leaning in so her chin grazed his shoulder. He squinted then, seeing a faint yellow mist ooze out of the rift. He had never seen anything like it before, but strange colors in the air were nothing to think twice about. The city dwelled in a murky haze most days. "I have a theory about the calor, you see," she said. "I think in this city—"

He ripped himself from her grasp. What was he doing? He had come here for a purpose and had instead been distracted by an idealistic zealot.

"No, you look," he said, satisfied when she took a step back. "I don't have the luxury of gallivanting across the Lower Tectonic spewing theories no one gives a damn about. I've got a city to run, people to feed, homes to hold up. You have already had far too much of my time, and now you better get out of my face."

"What if I have proof?" she said, jutting her chin out.

Iravan's temple throbbed. There was a strange smell in the air, hair and fat burning on top of yet another pyre. He glanced around for any sign of smoke, but everything looked normal. His mind was playing tricks on him again. "What proof?"

"There's evidence, outside of the journal you're all aware of, that a reserve exists, you see." Mariam's hands moved a mile a minute. "A buildup of calor in a specific location would cause inherent changes to the chemistry of the land. It's been getting hotter here, as it has everywhere in the world, but there's no calor anywhere else for me to analyze. Calor responds differently to heat, and its behavior within various containers differs based on the composition of the—"

"Am I supposed to understand this?" Iravan interrupted. The air around them darkened a shade, and they glanced up in unison. The vapor was more visible now, and people had taken notice, pointing up at the sky. Fucking great, yet another thing he had to deal with.

"This is bad," Mariam muttered, the light casting the lenses of her glasses in an orange hue. "We should continue this conversation later. You can find me in the Bow, I'm on the second street, in the house with the lavender door. But right now, you should get out of here."

Iravan blinked at her. Souls, she was serious, ordering him about. His disbelief transformed into a scathing glare. "Maybe you should get out of my city."

He walked away seething, but as his anger simmered down, her words took on a different light. The calor reserve, and proof of it? A load of shit, if you asked him, but looking at the desperation around him, he couldn't help but wonder. Mariam sounded like she knew what she was talking about, even if whatever she said about compositions and behavior went in one of his ears and out the other. Maybe Yadav could talk to her, translate her scientific babble. Despite the raids last night, they still did not have enough calor. The poor were robbing the poor, and soon they'd be fighting over meaningless scraps. A reserve like that could change everything for Tejomaya.

"Run!" someone screamed, knocking into him *hard*. His skull rang, and before he could gather himself, everyone around him was moving.

"What is it?" he asked, glancing around frantically.

"Look up!" a woman screeched. She elbowed him. "Get out of the way!"

Iravan stumbled into another panic-stricken passerby, sending them sprawling. His knees nearly buckled at the sight above their heads.

Where he had just seen that strange yellow vapor was a

vortex of air, spinning threateningly over their heads, up near the rift. The beginnings of a maelstrom, but something about this was different. Its edges blazed orange and sparked against the static violet of the sky, hissing as it touched stagnant air.

There, that smell of singed hair. An acrid gust, and the temperature rose several degrees. Sweat broke out across his back, a sharp pang of terror that rattled his spine. The flaming band grew wider, stretching toward the ground.

He was staring at a rippling wall of flame.

"Run!"

But it was too late. He couldn't look away from the monstrosity as the ring exploded, the sky emitting a carnivorous roar.

A rope of fire lashed down on the market.

Tejomaya was always hot, but in the space of a second, it became volcanic, turning so dark that he couldn't see a thing. Iravan's clothes singed his skin; everything ignited.

"Look out!" he yelled, as something whistled through the air and hit the area where he had just been standing. It was a burning beam of wood he'd dodged through sheer luck, and he'd dragged someone down with him. A man, who stared at him with the kind of fear that sent people jumping off sinking ships.

"Oh souls," the man cried, as someone stomped on his spine.

"Get up," Iravan cried, helping the man. They were going be crushed in a stampede.

Someone barreled into them, and just like that, Iravan was lost in the crowd, elbows and arms shoving into his stomach, his body thrust in every direction. His vision was filled with smoke—slippery, thick smoke that snaked into his lungs and choked him. It was like someone had stuck blades through his eyes, but he stumbled toward what looked like an opening between two tables.

A flaming cloth tumbled down from nowhere. A woman next to him, a slum-dweller who specialized in textured pots, shrieked as it swallowed her body in smothering heat. He tried to rip it off her, but he couldn't see, couldn't feel, couldn't tell where she was, whether he was helping, or if his arm was submerged in devouring flame. Tejomaya had burned once before, and he had always wished he'd been there to change the outcome of that day. Now he was in the heart of a fire, and he realized how foolish that hope was.

With a groan, he thrust the fabric as far from them as possible, ignoring his blistering palms. The woman's pleading cries overflowed with expectation, as though he had the power to quench these flames. Then, she pointed behind him and screamed.

Iravan spun on his heel, grunting as someone's knee drove into his abdomen. But there he saw her. A little girl curled up under one of the burning tables, wailing. Lufi, Mahini's youngest. She let out a heart-wrenching cry at the sight of him.

Iravan dropped to his elbows in front of her. By the souls' mercy, the table's legs weren't on fire, but there was so much smoke that he fell forward in a fit of coughs.

"Hold on to my hands," he called, fighting to hold his next breath. But Lufi kept crying and pointing behind him. He peeked over his shoulder, desperately trying to see past the pain knifing his brain. There, a doll, caught under the leg of the neighboring table.

For fuck's sake. Iravan swung around and wrenched the doll out by the head. He held his arms out to Lufi again, urging her forward. They had to move, or he was going to pass out on the asphalt.

This time, she wrapped her small hands around his wrists. Iravan pulled her to him until her body was close enough for him to hook an arm around her waist.

"Don't let go, okay?" he said, giving her the doll. It was impossible to see through the dense smoke, but he caught the glistening lines of tears down her cheeks. She coughed violently into his shoulder. Iravan slid them out from under the table, bent his knee under him, and lifted them both up and out. The woman he had helped was playing sentinel, batting away people so they wouldn't flatten him. Iravan gave her a grateful nod, then studied Lufi.

Copper blemishes covered her light-pink dress, but he couldn't see any obvious signs of burns or wounds.

"Where is your mother?" Iravan asked.

Lufi let out a resounding scream that nearly shattered his right ear.

"Okay, okay," Iravan muttered, rubbing a hand down her back.

A wave of heat slammed into them, and she cried even louder. For a moment, he stood there, and the world grew to a standstill. Everyone was running while fire leaped from surface to surface, greedily eating their hopes and dreams. Smoke rose to the sky in spires, a signal for help that would never be answered. Tejomaya groaned under the weight of debilitating sorrow.

Their day of reckoning had arrived, and when he thought about what was to come, he considered succumbing to it all. Maybe this was a gift, a way to reunite with those he had lost a decade ago, in a different fire. But he thought of Dev. Of Yadav. Of Lufi in his arms. Of the countless faces that leaned on him every day.

"I'm going to get us out of here," he promised.

He pulled her to his chest and shoved his way through a sea of writhing bodies.

CHAPTER SIX

Anastasia

Anastasia stormed into Charvi's cottage.

"They raided our fucking boats," she yelled, slamming the door shut behind her. She hadn't had a chance to speak with Charvi since the Council session two days ago; her friend had been "too busy" with Baruna and the gatherers. It was more likely that Charvi was avoiding her because of her plans to attack the slums, which may have once instilled a prick of guilt in Anastasia, but not anymore. Not after she'd heard what the leeches had done to their calor supplies.

"They did not," Charvi exclaimed. She was in a familiar freeze-frame, midcleaning. A dark-blue book dangled from Charvi's right hand. "That's stupid, even for them."

Anastasia nodded victoriously. "It's exactly what I needed. They've riled the entire Council up. Petra is sending the blood-strippers out to arrest their precious leeches as we speak."

Charvi fell quiet. "I see," she said, then returned to cleaning. Loud thumps sounded as she stacked stray books on top of one another, before pulling at one end of the rumpled bedsheet so violently that it slipped out from under the mattress. She swore under her breath.

Anastasia frowned. "What in the souls' names is your problem?"

Charvi let out a small laugh. "They were our friends, Ana," she said. "More than that. Maybe Dev was molded from hell's feces, but Ravi—"

"He is not my friend," Anastasia replied, but the admonishment came out strained, animalistic. The sound of his name set her spine on fire, ignited the kind of rage that dictated the shape of her life and eventually became her entire existence. "We left because of him, and stayed away because of what he did. And even now, they just attacked our people at the harbor!"

"Your people," Charvi said, sharply.

Anastasia took a step back, stunned.

Charvi bit her lip. "That was uncalled for, I'm sorry." Anastasia's fingers were numb, but Charvi continued. "But I've been thinking, and I'm not just saying this for the safety of your—our people, but maybe you should consider what Jezeme said. About withdrawing."

Anastasia couldn't believe this. She had been born in Tejomaya. Yes, she didn't look like Charvi, but it was her home too. She wanted to see the city rise anew, wiped clean of the people who'd hurt her. Suggesting she withdraw, go to Gehanna, a country she'd never stepped foot in? "Never."

Charvi pleaded, "There's no calor left. For anyone here. You could convince Hamish."

"It must be easy to forget, when you didn't lose everything," Anastasia said, softly. It was a low, pathetic blow, but Anastasia had never been above it.

Charvi recoiled. Quiet sank into the chasm between them.

"I am grateful every day for what you did for me," she said. "I can never forget it."

The words were right but the tone was wrong. Before Anastasia could dissect it, a horn blared in the distance. They jerked apart, looking to the window. Anastasia couldn't remember the last time the island's alarm had been used. It was reserved for public crises, and here on the island where one could enter only with express Council permission, where Hamish ruled with an iron fist, those were few and far between.

It must be that someone hostile was on the Isle of Vis.

Anastasia's heart pounded as she reached for Charvi, prepared to make their way to the island's catacombs, as per procedure. But Charvi withdrew, her mouth parted for her sole concern:

"Baruna."

The island was consumed by a miasma of panic.

Everyone had rushed outside their homes, searching the skies for any sign of the horror that would elicit the horn. The sight of pale-faced bloodstrippers rushing to the ports was enough to signal that this was no test but something entirely legitimate.

The civilians moved like a swarm of bees toward the catacombs, except for one person.

"Charvi!" Anastasia screamed, as she wrestled through the crowd in pursuit. Charvi was running, dirt kicked up with every urgent footstep toward the stone forest.

"Get out of my way," Anastasia said, elbowing a couple as she kicked off her slippery sandals and continued barefoot. The rough gravel cut into her skin, but she would be faster this way.

Then, in the blink of an eye, she lost sight of Charvi. Her stomach tightened, her thighs screamed, and for a moment, she considered turning around. It was clear their once unshakable friendship had changed, even if she couldn't pinpoint when. Maybe when Baruna had been born, and the distance between them had grown, inescapable now. She didn't know if Charvi would come running after her if their roles had been reversed. But in that second, Anastasia considered a world without Charvi, the one person who had loved her through her worst. Who had stayed. Anastasia needed Charvi.

Matthieu stepped into her path. "You cannot go after her, Drakos."

Souls, this man was as repulsive as he was unflappable. She remembered the last time she had stood this close to him, smelled the excessive spice-scented cologne he surely bathed in. The trajectory of her life had changed course, and he had remained impassive to her tears. Now, his shoulders were stiff, face wiped clean of his usual condescension, but the stench of pepper still made her gag.

Anastasia ignored him. "Varun!"

She waved at the gatherer she had spotted in the crowd. "Did you see where Charvi went?"

Varun looked warily between Anastasia and Matthieu. None of the gatherers liked Matthieu, or any of the Upper Tectonic civilians who stayed on the Isle. Anastasia was the exception, by virtue of her friendship with Charvi.

"She just ran past," Varun said. "I can go get her."

Anastasia shook her head. "You go follow protocol, I'll get her. Where did she go?"

Matthieu said, "You will do no such thing."

Varun pointed at the stone forest.

"Thank you," Anastasia said, patting his shoulder. He gave her a grateful smile before heading to the catacombs.

"Miss Drakos," Matthieu said, stepping into her path. "I must insist that you—"

Anastasia snarled in his face. She knew Matthieu couldn't care less about her safety, but maybe Councilmember Petra had asked the Finzish bloodstripper to keep an eye on her. "Get out of my way. I won't ask again."

Then Anastasia was off, like a deer breaking from the herd, as she chased Charvi into the heart of the island.

The stone forest was sprawling and serpentine, a lush terrain of flora turned into hard, unyielding rock, and Anastasia worried she wouldn't find Charvi among the spires. But the moment she stepped under the heavy, groaning canopy, she saw Charvi hurtling through the trees.

"What the hell do you think you're doing?" Anastasia screamed, her torn cries echoing. Once, this run would have been child's play, but her body was crumbling, and each breath battered her shriveled lungs. "Baruna has probably been taken to the catacombs already."

She wanted to be at the catacombs, not here. Emergencies were the only time they were allowed in the twisting, half-collapsed tunnels. The one opportunity she had to explore its depths was being stolen by her deluded friend.

Finally, Anastasia caught up to her, but if Charvi noted her presence, she showed no indication of it.

"I have to find her," Charvi said, her breaths labored after the sprint she'd made halfway across the island. At least she had stopped now, her head instead moving jerkily as she scanned each direction. "What if they didn't bring her?" Her voice rippled, thin and strained.

Anastasia huffed, wiping her face with the low neckline of her blouse. "Don't be stupid, of course they brought her. You always believe the worst in people." She reached out for her friend, but Charvi lurched out of range. There'd been only one time her friend had been so possessed by fear and need, a long time ago. She had run to Anastasia with a sick infant in her arms, begging for help.

"Did you know when it rains, they push Baru into the puddles so she comes home bathed in blood?" Charvi sounded like she had swallowed dry sand. "Did you know one time, they locked her in a turbine cell, said she belonged in there and not with them?"

Charvi did not specify who "they" were, but it wasn't required. Baruna was one of the only gatherer children; most remained childless, and any other Janmiri youth were much older or younger than Baruna. Everyone her age was from the Upper Tectonic, and she stuck out like a sore thumb, her brown skin so dark it could be picked out from miles away.

Anastasia did not know, and it must have shown because Charvi barked a cold laugh, sticking her finger into Anastasia's sternum.

"They could have left her here," she said. "And the only person who would care to look is me. You of all people should understand, after what happened."

Anastasia stepped back, heat coursing through her body. Charvi had never told her any of this before; she knew Anastasia only tolerated Baruna, but she could have stepped in with the bullying. She was a Drakos; they would listen to her. "Then why would you send her to play with them?"

Betrayal etched itself on Charvi's face. "What am I supposed to do? Lock her up in our cottage? Not all of us have the Drakos name protecting us, Anastasia. She has to learn how to hold her own in this world, because the souls know I won't always be around to do it."

Anastasia opened her mouth to tell her she was wrong, but Charvi wasn't done.

"And if you think it doesn't rip my heart out each time I send my child to a place that will hurt her, if you think I don't lose sleep every single night wondering if there's any other option, then you don't know me at all."

Anastasia had never been deluded enough to believe that Charvi had left Tejomaya solely for their friendship. When Baruna had fallen sick, Charvi's desperation for medical attention had led her to Anastasia, and it was only with her friend's help that they had procured the required care from the blood-strippers, and later on the Isle of Vis. The island was meant to give Baruna the better life that Charvi wanted for her, but her clear resentment for their new home was glaring.

"If you'll excuse me," Charvi spat, "I need to find my child."

"Miss Drakos?" someone called, insistently. A bloodstripper. Anastasia was thankful for the interruption. Perhaps Hamish had found it in himself to give a shit about his daughter and insisted someone retrieve her. At least it wasn't Matthieu.

"What is it?" she responded, ignoring Charvi as she walked toward the exit.

"It's Tejomaya," he said. "Reports are saying a maelstrom descended over their underground market. It's—"

But Anastasia was running, running out of the forest, and her breath left her as she saw a mass of flame descend upon the city across the pale-gray waters.

CHAPTER SEVEN

Zain

The sky exploded, saving Zain from the longest lecture of her life.

Fortune favoring Zain Jatav? Surely the world was ending.

She had been at the slums earlier that day, cursing herself for not being quick enough to pilfer five vials of calor from the cases she had transported. It was the *perfect* opportunity to meet the Anniversary deadline with little skin off her back. Souls damn Iravan Khotar for yanking her lifeline out of her hands.

She'd been helping Gayathri with patients when Bilal tore his stitches and bled all over her, leaving red splatters down the front of her tunic. When she eventually returned home, Kanak had stood there with their mouth open. Samiah's glower had quickly turned homicidal, and she was a second away from committing murder with her favorite brown scarf when a wave of heat nearly knocked them off their feet.

One look at the blazing maelstrom and Zain acted on instinct, shoving Kanak through the rusted trapdoor near their dining table before following them. Her body tingled, numb from shock. Tejomaya was not prone to tornadoes, but its seaside geography did grace them with rare typhoons. Kanak was one of the last Tejomayans with a large home in the Bow—most had been bought by the Gehennese, but the ones closest to the slums had been left under acolyte ownership—and it was fitted with a cellar. It helped that Samiah's clothing business was one of the few that still thrived in the city. The Gehennese loved her work.

Zain used to be embarrassed by the social disparity between her and her friends, but she couldn't fault it now. Samiah's bare feet appeared a moment before she hopped inside and pulled the door shut above her head, leaving them to stew in inky-black terror.

"What was *that*?" Kanak cried. "On my soul, what about the neighbors?"

Samiah soothed them. "They're usually home at this time; they will find shelter."

Zain nodded. "I didn't see them out either. I mean, maybe they were in town, but maybe the storm missed them. Maybe . . ." Her voice faltered. Their neighbors may be safe, but the rest of Tejomaya, all the people with no protection . . . The possibilities for disaster were endless.

"Were you at the slums, then? Is that why you're here, covered in blood?" Samiah asked. She sat in the far corner, away from Zain, veiled by darkness, but her admonishment bore enough presence on its own. "How many times do we have to tell you not to get involved with the scum of this city?"

"This is what you want to talk about?" Zain yelped, dizzy from the rising heat. "We're quite possibly about to die!"

If a firestorm couldn't save her from her guardians' wrath, then she was shit out of luck.

"You've been avoiding us since it rained two days ago, and

we haven't seen you since the raids last night," Samiah said, preparing for what was sure to be a legendary tirade. "Raids! On the *bloodstrippers'* boats! You aren't going anywhere without giving us answers, don't you dare even try to leave."

But Zain couldn't speak. She was thirteen again, watching the Temple of Many-Souls burn before her, rivulets of blood running down her clawed arms as her insides screamed with agony. The tips of the fire had been blue. Ten years later, and she could still see its cerulean hue, its cold sapphire heart that burned so fiercely. Her chest constricted and she couldn't quench the image even in the impenetrable darkness of the underground. Then a hand found hers, and Kanak squeezed her lightly, three times.

They had done this many times before, she and Kanak, the acolyte inviting the orphan into their warmth without asking for anything in return. Zain had been a leech long before she had found the streets and slums and the business of stealing blood; she had leeched off the kindness of someone far better than herself.

"Two days ago, you and Dev . . . ," Kanak trailed off. Their house was possibly burning down, but their concern for Zain remained first on their mind. "Why do you go near those men?"

And there it was. The moment where it all fell apart. She couldn't tell them she didn't *want* to work for Dev, because it meant she would have to confess her own crimes, expose her shame. Zain couldn't bear it if Kanak looked at her the way Zain saw herself. Sometimes, the only thing that kept Zain afloat was when Kanak looked at her like she might be worth something someday.

A loud roar aboveground ripped through the air, sending them flying into each other. Zain held Kanak's and Samiah's shaking hands until the commotion ceased.

"It's not what you think," Zain said, sitting back. She would rather come up with a crackpot of lies than deal with the present. The cellar was a kiln. They all needed the distraction. "I was in the square that day when a bloodstripper saw me and I panicked. I went to the slums for safety, and Dev was walking me home. And today, I was helping someone who got hurt. This isn't my blood."

There. It wasn't all untrue.

"I believe you," Kanak said, quietly, despite Samiah's undisguised snort. "But when we see you come home covered in blood after the rains, it takes us back to a bad time. And now you're at the slums again. We almost lost you to all this before."

Zain's composure strained. Kanak had never raised their voice in anger, had never raised a hand in violence, no matter the brutality they were faced with. Even when they had been unjustly ousted from the Temple for reasons Zain suspected had to do with her, even if Kanak harbored any resentment toward her for their pseudoexile from the Temple, they had tended to Zain with such care. They would never understand why Zain refused to put her gun down. It didn't matter that it was never loaded.

All Zain had wanted when she was younger was to be like her guardian, but she was destined to fail at every turn.

"I will never be lost to you," she promised. If every truth felt as comforting as this one, then she would never tell another lie again.

Samiah fidgeted. "The heat's subsided, I'm going to go check upstairs."

A slice of light illuminated her deep-black skin, then the cellar, as she pushed the trapdoor open. Noise flooded the basement instantly. Zain followed her guardians.

The area outside the house was *razed*. In seconds, Zain was covered in flaky ash, sticky as smog against her dark-brown skin. Sparks from little fires still sliced through the air. Where the smoke thinned near the ground, bodies thrashed, skin mangled in patterns of red and black, bones charred to the core. And the smell—under the thick, choking smoke lay the cloying, rotten odor of burning flesh. Zain heaved over the side of the road, coughing until her stomach emptied, a sickly yellow splatter on top of black ash.

Kanak yelled, "We need water!"

"Go!" Zain told Samiah, wiping the string of drool from her mouth. But her guardian rubbed soothing circles on her back until her gut had nothing left to give.

Then, they leaped into action, heading for the courtyard. It helped, running next to Samiah with a goal in sight, while everything around them crumbled.

The square was even worse.

The twin minarets were wreathed in smoke, the beautiful engraved architecture transformed into a gateway to despair. Ropes of fire rose around the bulbous domes, and any intact structures were concealed by swirling ash. Only the bells lay unscathed in the middle, but the brass glowed ember red. A horrific groan from a flaming building sent people scattering like ants from a kicked anthill. Any impression of the courtyard being an open space was gone. Fire poured through pillars, soaking the air with the taste of death. If it was this bad here, what was happening in the slums? Gayathri, Laila, Bilal . . . Zain's stomach hollowed.

People wailed, hands reaching out aimlessly, begging for help. Some were desperately throwing buckets of water onto the closest buildings, their efforts doing little to subdue the rabid flames. Samiah thrust a broken metal bowl into Zain's arms; it burned her palms but she gritted her teeth, wrapping her hands in the hem of her tunic before rushing to the nearest well to fill the bowl with water.

Not enough. This wasn't going to be enough. Zain threw the bowl near her feet, then flinched when it bounced off the ground with a sharp metallic click. There, a piece of pipe jutting from the ground. She didn't give herself a moment to think; she picked up the bowl and brought it down on the pipe joint.

She bellowed and hit it again and again. She had to save them, to help her city this time. She had failed once before and the fire had never gone out, not in her memory. She couldn't burn any longer.

By now, the people around her noticed, and a man joined her. He held a large rock, and on his next hit, the pipe burst open, gushing water. Someone exclaimed, and word spread; soon, water spurted from parts of the ground, the fire hissing, then dimming. Under the shrill exhale of metal, she swore she heard the city sigh with relief. They would pay for this later, the lack of water that was to come; but right now, they needed to survive.

"Zain!"

Someone barreled into her back with a broken whine. Laila was crying into her tunic. Angry red burns patchworked her arms.

"On my soul, Laila, what are you doing here?" Zain asked, dropping to her knees.

"I can't find Lufi," Laila wailed. "Mama left us at the market while she packed up our stall, and then everything caught fire. I was trying to get Lufi's doll, but I dropped it in the crowd and"—Laila gulped for air, clutching at her necklace as though it were choking her—"I lost her. I don't know where she is, I thought she came here."

"Shh," Zain said, ripping off a piece of her tunic and soaking it in the water gushing from the pipe. She gently placed the rag on Laila's burns. These were bad, far worse than Laila had realized. She was in shock and needed medical care.

"Guards!" someone cried.

Zain covered her mouth as a group of bloodstrippers entered the square. Aid. The guards had resources, manpower.

Laila let out a guttural scream. "Help!"

Zain got to her feet and echoed her call. "Please help!" She couldn't summon even the slightest shred of guilt for pleading to the people she hated. For once, they were on the same side; if this city no longer existed, there was nothing left for them to rule. Around her, people waved at the bloodstrippers, cries amorphous, but the guards came to an eerie, chilling stop. Observing the pain around them like predators who played with their prey. Like torture was a part of the kill.

The first guard pointed at a leech, a boy who was bent over an unmoving body, sobbing. Two bloodstrippers rushed him from behind and shoved him to the ground, pinning the leech's wrists behind his back. The people around him yelled in protest, but the guards raised their guns, fending off the outraged crowd.

Arrests? During *this*?

Zain was going to be sick.

"Laila, hold this to your burns," Zain ordered. "Get out of here, go find Gayathri. Check the slums, I don't think the storm went there."

"What are they doing?" someone shouted.

Zain twisted on her heel in time to see them drag the leech off to the side. She searched for the slumlords who presided over the area. In that moment, she'd even take Dev. But faces melted into one another, covered in soot and blood and identical expressions of anguish. The bloodstrippers broke out in pairs and began their systematic assault.

People who hadn't noticed the attacks were caught unawares. They were tending to their wounded, putting out fires, and fighting for fresh air, and now the souls were punishing them with yet another enemy. No one could withstand attacks from so many sides. The man who helped Zain break the pipe leaped forward, protesting, but the nearest guard whipped him with a baton, sending him falling to the ground. An unnatural cold seized her as she noticed the guards' targets. Leech after leech.

Zain looked at Laila, who was struck with the same realization. "Laila, I—"

"Go," Laila whispered.

"Find Gayathri," Zain commanded, then rushed behind the nearest column that wasn't on fire.

Coward.

She shook her head, trying desperately to stifle the growing pressure in her chest. Her thoughts were a mess, her body hurt, and even the sharp cut of adrenaline couldn't help her make sense of what was happening. This—attacking her people when they were battered down—was a new low from the Gengs.

No one would be able to come after any of those arrested. No one would even care, not when the city was in shambles. Zain's ribs threatened to crack when—

"Zain?" Samiah appeared to her right.

Zain bit down on her cheek to keep from groaning.

"What are you doing?" Samiah hissed. "Do you see what's happening out there?"

Zain's mouth dried. "They'll take me."

Despite the smoke, Zain could measure how far Samiah's

face fell. She braced herself for the reprimand, but Samiah unwrapped the scarf around her neck and handed it over. "Put this on," she instructed. "We walk out of here together, and straight home. Do you hear me? Do not look up, do not speak."

Zain shook her head. She couldn't leave in the middle of *this*. Samiah ignored her protest.

"Stop shaking like that," Samiah said. "You'll give yourself away." She wrapped the fabric around Zain's shoulder, passing one side over and around her head to conceal her profile. Samiah squeezed her hand and led Zain onto the path home.

"There!"

"Hurry!" Samiah cried, nearly dislocating Zain's arm in an attempt to drag her away. But it was too late. Zain was tackled to the ground, wrists crushed in an iron-clad grip, sending a sharp blade of pain to her shoulders. Bony legs pressed her into the gravel, hot as coals.

Somewhere behind her, Laila screamed.

"I got her," her captor called. Zain knew that voice.

She knew that bloodstripper.

CHAPTER EIGHT

Zain

Jail smelled worse than searing flesh.

"You fuckers, let us out! People are dying out there!" someone yelled, banging on the bars of their prison. Most of the leeches had been split into different cells the moment they'd arrived. Some had taken a beating from trying to fight back, but even the older, stronger ones had been drained from helping the city after the fire. Zain leaned against the stone wall of her enclosure, panic and rage mixing to induce complete immobility.

Everyone had their way of coping. Across from her, Bilal sang a popular tavern tune under his breath while nursing a black eye.

> *Old Vicky, he came home with salt in his*
> *   beard*
> *And sopping full balls he'd forgotten to shear.*
> *Our loyal Vicky, he headed straight home.*
> *His missus took one look and said, "Please*
> *   be gone."*

"Will *you* please be gone," Zain muttered, but Bilal did not falter.

"My love," Vicky cried, so full of dismay.
"How are you so callous to turn me away?"
She said, "Your white hair's so tarred it's
    turned a rat black,
"And you've still got salt stuck in your ass
    crack."

He assumed the high-pitched squeak that most men employed when delivering Vicky's wife's reprimand.

"Be serious for one fucking second," Zain said, louder this time.

He said, "Give me a break darlin', I'm soaked
    to the bone."
She said, "I'll warm your bed if you came
    drenched in stone."

After his last note died down, he whispered, "You know, that last line never made any sense to me."

A guard yelled at them to shut up. Zain's head throbbed from the commotion. "It's not supposed to, you thickheaded buffoon," she said. "She never *wanted* him in her bed."

Bilal considered that, then gave up all pretenses. "How bad was the Bow?"

Zain shook her head. The last few hours were a blur. "I think it missed our place. The artery probably got it the worst. The underground market was hit bad, I don't even want to think about how many people—" She gulped for air. Bilal slid toward her, wincing, and put his hand on hers.

"That might be the most I've heard you speak since I had my tongue down your throat."

Zain groaned, halfheartedly batting him away. "That was ten years ago. Either I made an impression, or that was the last time a girl had the misfortune of having you breathe in her face."

He laughed, and she was transported to a different time, when the heat beat down on her brow while she leaped through the streets, her face stretched into a rare smile.

Bilal read her mind, pulling her closer. "We used to have so much fun, our whole group. You were one of Dev's favorites too, always chosen for his secret missions. Then, you stopped hanging out with us, and six months ago you just vanished."

"I did not vanish," Zain protested, resting her head on his shoulder. "I'm right here. I was your *partner* the other day."

He tensed, and the low timbre of his voice reverberated through his chest. "Come on, Zain. We're stuck here for souls know how long, and neither of us can tolerate thinking about what's happening out there."

In all these years, no one had asked her why she had distanced herself from the slums and then abandoned them entirely at the first signs of a drought. Samiah and Kanak were all too happy to see a shift in her company, and everyone else had been left to wonder. She had imagined this, though, a time when someone would care enough to ask.

"I grew up," Zain said, hoping it didn't sound like she had rehearsed this during long nights when she couldn't fall asleep. She curled into a tighter ball against Bilal, concealing her face. "We were children. I found different things to occupy my time. Leeching wasn't sustainable—for me." She amended the last part, knowing full well that Iravan and Dev had sustained beyond what anyone had imagined.

It simply wasn't sustainable for her to be around Dev. It wrecked her and confused her, being near a man who was like a deck of cards, and she never knew which face she would draw. At first, she had felt so special, and it made all the other leeches love her, hate her, and want to be her. Zain had never experienced this, not even with Kanak, whose love was quiet and soft. As a child, she had craved something more vibrant, something that cut through her veins.

It was too late when she realized that Kanak's love insulated while Dev's suffocated. She lost piece after piece of herself, until she had nothing to give to anyone else, and that was before she'd learned he was dealing with the Council on the Isle of Vis.

"That makes sense. You never really belonged with us anyway," Bilal said. She recoiled, and he quickly added, "I just meant that you had Samiah and Kanak, you know? You lived in the Bow, had a proper house and things. You always had one foot in and the other out. But I'm happy it was your decision. I thought it had to do with the Temple burning down—seems like that's when things changed for everyone."

The fire a decade ago had marked a cataclysmic shift in Tejomaya. The Temple had not just been a beloved monument, but a symbol of community. It was the last one standing in Janmir; the Gehennese had knocked down all the others. People had literally laid down their bodies in front of its walls to defend it. Regardless of religious belief, one could go there for weekly sermons, to seek guidance, to get married. Its loss unraveled Tejomaya, turning the acolytes into figureheads, confining spirituality to people's homes. The threads that bound them together vanished as each year passed and nothing rose to replace it.

The Temple's loss unraveled Zain for other reasons.

"What a freak accident," Bilal muttered, resting his head on hers. "Wait, you were there, weren't you?"

Her vision flashed blue, then warm, then splintered into screams, raking down her soul. Suddenly, she wanted him to sing again, to bellow until the ground above them shook in the hopes that it drowned the loudness within her. Sweat pooled in her curves and folds.

One Tejomaya...

Two Tejomaya...

Three Tejomaya...

"I was," she confirmed.

"Wow," he said. "I can't believe we've never talked about this. There was supposed to be a meeting there, right? Dev wanted to talk with that Anastasia Drakos and the acolytes. I knew it wouldn't work, but for people to die... Were you inside when the Temple caught fire?"

She pushed him away, desperate for air. "Can we not talk about fire right now?"

Suddenly, a door above them slid open, letting in a sliver of light. The cell undulated around her in bulges and divots, mud caked to every inch. Red splatters from betel nuts stared at her, arranged like the markings of a prisoner counting their days.

Bilal fell quiet; they both strained for the warning sounds. Two guards, if she could wager a bet. The other cellmates resumed their ruckus, howling to be let out.

"... are you certain about this?" one guard asked in Gehennese. Thank the souls that Samiah had insisted Zain learn the language.

"Yes, Theron," another replied in exasperation, like he had been asked this question a million times.

Zain's ears rang. The guard from the turbines, again.

"I don't understand why this one in particular," Theron replied, deeper, angrier. "I just hope you know what you're getting yourself into, Leander."

"Because you haven't seen her," Leander said, clearly at his wit's end. Moreover, Zain realized, he was much, much louder. As though he were just outside their cell. "It's this one, I'm telling you. I've been watching her."

Her mind caught up to what her body already knew. The cuts on her palms stung from sweat, and sticky hair matted her nape. Her pulse was beating so fast it could race one of those fearsome jet planes that no longer flew.

I've been watching her.

A torch lit. And there, just footsteps away with only metal bars in between them, were two bloodstrippers, one unnervingly familiar.

The first was the man from the turbines, the one who had taken her here. The one who, she was now certain, had been watching her. She glumly noted that his skin looked unharmed from the vial of calor she'd smashed against his face. His companion brought her pulse to a halt. Where the first man looked young and, from her past encounters with him, a little bit naive, his partner was anything but. He was taller and broader, with uneven stubble coating his lower jaw. A silver scar cut across his face from above his right brow to the top of his cheekbone. No jacket on, but she'd bet he was more senior than this Leander. The one thing they did have in common were their eyes. Even in the torchlight, they glinted at her. *Like the vipers they are,* Kanak would say, *the lighter their eyes, the more absent their soul.*

"Someone will come for you shortly," the tall one said in stilted Janmiri to the people in the other cells.

The man from the turbines stepped forward and asked, "Is your name Zain Jatav?" His Janmiri was drawn out by an accent she had come to despise. Bilal's hand tightened around hers. She said nothing.

"I'm Leander Cleirigh," he said. "We are your assigned blood-strippers. We are hoping you can help us with something, if you would follow us."

Theron stepped forward, just as Bilal maneuvered his body in front of hers. "You're not taking her anywhere."

Leander pulled out his gun.

"Don't," Zain yelled, before Bilal could do anything bull-headed. As much as he got on her nerves, she had no interest in watching his head blown to smithereens. Bilal sat back, eyeing the gun with distaste. "I'll come with you," Zain told the guards.

"Zainy—"

"I'll be fine," she insisted, squeezing his hand. Bilal's brows furrowed the way they used to when she'd tell him she didn't want to eat more sweets. Behind the battered and bruised man was the boy who'd let her and Gayathri braid his hair. "Please, trust me."

He didn't look thrilled, but he let her go. Zain followed the guards as though marching to her death.

The bloodstripper quarters were much larger than she had imagined. Theron led her up the stairs and through a strange set of hallways before bringing her to a closed wooden door. She had barely adjusted to the light, so there was little she could gather about this place except how far her legs had carried her. Now, she was sat across from Leander, while Theron stood guard behind him, her wrists bound together and set on the table between them.

"As you know, the city has been experiencing difficulties with calor shortage," Leander said, carefully, like he was falling into a scripted speech. "The Council has asked us to conduct an investigation into the recent rainfall, study any patterns that might emerge. Given that the people from your side of the city tend to—how shall I say it—rely upon calor, we thought you might be helpful."

Zain's mouth was agape. Accent aside, this man's Janmiri was *good*. More than that, Leander had outright addressed that the slums had been taking their share of calor over the years. Of course, everyone knew this already, and while leeches could not afford to be caught in the act, the bloodstrippers generally left them alone. A compromise to salvage a modicum of peace.

That, or Dev had asked the Council to hold their dogs back.

"Expecting her to be helpful is like asking an animal to wipe its ass," Theron said in Gehennese. Leander waved him off. Realization—and annoyance—set upon her. This Theron didn't think she understood him.

"Just to be clear," Zain said in his language. She hadn't planned on deigning them with a response, but she couldn't resist the urge to see his face when her Gehennese came out flawless. Theron didn't so much as blink. "You want *us* to help you understand what is happening with the drought? Don't you have people for that? On *our* island?"

Theron snorted, prompting another fierce look from Leander. Their mirrored expressions were startlingly similar.

"Yes, we have extractors who study calor," Leander said. "But they are going down the wrong path. I have my own hypotheses, and with adequate testing, I might be able to find a solution that would aid all of us. For that, however, I need calor."

"So take it," Zain replied, brows furrowed. In her experience, bloodstrippers were concerned only with protecting the Council's calor. They didn't care about calor research. "Go dig around the harbor or the island. I still don't understand why you're here."

"There's a shortage," Theron said in pidgin Janmiri. "We can't just take calor."

Zain smirked at his poor linguistic effort and switched back to her native tongue. Easier for her. "You seem to keep taking it just fine." *Not just from the skies, but from the slums.*

Zain thought back to Dev's exchange with Dheera. The package he was referring to had to be calor—nothing else mattered in this city. He was dealing in calor with the Council.

Leander ignored her comment. "Whatever we can take isn't enough. And from what we have learned about you . . . you can help us get more."

Zain stared at him blankly.

He continued. "We want to find the Temple of Many-Souls' calor reserve."

Zain looked at him for a moment, then tipped her head back and laughed.

To his credit, Leander waited for her hysterics to subside. Theron, however, looked positively murderous.

"You do realize that's a myth, right?" Zain said. "It's more unbelievable than flight."

Every child in Tejomaya had grown up hearing about this purported reserve. Zain remembered huddling around an old archive book the slum kids had been passing around, filled with an acolyte's annotations on Tejomaya's history and customs. Gayathri had read every word out loud to an awestruck Zain and Bilal under a flickering candlelight. They'd been less interested in the politics of it all. Bilal yawned audibly when his sister told them about how Gehanna had entered the city nearly a century ago under the pretense of trade, offering to inject Janmiri markets with affordable advanced technology in return for the country's natural resources. In the decades that followed, the rest of the world latched onto Janmir's calor like a parasite, and the country's thriving economy collapsed as Gehanna cut tariffs on their own products.

Fifty years ago—and this was the part of the tale they knew—thousands gathered from across the Lower Tectonic to protest the blatant Gehennese occupation. The ensuing conflict split the sky and land, taking countless lives before blood began raining from the hideous rift.

But in the book, there was a private section on acolyte rituals and secrets. And of the hundreds of notes scribbled in the margins, one had captured the interest of everyone who had seen the book:

There's a calor reserve still in this city. Speak to Inas.

Inas, the Head Acolyte. That's all it had taken for the rumor to spread like wildfire. The handwriting was badly smudged and nondescript, and nearly every acolyte in the service had been accused of being the author. The story changed as often as new veins sprouted in the sky, but the heart of it stayed the same: the blood rains held the last calor in the world, and the acolytes wanted to protect it. The acolytes staunchly denied such claims, and the belief had faded into folklore.

The reserve was nonsense. A story told to give them unreliable hope for the future.

Theron took over. "You grew up in the Temple before being taken in by Kanak Jatav. Why would an acolyte adopt a random Janmiri orphan and leave the Temple? Why you, out of so many others in their care?"

"Because we shared a special bond," Zain said. It was true—Kanak and Zain had always connected. When the time came for Kanak to leave, they had taken Zain with them.

"No acolyte ever leaves the Temple unless asked." Theron leaned over her. "You got too close to the truth about the reserve."

Zain bristled. Yes, she sometimes thought Kanak left because of her—hated herself for it quite frequently, actually—but this reasoning was absurd. "I was *five.*"

The way he watched her stripped her to her core. How much did he know about her? About her family and her past?

"You can find out," Leander said, kindly. "As you said yourself, you have a good relationship."

Zain didn't even have to think about it. "I will never help you."

Leander sighed, then gestured at Theron to continue.

"The bloodstrippers would like to do this without causing a massive upheaval," Theron said. "The Anniversary of the Carnage is right around the corner. Tensions are running high. This is supposed to be the easy way. If you help us, we can do this quietly, and once we have our answers about calor, things can go back to the way they were without anyone knowing about our conversation and your role in it. If you don't help us, then we can always go to the acolytes." His finger stroked the side of his gun. "Put your special bond to special use."

"Don't you dare go near them," Zain said, struggling against her bindings. Theron's mention of the Anniversary sent a bolt of lightning through her heart. Her deadline with Dev was at the same time. Two parties wanted her to deliver calor she didn't have. It was also the day the don was planning something undoubtedly terrible. Would the souls give her a fucking break?

Leander placed a gun on the table. Her gun. "The cartridge is empty," he said. "You don't need to decide now. Meet me at the docks at midnight in three days with your answer. I would like if you would help us without needing to resort to any threats, but there is too much at stake here, and we'll do what we must."

CHAPTER NINE

Iravan

Iravan stumbled through unrecognizable streets, the world moving with the haziness of a dream but the terror of a nightmare. Lufi was drooped in his arms, her doll pressed against his chest as she cried into his soot-smeared shirt.

He headed toward Yadav's store, unsure what he would do if it had crumbled to ash. His gait was unsteadied at the sight of the shop, untouched by flames.

Harshit, a spice-store owner, emerged from Yadav's neighboring building. They looked in disbelief at the row of shops that sat in front of the Sickle.

"It missed us," said Harshit. "It went the other way, toward the Bow and then the Soulless Sea."

But the storm's aftermath had left no corner untouched. Names were bellowed frantically by those searching for loved ones; others were already discovering the depths of their losses. It was too familiar, this grief. It threatened to eclipse him.

"Sir!" someone cried. It was Laila and two other slum boys bolting in his direction. "You have to go—"

Laila skidded to a stop, a sodden cloth dropping from her hand. "Lufi?"

Lufi raised her head in her sister's direction, then let out a wounded cry. Iravan's chest loosened as he lowered her to the ground. Lufi hurtled into her sister's arms, which were bare to the elbows and covered in deep burns.

"I'm so sorry," Laila sobbed, dropping to her knees. "I didn't mean to leave you. I won't leave you again, I promise."

Iravan winced as Lufi's rough embrace disturbed her sister's scalded skin. He slowly pulled Lufi back an inch. "Be careful," he said, gently, pointing at Laila's arms.

Lufi looked stricken, tracing a little finger around the edges of Laila's wrinkled flesh. Laila flinched, a tear rolling down her cheek. Her whole body was shaking from adrenaline and pain and relief. It was a miracle that she could still stand.

"You should go get that checked out," Iravan said.

"I will," Laila said. "But we had to come find you first. The bloodstrippers, sir. They're arresting everyone."

The world dropped out from under Iravan's feet.

By the time he made it to the square, the bloodstrippers were gone. Smoke filled the air. Water pulsed from parts of the ground, but attempts to douse the flames had been partly abandoned. There was a fevered pitch to the city. People reached for Iravan, asking him where their children had been taken, and he couldn't do this—couldn't handle all this at once. He couldn't look at their ash-streaked faces and offer them hope because, souls be damned, he had none for himself. Iravan searched the crowd desperately for someone he could trust, but the eyes that found him were not the ones he would have chosen. Still, she was better than the people clutching at him for comfort.

As he moved closer, he realized Samiah Jatav did not possess her typical steadfastness. She was missing her signature scarf, that brown drab she made and sold to anyone who'd buy it, and her fingers clutched at her barren neck instead. Her steely gaze eviscerated him.

"They took Zain," she said. She stood still, but her eyes conveyed anarchy. "They did not say why, but we all know what those children have in common. You should have been here."

There it was. The accusation Iravan had been wrestling with, but no matter how much the reproach made him feel like a shrunken man, he stood taller.

"They're not children anymore," he said. "They can take care of themselves. And what about you, huh? What did you do while the bloodstrippers took your child from you?" Shame steeped his words, but was he not telling the truth? The city was in shambles, and he was stretched so thin he felt like a wraith, like anyone could walk through him. He'd rescued Lufi, and failed everyone else. "I cannot be everywhere at once."

For a moment, he thought Samiah would spit at him, the way she had ten years ago when his mistakes had torn the city in half. Was history repeating itself today?

"That has always been the problem, Iravan," she said, quietly, her eyes shining with sorrow. "You light the fire in all of us, but you're never there to watch us burn."

It was nighttime when Iravan went looking for Dev. Between putting out fires and dealing with immediate damage, the hot loo winds had blown away both ash and time.

Night in Tejomaya was dull; the sun remained concealed behind the rot, which took on a pungent black-and-red hue in the hours people slept. That night, no one was going to rest, and the sky reflected the city—ashen, with embers burrowed in its skin.

You're never there to watch us burn.

Samiah's indictment stuck to him like the blood rains. He reached for his coin, its surface roughened from the grime that accumulated in the bottoms of his pockets. Its touch was the only thing that allayed the thunderous roar in his ears.

A lone figure prowled along the stone wall that lined the outer perimeter of the slums, cigarette in hand, rage dripping from each movement. Iravan recognized this state, a person imprisoned by desire. Dev was his most dangerous self when he was like this—single-minded and relentless—and it wouldn't stop until he had an outlet.

Good. They both needed a fight.

"They've taken it too far this time," Dev said. His eyes were bloodshot. "You wanted to avoid confronting those motherfuckers, waste our time on the damn Sickle, but this was never a two-sided issue. Now they're here picking our kids off the street."

Iravan staggered. He expected anger, but not at him. It was no secret that, of the two, Dev had always pushed for a more aggressive approach toward the Gengs in their city. Iravan had never wanted to risk an outright rebellion, not when they were outmatched on so many fronts, and keeping balance had been critical to their success so far. They had never weaponized their differences against one another.

"You're acting like I welcomed them here with open arms," Iravan said.

Dev let out an empty chuckle. "You might as well have."

The recrimination slipped off his tongue like blood on steel. Dev dropped his cigarette on the ground and crushed it under his heel. Embers sparked on debris. Iravan saw red. They didn't have enough calor. The leeches had been taken. His city had been ignited.

And he was useless.

Iravan needed to move or he'd punch Dev in the face, and that would do neither of them any good. He set off toward the Bow. Dev caught up to him in seconds.

"Where the fuck are you going?" Dev asked.

"To break them out," Iravan replied. They were approaching the ashes of the Temple. His body trembled at the sight. The leeches he could get out, but it would be a measly stopper on a souls-be-damned tsunami of problems. The answer was calor—and he didn't know where to get more. Unless . . .

Dev pulled Iravan's arm. "Is that all you're going to do?"

Iravan's head buzzed. Mariam's voice echoed in his mind. The calor reserve. How dire things must have gotten for him to revisit that absurd idea . . . but he couldn't afford to write anything off now.

"No, it's not all," Iravan said. But he couldn't tell Dev about the reserve, not before he had proof. And a small, selfish, rash part of him *wanted* to do this on his own. He thought of Dev and Yadav, always conspiring together, treating Iravan like he was made of glass. It was time to remind everyone that his broken edges could still draw blood. "But I need to speak to some people first."

They came to a stop in front of the Bow. Iravan could see where the storm had hit. The houses that had narrowly escaped looked almost comical against the charred remains of the less fortunate. People roamed outside, crying, melting into one another in the ghastly routine of a community that had suffered time and time again. Iravan was sick of it. One more loss and he would split apart. Souls only knew what would be left inside him.

A toddler waddled in front of them, veering just far enough from her family before her mother swooped her up, chubby arms grasping at air. Iravan's breath caught.

"You haven't been the same since she died," Dev said, observing. Iravan resumed his march.

"I know it messed you up," Dev continued, keeping pace. "I promised you then that we would get through it together, but I still need your support. She would want you to fight for a better world, Ravi. Imagine if she were still alive—she would be almost, what? A teenager? A whole-ass person suffering in this shithole, and you would move each hut in the slums by hand if it meant changing that."

"I already said we'd fight!" Iravan bellowed. He regretted it immediately. Around them, everyone fell quiet, watching him. Their attention was stifling. It was okay for everyone to disintegrate in their grief, but one loud word from him and the spotlight was on. Blinding. "Don't speak of my daughter like you know what she'd want."

She'd never had the chance to ask for anything.

Dev winced, then led him away from the crowd. "You can look into whatever it is you have in mind," he said. "But I have something that is ready. Yadav and I have been working on calor injectables."

Cold sweat broke across Iravan's forehead. Bare contact with calor through the rains caused a brief heightening of senses, a stimulating effect on humans, but any experimentation had proved too dangerous. Before calor scarcity grew, before the Gengs invaded countries like Urjan to steal their reserves, before the sky bathed the world in blood and fury, it had been outlawed for use in humans. It caused far too much damage, prompting bodies to combust when they absorbed too much.

"*We* never talked about it," Iravan said, but the accusation in his tone was whittled away by curiosity. "Do they work?"

Dev hesitated. "We need to test them. On people. And we need more calor."

A few weeks ago, Iravan would have shot down the idea right away—it was far too dangerous to risk losing people during testing—but the last few days had rewired his thinking. He let himself consider it. Power in their reach, a city they could restore. His daughter smiled at him from his mind's eye. One thing was for certain: each moment he had was a gift others had not been given. And he did not intend to waste any more.

"Fine," Iravan said, and Dev's face broke into a terrifying smile. "But we do this safely. With agreed-upon terms. No person goes through this without knowing the risks. We're losing people in droves, and we don't need to be the cause of more loss. Let's discuss tomorrow."

The delight on Dev's face faded. "Tomorrow?"

"We are needed out here." Iravan gestured around them. Now, a little farther from the crowds, they could see how lost everyone looked, like bits of lint tossed around in an aimless wind. "They'll be looking to us more than ever. You should inspect the slum lines, check on Yadav."

Dev nodded curtly. "Can you handle the jail alone?"

Iravan tried not to bristle. "I'll get them out."

Then he would find this calor reserve and save his city once and for all.

"You gave them the *Sickle*?" Bilal asked, his long legs moving rapidly to keep up. Behind them were the fifty or so leeches who had been arrested, all released without issue—proving the Gengs were just trying to exacerbate their suffering—and making no pretense of hiding their eavesdropping.

All except one. Zain, whom Iravan had noticed right away by her mane of hair, had a glassy look to her.

"Do not use that tone with me," Iravan said, and Bilal's open jaw clamped shut.

Relinquishing their battle over the Sickle to the Gengs, a fight that had simmered during the drought, was a simple way of getting their people back and presenting a peace offering. Tejomaya could not and would not be won with brute force; the upcoming Anniversary of the Carnage was another reminder of that. At least he was almost home and this hellish day was nearly over.

Iravan faced the group that trailed him, feeling ancient. He was only twenty or so years older than they were, but they all looked so young. It was the flush on their still-plump faces, the optimism to their steps—like they weren't sprinting in place like he was, burning out on a path that led nowhere. "What the hell happened?"

"Apparently the Council ordered arrests, sir," Bilal said, cupping his broken nose. "In retaliation for the boats. I think it was Drakos's orders." The name had a chilling effect on Iravan. This was not Hamish Drakos's style. The Council Head was like a boa constrictor, wrapping around the slums and squeezing, slowly. This was a bite, and there was only one person who knew just where to sink her poisoned fangs.

Fucking Anastasia.

Do you ever think before you act? Yadav had asked her once.

She had smirked, flipping her long hair behind her shoulder. *What's the fun in that?*

Iravan had pulled her in by the waist, drunk on her laughter, mesmerized by how it sounded like wind chimes and fractured glass at the same time. He didn't have to wonder when things had gone so wrong between them, not when he'd marched right up to the bloodstrippers and handed over her pain on a silver platter. And she'd struck back, singing like a canary that'd been locked in a cage with all his secrets.

Now her laughter sounded like drowning, a constant gasp for air.

"No, it was the Finzish," one of the other boys drawled, oblivious to Iravan's inner turmoil. "They were talking outside my cell. We got their boats that night."

So the Council was tearing itself apart. "What else?" he asked, feeling for his coin in his pocket.

It became clear they were all shaken. They peppered him with questions of deaths and damage. The darkness concealed a lot of the destruction, but maybe that made it worse. Knowing the horrors the day would unveil.

"Go home," he said. "And meet at the square tomorrow at noon. We have work to do."

No one had to be told twice.

"Not you," Iravan said to Bilal. The boy perked up. "I want eyes on our borders, all times of the day. Report on anything—or anyone—suspicious around the area."

Bilal frowned. "That's not very specific."

"I know," Iravan said. Reluctantly, he added in a low voice, "But you're the only one I can trust. There are rumors of"—*Souls, I'm doing this*—"a calor reserve."

Bilal looked as confused as Iravan was disgusted with himself. "The thing in the book?"

Iravan massaged a tender point in his temple and nodded. That ridiculous book had driven him up a wall when it first spread

through the city, sending everyone into a tizzy. He couldn't believe he was legitimizing this.

Bilal gaped at him. "Is it real?"

"I intend to find out," Iravan growled. "Just keep your eyes
and ears peeled. Especially if other people are looking. And not a
word of this to anyone else—not even to Dev."

If he was surprised, Bilal didn't show it. With a quick salute,
he hurried after Zain, who was steps behind the others, braiding
her hair. Which reminded Iravan . . .

"Jatav!" Iravan called. Bilal and Zain both turned, but his
beckoning fingers were only for her. There was something off in
her expression. Not exhaustion or fear, like the rest of the leeches
who'd been arrested. Something darker. She dragged her feet toward Iravan, as Bilal joined the other leeches.

Iravan had known her since she was seven, when she and
all the other kids had panted after Dev like dogs. And then she
had faded away. Making short appearances at meetings over the
years, exchanging a quick word with the other leeches, mostly
sticking to the periphery. Iravan had always attributed her disap-
pearance to Samiah and Kanak.

"Is there anything you're not telling me?" he asked, too tired
to beat around the bush. He wasn't expecting a straight answer
either way; instead, he studied her face.

Zain looked down at her feet, and he wanted to yank her
head up.

"Not really," she said, after a moment. "They wanted to know
where we get our calor for testing. I told them about the turbines
in the Sickle. Sounds like that won't be a problem."

"Testing?" he asked.

Her face was placid, unyielding. But Iravan was no longer

focused on her expression. Zain had been paying attention during their walk.

"They want it to rain again, but I didn't understand half of what they said. All I know is they want calor and they won't tap into their own supplies. I'd watch out," she said.

"*We* need to watch out," Iravan said. And then, because the day had grown so long and muddled, he asked, "Why do you still work for us?"

As the seconds stretched between them, he regretted asking the question.

"I don't know," she replied.

It might have been the only honest thing she'd said to him.

CHAPTER TEN

Anastasia

Anastasia liked the way her face cracked open in the shattered mirror.

It was one of the only times she met her own eyes. She liked how her thin lips appeared disfigured along the dark crevice, distracting from how her dark-brown irises held nothing. No emotion, no light, no command.

Once, people called her beautiful; only a decade ago, she had been heralded as the Council's dazzling leader to come. She had the intellect to match—that, of course, remained unchanged—but the years had twisted her plump skin, drained her caramel hue into something waxen. At first, she had resented it, the relentless assault of time and life on precious, fleeting beauty, but soon she forged it into her armor. There was something haunting about her now, something that stayed with people long after her presence was but a memory.

Watching Tejomaya burn had left her raw. Charvi had fled to the other gatherers, but Anastasia remained rooted to her place by the forest. It was strange, like the souls were taking her back to the day she had left the city, her true home, with fire in her wake. The person that had risen from the ashes was unrecognizable to her. Anastasia had no interest in returning to that person, but that was what her father was asking her to do.

"Are you worried about the bloodstrippers?" Hamish asked, aligning stacks of parchment on his desk. He was in a foul mood after how terribly the evacuation went. Apparently, no one was able to get into the catacombs, which had "inexplicably sealed up," according to the messengers. "May I remind you that you *wanted* to go to Tejomaya?"

Anastasia tried to feign nonchalance, all while the knot in her belly tightened. "That was fifteen years ago."

Her father couldn't possibly be serious. He had been furious at her for staying in Tejomaya as long as she had. Furious at the reports that Matthieu had brought back to the Council, her secrets cheapened by his retelling. Hamish had mocked her for becoming one of *them*. As if she hadn't always been one of them in some ways. He was the reason she'd been born on that soil. "It will be different now, especially after the storm."

"That is the point," Hamish said, slamming his fist on the desk. "We need someone to oversee the turbine inspections and validate the reports we're getting. There will be parts to order and replace. The bloodstrippers also described a strange vapor coming from the sky before the storm, and they think it might have something to do with Dheera's death."

Anastasia fumbled for an argument, but came up empty. Hamish Drakos never let his thoughts crumble, not even in front of her.

"The maelstrom had to hit right before their platter of anniversaries," Hamish continued, but the distant look in his eyes made it seem like he was talking to himself. "You know, when horrible things happen to your city, you might learn something. The rift happened because they couldn't learn to cooperate, and forty years later their precious Temple burns down the same day. Bunch of savage freaks."

Anastasia's tongue dried. She hadn't been in the Temple that day, but sometimes she woke in a cold sweat, her body imprisoned by burning walls, rubble crushing her skull.

Hamish remained oblivious to her despair. He rested his chin on interlocked fingers, pressing his eyes shut as if to restore an unattainable calm. "As you know, the Anniversary is a sensitive day for the people of Tejomaya. Matthieu told me he's hearing plans of a potential rebellion. It's why he was here."

"Matthieu knows nothing," Anastasia said, shakily. Matthieu had been suspicious of her since her time in Tejomaya. She was certain he was in Petra's ear, dissuading her from backing Anastasia for the Council. Going back to the city would not help her case. "I know you all think little of the dons, but they are not deluded enough to risk fighting our forces."

"And how would you know what they would risk?" Hamish sneered. "You poked at a sleeping beast, urging Petra to order those raids after the storm. Devraj Basu will be incensed—at least we don't have to worry about his partner. Sounds like he's a shadow of his former self."

Anastasia felt ill, and it wasn't because of her ailing body. This was the closest Hamish had come to saying Iravan's name. "What does it matter what Dev thinks?"

"I don't care what he thinks," Hamish said, looking affronted. "I care what he will *do*. And in case you've been too busy to realize, our Coalition is vulnerable. Petra wants another Finzish delegate to take the open Council seat. As much as I wish I had another option, I want it to be you."

She would never be his first choice, but the gravity of his declaration was still overwhelming. Her father had never backed her before.

"I can make my case here," Anastasia insisted.

Hamish shook his head. "Petra and Jezeme have been increasing their bloodstripper presence in Tejomaya, and I worry about them running rampant. There is only so much I can do from the island, and it is imperative we maintain Gehennese control. Things will go south soon, and I want us to be on top when it does."

"When what goes south?" Anastasia asked. *Tell me*, she wanted to plead. Hamish moved uncomfortably in his seat, like he'd given away too much.

"When the rebellion begins," he said. "For the love of the altar, Ana, can you pay attention?"

His ire was a facade. Her father was hiding something. He wanted to keep an eye on Tejomaya, and now she wanted to keep an eye on him. She scoured for a way out—her father understood only action and solution.

"What if I get us information on the rebellion without me leaving?" she asked, loudly, hoping her false bravado belied her fear.

Hamish lifted a brow in question. "If you can get us information on the plans, you can do as you wish."

"Fine, but I have one condition."

She was pushing it, but she had squandered enough time. She would dig herself a hole, claw her way out, and land right where she wanted. "If I deliver prior to the Anniversary, you call a vote for the Council position immediately."

Hamish looked aghast. "That's in a week. You don't have the votes."

"I'm the only option at this time," she said. All the theatrics at the meeting weren't just for fun. "And I've built my credibility over the past ten years. Who smooths over any troubles with the gatherers? Who extracted sensitive information on the slums and handed it over to the bloodstrippers, redesigning their patrols and strengthening our foothold in the city? Who stepped in during that failed meeting between you and Petra and negotiated a new calor deal?"

"Listing your accomplishments won't change their concerns," Hamish warned.

She'd never been able to get past the concerns about whom she had spent time with, whom she had loved. They didn't see that when she returned from Tejomaya heartbroken, she'd fashioned the pieces of her heart into something lethal.

"The sooner we do this, the less time they have to put forth a viable candidate," she said.

Hamish grimaced. "You'll have to get us verified reports in a week, and if you fail, you leave for Tejomaya immediately. I will trust only a Drakos to do right by us. Remember who we are."

How could she ever forget? Hamish Drakos had spearheaded the technology to extract calor from blood and had moved the ruling body of Gehanna to the Isle of Vis. The Council had ratcheted up another level under his guidance, and he had managed its complex geopolitics with finesse throughout the years. His power may now be waning due to Finzish and Nohri intrusions, but he was still indomitable. History would never forget the Drakos name, forever entwined with the zeitgeist of calor depletion and the revolutionary act of prolonging the Upper Tectonic's lifespan.

"Fine. Do we have a deal?" Anastasia asked, this time flashing him the briefest of smiles to hide the sear of a long-lost memory:

a brutal heat wave, the air hazy and thick. Her voice, more than a decade younger. *I'm a Drakos,* she had said proudly. *That means "dragon" in our tongue. We were built for the heat.*

Then came the taunt.

You're in Tejomaya, Drakos. Your name means nothing here.

"You have my word," her father said.

Anastasia bowed her head. "You should get that fixed," she said, gesturing toward the cracked mirror that hung to his left, the one that showed an unnerving reflection of how broken she was inside. Anastasia left the Head Councilmember's chamber, doing her best to ignore the memories.

One thing was for certain: whether in two weeks or in two decades, she was never going back to Tejomaya.

Night fell over the island like a lover's last breath, sudden and insufficient. Anastasia watched the city beyond the waters vanish entirely behind the thick fog, and she wished her thoughts would do the same.

Yet they persisted. Insufferable things.

Her meeting with Hamish left her walking aimlessly, away from the marble mansions and general island populace.

The deal she had struck was all well and good, but her promise was not one she knew how to uphold. How was she supposed to retrieve information on the rebellion? The offer had sprung from a place of desperation. Now she had to find a way to follow through.

Bang.

Anastasia was on the opposite side of the stone forest, on a part of the island that was home to a dilapidated toolshed. The shack held equipment to fix turbines and calor lines, but no one on the island knew how to use them, so they defaulted to assistance from the mainland. As a result, this corner of the Isle of Vis was left without much life. Except one person.

Anastasia had put this off for too long. Something had to give.

Bang.

It grew louder, harder, the grinding crash of metal on metal. It was difficult to see in the dark, but Charvi's figure, hunched over the plains, was something she could always pick out. Another sound rose in the quiet—hushed voices.

Charvi was not alone; two figures accompanied her. One was small and squatting on the ground, and the other was emerging from behind the crooked slats that made up the walls of the shed. Anastasia drew closer, slowing to hear the tail end of their conversation.

". . . leave it here. What about the next one?" Varun asked, dusting his hands.

"Tejomaya will send word," Charvi replied, face tilted up at him.

Gravel crackled beneath Anastasia's feet, prompting the unsuspecting subjects of her surveillance to look her way. Was she imagining the rictus smile on Varun's face, the stricken tension in Charvi's? Baruna sat on the ground next to her mother in a pale-yellow variation of her usual cotton dress, drawing something in the earth.

"Your hair's getting long," Anastasia commented, studying the long waves that curled under Varun's ears as he drew closer.

He raked his fingers through his hair. "That it is. Want to cut it for me soon?"

The corner of Anastasia's mouth twitched. She hadn't spent

time with the gatherers in a while; sometimes it felt like being back in Tejomaya, a fact that landed uneasily on her heart. "Sure you can afford it?" she joked.

This was usually when Charvi chimed in, pulling Anastasia's leg in a way none of the other gatherers ever quite managed. *He pays for it by spending time with you* or *My child could do a better job for free,* she'd say.

Charvi said nothing.

Varun's easy smile faltered. "I'll have to work something out."

He bowed his head in farewell, then angled away.

"You don't need to go," Anastasia said, reaching for his elbow. She glanced anxiously at Charvi, who scoffed lightly under her breath.

Varun gently pulled his arm from her grip. "I have to get back to packaging our latest calor collections. Charvi and I are leading distributions this week."

"Weren't you in charge last week too?" Anastasia asked. All gatherers had high-exposure, high-risk jobs, and most had accepted that it was the price they would pay for their life on the island, but the packagers and distributors had it worse, coming in contact with fully processed calor. "I can speak to my father, ensure rotations are taking place as planned."

"No need," Varun said. "The extractors brought us new protective equipment; Ronin said these new gloves are impenetrable. Besides, we have a system in place that should make this go quickly. We'll be okay, but I must get back."

He waved goodbye to Charvi. Her mustard shirt, torn slightly at the neckline, clung to her sinewed arms as she resumed work.

"Are you building too?" Baruna asked Anastasia, noticing the tension.

Sometimes, Anastasia forgot how much more vocal the

reticent child became when she was alone with her mother. Maybe she would be a bridge to reconciliation.

Anastasia pressed her palms into the sides of her mid-length skirt. "No, but I come here when your mother is working. Did you know we used to do this when we lived in Tejomaya?"

Charvi's head twitched, but she continued her work.

Anastasia went on. "We had a favorite place there too. By the foothills, where the mountains descended into the plains. It was quite beautiful. All our friends would go there or to the harbor after we were out to drink—I mean, out for fun."

Charvi snorted. "We took you there because you got into fights at the tavern and needed to be removed from civilization."

"That's not fair. One time, I had to pull *you* out of a brawl," Anastasia said, smugly.

"Mama?" Baruna asked, with a hint of awe.

"Shush, Ana," Charvi said, then wagged her finger at her daughter. "No fights, Baru, or you will hear it from me. Besides, that was an exception. He swung at me first."

It was true. It was how they had met. Anastasia had been new to the city, shadowing a bloodstripper at the local tavern everyone frequented. She was about to leave when a large man sent his fist into Charvi's cheek. He'd groped her and lost his temper when his unwelcome advance was met with rage. Charvi hissed in his face before leaping on his chest. Anastasia was entranced. She had never seen anyone behave so wildly, so unencumbered. Anastasia always thought that she'd rebelled against those constraints, but it wasn't until that moment, when she watched Charvi snarl in the face of a man twice her size, that she realized she was still living within the established parameters of her life.

She had jumped in, pulling the man's arms behind his back, and laughed with glee as Charvi got her own punches in. They bolted out of the tavern together, cackling, inseparable ever since. People, unable to comprehend such an unshakable friendship between unlikely allies, sometimes wondered if she and Charvi were romantically involved. Their bond ran parallel to blood.

"What happened to your friends?" Baruna asked her mother.

"People grow apart," Charvi said, putting down her tools. Her gaze lifted to Anastasia's. "Some friends are the kinds you share memories with, others become those memories. Now, off to bed. It's late. I'll clean up and be home soon."

Baruna stood obediently, dusted off her dress, and gave her mother a kiss on the cheek before heading to their cottage, leaving a deep silence in her wake.

"I came to apologize," Anastasia said, smoothing the back of her skirt before settling on the ground in front of Charvi. Despite their fight from earlier that day, Anastasia only wanted to talk to Charvi about her conversation with Hamish. No one else would understand.

"No," Charvi said. A glint of a smile flashed in the dark. "You came because you need something. But I'm glad of it anyway. I wanted to see you too, after today."

Anastasia could barely breathe through the heavy sadness that fell over them. The storm that hit Tejomaya would have triggered memories in Charvi as well. Her friend must have been drowning in worry for the people she had left behind on the mainland.

"Have you heard anything?" Anastasia asked.

"No," Charvi said, then lifted an angular tool. A screeching sound followed as she pounded large objects on the ground. Three years, and Anastasia still didn't know what Charvi was building out there, but it grew bigger with each visit, nearly the size of the shed itself now. *A dream,* her friend had said when she'd asked, chest puffed with pride. *I'm resurrecting the past. Do you want to know how?*

No, Anastasia had said. *Surprise me in the future.*

"I'm sure they're okay," Anastasia said, but the sentiment was hollow. From what they had seen, there was no guarantee anyone was okay.

Charvi shook her head. "Can we talk about anything else? I can't—I can't go there."

Anastasia obliged, filling her friend in on her conversation with Hamish. The only insight Anastasia had into Charvi's reactions was in the way her movements halted in surprise, then flowed again. When she finished, Charvi retrieved a drill from the toolshed and set it down between them.

"So what are you going to do?"

"I don't know," Anastasia said. "I was thinking of speaking to one of the messengers, see if I could pay them to infiltrate the slums for me. Dev probably has the same men around him, Iravan too." Saying his name was an exercise in torture.

"It's been ten years, Ana," Charvi replied. "It's very different now."

Anastasia sunk her head into her hands. "He said the same thing, you know. It's like he's taunting me. All these years, I have worked to leave that life behind, have been prepared to give up anything to get a damn Council seat. First, they said it would be nepotism, and so I volunteered to join the bloodstrippers, away from this island. To prove myself outside my father's shadow. Then, when I came back, Iravan told Matthieu—" Anastasia's breath hitched, like someone had taken a scissor to her thoughts. She tried again. "When I came back, they said I had spent too much time away, that maybe I could not be trusted to act in the best interests of those who lived here."

Ten years she had spent paying the cost of Iravan's actions, earning back the Council's faith, their respect. All for what?

"Your father is an asshole," Charvi said. Stones clattered as she moved closer, the warmth of her body pressing up against Anastasia's side. "He knows this is an unreasonable ask, at an unreasonable time of year. A cruel test."

"One I'm failing," Anastasia said, looking up at the amethyst canvas staring down at her. Perhaps the sky had rotted because of everything it had witnessed below. Perhaps it wept because the pain was too much.

"No," Charvi said, quietly. "You're not. I have an idea."

"What?"

"I could go to Tejomaya."

Heat leached from the space between them.

"No, you couldn't," Anastasia said. "You can't just go there." *You would never come back.*

Charvi's hands touched hers, coarse and warm, blistered from hours of work but tender against Anastasia's palms.

"It's killing me to be here after today," Charvi begged. For the first time, her composure cracked, revealing the frightened woman beneath. "And none of the messengers would manage what you need them to do. I know how to spot Dev and Iravan's men, and I can disguise myself. I'll avoid the slums, stick to the taverns, see if I can hear anything. I can check on everyone from afar and be back with the information you need."

It was too good to be true. "But Baruna?" Anastasia asked. If Baruna left with Charvi, she could not let them go.

Charvi shook her head. "I'm not taking her into whatever is going on there. You can watch her."

Anastasia's jaw dropped. Charvi barely let Baruna out of her sight. To leave her behind entirely was unfathomable. Anastasia flashed back to Varun's strange behavior, measured that against the docile Charvi sitting in front of her.

"Is something wrong?" Anastasia asked, baldly. "Did you hear something? I heard you speaking with Varun earlier, about something from Tejomaya."

Charvi worried her lip. "Maybe. I just need to go see for myself. Please, Ana."

Wasn't this what she wanted, a miracle lifeline to help her achieve the demise of the people who had hurt her? Why did this cold fear settle so painfully in her bones? It was the city, she decided, that hurt when she did not want it to. She cared about the land, her home.

Anastasia cleared her throat. "And what if they're not okay?"

Charvi looked down. "Then at least I'll know."

Silence stretched taut between them.

"About Baruna . . . ," Anastasia trailed off.

"Don't think I forget she is here because of you," Charvi said, patting Anastasia's knee. "I trust you."

Something curdled in Anastasia's chest. She did not want to be trusted with the child, could barely stand to be in the same room as her most days. But she'd take a lifetime of watching Baruna over going back to Tejomaya.

"Two days," Anastasia said, firmly. "You go in on the morning boat and you're back the next evening. You can't stay longer, you know that."

Charvi nodded and gave her a weak grin. "On Amu's ashes, Ana. Two days."

Surely, she could manage that.

CHAPTER ELEVEN

Iravan

"**W**hat if we kidnap one of them to test it on?"

It had been two whole days of arguing with Dev since he'd rescued the jailed leeches, and Iravan was ready to take a gun to his own head. He was sitting across from his partner, wondering how they had gotten to where they were now, crammed in Yadav's back room. The old mechanic leveled the most morose expression at them in the midst of scribbling in his journal.

What happened to your face? Iravan had said to Dev when they'd first met. They'd been just two of the city's countless orphans. Dev's face had melted into the sea of many until that moment, when the blood vessels around his right eye had filled with ink and the side of his jaw had swollen to the size of a small stone.

Dev had spat a wad of blood to the ground and then—in a way Iravan still found remarkable—flashed a toothy grin at him. *A Geng beat me up.*

Why?

Dev had shrugged. *I made them angry. It's fun.*

Iravan had shaken his head. While this boy, who smiled

through a grotesque gash, should have scared him back then, Iravan was instead curious.

You're crazy, he had said.

Maybe, Dev had replied. *But no one will call me crazy when I get my revenge.*

The boy who dared to dream, Iravan had called him, and soon they became thick as thieves. He shared his own dreams— of safety, security—while Dev found someone with whom to stoke his anger and resentment. They were yin and yang, water and fire, order and chaos. They made the perfect team.

Ten years ago, Dev would never have challenged him like this in front of anyone, least of all another business partner. It was their unity that gave them credibility when they started leeching blood from the guards across the city. They'd gone to Yadav with their loot, and together, the three of them had centralized the slums' disparate power lines, which never had enough calor. They recycled sewage to increase access to clean water and provisioned healers with adequate supplies to mitigate rampant disease. They'd won the people's hearts. But Iravan hadn't realized just how much ground—and authority—he had lost since his daughter's death. They were falling apart.

"We can't just kidnap a bloodstripper," Iravan said, wondering why the hell he had to spell this out. "How would we do that?"

"We call a meeting," Dev said.

"Like that went well the first time around," Yadav commented.

Dev leveled a glare at him. Yadav never let Dev forget that it was he who'd set up the meeting with Anastasia and the acolytes.

Iravan moved the conversation along before either man could snap. "Where would we keep them?"

"Downstairs," Dev exclaimed, gesturing at the innocuous

rug that stretched across the corner of the room. The one that concealed a trapdoor.

"And let them escape through the damn tunnel?" Iravan retorted, slamming his hand down on the table. Years back, they had dug an escape tunnel from Yadav's cellar out to the foothills, but they had vowed to never use it unless absolutely necessary. It was their trump card, and Dev wanted to invite the enemy inside. A precious syringe teetered dangerously close to the edge of the table. Yadav stopped writing in his journal and snatched it, frustration simmering.

"Both of you need to get it together." Pointing at Iravan, he said, "You need to be willing to take risks. You said no testing on our people, and I agree. I will not risk any Janmiris on this, especially not at this stage, but we need to do something before we run out of time."

Willing to take *risks*? Everything they did every single day was a souls-cursed risk. Iravan opened his mouth to say as much, but Yadav had already turned to Dev.

"And you," he said, "need to have your head screwed on right. Iravan's right about the bloodstrippers—we can't just take one of them off the streets and not expect retaliation. With the Finzish and Nohri getting involved, the Gengs are defending against multiple powers. It makes them more dangerous, desperate. And if things do go well, it's too much of a risk for a guard to have calor-charged superhuman powers!"

"All I hear is you having absolutely nothing to contribute to this conversation," Dev said. "Why don't you stick to your little workshop and let us do the thinking?"

Yadav's stare could cut steel. "I have guided you since you were a bunch of idiots looking to make a difference," he warned.

"Every day since, I have asked myself if I made a mistake, and I have always decided that I did not, because you were stubborn assholes ready to light the world on fire for your people and if I could be but a shadow in your legacy, I would die a proud Janmiri man. Lately, my answer has been different. Keep going this way, and you will ruin us all."

Yadav picked up his journal and left.

"Souls, he's getting old," Dev said, pushing on the table so his chair hung on its back two legs. He gave Iravan a lazy smile, so deceptive that for a second, he saw a flash of the old Dev. "Was he always this mopey? *My answer has been different*," Dev imitated, then pulled out a cigarette from his jacket. He offered one to Iravan, who declined, watching as Dev lit the end.

"It's harder for him, you know," Iravan said, against his own will. A small part of him enjoyed this rift between Yadav and Dev—it put him back on Dev's side, where he belonged. But they couldn't fight each other like this. Iravan continued, "He was alive when the rift happened. He lost friends and family in the massacre. The Anniversary is right around the corner, so let's leave him alone."

Dev tapped his rings against the edge of the table. "Come on, we don't have time for his shit. What does he want us to do? No bloodstrippers, no Janmiris. I say we ask for volunteers and get this thing inside them. You know they'll line right up."

They would, but Iravan did not want to gamble with his people. If they were going to do this, they needed to make sure it hit those Gengs where it hurt most. He thought about how the bloodstrippers had dragged his people off the streets, how the Drakos family stretched their arms across the Soulless Sea, like the world was theirs for the taking. He had seen how far

Anastasia would go for power—and he would go further to ensure she didn't win.

As Dev rocked back, blowing halos in the air, Iravan remembered the smoke that etched the sky on the day of his greatest loss. Dev had put him back together, taken over leading the city to make sure they wouldn't lose all they had worked for. At every step, he had relied upon his friend, and now he had the opportunity to do the same in return.

"I know what we can do," Iravan said, the pieces shifting into place. It would hurt everyone, this plan, but if it went well, it would hurt the Gengs more. Dev looked delighted as Iravan laid out the nightmare he had concocted in his head.

"I've been talking to people who can help with this," Dev said. "But Yadav won't like it."

Iravan contended with a pang of guilt. "Doesn't matter."

Just then, Yadav barged back in, terror convoluting his features.

"There's a problem," he said.

A crowd had amassed outside Bilal's hut.

"Move," Dev barked.

"Get all these people out of here" was all Iravan said, as he entered Bilal and Gayathri's home. He slammed the door shut.

The inside of the hut was threadbare; a tattered mattress sat in the middle of the room, a hodgepodge of belongings scattered around it. Bilal lay on the bed, his eyelids fluttering while his sister cooled his head with a soaked rag. Water dripped down the side of his face, splotching the pillow.

"How long has he been like this, Gayathri?" Dev asked, dropping to Bilal's other side.

"He said he wasn't feeling well this morning," Gayathri said, fighting back tears. "But I thought he just had too much to drink last night. When he kept complaining in the afternoon, I told him to sleep it off. I had work to do. I was teaching classes this evening. I got back and found him here, drenched in sweat."

"Same symptoms?" asked Iravan. He remained by the door, unable to move any closer.

"Not all of them," she said, raising the rag. Tufts of Bilal's hair clung to it, and when Iravan looked closely, he realized her arms were covered in strands of black. Not *yet*.

"I should have known," Gayathri continued. "I've been treating people for soul-sickness for weeks, and in my own brother . . . in my own brother, I didn't see it happening."

"You couldn't have known," Iravan said. *And it wouldn't have made a difference.* They had all watched this happen before, over and over again. The fever, the trembling, the loss of hair. Soon, Bilal's skin would peel off in neat strands, a macabre sight. When one of the first victims had suffered through the disease's trajectory, Iravan had suggested they slit his throat. He'd meant it too.

"Where has he been lately?" Iravan asked, resisting the urge to run.

Gayathri wiped her face with the sleeves of her kurta, but the withering look she delivered him was fierce. "You should know. He was out on your orders."

Bilal moaned.

"Hey," Gayathri whispered, exhaling as his eyes opened a smidge. "Can you hear me?"

A weak smile touched the corners of Bilal's lips as he noticed

Iravan and Dev. "I've never felt so special," he said. "To have both dons at my deathbed."

Iravan fought the brick in his throat, but Dev grinned. "You *are* special," he said. "Only you would be this annoying on your deathbed."

Bilal let out a strangled laugh. "I was by the foothills," he said to Iravan, "near the back of the slums. Didn't see anything."

No reserve, then. But in that moment Iravan didn't care.

"Did anyone else go with you?" Iravan asked. They would have to track down who'd been near Bilal, near his food and water.

Bilal shook his head. "Not enough people," he gasped, and his facade shuddered, giving way to the face of a dying man. "I hoped to help more. Too tired. It's too hard." His neck slackened.

No, Iravan could not do this.

"Where are you going?" Dev called, as Iravan opened the door to the hut.

"To find a fucking cure," Iravan said, looking over his shoulder. "Don't you dare die on me."

Iravan muscled his way through the crowd, ignoring Dev's cries for him to stop and Gayathri's pleas for him to wait. He knew what they would say. He and Gayathri had spoken to every person with the barest knowledge of healing, had scoured the old acolyte records that dated well past the colonization of Tejomaya, and had even broken in to the bloodstripper quarters to see if they had any similar cases. Every effort had been as fruitless as the dried-up sky. But one voice had taken up residence in Iravan's brain, a pesky Urjan woman's, with too much to say.

You can find me in the Bow, I'm on the second street, in the house with the lavender door.

He hadn't taken her seriously yet.

When he got to the door—more a dusty gray than lavender—it was an effort for him to not tear it down. Mariam answered on the third slam of his fists, wearing a midnight-blue dress that ballooned around her. Her glasses nearly slipped off her nose in surprise.

"I wasn't expecting—"

"The cure for the soul-sickness," Iravan said, resting a hand on her doorframe. "You said, that day at the market, that you may have something. I need it. You can ask me whatever you like, tell me to do whatever you want. But I need the medicine now."

His heart hammered, rattling his ribs. He hadn't had time to think through how he'd ask, what he'd offer, just that he would pay any price. Iravan had committed many crimes in the name of his people; he had killed, maimed, and torn away parts of himself until he was nothing more than a vessel for battle. In front of Mariam, he laid down what he had left: his pride.

A knot formed between Mariam's brows. "I may have something," she said. "But it's not a cure."

"I don't care," Iravan said, hoarsely. "Please."

She studied him. "Wait here."

Everything was moving too fast and too slow at the same time. He heard the sounds of drawers opening and closing, paper tearing, but all he saw was Bilal. Bilal with his eyelids heavy, body skeletal. *Not him. Please not him.*

When Mariam returned to the door, she held a small bag filled with a white powder.

"Mix this with water and feed it to them," Mariam said. "It should help, but I have to reiterate that this is not a cure."

Iravan was already calculating the fastest path home as he pocketed the substance. "What do you want in return?"

Mariam shook her head. "I do not hold a bounty over aid. But when you are up for it, I would appreciate a conversation."

Iravan was hardly listening. "Thank you."

As he turned on his heel, Mariam asked, "Who is it?"

An involuntary cry slid from his throat. He didn't dare meet her eye. "My family."

By the time he got back to the hut, the crowd had dissipated. The remaining stragglers—mostly kids, including Laila, and a few leeches taking turns trying to look through the crack in the door—parted as he raced toward them and through the door of the cottage. Gayathri and Dev jumped from their places on either side of Bilal's bed as he held out the bag, brandishing it like a sword.

"Mix it with water and give to him," Iravan commanded, shoving it into Gayathri's hand. Behind them, Bilal moaned. Fallen hair coated every surface near his body.

The healer stared at it with red eyes. "What is it?"

"Something that should help," Iravan said, raking his hands through his hair. "I got it from an Urjan I met a while back."

Dev and Gayathri gave him blank stares.

"Do you have a better idea?" he snapped.

Quietly, Gayathri followed his instructions. She summoned Laila to bring them a fresh cup of water, the girl's bandaged arms shaking as she mixed in the powder while Gayathri and Dev helped Bilal sit up. Iravan sent the kid away, taking over her job. She had enough fodder for nightmares already. He tipped the liquid into Bilal's mouth. Bilal gagged violently over the medicine, but after a few minutes, his breathing slowed, his muscles eased.

"The pain," Bilal moaned after a few moments. "The pain is gone."

Was that all the powder was? Something to numb the pain?

It's not a cure, Mariam had said, but he thought it would at least buy them time. Bilal's skin grew more ashen by the second.

The concoction of Bilal's piss and sweat and rancid sickness threatened to make Iravan ill right there. Was this his only destiny? To fight and claw for scraps? To sell his soul, let the world tread over him, only to buy them a morsel of dignity in a still-assured death?

"You should both go," Gayathri said. "They'll need you out there."

Dev rested a hand on her back in farewell.

"You should ask one of the others to come watch him when things progress," Iravan said.

"I do not abandon the ones I love," Gayathri said, and it was the same accusation Samiah had leveled at him after the fire. Women who knew nothing of all he had given, all he had abandoned for the sake of their futures.

Gayathri moved her fingers through her brother's hair, her jaw ticking as more strands fell out like plucked eyelashes. Iravan said nothing. He felt nothing. The world turned black with his departure, and he shook off Dev and all other company, opting instead to sit alone in his home, staring at the ashes of the burned Temple.

Hours later, when people began returning to their huts, disturbed and frightened, one of the leeches announced that Bilal had passed.

Gayathri, Iravan was told, stayed until the very end.

CHAPTER TWELVE

Zain

In recent years, Zain had cultivated a reputation for disliking other people, but the truth went deeper.

As she settled on top of the crooked barstool, she was acutely aware of the gazes burning holes in the back of her neck. Most visitors to the tavern came to find companionship and joy or, at the very least, a safe place to hold conversation. In a strange way, the tavern had assumed the role of the Temple of Many-Souls, becoming a foothold for community.

Today's tavern visitors were possessed by a fevered energy, but she was a deep, dark stain, an abyss of quiet. Normally, she sat in the back, hood pulled over her head as the singer on the makeshift platform rattled the thatched roof with each swelling, haunting note, but today she needed a drink. And she wasn't alone. A hooded woman with bushy hair sat to her right, equally quiet, and they were both content to respect each other's solitude.

"Thank you," Zain muttered to the elderly barkeep, who slid a goblet her way before tending to her neighbor. She swirled the spiced red liquid until it sloshed just below the iron-wrought rim, wondering whether it would be a better decision to finish it in one go so she could leave. The answer would usually be a resounding yes, but she knew what was waiting for her outside those doors, and she wasn't quite prepared to face it.

Bilal was dead.

Laila had delivered the news. Zain had stood, stone-faced, while the girl wept into her kurta. She'd stroked Laila's hair with a hand that didn't feel like her own. Kanak had cried too, and Samiah had closed her eyes, tapping her wrist with two fingers before bringing them to her forehead. An Urjan prayer for a soul taken too soon. After Laila left, Zain had strapped her gun to her holster and gone searching for a way out of her dastardly head. Now, her fingers traced the outline of the barrel.

Three days had passed since her release from jail. Three days during which she'd mulled over her strange conversation with the green-eyed bloodstrippers and their threats. Three days since she'd learned that Iravan Khotar was looking for the calor reserve too, and then lied to his face.

What scared her was that she had almost told the truth.

When he'd called her name, she was sure he had caught her eavesdropping on his instructions to Bilal about the reserve. She had been *so* close to telling him that the bloodstrippers were after the same thing, but something held her back.

Iravan had looked so tired. Entirely human. As though the fear that devoured her had taken a bite out of him too. When he asked why she still worked for them, she almost told him about Dev, about the fire, about everything.

Go ahead, tell them, she heard Dev laugh. *Who's going to believe you, Z?*

No one. No one would believe her, certainly not the man who was practically Dev's brother. It was why she had tried to take matters into her own hands once before, only for everything to go terribly wrong. Kanak used to say revenge was seductive, but the risk of being consumed was always higher than the brief reward of release. Since then, Zain had earned her suffering, found comfort in it being her sole companion. But maybe there was another option.

There was an old Urjan saying: *The rocks that break ships spill treasure.* Samiah told her stories of children who would find gold and gems buried in the Urjan white sand beaches, near toothy rocks notorious for shipwrecks. She knew Dev communicated with the Council, possibly through bloodstrippers. Her arrest could be her rock and treasure. Maybe sticking around the guards would lead her to the same people Dev worked with. Maybe she could finally find proof.

If she rejected the bloodstrippers, she would also put Kanak in danger. Zain had dismissed asking her guardian about the reserve—they had enough on their plate with helping the city recover from the storm—but the guards would not be as considerate. The bloodstrippers needed her, and if there was one thing Zain had learned, it was that needing was a weakness. Something she could use to her advantage.

Four days until the Anniversary.

A sign. She needed a sign.

"Another drink?"

The barkeep made her realize she had consumed the last drop of her goblet. A warm buzz penetrated her mind, a set of fingers unraveling the coils of her worries, smoothing out the folds of her fears.

I could I could I could.

Zain pushed her goblet toward the barkeep, who filled it to the brim from a carafe.

"You seem like you need extra," they said. She didn't respond but instead fished in her trousers for a coin. The metal burned her flesh as she placed it on the table, but the barkeep shook their head.

"Keep it," they said. "It's past midnight. Everyone's covered."

Bilal's funeral was the next day. Someone must have paid for celebrations in his memory.

Zain grimaced as she swilled the beverage, ignoring the barkeep's snicker. The crowd grew louder and the air stickier with each passing second. She abused the free liquor. If she couldn't make a decision, then she could at least drink herself into a stupor and delay having to make one.

Then, the mood transformed, a distinct rumble rolling through bodies following an exultant cry. The woman sitting to her right got to her feet so quickly, Zain nearly toppled off her stool. The door crashed open. Iravan and Dev had arrived.

"Sorry we're late, we had some business to attend to," Dev drawled, as Zain pulled her scarf over her head, seized by a sick urge to play voyeur.

"You're not the only ones," someone said. "There are so many fucking bloodstrippers everywhere. They're stopping us at random for questioning, getting in the way of repairs."

The whole city had come together to help rebuild what they could from the ashes, but they were running on fumes. The tavern rattled like a pot left on a stove too long, and voices fought to the surface.

"My ma has been talking about leaving," a voice chimed in. "She's terrified the storm may happen again."

"She's not the only one. My sister met with some Urjan who was talking about calor alternatives."

"What alternatives?"

"My brother's been screaming in the middle of the night—"

"Go *where*? To the Upper Tectonic—"

"Doesn't look like the sky's going to give us anything, rain or fire," Iravan interrupted, and a hush fell. "It's been stale, unmoving. There's no reason to believe the storm was anything more than a rare aberration."

The aberration had razed their city, flooded the acolyte service with orphans to care for, left parents sprinkling their children's ashes into the sea. People were without property and income. Zain fixated on the liquid in her goblet.

"Well, these problems won't grow legs and run away," Dev joked, but there was a warning threaded in his jest. "We'll deal with them tomorrow. Tonight, we honor our ancestors, and the ones who have passed."

One by one, uncertain clinks punctured the air, a temporary guise of peace. There was a monster in the room, but for the evening, they would throw a curtain over its body and pretend it wasn't there. Zain bit back tears as she looked up. The sight of Dev smiling, arms slung around the people he was actively betraying every day, riled her temper.

She'd asked for a sign, and she'd received one.

Zain left her unfinished drink on the counter.

Zain tasted salt in the air as she ran past Yadav's store and down to the harbor.

The streets were quiet, and the silence was a taunt, as though the city was watching her betrayal. Only the sweet numbing of terrible decisions kept one foot in front of the other. Leander had said midnight, which had already passed, but surely they hadn't left yet.

She halted on the abandoned boardwalk.

Your turn, Bilal laughed in her head. She was nine again, standing across from him and Gayathri on the creaky planks. They were playing a twisted version of roulette, jumping on the rotted platform to see who'd fall through first, always terribly disappointed when it never happened.

The souls have marked you as their own, Yadav said, distraught by their antics.

Well, the souls' marks had been tenuous at best. Zain squatted, tracing her fingers along the gaps between the beams. Age had made a mockery of their childlike invincibility.

Footsteps tore Zain from the memory, and her hand flew to her hip, only to find that her holster had shifted. In her trance, she hadn't properly threaded it through her belt loop.

"You make that look very convincing when we both know your gun isn't loaded," Theron said in Gehennese, as she searched for the misplaced gun grip, alcohol wreaking havoc on her coordination. "A strange and pointless choice."

She clumsily flicked the weapon at him and slurred, "You confident about that?"

Even in the dark, she could read the disgust on his face. "How much did you drink? I can smell the alcohol from here."

She grinned, the wine teeming with her movements. As Theron's luck would have it, he always caught her at her worst. The bitter taste of the beverage dried her tongue out. "Thought you'd know better than to piss off a drunk."

He stalked toward the darkened alleys adjacent to the Sickle.

"Thought you'd know better than to turn your back on a weapon as well," she grumbled, following him into neutral territory.

"Sure, if it's loaded," he replied, coming to a stop. Her cheeks flushed as she fixed her holster and stowed the gun. Those drinks really were getting to her head. She couldn't say a word to the decent slumlord, but she could swing a gun at a bloodstripper. Splendid.

"Where is Leander?" she asked, once they moved out of earshot. Tejomayans speaking with the odd bloodstripper was no cause for concern—coexisting in the city had certain requirements—but neither of them wanted to be seen. It would raise too many questions.

"My brother is busy," Theron replied. Ah, she was right about them being related, then. The guard stared over her shoulder at the city that jeweled the hills. Whispers of a dulcet song played in the air, echoing across the distance, but between them was a devastating silence.

"I assume you have come to take us up on our offer," he said.

Zain swallowed at the casual way Theron recognized her cowardice. All the wine-fueled confidence shed like silky darkness from the crimson sky.

"Do you have a location for us?" he prompted, scratching his neck. The movement drew her attention to the emblem on his uniform, the recognizable Gehennese pillars, much smaller than she would have guessed.

"No," she said, blinking rapidly, certain her vision was afflicted. Now was not the time for her to ruminate on Theron's bloodstripper rank, not when she couldn't count fingers if he were to hold them up. "My guardian, Kanak, doesn't know where it is either. None of the surviving acolytes do."

Forget a location—no one even knew what the reserve *was*. When Gayathri had read from the strange book, Zain had always imagined a large tanker or a reservoir dug between two hills. But where would something of that size lie concealed in a city that had been dismantled stone by stone? It had to be smaller, if it even existed.

"I know that's not true," Theron said, accusatorily. "We know about the acolyte's book, the one with the truth."

Zain snorted. *One* throwaway line about a reserve along with hundreds of other notes in the rest of the book. Whoever wrote it had just been speculating and hadn't realized what they would unleash upon the city if word ever got out, which of course it did. "Well, I don't know whose book that was."

"I'm not sure that's true—"

"I don't know if you've heard of the fire of the Temple of Many-Souls." She cut him off, sick of his unimpressed airs. Blue shimmered at the edge of her vision. "The Head Acolyte who passed during the accident, Inas Shah, was the last keeper of the secret." Even that partial confession was a spear carving "traitor" into her skin. If he'd seen the book, then he knew this aligned with the ridiculous note. "They didn't have a chance to pass the knowledge onto anyone else, given the . . . nature of the event that took place. At least, not to any of the acolytes I know. But there was someone with them on the evening of the fire. At the peace meeting in the Temple, between your people and ours."

"So you're saying whoever got their hands on the book and knew about the reserve was outside the Temple?" Theron asked, looking deeply skeptical. Souls, he would not let go of this book, would he? Even Bilal hadn't been this bullheaded about the reserve when he was younger. The thought of him made her hiccup.

"Yes, and I have it on good authority that he is also searching for the reserve," Zain lied, blinking away her despair. "I heard him myself the other day."

"Who?"

Zain cleared her throat. Iravan's quest was foolhardy—he

must have truly gone off the edge to be looking for the reserve—but it was going to be the veil of truth over her ploy. One of the slumlords was hunting for the reserve, and he would have a target on his back. But she didn't need to be honest about which one.

"Devraj Basu. If you can get him, you'll have your answer."

CHAPTER THIRTEEN

Anastasia

harvi was a day late, and Anastasia was seconds away from taking to the city in search. Only a desperate sense of self-preservation kept her on the island.

When Charvi hadn't arrived on the expected boat, Anastasia had dissociated. Foolish—it was profoundly foolish that she had agreed to this plan. Souls only knew what would happen if she'd been recognized, and each grisly possibility tipped Anastasia further over the edge. Charvi wouldn't leave Baruna behind.

Which meant something had gone wrong.

Unnerved, Anastasia ran her hands along the polished marble counters that lined her kitchen. Her coolers were on, but she was still sweating from the near-constant fever simmering beneath her skin. A large antique clock ticked ominously across from her, its spear-shaped hands carving time from its faded face. It was early afternoon, and there would be no boats for the next few hours. She would give it till this evening. A day felt reasonable, expected even. Maybe the damage from the storm had delayed Charvi, or maybe someone she knew had been hurt.

But Anastasia couldn't stay home or she'd go mad.

Outside, routine was well underway on the Isle of Vis: extractors were assessing calor supplies, councilmembers were politicking, and residents were going about their daily chores. The port swarmed with gatherers preparing shipments. Anastasia glimpsed Varun by the dock, dressed in his gatherer browns, wisps of hair moving lightly with the languid breeze. He was gesticulating wildly at two gatherers whom Anastasia didn't recognize. Perhaps they were new. She beelined toward them.

"Have you heard from Charvi?" she asked, noting tangentially how they fell quiet upon her arrival. She was certain Charvi had told Varun where she was going, even if she hadn't provided details as to why.

Varun gave her an easy smile, but his eyes skittered, reflecting her own worry back at her. "Not yet, but I think she'll be here with the next boats."

"She said she'd be back by now," said Anastasia, feeling like a broken record.

One of the other gatherers, a short brown girl with two braids, worried her lip. The other stranger, a man with deep-set brows and thick, curled lips, was looking at Anastasia oddly. She'd never felt this uncomfortable around the gatherers before. Then again, she hadn't spent much time around them without Charvi.

Varun squeezed Anastasia's elbow. "You should go rest. You don't seem well. This trip would have been difficult for her. I'm sure she's collecting herself, preparing to return. We will be here all day and can send word when she arrives."

From their rigid body language, it was clear she wasn't welcome. As Anastasia walked away from the port, she became painfully aware, now more than ever, of how few people she had in her corner. Were people born this way? Alone, miserable, and with barbed walls built high? She'd found people who would risk the pain of reaching out to her, ones who didn't just deem her worthy but savored the lethal edge she brought to their lives. Charvi, who leaped into bar fights with her. Dev, who met her every harebrained scheme with something more devious. Iravan, who saw right through her brash front and had held all of her with unguarded delicacy.

It had made it so easy for him to destroy her.

They'd turned their backs on her, one by one, all except Charvi. And now she was gone too. Anastasia's knees quaked as she set upon a path she normally avoided. Maybe things would have been different if she'd had a mother like Charvi was to Baruna, but all she had was a father who'd thrown himself into research when his wife had died in a calor-plant explosion. Everything and everyone she loved either died or turned to poison, killing her slowly. Who could blame her for what she'd become?

Anastasia came to a standstill, realizing where she was. A cream-colored stone bungalow gleamed against the brown and gray scenery. The awning windows on each wall were sealed shut to keep the cool air inside. It was notably smaller than the homes of the councilmembers, containing three, maybe four, rooms. Anastasia wouldn't know. She'd never been inside this place, the island's school.

Perhaps she had already gone mad, she thought, as she reached for the brass doorknob of the entrance. A dark, narrow corridor greeted her. Voices rose from her left, and she followed the chatter to the first wooden door. It was unlocked.

Twenty eyes pinned her under curious stares when she entered the classroom.

"Miss Drakos," said Ronin, the extractor in charge of lessons that week. He stood in front of a large blackboard, holding a small piece of chalk that had been worn down so much, his thumb and index finger could only precariously grip its edge. "Can I help you with something?"

Whispers rustled around her. Nine pale faces clustered in twos and threes. A solitary brown child sat at the back. Baruna picked at her hand, oblivious.

Did you know when it rains, they push Baru into the puddles so she comes home bathed in blood? Charvi accused. But for all her rage, she had said something different to Anastasia before leaving for Tejomaya. *I trust you.* Souls, if something had happened to Charvi, then Baruna would become her responsibility. Her throat burned.

"I'm observing," Anastasia said, ignoring Ronin's baffled face. "Please, continue."

It became clear very quickly why none of the children paid attention.

The man was brilliant—there was little doubt about that—but he was also loquacious, pompous, and hyperbolic in his movements, a pathetic attempt to appeal to an audience he did not understand. And even if he were able to communicate complex topics to the young islanders, the contents of that day's lecture would have driven Anastasia away even sooner.

Science. She detested science.

Only those who hadn't walked under the rains could distill calor knowledge the way Ronin did, from how its properties changed with heat and pressure, demanding constant improvement of technology, to the first rudimentary processing instruments, to the era of Hamish Drakos's advanced tools.

But Anastasia had felt calor on her skin, whispering its secrets to her. Back before everyone started avoiding calor exposure, others had reported similar sensations. Now, these anecdotes were increasingly rare, for most frontline workers had protective gear to limit skin contact with calor. It was something science could not explain. She was flirting with blasphemy, her continued dalliances with calor, but it felt near divine. Like magic.

"Is it true we could fly?" one of the boys in the back asked.

Ronin scowled. "The era of aviation was magnificent, but the amount of calor required to fuel flight no longer exists. Dwell in the present, little ones, or you will be forever miserable."

So these classes were both convoluted and depressing.

Anastasia interrupted. "I must say I disagree." The extractor looked stunned at her rebuke—Anastasia wasn't sure what had come over her either. But if she stayed quiet too long, she would think about Charvi. "If you look at the real history of calor, there is much there that is magnificent. Violent, yes; brutal, even more so. But also inexplicably magnificent. Tell them about the rift."

The children sat straight, murmuring as they glanced at the scarlet sky.

Ronin pushed his glasses up his nose, laughing nervously. "The rift, miss?" he asked, glancing between her and the students. "Are you certain?"

Anastasia shrugged, but secretly she cared. These children deserved to be fascinated.

Ronin spent an inordinate amount of time laying out the long history of calor that predated not just her existence but her father's and his father's. A time when calor had lain in abundance in the skies, and nations around the world had developed methods to mine it from above. It had fueled their homes, their transportation, their communication systems. "Yes," Ronin sighed, "including aviation. We used to visit the sky."

Anastasia could hear Charvi snipe at each of Ronin's points. "We long harnessed the power of the skies," he continued.

We've abused the sky and the land, spread war and crime and disparity, Charvi's apparition said. *And trust me, they remember.* Janmiris thought of their world as sentient. Each time they walked past the stone forest, Charvi would say, *The forest was betrayed.*

"Gehanna decided to take matters into our own hands and manage calor on the world's behalf," Ronin said.

Anastasia didn't need a phantom Charvi to tell her how distorted this tale was. The justifications used for their continual invasion of land after land, leaving it in shreds, all in the name of knowing what was best. Urjan had been one of the first to fall, the country left inhospitable after the Gehennese drained them of their calor, sending masses of refugees across the Upper Tectonic and to the south, putting immense strain on Janmir and its neighboring nations.

"What about Finze?" one of the children asked. "What did we do?"

Made things worse, Charvi scoffed.

Anastasia really needed her to come back. She couldn't live with her friend's ghost.

Ronin looked pleased with the question. "Gehanna has always valued our allies. To ensure calor distribution remained equitable, the Upper Tectonic Trade Agreement was signed between Nohri, Finze, and Gehanna, part of which required two of the eleven Council seats to be held by a Nohri and a Finzish member each."

Anastasia bit her tongue. Ronin's version was laughably rosy. The agreement had been tenuous, a meager compromise made by a country that did not have the resources to maintain power over the Lower Tectonic while fighting the larger nations of the Upper Tectonic. The encroachment of power that had come since was only fodder for the Gehennese faction who believed in a purely Gehanna-held Council.

"And then came the rift," Ronin said, then paused. She waited for him to continue, but he instead patted his dry brow with a handkerchief. He had no idea how to tell this part of the story. Had it never been taught before?

Go ahead, Charvi goaded. *Tell them the truth. It's the least you can do for me.*

Anastasia stepped in front of the classroom. It was a strange sense that overcame her then, a knowledge that she was, in that moment, straddling a no-man's-land, caught between two realities. A tug-of-war between the beliefs she had accumulated over the years—the ones Hamish had spewed, the narratives she'd internalized during her time in Tejomaya—and it was only as she laid them out one after the other that she confronted how they would never fit together.

"The rift occurred nearly fifty years ago," she started. "The Anniversary of the Carnage is in a few days, and it is also when the rift formed. After we entered Janmir and moved south to Tejomaya, there were many who were unhappy with our plans for calor. They did not understand that we had studied this, that we knew how to preserve and use calor most efficiently for the benefit of the entire world. There was a protest that day; thousands gathered in Tejomaya from all across the Lower Tectonic, beyond the harbor."

"Beyond the harbor?" one of the children asked. "But that's water."

"It is water now," Anastasia said. "The protests escalated, and no one quite understands this next part. There were few survivors. But the conflict led to an explosion, tearing away this island from the city itself and creating a rupture in the sky."

There was silence, filled only with Ronin mumbling, "We are still studying the rupture."

"So the island was once part of Tejomaya?" a student asked.

Anastasia nodded, her heart shriveling as she remembered what Iravan used to say. That he'd find a way back to the lost part of his city.

"What happened to the people?" another girl asked. She was so young.

"It's called a carnage, stupid," one of the boys said, but even this riposte lacked punch. They all glanced at Baruna, who curled further into herself. So much for protecting her.

Anastasia understood then why Ronin never told this part of their history. The words tasted like ash.

Now you see, Charvi said. *You see why I find you so difficult.*

Anastasia rubbed her forehead, desperate to exorcise her friend. This evening would be too late, she needed to—

"Miss Drakos," someone called from behind. A messenger, peering through the open door. "One of the gatherers is looking for you. Said she's finally returned from Tejomaya."

Baruna leaped to her feet and fled the classroom, knocking hard into the indignant messenger. Ronin scoffed but Anastasia held her hand up.

"You can take it from here," she said.

She fled too.

CHAPTER FOURTEEN

Iravan

The day was suffocating.

Iravan rose, tasting the bitter regret of a drink too many. He stared at the white kurta pajama set he had left hanging over the back of a chair. He detested how the harsh grass-woven fabric rubbed against his arms, the stitching coming apart from wearing them one too many times. He smoothed down the sleeves, vowing once more that he would burn the clothes at the end of the day, knowing full well he wouldn't.

Every morning, he was greeted by the ashes of the Temple of Many-Souls, and every morning, he paused in remembrance. Today, Iravan stayed a while longer, feeling his insides decay. People always asked why he chose to stay here of all places, among the skeletons of his ghosts. Punishing himself for the mistakes he had made.

Among the living, he felt adrift.

He found Gayathri waiting by her hut, Dev's arm wrapped around her in comfort. She wore a thin cotton salwar kameez with her head wrapped in a dupatta, its folds shadowing her bloodshot eyes. Around them, slum-dwellers and merchants alike snaked through the ramshackle huts in their own funeral whites, making their way to where the land met the mountains.

"Nice of you to join us," Dev said, slicking back his freshly cut hair with a small hand comb. Iravan resisted the urge to brush through his own wildly growing waves. He hated getting his hair cut, loathed the feeling of someone else's fingers on his skull. Only one person had earned that privilege, and look how that had turned out. "Between you and the missing acolyte, it's a wonder how we're going to get this done."

Iravan pushed away his thoughts. On days like this, it was too easy to walk into the cobwebs of his past. "Where is Kanak?"

Dev shrugged. "They were supposed to be here an hour ago, but I haven't seen them or any of the other acolytes."

Finding someone when they all were dressed the same would be a hassle. "Have you seen Samiah? Zain?"

"Zain?" Dev's voice pitched strangely. "Is she still alive? Haven't seen her in a while."

"Why don't you head over to the procession?" Iravan said to Gayathri, ignoring Dev's twitchiness. "We will make sure your brother is ready."

He couldn't bring himself to call it a body just yet. Gayathri left, looking like a child who had lost their parent in a hoard of people—not at all like a healer who had spent the hours after her brother's death tending to the masses of burn victims from the storm. He should have helped her with the injured, but her desolation was his personal faith. Grief was a mirror that eclipsed time and space. Behind the present funeral procession lay a different one in the recesses of Iravan's mind, one he could barely remember but that stayed with him every day.

"Are we still on track for the Anniversary?" Iravan said, keeping his voice low so as to not reach curious ears.

Dev nodded. "I'm making the trade tomorrow. Don't trust anyone else to do it."

At least something was going according to plan.

"Come on," Iravan said, even though all he wanted to do was run away. "Let's get this over with."

To his relief, Kanak showed up right before he was about to send people out to look for them. Samiah flanked them, emanating anger. Iravan prickled under her stare but opted not to engage. This day was not about him and his thorny past.

"I'm sorry," Kanak said, huffing as they entered the hut. "We were helping with food rations down by the artery. A lot of the power lines in the Bow still aren't working after the vortex, and I thought I'd help the acolytes with distributing aid."

Their apology was easily accepted—they had all been occupied with the aftermath of the storm. What they didn't discuss was that this was Kanak's first time entering the slums in ten years. Other acolytes had cared for the bodies of those who'd died before, and as Kanak was no longer formally with the Temple, they would typically not be the first choice for such an occasion. But Kanak had known Bilal from all the time Zain had spent with him, and they'd felt inclined to take up the mantle one more time. Gayathri had agreed, despite the discomfort the decision sowed in Iravan's chest. He did not like involving people who made their distaste for him and what he did so apparent during a time meant for community.

Those who lived in the Bow were not community.

"That's okay," Iravan said, guiding them into the hut to where Bilal lay, face up. He wanted to get out of here, far from the corpse of someone whose life had been twined with his like the old ivy that once clung to Yadav's home, now dry and acrid. Nothing in Tejomaya was meant to last.

Kanak got to work, chanting while cleaning the body, facilitating the soul's ascent from their torn land to the skies. Iravan fell into unthinking motions as Kanak covered Bilal's corpse with a white sheet and lifted him onto a pall. Dev and Iravan took the front, while two of their men shouldered the back. Samiah and Kanak trailed behind as they made their way to the foothills.

The slopes were painted white by hundreds of bodies sheathed in ivory, swarming over the browned grounds. The sky hummed above, and Iravan pictured maggots in a wound, bustling to create a life within its rotting parts.

The image made him want to tear his kurta off by the time the body was set in place. The air was heavy with despair; it stank of tears and rage, blood and sorrow. He backed away as Kanak presided over the ceremony. He was envious of the way people hung to Kanak's every word, as though the promises in their prayers and mantras had ever shown any signs of being substantial. He had lost comfort in spirituality a long time ago—it was no better than looking at a glass house with all its walls boarded up. From the outside, he could see what existed beyond religion, but to everyone within the house, nothing else mattered. He craved the illusion, mourned the shattering of his reality.

Gayathri stood across from him with a few other women, their bodies shaking with grief. Laila and Lufi hid in the folds of Mahini's white salwar. A memory unfurled, of Dev holding him up. Of him searching the crowd for someone who had abandoned him at the first sign of tragedy. It grew difficult to stay upright. He fumbled for the coin in his pocket, but his fingers slipped over it, unable to find grounding.

Gayathri laid a stone rose on Bilal's chest. Iravan followed suit, with Yadav right behind him. White roses used to be the way of their people, but those were now too rare. Iravan hadn't brushed his fingers against soft petals in over two decades. They had all turned to stone.

On his walk back from the pall, gooseflesh dotted his nape. Yadav caught up to him, equally unsettled, pointing to the area behind them where the crowd surged near the ashen parts of the Bow.

"Is that who I think it is?" Yadav asked.

In their black uniforms, the bloodstrippers nearly blended in with the slate backdrop. Ten years ago, Iravan had been at another funeral, acutely aware of the guards present, the ones who'd watched him fall apart. That time, he had brashly marched up to Matthieu, told him things he wished he could take back, and set into motion a decade-long battle he'd been too weak to fight.

"You make sure Dev doesn't see them and do something stupid," Iravan said, forcing a rictus smile when Dev looked over, curious. By the souls' mercy, the bloodstrippers were out of his partner's line of sight. "I'll go deal with them."

But when Iravan drew closer, he realized this wasn't a normal group of bloodstrippers. Because there, in the middle, was a councilmember.

Iravan ducked behind the nearest tree, his chest heaving. What was a councilmember doing in Tejomaya, near a funeral? He stole another glance. The councilmember was speaking to someone he couldn't see, a familiar figure in a bright-orange kaftan dress with long dark braids curtaining her profile as they both knelt on the ground. It couldn't possibly be.

Mariam held something up for the councilmember to see. Minutes later, they stood, exchanging final words before the guards escorted the councilmember away. The woman lingered behind, scrutinizing the ground as she fiddled with the gold bracelets that shone on her arms like scars.

Heat flushed through him. What was *she* doing, speaking to the Council?

Iravan strode toward Mariam, mind made up, and clasped a hand over her mouth. He felt the soft escape of surprise against his palm as he broke off her scream.

He didn't care about the murmurs as he dragged Mariam away. Let them talk. Once they were out of sight—and, he hoped, out of hearing range—he released his one hand covering her face but maintained a firm grip on her shoulder.

"What are you doing?" Mariam hissed. He took her in then, his disbelief warping reality. He summoned the recollection of when he'd last seen her. The powder she'd put in his hand, the one he'd given the friend who now lay dead.

"What the hell are *you* doing?" he asked. "Speaking to the Council?"

Her thick eyebrows furrowed with confusion, her jaw tense and stiff. Looking at her pulled on his memories like a bucket tossed into a well with no hopes of water in its unseen depths. A bead of blood swelled on her bottom lip, and he had the urge to corkscrew her flesh between his fingers, see how much she might bleed.

"I was telling them what I've been trying to tell you," she said, with the same impertinent tone that made his beastly temper stir. "The reserve—"

"You told them about the reserve?"

She fell silent. His ire went from a simmer to a boil. This woman, this Urjan trespasser, dared bring the Council to the place where he was putting his friend to rest.

"Take your hands off me," Mariam replied. She was clearly doing her best to sound calm, but her shoulder quivered in his grip. She lifted her dirt-caked hands as if to push him off.

Iravan dug his fingers into her back in warning. "What were you doing with the soil?"

Behind them, a conch shell sounded, signaling the end of the ceremony. The peal summoned the images of Bilal's wan face disappearing beneath a worn sheet, of his own daughter's remains, each snapshot spilling through his fingers like sand. "What was that you gave me the other day? Are you behind the plague? Were you working with them to kill us?"

Mariam recoiled, her mouth agape. "Kill who?"

"Bilal!" Iravan sensed himself losing control, but everything came together in a grotesque supposition. "Him, the others. The sickness. You, here, at the foothills with a councilmember, after telling me you could help. He told me—he told me he was here before, before all this happened."

It was falling into place, and the pressure at his temples swelled. When it grew too painful to articulate his emotions, his body wanted to take over. He would end this. He would end this now. He wanted to wrap his hands around her neck and squeeze.

His thoughts shattered as Mariam punched him square in the jaw. Iravan stumbled to his senses, like a man in a dark cave thrust into daylight at last. What the fuck was he doing?

"I-I didn't—" Mariam stammered, hurrying to put distance between them. "I didn't kill anyone." Fat tears fell from her face.

Of course she hadn't killed anyone. The only killer between the two of them was him.

Mariam turned and ran.

CHAPTER FIFTEEN

Zain

Of the many things that kept Zain up at night, imagining her death often topped the list.

She had entertained nearly every option Tejomaya had to offer: drowning in the Soulless Sea, getting shot by bloodstrippers, being shredded by a maelstrom, losing her hair and skin to the soul-sickness, burning in yet another building, and even being buried alive. What Zain had remained blissfully unaware of was death via the company of Theron Cleirigh, *voluntarily* sought.

She slung the fifth bag of grains she had painstakingly filled onto the slow-growing mountain of foods, all perfectly edible, all meant for the Gengs on the island.

"Are you certain he is going to be here?" Theron asked, his gaze set resolutely ahead as he imitated her motions with far less difficulty, evidently immune to the popped blisters that left her hands raw. He hadn't spoken all day, leaving her to wonder about his small insignia once more. The high-and-mighty guard was low ranking. His attitude was merely compensation for a bruised ego.

She gritted her teeth. "I have told you several times already, I do not have Dev's schedule on me."

He snorted, but she'd take his dismissal over seeing how nervous she was.

Zain had studied Theron and Leander for a response to Dev's name, in the hope they knew of his relationship with the Council, but the brothers' expressions remained professionally schooled. The only suspicious behavior she had seen was Theron shifting away from patrolling bloodstrippers, clearly unwilling to be seen out with her. Strange, for men who claimed to be working with her on official orders. So, she'd started plotting, beginning with a stakeout at the harbor. The Anniversary was two days away, the day Dheera had said there would be a package exchange. She had to dig up the chain of communication between Dev and the Council, uncover what he had planned, ideally see the exchange for herself.

And there was no better place for her fanciful plans of espionage than the harbor. On early mornings, the boardwalks spilled with morning messengers from the Isle of Vis who traded news with bloodstrippers, Tejomayans, and visitors from the Upper and Lower Tectonic passing through the port. Janmiris weren't allowed to enter the Isle of Vis, not unless they were gatherers, so the information that traversed there through word of mouth was as precious as calor. What better place to eavesdrop than this estuary of communication, where word could be passed between foes with not an eyelid batted?

". . . Jezeme has been pushing to withdraw again," a passing messenger said to a port bloodstripper. "Says the damages to the city from the storm are insurmountable."

The guard's Finzish insignia glittered. He replied, "Wouldn't Petra love that. One less person for her to worry about."

Council politics had never interested Zain, but she paid close attention for any mention of the dons. She was well versed in the other circulating stories. How the food-ration queue at the artery still grew, how another burn victim had succumbed to their gruesome injuries, how Yadav didn't have enough equipment or materials to help with rebuilding, stalling repairs across the Hammer. Besides the occasional whispering of a rebellion—when weren't those rumors thrown about?—most Tejomayans cowered, studying the sky like they expected it to turn on them at any given moment.

Theron, of course, thought they were here to look for Dev. As if the don would come down there himself.

At least Leander would have struck up a conversation, maybe let a hint of his agenda slip. But no, the prodigal bloodstripper had other jobs to do, and for reasons she had yet to understand, that meant she was stuck on scout duty with the surly older brother.

"Oi!"

Sullenly, they both turned. The helmsman they were help ing had returned from his smoke break. He was short and clearly had a complex about it, standing on the food crates to tower over them. His hands slid into loose brown pants as he appraised their work, his dark mustache rising and falling with each barbed criticism. Of course, he directed his ire only at Zain.

"You filling those up to the brim?" His Janmiri was so awful, it took her a minute to decipher the question. His tone was accusing, but Zain swallowed her retorts. She knew how to deal with people like him—no eye contact, no speaking, all subservience. She just had to get through the next few hours, and then who knew, maybe she would take a hammer to his boat. She rammed the shovel into the open food crate and heaved a serving into an empty sack.

One Tejomaya . . .

"You make sure she ain't thievin'," the man continued in Gehennese.

Two Tejomaya . . .

When Theron didn't reply, the helmsman said, "Their kind got nothing else to do. I hear they runnin' around stealin'. Reckon the bloodstrippers ought to whip them into shape. This one would be a sight, stripped down and lashed." He laughed, as though he were describing an animal being trained, then left.

Three—oh, the counting was pointless. Zain needed to hit something, preferably the helmsman's face. She threw her body into her movements. It wasn't the first time she'd heard Gengs speak about her in this way, but she'd never had to stay through their taunts. As Samiah and Kanak's ward, she was sheltered, and as a leech, her masters at least looked like her. It rattled her, and the fact that Theron had been there to witness it all was rankling. She did not want to discuss it, but each passing second he said nothing was infuriating in other ways.

Another sack landed on the heap. Her palms tore from the force, and she rubbed bloodstains on her tunic.

Theron spoke. "If you're not going to pay attention to your surroundings, you might as well go back."

She tucked stray curls into her scarf, cringing as their sweat-coated ends caressed her neck. For the first time that day, he was actually looking at her, albeit as though she were the biggest fool he'd ever come across.

"We are here for a reason. If you're going to be distracted, then this is a waste of our time."

"*You* are a waste of my time," she shot back, immediately embarrassed by her own petulance. He was right. She'd tunneled into herself. The morning boats were nearly done loading, and soon the crowd would disperse until travelers returned in the evening. Their disguise would vanish.

This was poorly planned at best, reckless at worst. She had no idea where the exchange would be taking place, and the harbor was too public. And even if she did overhear someone from the island pass on a message to a leech, or vice versa, what was she going to do about it? Unless Theron acted as an eyewitness—Zain nearly guffawed at the thought—none of what they were doing would help matters.

"Fine," she said. She dusted her hands, prepared to rip her scarf off and escape the grimy helmsman and all the other men who had leered at her as she worked. She would think of something else. "Let's head back to your brother. I don't think—"

Theron pinched her so hard it sent a shiver of pain through her bones. She bit down on the knuckles of her free hand as she followed the path of his pointed finger. A man came down the boardwalk, his figure unmistakable despite the hood over his head. Dev's broad shoulders filled the narrow width of the walkway. Against the bloody sky, he looked like a terrifying omen descending upon the harbor.

To her surprise, no one else noticed. He passed by quietly, quickly. Alone.

She had rarely seen Dev out alone. She opened her mouth to tell Theron this, but he spun her by the shoulders to face him instead. Dev vanished, replaced by a boat bobbing on the murky waters, weighed down by the mound of food. The island peeked from behind the thick mist.

"We have company," Theron said, quietly, in broken but

unarguably clear Urj. Zain struggled against his iron-clad grip. This man's multilingual abilities were annoyingly impressive. He added loudly in Janmiri, "Finish loading these up."

She was about to snap at him, desperate to catch sight of Dev, when the helmsman reappeared atop the crates.

"I'm watching her," Theron said, very irritated, in Gehennese, and maybe the helmsman didn't quite believe the bloodstripper, because he stayed. Zain mentally snapped every finger of his as she bent to his will. Her kurta was too large, impeding her mobility. The air pounded her lungs, bruising it with the smog of salt and toxins that hung low over the harbor. She was a doll on display, and she wanted to shatter her case. Each motion felt like an insult to her people, each second that man watched her aiding his cause was enraging. She needed to see Dev.

"He's talking to someone," Theron whispered in Urj, and the rage ensconcing her diffused to worry. The helmsman was right there. "Has a package."

She tuned out the helmsman. Theron didn't say more, but he had given her enough. Dev was here, carrying out the exchange. But who was he meeting? What was the item? Who else knew?

"Gehennese?" she whispered. She sounded so desperate, but she couldn't help herself. She had to know.

"No," Theron replied, to her surprise. A moment later: "A woman, gatherer robes, but she's trying to hide her identity."

"Enough talk!" the helmsman called, but it didn't matter. Zain's thoughts had come to a standstill. Something heated in her chest, then burned with dismay. *Stupid,* she told herself, *stupid to be so surprised.*

She knew the man had secrets. She was one of them.

Leander waited for them back at the turbines in the Sickle, gleeful.

Just a few days in his company, and the boy who'd interrogated her was nowhere to be found. He was young, only seventeen, and very intelligent. He was also a little dissociated from the rest of the world. His mind homed in on a particular task, rendering him unable to see beyond its scope, but she could rest assured that what he put his mind to would be completed. Even now, he didn't ask how their day at the harbor went. He had forgotten about Dev entirely. Instead, he pressed a strange contraption into Zain's hand.

Her lips curled. "What is this supposed to be?"

"It's a mask," Leander replied, proudly. "Here, try it on!"

Zain lurched back, slamming into Theron. Leander frowned. "Oh, no, it won't hurt you, see—"

He put the mask over his head. It was a funny-looking thing, made of a dark material she could not identify. It wrapped around his entire face, leaving holes only for the eyes. A muffled sound came from it.

"We can't hear you," Theron said, dryly.

Leander cocked his head, then took his mask off. "Sound transduction issues," he muttered to himself. "But this will keep you safe from the air. You know, I met this interesting Urjan prophet recently, fantastic calor research. We agreed that the air has been terrible for a while. You'd think they would have made something for us sooner, what with the air being orange and brown and it getting so much hotter. It's killing us slowly, the particles are . . ."

Zain couldn't follow along when Leander went on tangents, often switching rapidly between Gehennese and Janmiri when he got into complicated explanations. She wriggled out from between the brothers, needing air.

"Can we move somewhere more inconspicuous?" Theron asked, interrupting Leander's spiel. "We need to debrief, and I don't like the odds of someone finding us here."

Zain agreed, but she was up to her neck in doubt. The other guards were also searching for calor, so why was Theron so intent on not being seen? The disused machines whirred above their heads, blotting the dormant sky.

"It won't rain again," Leander said, matter-of-factly, reading Zain's quiet observations. "The weather parameters do not line up. It has been getting hotter, and air pressure is higher. Calor doesn't like to come down on days like this, and it's been a long stretch of them."

She stared at him. She'd heard these words before but didn't pretend to understand.

"All the more reason for us to make our move soon," she said, eager to shift the conversation back to her goal. She and Theron hadn't spoken on their way back. He had probably exhausted his verbal quota for the day. She was shocked when he cleared his throat.

"Dev was at the harbor, meeting a woman from the Isle of Vis. I couldn't get a good look at this person. She was hooded and stayed behind one of the beams. My guess is it was one of the bloodstripper spies they've hired," Theron said.

"Oh yes, we know all about the spies," Leander said, sagely, when Zain flinched.

They certainly didn't know about the network of bloodstripper spies, and Zain was starting to believe the brothers didn't know about Dev and the Council either. It made sense, since he was doing his own dirty work at the harbor, but it meant there was nothing Theron or Leander could say to indict him.

But how would the bloodstrippers react if they learned their

Head Councilmember was working with a don behind their backs? The Council oversaw all gatherer movements to and from the island, so the woman must have been meeting Dev on their orders. Maybe no one would believe Zain, but Iravan wouldn't be able to ignore the accusation if it came from the Gengs themselves. And, souls, did she need Iravan—anyone else would be powerless. She needed Dev to lose the unearned adulation and trust of the city.

Theron continued in the clipped tone of a soldier providing a report. Again, her eyes darted to his insignia. "He brought a package wrapped in fabric. Handed it to the spy and left. It was quick."

Leander frowned. "So we think this may have been calor? From the reserve?"

Zain shrugged, unwilling to launch into the litany of reasons why this reserve did not exist. Whatever kept these men occupied while she sought a path to Dev's demise.

"I am not sure what it was, but we should return again tomorrow," Zain said. "This morning, he was alone, which is not normal. He is usually with Iravan, Yadav, or some of the grunts, but now that we know this is something he does by himself, we can capture him and—"

"*Capture?*" Theron asked incredulously. Leander's expression was pitying.

"Well, if you get him on his own, you could coerce the location out of him." Zain made her best attempt at bluster. With any luck, Dev would use his relationship with the Council to weasel out of torture, revealing his relationship with the head Drakos.

"Not by hurting or arresting him without due case," Theron said, with finality. "Hell, even with cause. It would disrupt the entire city, turn over the long-standing relationship between the guards and the slums. It would change everything."

She *wanted* to change everything.

"You have more power than he does," Zain insisted, growing more flustered. "And he's not sloppy. He won't just lead you to the reserve."

Leander piped up. "I think you should keep tailing him, but I agree with Theron. Dev cannot know we are onto him. Besides, we don't even need him to bring us to the reserve. I have something else to tell you both—I hear he's been embezzling calor."

The blood drained from Zain's face.

"Like a personal stash?" Theron asked. "It's not so shocking he'd want more for himself. Look at the Council."

Leander shook his head. "It's more than that. He's gathered an enormous amount for research, and it's being stockpiled somewhere. If we find it, it might be enough for my purposes, and we can leave the reserve hunting to the other guards."

That confirmed it—whatever Theron and Leander were doing wasn't in line with the Council's orders. But Zain was too busy panicking. She pushed her hair back, willing her flaming skin to cool. The news about Dev's calor cache was unsurprising, but this battle of motives was getting too unruly and too unpredictable. What had she been thinking, agreeing to work with these men?

"We should do it on the Anniversary," Theron said. "Everyone will be out of their homes, and both he and Iravan will have to be in public places for the various processions. If we can find out where he's keeping the calor, that will be the perfect day to strike."

Leander snapped his fingers. "That's perfect. Where are you on duty this week?"

"The jail, but I can swap with someone for the artery. No one likes that rotation, it shouldn't be a problem."

The Anniversary would be cutting it too close. He would

come that night, either to collect his dues or inflict punishment, and none of this would protect her. Time—she needed a moment to gather herself, to think. There had to be a way to redirect their cause. Not only was she unwilling to let bloodstrippers into the slums to violate their space, but she had no interest in helping them with calor at all.

Yet she nodded under the pressure of their scrutiny. *Coward.*

Leander looked pleased with her acquiescence, but Theron studied her with unnerving care. She let her hair fan her face. She was too close to back away now.

"We have to plan more carefully," Leander said. "I'm going to come up with options. Zain, I'll need your help."

Zain nodded absently. The Anniversary was two days away, and she needed to find a way to end Devraj Basu. Again.

This time, she could not fail.

CHAPTER SIXTEEN

Anastasia

This was Anastasia's third time in a private Council session.
The first had been colored by the dreams and illusions of
youth, when she'd stepped boldly into the barren chamber and
made a demand, the first in a long series of moments that would
define her legacy. She'd asked for the opportunity to lead, to
embark to Tejomaya and shadow the bloodstrippers, when the
demarcations between island leadership and its sprawling grunt
force were as impervious as the Soulless Sea's trenches.

The second session had marked the shattering of her dreams,
when she had returned from her time in the city hungry for
blood. Her dreams had gone up in a raging fire that had cost her
everything, her reputation sullied by the secrets Matthieu had
relayed from the mainland, handed over by the only people she'd
ever trusted with her heart.

So, Anastasia took the faith Tejomaya had put in her and
crushed it beneath her heel. She told the Council about the power
of the dons, how the leeches operated, which turbines to guard
against their attacks, where to increase patrols.

Was it a coincidence that two of her most pivotal moments had taken place in this very alcove? Or perhaps it was simply foreshadowing, the gray stone of the thrones a reflection of how empty the slate of her life had been, its engravings determined by the conversations to come. Anastasia was determined that the vultures perched on the stone thrones would not set the course of her path ahead. This may be her third time facing the Council, but it was the first time she bore the upper hand.

"Anastasia Drakos," said Petra, who was presiding over the session instead of Hamish. Some bullshit about bias. Hamish, at Petra's side, surveyed his daughter over crossed arms. Thirty-five years old, and yet a piece of Anastasia still cowered under the weight of his stare, which dripped with more expectation each year that passed. "As you know, we are now two days away from the Anniversary of the Carnage. The Council had initially discussed sending you as emissary to Tejomaya to oversee the week prior and act as an extension of us in negotiating matters of peace and stability."

The way she said "stability" was like a gavel being brought down.

"You declined our orders," Petra said. "Is that correct?"

Anastasia fought to keep her annoyance in check. "Councilmember Aguilar, you have been informed correctly of my decision. However, I am certain you have also been told of my proposed approach, or I would not be standing before you at this moment."

She couldn't help the impertinence. None of them had time to waste on foolish formalities.

"I sent one of the gatherers to Tejomaya instead," Anastasia continued. "She was a resident of Tejomaya prior to joining us on the Isle of Vis. She is familiar with the city's unique politics, and

I was sure to brief her on our priorities as it concerns the city. Regardless, she has earned our loyalty."

"We are well aware of your decision to send a gatherer to the city in your stead," Petra said, steepling her fingers. "Your loyalty she may have gained, but ours she has not. It was thoughtless of you to move forward with such a reckless act that was not, and would never have been, sanctioned by the Council. She could have defected, taking with her valuable knowledge regarding our gathering processes and island infrastructure."

"She did not," Anastasia reminded them.

"No," Petra said, arching a thin eyebrow with impressive dexterity. "But she could have. Tell me, Miss Drakos, how do you know whom she met while she was there? What stories she might have told? Some of us believe your decision demonstrates a lack of maturity and a complete absence of the kind of strategic vision we require in our councilmembers. Moreover, had this happened with a different person here on the Isle of Vis, we might have deemed them unfit to reside here and considered stronger action. Like excommunication."

Hamish looked pointedly over Anastasia's shoulder. Petra smirked, transparently delighted at bringing the hammer down on the insolent Drakos heir and spiting the Head Councilmember in the same breath. "Ah yes, and you know as well as we do why that will not be a viable option in your case, do you not? The name Drakos, after all, means something here."

The words slammed into Anastasia.

Your name means nothing here. She forced the memory out.

"As you know, I have not been to Tejomaya in a decade, and I do not intend on returning. You may find me strong-willed in matters of direct orders, but you will find me equally stubborn when it comes to accomplishing what I set out to do. Something

I have learned from my father." Hamish remained passive, but she knew that would please him. Let the rest of them tell her she hadn't earned her position. "And perhaps before you lecture me on Council responsibilities and trust or condemn me to solitude in a remote Janmiri province, you might want to hear what it is I have learned."

"Very well," Petra said, exchanging a brief glance with Gohren, the other Finzish councilmember.

"It should come as no surprise that those in Tejomaya share our concerns about calor," Anastasia said. "It has not rained since the drought broke, and our extractors are still uncertain as to whether this signals the beginning of a new drought or a pattern we do not have the data to predict yet. There are other challenges plaguing the city as well, a strange sickness near the slums and the maelstrom that formed right after the rains. People are afraid that the little they have is being taken away from them."

It was subtle, but each councilmember leaned forward.

"There is a planned rebellion on the Anniversary," she finished.

The Council immediately broke into cries of outrage.

"Preposterous!" Gohren called.

"With what force?" Jezeme asked.

Hamish and Petra remained quiet.

Anastasia hesitated. The knowledge she held was going to shift the paradigm of Tejomaya, the way the Council operated and controlled the unruly municipality. She had hardly processed it herself.

"They have developed calor injectables, ready for use during the Anniversary. They will storm the bloodstripper quarters after the morning traditions and take back the city. We are not certain of the effects or effectiveness of these injections just yet—our gatherer was only able to retrieve so much information before returning—but I would urge the Council to treat this matter seriously."

Their silence pressed on her like a grueling heat wave.

"How is this possible?" Petra asked. "I thought calor in the body produces a burst of energy, destroying everything in one's surroundings. It's suicidal."

All valid questions. The combustibility of calor in human blood was a hard-earned, well-documented, and bloody fact. "Hard circumstances breed desperation," Anastasia said. "Desperation breeds innovation."

"We should arrest them now," Gohren said. "Raid the slums and stores. Find their supplies."

Jezeme shook their head. "Maybe this is a sign to withdraw. I recently met with an Urjan prophet—"

Petra scowled. "As we have repeatedly said, Nohri is welcome to withdraw."

Jezeme stood, drawing the upswing of chatter to an abrupt close. "That is what I was going to share with you. I have spoken with our parliament, and we will be pulling our forces. Nohri will continue supporting the Coalition, but we have decided our national interests lie elsewhere, in exploring opportunities outside of calor. The sickness in the city is of concern to our guards— and if you're listening to your people, you will consider leaving as well."

"As you wish," Hamish said, following a beat of silence. His voice was restrained, evidently trying not to sound too eager. "What is the timeline?"

Jezeme looked to their fellow Nohri councilmember. "Rozida and I will remain behind to oversee the transition. We will take our leave now and meet with our bloodstrippers, seeing as our opinions are no longer needed on the matter at hand."

Petra raised an eyebrow. "And you don't wish to find a replacement for your Council seats? You would leave like this?" Anastasia read the underlying message, the calculation that her father was working out as well. Two empty seats. Three, if she counted Dheera's. If all those seats went to Finze, the impact on Gehanna would be cataclysmic.

Jezeme looked strangely sorrowful. "We came here to help manage the little calor left in the world, to ensure equitable distribution of an important resource. That has failed for a while now. I believe there is nothing left for us to do," they said. "In peace, we will part."

No one said a word as the two Nohri made their exits.

Anastasia picked at the skin beneath her fingernails. Nohri had been a proponent of withdrawing for months now, but to come to such a rapid decision . . . It left her unsettled. She couldn't fathom abandoning decades of work in a single moment, walking away from it all. Was there a variable she wasn't accounting for?

No, she couldn't go there.

"I think we should stay put," she said, after a reasonable period of time had passed. The other members looked like they were still deep in thought, but she could capitalize on the distraction. "We do not know how many of the injectables they have, or how effective they are yet. If we deploy our forces all over the city, we will be stretched thin. If this is as large a threat as it could be, our guards will be overpowered in no time, especially without Nohri. Our advantage in numbers will be lost within moments."

"Surely not," Petra said. "I agree with Gohren. We need to be more aggressive."

Anastasia held up her hand. "I wasn't done. We should send all bloodstrippers to Tejomaya and set tails on the primary men of concern, Devraj Basu and Iravan Khotar. I can guarantee they are responsible for this plan but will not have the supplies on their persons. Watch them closely on the day of the Anniversary, and when they move, we seize them. Our men versus the two of them will not be a problem."

"How would that stop the attack?" Gohren asked. "How do you know their people will not go ahead with it?"

This was Anastasia's time to flex her knowledge, but she wasn't prepared for the warning that swelled in her bones. A phantom hand wrapped around her throat. She tamped down on the instinct to keep quiet.

"I have lived with the people of Tejomaya," Anastasia said, as though they needed reminding of her traitorous past. "They worship those two men like gods, especially the ones who work for them. They will not act if they believe either Iravan or Dev to be in danger."

Many things had dulled in Anastasia's memory—how the humidity in her apartment had plumped her hair, how the drinks at the tavern had tasted like spice and honey, how people's reception of her had started cold, then turned genuine. But she never forgot their devotion.

"Cut off the monster's head," Petra murmured. "That works."

Anastasia gave her a cold smile. "Some might even call it visionary."

"There is still another matter we must discuss," Gohren said. Again, he looked at Petra, who nodded subtly.

Hamish frowned. "What else is there?"

"I met with Matthieu recently, and he has uncovered valuable information," Petra said. "He has reason to believe the rumored calor reserve in Tejomaya is real."

Anastasia couldn't swallow her scoff. She remembered distant talk of the reserve during her time in Tejomaya, whispers carried on the wind. There'd been an old acolyte book with an unspecific mention of a reserve, perfect for keeping children entertained. "That's bullshit."

The smug look on Petra's face grew. "Oh, but it isn't. Apparently, some of the Gehennese guards have been investigating on their own. Funny, I don't recall you sharing this with us, Hamish?"

Hamish cupped his chin in unhurried thought, but Anastasia knew that when he grew nervous, his lower jaw twitched. He was hiding it from sight. "I was not aware of this."

Petra raised her eyebrows. "So your guards are working without your orders? That's more concerning."

Hamish gritted his teeth, and that's when Anastasia knew, without a shadow of a doubt, that her father was lying. "And we can be sure I will see to this matter."

Gohren intervened. "Regardless, this is a lead we must follow. We have asked Matthieu to find the reserve. It would solve many of our problems."

If it weren't for the other councilmembers eagerly nodding their heads, Anastasia was certain her father would have imploded. But Petra had him like a mouse caught in a trap, and he was forced to sit back as the Council signed off on the Finzish plan to pursue a myth. There was a dim buzz in Anastasia's ears as the session wrapped. It persisted as she followed her father to his office, until the moment she slammed the door behind them.

"The reserve?" she hissed. "And don't you dare lie to me."

Hamish punched his desk with a shocking force that peeled the skin off his knuckles, leaving a bloody streak on the dark wood. Anastasia stepped back, her heart a hummingbird in her chest.

"What is it?" she asked. She had never seen her father like this, not even when her mother had died. "What have you not been telling me?"

"How long do we have?"

The room took on an unusual chill, the kind of cold that wrapped around one's bones. Hamish was coiled so tight, Anastasia thought he may snap in half if unleashed. "We are family," Anastasia said, gently. "I am your daughter, you can tell me—"

"You don't get to choose when to be my daughter," Hamish growled. His words were poisoned darts, aimed true. "You waltz in and out of here, and I never know which day you'll leave again, so don't you dare use that to demand answers from me. How am I supposed to trust you?"

Anastasia's chest rose and fell. Her breathing matched her father's, heavy with anticipation, rife with distress. They had clung to each other with ragged claws, not realizing they were tearing each other apart in an attempt to stay close. "I left once," Anastasia said. "And I came back, didn't I? Our—you're one of the only people who matter to me anymore." Her voice broke. She couldn't remember the last time she had been vulnerable with her father. She half expected him to sneer, but he looked down at his desk instead.

"I wish you didn't have to lose everyone else first," he said.

Time had taken so much from her. Anastasia steadied herself against the wall, waiting. Hamish visibly collected himself, and she tried to mimic him the way she had as a child. Stand upright.

Shoulders behind your back. Head held high, because how else would you see the world at your feet?

"They weren't supposed to find out about the reserve," he said, finally. "Those good-for-nothing guards must have let it slip. This is why I handle things on my own."

"You wanted the reserve for us," she said, slowly. Of course he did. Calor was limited, and it wouldn't be replenished anytime soon. Her father had never liked the Coalition, but she hadn't realized he had active ploys against them. However, this wasn't what bothered her most.

"How could you even believe in this?" she asked. "Everyone knows the reserve doesn't exist."

Hamish tapped his desk, then let out a low laugh. "Everyone except the people who know it's real. Truly, Anastasia, you're the one who spent all that time with them and never told me. *This* is why I could never fully trust you, knowing you never came clean with me."

She frowned. "What are you talking about? Who told you about the reserve?"

Hamish bared his yellow teeth. "Your old friend Dev."

Anastasia's blood ran cold. "What?"

"He let slip once that he was looking for it," Hamish said. "Thought he was being slick, tried joking about it the way you are now and telling me it isn't real. But none of you can fool me."

"You're working with Dev?" Anastasia whispered, the rest of her father's words nothing more than garble.

Hamish waved her off, as if he hadn't dropped a grenade in her lap. "We've developed a mutually beneficial relationship."

She couldn't believe this. "How long?"

"Years."

The chamber spun. She couldn't bridle her distress. "What

possible reason could you have to do this? To work with one of the two men we have been fighting against for decades?"

"Calor!" Hamish cried, pushing the papers off his desk. They floated to the floor with unnerving delicacy. "You have no idea how bad it's gotten in Gehanna. And the fact that we have to share the little calor left with Finze and Nohri? I even looked into this alternative bullshit Jezeme has talked about, but it'll do nothing for the lives we want to live. The calor shortage will kill us, Ana, unless we can find the reserve."

"He's giving you calor," Anastasia repeated. "And what, for the love of the souls around us, are you giving him?"

He was quiet for a second too long. "I gave him some of the materials for the injectables."

Anastasia covered her mouth. Hamish talked as if his voice had been stolen and only just returned.

"This is good for us, you will see. Dev agreed to target the Finzish and Nohri guards. The different emblems help. They'll wipe out the Coalition, and we can gain sole control over Tejomaya."

Anastasia could see now, the domino her father had flicked to bring the whole city tumbling down. She understood why he thought his plan was ingenious, because she knew the way he viewed the people of Tejomaya. But her father was a wolf that had never been among sheep. He didn't know their wool was made of barbed wire.

"You're a fool," she said. "You're trusting a fucking don to do your dirty work for you? Do you realize they'll come after us next?"

Hamish shook his head with disgust. "I've made sure our bloodstrippers are aware and ready. I have him under control, and you will know your place and stop questioning me. You've done nothing but damage us over the years, while I have held us together."

Anastasia needed time to process this, the depths of her father's delusion. "You will ruin us," she said. "You don't know him."

But I do. She was supposed to have been with Dev the night she disavowed Tejomaya, and if she had made it to that meeting in time, everything would have been different. Maybe the Temple would have still burned, but her life wouldn't have gone with it.

Hamish looked disappointed. "And you don't know me," he said, quietly.

He turned his back to her in dismissal.

Anastasia couldn't sleep that night.

The tangle of her thoughts prodded her like a thorn stuck in her shoe. Her father and Dev. It was grimy, two parties boxing out a third to scrape a thin layer of flavor off the top of a decidedly rotten pie.

She sat up, cheeks flushed, searching for solidity, for surety in the dull darkness of her bedroom. The door beckoned, a traipse through a memory she had been unwilling to face but that was now a preferable alternative to her current plight. In just her thin silk nightdress, she relished the press of the cold ground against her bruised feet.

The night throbbed the way it always did, in invisible pulses. The faint residues of red spindles carved the sky, the ones that would brighten as day broke, or some miserable variation of what the extractors called day. Their world was never-ending night, and the only reprieve was to cast out their horrifying truths for all to see.

Anastasia wasn't the only one facing the music. Tejomaya was invisible beyond the hoary opaque fog, but she could make out a figure sitting on the wooden jetty, legs dangling just above the water.

"I didn't know you had a desire to lose your feet," Anastasia said, propping herself up on one knee as she swung over the edge of the platform. The silk of her gown caught on sharp splinters that sank into her thighs.

"You and I always did have a penchant for pain," Charvi replied, staring ahead, still in her day clothes. Wordlessly, she passed her lit cigarette to Anastasia.

They had barely spoken since Charvi had returned. When Anastasia met her at the harbor, she had expected the worst. Her friend rocked Baruna back and forth before finally relaying her harrowing learnings. Upon sending an update to the Council, the two had been ordered to separate.

Anastasia had been incensed, but Charvi had appeared relieved. *I need to rest,* she'd said, but this was what Anastasia had feared. That Tejomaya would wrench them apart, their relationship a broken bone that would never set. Despite this, she had so many questions. Had Charvi seen the dons? Did she know about the reserve? Had the ashes of the Temple stained the land, or had time taken care of the imprints of tragedy in a way it never had for Anastasia?

Distance may have been for the best. Still, they could never stay apart during this time of year. Even in Tejomaya, the two of them visited the harbor after the Anniversary proceedings. They would toss rocks into the water, see who could skate their pieces farthest, dreaming of the day the ripples of all they'd done would be felt. And after they'd left, well . . . A phantom boat appeared in the corner of Anastasia's eye, three figures trapped in the confines of time. Charvi manning the helm with a baby in her arms, Anastasia at her side, her soul scattering to the sea as the city behind them burned, taking her loved ones with it.

"Do you ever wonder what is next?" Anastasia asked, letting the mirage fall away, knowing full well it would reconstruct to taunt her another day.

"I have only ever wondered what is next," Charvi replied. "But I think that question has been answered for myself. It is—it is Baruna who I wonder for."

Anastasia nodded, anguish stoppering her throat. She did not want to tell Charvi what had happened in the classroom. *I see,* she wanted to say, but did she, when she had never gotten the chance to worry after a child's future? It was easier to leave that stone where it lay.

Charvi dropped the cigarette into the water and stood, Anastasia following her lead to the shed where she often worked at this time of night. Charvi's creation had grown so tall that she had to stand on a makeshift platform to work. She brought a hammer down on two metal plates, the sound a violent rupture in the silent night. Years of rage flowed through the practiced motions she had learned from her mechanic father, and Anastasia wanted to ask if she could wield the hammer too.

"I heard you met with the Council today," Charvi said. "Is that why you cannot sleep?"

"No, I have that part under control."

It was everything else, the lack of purpose that followed accomplishing a long-held goal. Charvi had confessed that the question of what was next had been answered for her. Anastasia would have readily agreed, but now that death's embrace neared, she was suddenly uncertain. "How are you feeling?"

The hammer came down once, twice, a third time.

"As well as I can be, I guess. It was strange, you know. In some ways, the city is exactly how I remember it. In other ways, it is entirely different. Like a riverbank eroding over time, exposing more layers than you thought were possible."

Anastasia was hungry for more, but she didn't know how to ask, not when Charvi was behaving as if her decision to attack the dons meant she lost her right to love the city. As if her quest for vengeance hadn't started with love.

"Poetic," Anastasia said. "Which layer surprised you? The rebellion or the injections?"

"I don't think one would be possible without the other," Charvi said, her voice dripping with worry. "But I suppose those things do not surprise me at all. Rebellion was always the end of this road."

"You really think so?" But Anastasia knew her friend was right. "At least you and Baruna will be safe here. I'm glad you got out before the Anniversary. It seems like it will be one to remember. I still can't believe they're going to go through with this. I wonder whether they would if they knew about the vote. We'll tamp it down in an instant."

"So they're offering you the position?" Charvi asked, after a moment.

They breathed in unison, two hearts touching for a moment in time.

"The Council votes the day after tomorrow."

Silence then.

"They will anoint you on the Anniversary." There was no question there, and Anastasia did not want to respond. She knew this would be complicated for Charvi. Even if Anastasia could no longer think of Iravan and what they had shared without falling apart, he had been like a brother to Charvi. If Baruna weren't in the picture, if her safety hadn't been Charvi's first priority . . . would their friendship have withstood the test of Charvi's rage? Would they be sitting here together, holding each other's secrets in the dark like children huddled around the last candle in a storm?

Charvi switched to rubbing down the edges of her work, the grating noise subdued to something smoother. A promise of something new. After a few more minutes, Charvi stood, leaving Anastasia where she was. She exhaled an arduous breath, then spoke, so indiscernible that even languid waves sang louder.

"May your soul find peace beyond the fallen skies, Ana."

Anastasia didn't have the heart to tell Charvi that her soul could find peace only in the ravaging of the world, knew justice only in a ruined place.

CHAPTER SEVENTEEN

Zain

"**T**his is a terrible idea."

The irony that Theron was the one nodding in agreement was not lost on Zain.

"It is the best chance we have," Leander said. He had spent the last day poring over plans and maps and a whole host of items that muddled together. It was like the time Samiah had spent an hour answering Zain's innocent question on what loom she should use to stitch a wrap for Kanak's birthday. Leander had weighed the pros and cons, visited his calculations, asked Zain a multitude of questions she had hesitantly answered—with most of the truth, anyway—and revisited his hypotheses.

All the while, she had racked her brain for a way out of the puzzling knot she found herself in. No matter which end she pulled or how hard she thrust her nail into its core, the knot wouldn't budge. Only something drastic or disastrous—or both—would save her from the predicament with Dev.

As planned, Theron had been stationed along the artery, and according to his infuriatingly correct reports, Dev concerned himself with only a handful of locations: his hut, the harbor, the mechanic's store, and the tavern. He rarely left his home by himself and was typically with Iravan or Yadav. In short, he would need to be lured out of his hut. There was something unsavory about the way Theron relayed his findings, and she couldn't put a finger on why it bothered her to hear Dev described the way she saw him: lazy and entitled.

Leander was positively thrilled. "This makes us acting on the Anniversary even more crucial. It will be difficult to execute our plan on any other day."

"Dev will probably be home after the parade," she added, imagining the machinations of his downfall. "He's not out and about on the day."

Unless he was involved with whatever was going to happen, but she kept that tidbit to herself.

"What? Why didn't you say something before?" Leander asked.

"I was trying to talk you out of this," she said, shrugging. "But since you won't listen to reason, hear me when I tell you that Dev will be home after the parade tomorrow."

"Then we go in during the parade," Leander countered.

"I am expected at my guardian's side," Zain said, "They're leading the procession. So unless one of you can go in there at the exact right time, I will lose my alibi."

"We can't go either," Leander said, and his downcast expression nearly made her regret her omissions. "We're expected to man the procession. Every guard must be accounted for."

Bloodstrippers had never been near Anniversary proceedings. It was one of the unspoken rules of their truce. Tejomaya had been given one day to grieve.

"Man the procession? That is preposterous," Zain replied. "People will riot."

"That is exactly what the officers are expecting," Theron said, coolly.

The bloodstrippers had been more unsettled and aggressive than usual, given rumors of the rebellion. Every moment between the three of them was stolen, their schedules tighter. But she had not expected it to bleed into their sacred day.

People spoke of rebellion like they did about good habits—insistently and with no intent. Zain had stopped entertaining the idea a long time ago.

"If we can't go in during the parade, we get him out of his hut after. There is a shift change an hour later, so at least one of us can take advantage of that," Leander said. "Or better yet, one of us can pull him aside after the parade, leaving you to go in."

Zain was already shaking her head.

"Why not?" Leander asked, throwing his hands up in the air. "You will be a lot less inconspicuous going into his hut."

"No, I won't," she snapped. "Why would you think that?"

"Don't you work for him?" Leander asked.

Her mouth spasmed. "I used to."

Theron snorted, and, souls help her, she was not a violent person, but she wanted to punch him. Leander had been more patient than she had expected, pushing her to consider an approach of her own, but no matter how far she stretched her thoughts, contorted the boundaries of her capabilities, there was nothing she could think of that would allow this to end in the way she wanted. She needed Dev exposed, not robbed.

She knew him. If she did not deliver her five vials the night of the Anniversary, he would come to the Bow. She didn't need proof of the man's violence; she carried it on her body. He couldn't be allowed near Kanak in that state. But the thought of going to him, taking the brunt of his rage, made her want to jump into the Soulless Sea.

She would not allow it to happen this time.

This time.

"Then what is it you propose we do?" Leander asked.

Zain buried her head in her hands. "I don't know."

"Useless," Theron muttered.

"I don't see you coming up with any stellar ideas," she snarled, surprised by the venom in her voice.

"I'm not the one who knows who wrote about the calor reserve in the acolyte's book," Theron returned, calmly.

"On my soul, can you *stop* with the fucking book?" Zain cried. *There is no reserve,* is what she wanted to scream, but that would do her no good here.

Theron continued, "I'm also not the one with a relationship to the slum dons." He didn't have to be loud or angry for the meaning to hit home. "If you weren't such a coward, you would have proposed the most obvious solution. Or did you forget who is at stake here?"

Zain had enough of people threatening her guardians. "I have no relationship with anyone."

"Not just a coward, then," Theron said, ignoring Leander when he tried to intervene. "A liar too. An absolute fucking waste of life."

"Shut up!" Zain screamed, and got to her feet. Her cry was so enormous, she couldn't believe it came from her body, couldn't believe it was directed at a guard, but her logic had flown to Gehanna. Red filled her vision at the sight of him—this tall, pale Gehennese calling her a waste of life when he existed because of the pain she had endured.

"Why are you even here?" she yelled. "Why are you here when you hate me so much?"

Theron was unblinking. "Some of us do things we don't like. It's called duty, obligation—concepts you know nothing about."

"Oh, it's obligation that brings you here?" Zain said. Something came over her then, a boldness that had long nested in shadows. She advanced toward Theron, tilting her head up so she was inches from his face. "Is it obligation that has you seeking help from a leech? Is that what you'll call it when your commander asks why you hide each time you brothers are out on patrol?"

It was true. He thought she was some stupid rat, but he didn't know all she saw, all she kept to herself. The way he had ducked out of sight at the harbor. The way he and Leander stepped out of the streets when bloodstrippers patrolled the area. The way their plans for calor seemed more personal to Leander, rather than to the Geng cause. If Zain didn't have her own plans, she would have called him out a long time ago.

His eyes flickered. She hated how transparent they looked. She wasn't used to seeing herself reflected back. Her face was warped with all the anger she normally fought to keep inside.

Theron didn't flinch. He didn't grace her with even a scowl. Instead, he faced his brother, Zain already forgotten. Rather than a surge of rage, something in her chest plunged into a freefall.

Theron said, "You have until tonight to figure this out if you still want my help, but I can't sit here and listen to this anymore. I need to get ready for the market tomorrow evening to pick up parts for your masks. And if you come up with nothing by then, we're pulling the plug. I'm done."

Zain's nails dug deeper into her palms, as if the pain could cut through Theron's cruelty, through the way she had faced him, speaking up when so often she stayed silent only to be met with utter indifference.

Once upon a time, this wouldn't have been strange, her voice stepping in when her body couldn't, her system compensating. As a child, she had been demanding, but Dev and the fire and all that followed had made her taste regret. How many times could you choke on your own shame before choosing to lock it inside? At least her shame would be her own to bear, not offered up on a platter for people like Theron to pick apart.

"This could help your people," Leander said, softly, gesturing at Theron to back off. "I think the rains are tied to the soul-sickness plaguing the slums. If you help us here, it would benefit us all."

It wasn't as if she hadn't heard this before, the idea that the Gengs would help her people. They had never done so.

But every nightmare of late involved Bilal, the smoke from his funeral a smothering force that made her lurch up in bed, panting. She remembered Gayathri's face when she went to see her afterward, the healer's face sunken, aging too quickly. She thought of Laila and Lufi, who'd lost the light in their eyes since the storm. There were so many ways for people to die in Tejomaya, but grief was the first thief of life.

The old Temple of Many-Souls shimmered in her mind's eye, glorious and devastating as flames licked its sides.

An absolute fucking waste of life.

If only Theron knew.

"I'll get Dev out of his hut," she said, her mouth dry. Her resolve had shown steel the second Leander said he could help her people. She had sworn to do anything to alleviate the burdens for the slums, and well . . . she was here already, wasn't she? She couldn't go back to the way things used to be. "Theron is right.

I know Dev. It won't be strange if I retrieve him on the day. It'll leave the coast clear for you to storm the hut."

Surprise passed over Theron's face, followed by something she couldn't quite read.

Alone with Dev. She had been alone with him many times, but this would be different. None of this plan was how she had imagined it would be, but her fingers traced her woefully empty gun. Alone with Dev, away from the slums. Maybe this was how it was supposed to go.

"Works for me," Theron said. "I'll see you both tomorrow."

He stalked away, down to the harbor where the gray waters met copper land. Her anger had fizzled into hollow nerves. For once, she had set things in motion, and it scared the shit out of her.

"I know it doesn't seem like it, but Theron wants us to succeed," Leander said.

Zain scoffed. She didn't really care.

"Did you know we're half Urjan?" Leander asked.

"What?" She studied his face up close, but her observations remained the same. Pale skin, light hair, eyes a shocking green.

Everything was dull, but dull was home. Green was danger.

"Our mother was born there, near the Janmiri border. Her parents brought her to Gehanna when she was two, so she was Gehennese in all ways except how she looked. Theron's always been a little obsessed with Urjan, though, trying to learn the language and culture."

With a start, Zain remembered when Theron had spoken to her in Urj by the docks, and all the other pieces fell into place. She had heard of the Southern migration, when thousands had left to the Upper Tectonic during falling calor supplies. Sights had not yet fallen on Tejomaya then. When mining the skies in the Upper Tectonic, people thought it would be best to build a life there. She wondered how Leander's mother would feel now, knowing she left the place that had caught the unwanted attention of the very people her family had hoped to join. All roads led back to Tejomaya.

"And your father?" she asked.

"He died when I was three, when Theron was ten," Leander said. "I hardly remember him, but he made sure we were set up for success. Our mother was able to admit us to top schools, give us the best of everything. He had money and he left it for us."

A peculiar feeling ebbed in Zain's chest. Although their circumstances could not have been more different, this resonated with her. Hadn't Kanak done the same for her? Their love was boundless, and unlike Leander and his parents, Zain still had the blessing of being in Kanak's life. Yet here they were, two people who had been given everything, alone and lost.

"Why are you here?" she asked, but her tone was markedly different from when she had asked Theron the same question.

"I showed a great deal of promise as a child," Leander said, fiddling with the pilling sleeve of his uniform. "My teachers had their eyes on me from a very young age. I had a way with materials, grasped concepts of calor early on. It grabbed me in a way nothing else did. So when the army began recruiting bloodstrippers, I was recommended for my expertise."

"Were you given a choice?"

"Of sorts," Leander said.

An awkward silence hung between them. Zain did her best to make sense of all she had been told, reconciling it with what she knew.

"What about your brother?" she asked.

"He came for me."

CHAPTER EIGHTEEN

Zain

Leander must have given his brother quite the talking-to, because the brute wasn't saying a word in protest of this ridiculous idea.

"This wasn't part of the agreement," Zain argued. "I did not sign up to help you with your inventions."

Only a day had passed since her big fight with Theron, so Leander's request that she accompany his brother to the underground market that evening was met with great incredulity. Apparently, there were merchants in town with controlled materials from Gehanna that would help him with his masks.

"Why can't I just go alone?" she demanded. "I know the market like the back of my hand. I can make the trade for you."

"I said the same thing," Theron muttered, polishing his gun for the umpteenth time.

Zain fought the urge to snatch the weapon from his hands. "Oh, now he talks."

"Because," Leander interrupted, giving his brother a

meaningful glare, "they won't sell it to you, Zain. You're not . . . well . . . They won't sell it to a Janmiri."

She couldn't possibly have heard that right. "Then why are the merchants attending the underground market?"

"To sell other things!" Leander said, gesturing dramatically with his hands. "Look, this is a common occurrence. The vendors go to the market with specific goods they're willing to trade with locals, but I know they have what I need because they're bringing supplies to the bloodstripper quarters later. The problem is that supply is very carefully controlled, and I'm already at my quota and Matthieu won't give me more. Zain, you don't understand— if I can get ahold of enough of this rubber, it'll help me improve the vacuum suction on the masks."

Zain cut him off before she was subjected to yet another soliloquy on mask mechanics. "Okay, I'll do it, but if he says one more thing—"

"He won't!" Leander exclaimed, and wrapped her in a deep hug. Zain tensed, the feeling so wholly foreign when coming from someone who was not Kanak that her bones felt stupendously fragile. He let go when her arms stayed limp, and the air she sucked in after was sweet and bright. She blinked, a not-entirely-unpleasant sense of warmth rushing through her when Leander said, "Thank you."

The feeling lasted only a minute before she realized she would have to spend her evening with Theron Cleirigh.

If the market was the city's heart, tonight it was suffering from some sort of arrhythmia. Zain anticipated this, what with it being the evening before the Anniversary, and had timed their arrival well after the first flock of attendees had descended. Many Tejomayan merchants were still recovering from the storm, but plenty had traveled from outside the city for the special occasion. The air crackled around the merchants with the most prized artifacts, from casks of aged wine to handcrafted furniture.

"There are a lot of people here," Theron said, as he surveyed various stalls.

"Yes, and plenty of them are friends and family," she said, yanking him into an aisle of Urjan food stalls, where the air carried a hint of toasted chapatis and fava bean stew.

He glanced down warily at where her hands manacled his wrists. "Don't want to be seen with me?"

Theron had shed his bloodstripper uniform for a spotless linen shirt and charcoal pants, but he still drew suspicious glances from passersby. Must be the asshole oozing from his pores.

Zain let out a high-pitched laugh. "You're the one who should be worried. If Samiah saw us together—never mind. It's best if we lie low, get this over with, and leave."

The area behind her was strictly off limits—that's where Samiah, Mahini, and most of the other local booths would be. For once, she was thankful the market was segregated. The Gehennese traders were set up in the opposite direction, and she scanned the rows of peddlers until she found them, figures robed in royal blue, wearing perennial expressions of superiority. Her heart stuttered as she caught a glimpse of what used to be her favorite stall a couple of positions down—a table with a model plane.

"I'll wait at the plane booth," Zain muttered. "Don't take too long."

Theron raised his brows. "Can I look at this plane booth?" He tugged at his wrists, which were still ensnared in her steely hold. Souls, she was holding on so tightly, she could feel his pulse against her palms.

"It's hard to miss," Zain said, quickly releasing him, wincing at how her hands came away clammy.

Mercifully, he pocketed his hands and departed with a brief nod.

She watched with malicious envy as Theron maneuvered through the crowd toward the Gehennese stall, making his way to the front with ease. In contrast, she had to elbow open a path, muttering apologies in her stead. Her head swiveled like a broken lighthouse in search of people she might know, a price her neck would pay for the next morning.

By the time she got to the plane booth, Theron was speaking urgently with the Gehennese merchant, who looked smugly satisfied. Theron reached into his bag to retrieve an item as the merchant dipped under his stall, but they hadn't made the trade. Trust Theron to unearth the ability to make small talk now, precisely when she wanted to leave.

"The last models had jet engine systems that supply calor to plane motors."

Irritated, Zain brought her attention to the man at the plane booth. He was an eccentric recluse who lived on the outskirts of the city and made rare appearances at the market. When they were ten, Bilal and Zain forced him into letting them help. Then, Bilal had almost broken off a yoke in the middle of a demonstration, bringing an end to their assistant days. She'd do anything for him to be here now.

"This is the flight control. To take off, you press this knob and push the throttle forward. The yoke controls direction." He went on to describe the flying mechanisms Zain could rattle off by memory at this point. She idled in the back, not wanting to be recognized. As a child, she'd been fascinated by planes, but now

it hurt to think about. What use was a silly model when the real
thing would never return?

"Roses!" someone cried. "I've got colors you've never seen
before!"

Zain whirled at the call of the flower peddler, gasping at the
bundles of roses displayed on his otherwise unadorned table. It
didn't matter that he didn't have a beautiful tablecloth or an eye-
catching sign—the flowers were breathtaking on their own.

Jostling through the small crowd gathered around the stall,
she ran her finger along the stems, her nerves tingling at the
light brush of thorns. Most of the buds were hues of pinks and
purples, but there in the middle was a small bunch of red roses.
Zain's lips parted. Red has always been the color of nightmares.
The sky, fire, and blood had forever altered its connotation for
her. But she had always wondered if roses would be able to turn
the color into something beautiful.

Standing there, where the fragrance reached her in gentle
wisps, she was certain they did.

"Zain?"

Her breath whooshed out of her at Mahini's voice, right as
Laila and Lufi slammed into her body.

"Oh, hello," Zain said, seized by bone-breaking panic. Souls,
this was just her luck. She glanced for any sign of an approaching
Theron, but he was still with his merchant. "What are you all
doing here? Shouldn't you be at your stall?"

At closer glance, Mahini and her daughters appeared just
as dazed. Lufi was sucking on her thumb, while Laila scratched
around her still-healing burns.

Mahini gave Zain's cheeks a light squeeze. "We didn't set up
a booth today. Not a lot of ingredients, so we just came by to look

around, see if we could trade for something helpful. Things have
been tough lately."

Didn't Zain know it. Ingredients, materials—everything was
tough to find. Samiah was limited to the local grasses she could
gather, dreams of silks and cottons long gone. Zain's maroon
tunic was a recent experiment, and it itched constantly.

"You could make delicious food with anything," Zain promised, looking nervously between Mahini and Theron. Her breaths
grew labored as he pocketed the materials from the trader's table,
then met her gaze.

She wondered if she looked as stricken as she felt. Her heart
bleated as Theron frowned at the back of Mahini's head before
realization flooded his face. *Please wait,* she told him with her
eyes, then turned her attention back to the family.

Fortunately, Mahini was busy reprimanding Laila for
scratching at her wounds, with a sharp "I told you not to do that."
Both mother and daughter shared a look marked with tenuous
compromise before Mahini shifted her attention back to Zain.
"Yes, well, you have to come by and try my latest recipes. It's been
too long. We miss you."

"Of course," Zain said, scrambling for a way out of there. But
her attention snagged as Lufi reached for the flowers on the table,
turning pleading eyes up at her mother.

"We can't afford that, Lu," Mahini said, ruffling Lufi's hair.
There was a weary, exhausted sadness that clung to her like a reaper.

"I could trade this," Laila offered, pointing at the beautiful
pendant that sat in the hollow of her neck. Zain's breath hitched.
It was the one valuable item their family possessed. She waited
for Mahini to object and tell her *absolutely not,* but she only let
out a deep sigh.

"There are other things that could get us," Mahini said. "The flowers won't last."

The vendor, who had been eavesdropping, shot them a dirty look. He was accustomed to hearing similar excuses, Zain was sure. Still, she was reeling. She knew things had grown dire, but this somber version of a family that had always found a way to laugh, that continued to feed her and their neighbors when they had so little themselves, that shared their boundless spirit with everyone was her breaking point. Zain remembered when Kanak presented her with the rose seeds. How terrible that they had learned to diminish beauty, to discard value, and to base need on utility alone. She could not fault Mahini for her priorities, not when the two children by her side needed food on the table, but she still mourned.

"Here," Zain said, reaching for the few coins Samiah had given her. "It won't get you the whole bunch, but maybe a few?"

Lufi's face instantly lit up. "Really, Zainy?"

Hearing Bilal's nickname for her made Zain ache.

"Oh, we couldn't," Mahini said, but Zain pushed the coins into the vendor's hand.

"For all the times you've fed me," Zain said, returning Laila's and Lufi's hug. Their cheeks dimpled as the vendor handed each of them a lush red rose.

Sometimes, beauty was enough. Sometimes, it bred wonder, and what was hope if not a continued belief in wonder?

"You must come by after the Anniversary," Mahini said, patting Zain's cheek. "I have to get Laila's wounds redressed, but promise?"

"Please, Zain," Laila begged. "We haven't played hopscotch together in so long."

Zain swallowed thickly at the spark of life in Laila's eyes. "I'll try."

She looked for Theron as soon as the family disappeared, but he was no longer at the Gehennese merchant's booth. Great.

"Do you want one for yourself?" the vendor asked.

Zain shook her head. She didn't have anything of value left on her person to trade, but she did feel a renewed sense of determination to plant Kanak's seeds once she got home. *After the Anniversary*, she told herself. The thought halted her in her tracks. She was thinking past her deadline, as though there was a possibility beyond tomorrow. Somewhere in the wreckage of the week, she had found hope.

She was doing this. She was going to face Dev.

"I'll take one for her."

Zain spun to see Theron, holding out a bag of dates. Her mouth watered. Dates were not found in Tejomaya, but she had tried one from Kanak after a bloodstripper had traded with an acolyte. They were utterly precious.

"No, thank you," Zain said, politely. She had no interest in getting anything from Theron, but the vendor, his face ghostly white, appeared to have recognized the guard. He ignored Zain, handing over a rose to Theron with a bow of his head. Theron held the stem out.

She crossed her arms, too aware of the fact that the vendor was watching, as were the remaining bystanders, all looking a little too eager. This city was full of gossipmongers, and word could spread as surely as calor to a dead man's brain. Oh souls, what if Mahini and the girls were still around? Zain turned on her heel and set off toward the exit, willing the crowd to swallow her in its humid, spice-dusted melee. The market spat her out along the artery, where the night landed darker, quieter, promising anonymity. Theron caught up to her.

"Will you just take it?" he asked, shoving the rose to her

chest. Zain yelped as a thorn pricked her flesh and instinctively took the flower.

"Is this supposed to be an apology?" she asked, exhausted from being on high alert. "Because you made up for it by not screwing me over back there."

Theron clicked his teeth. "Is that all it takes?"

"Well, no," she protested, feeling quite chagrined. The noise from the market had faded, the buildings around them serving as eerie watchers. "But I appreciate it. That would have been a mess, had they started asking questions."

The guard shrugged. "I was told I should be worried."

Zain nearly tripped over her own feet. Were the souls deceiving her, or did Theron just try to *joke*? She hadn't thought it possible, and she studied his stoic profile for any sign to suggest she was right. His scar appeared longer at night, casting a shadow across his jaw. Absentmindedly, she tapped her finger against the sharpest thorn.

"In Gehanna, those come with the thorns stripped off," Theron remarked, catching her mid-assessment.

Zain flushed, mildly embarrassed by how she'd been momentarily captivated by his face. She did not doubt that life was vastly different in Gehanna. How could it not be, when they had plundered the Lower Tectonic and taken all their resources home? It was the one place that was fooled into thinking the world was different, its reality held together by the wars that raged outside its borders. She felt guilty for wanting to know more, but wasn't she owed a kernel of their illusion?

"Did you like it back there?" she asked.

Theron contemplated her question for a long moment. "It's not what you'd expect. Beautiful, of course, but less an oasis and more a museum. Like everything we once had is now there in this one place, still available for some to enjoy. But mostly, it's lonely."

Zain was surprised. "Lonelier than here?"

Theron's jaw ticked. "Leander and I may look Gehennese to you, but there, we look more Urjan than you'd think. People could always tell."

"But you were recruited into the force," Zain said.

"Recruited is one way of putting it," he said. "I'm sure they believed we would blend in, with the way we look. If I'm honest, I wondered that too, if we'd fit in here."

"Maybe if you came without a uniform," said Zain, impetuously, remembering they had money. "That might have helped matters."

"You're right," Theron said, letting out a shuddering breath. "We should have left before they roped Leander into a situation he—we—couldn't leave. But here we are."

There was a stark sadness to his statement that caught her off guard. She remembered what Leander had said about Theron's curiosity surrounding Urjan, the other parts of his ancestry. The tiny insignia on his uniform. She imagined for once what it would be like to belong to two places but neither at the same time. For each side to believe you weren't truly theirs. Zain had felt caught between the Bow and the slums, but she had still been loved by both, still been part of the two sides of Tejomaya. Theron and Leander were fractured across the world. Everything she had felt—anger at who she was, anger at how she had been born, anger at the way life had shaped itself around her—emerged in a new light.

"Did you hate your mother for it?" she blurted out. It was the first time she had hinted at her ugliest thoughts, her resentment that Kanak's shelter had isolated her from the other children, whom she may have bonded with had things turned out differently. Maybe if she'd had friends, she wouldn't have gone to the leeches. She wouldn't have fallen in with Dev. She wouldn't have the guilt that consumed her after simply entertaining such thoughts.

For some reason, his answer mattered.

"At first," he admitted. His voice was low, and he wouldn't look at her. "But I realized it wasn't her I hated. It was not belonging."

Zain mused on whether this was the first time he had said those words out loud. Silence pressed down on them, the streets quiet as they wound around the farthest end of the slums and toward the edge of the Sickle. Suddenly, the walk felt like it had been lifted from a dream, a delicate thing she didn't want to end. One more question, and for once it didn't fill her with anger.

"I have always wondered," Zain said, "about the sun. Is it really so beautiful when it disappears?" She had never quite believed it, not when Janmir had never returned from the vanishing sun.

"Everyone says they love the sunset," Theron replied after a moment of consideration. "But the sunrise is far superior. Not necessarily in beauty, but in the intimacy of it all. Sunsets are observed by lovers, friends, and families, all locked together in awe of its magnificence. Not everyone is awake for the sunrise. It's you and the glorious, blazing sky, watching as the light shatters the darkness above your head."

That night, her nightmares quelled for the first time. Instead, Zain dreamed of a sky she'd never seen, of a light that broke across an invisible horizon.

CHAPTER NINETEEN

Iravan

" **S** top fidgeting."

Iravan scowled at Yadav. The mechanic's usual gray-blue Anniversary kurta was hanging loosely over his knobby shoulders. Yadav had lost even more weight in the days since the storm, spending every spare hour helping rebuild stores in the Hammer. Dev peeked around Yadav quizzically, then dragged his eyes to the ground, where Iravan was tapping his feet away to "Old Vicky."

"People are watching you," Yadav murmured, clasping his hands together, a portrait of peace while his words conveyed wrath. "Pull yourself together, and stop singing a bar song in your head."

"That's the damn problem," Iravan said, hating that they'd been thrust to the front, clearly identifiable among the city people assembled to watch the cavalcade passing down the artery.

Yadav let out an exasperated groan. "They watch you every year."

Dev concealed a laugh with a cough, which Yadav rewarded with a hard smack to his back.

Iravan contemplated Yadav's words, wondering what felt so wrong this year. He had been at the Anniversary mourning ascent every year he could remember, watching the acolytes proceed down the artery from the eastern harbor, past the Hammer and the slums, all the way to the Temple.

Things had changed, of course. For one, Iravan used to be a boy hovering at the back of the gathering, but he and Dev had steadily moved forward, eventually flanking Yadav at the front of the crowd with the last remaining survivors of the final stand. Only a handful of those survivors remained now: the man who did the plane demonstrations at the market, the woman who laundered clothes near the Bow. The last people with any memory of a free Tejomaya, of a self-sufficient and prosperous Janmir.

The family members who stood by the survivors now knew only soil that reeked of death, and art that sang of pain.

The Temple no longer stood. And the path they walked was fringed by ash, no amount of wind strong enough to remove the blackening from the soil. He wondered if, ten years down the road, there would be anything left to burn.

Kanak walked by, joining the acolytes for the annual procession. Iravan had been preoccupied with Dev and their plans for the Anniversary, but he had spent his free hours with the acolytes, trying to track down the infamous journal with the note about the reserve. It wasn't like he could ask outright—word of a slumlord's interest in a myth would spread far too quickly—but he hoped there would be another hint in the acolytes' hermetic correspondences. No luck there, though.

Dev guided Iravan and Yadav toward the burned-down Temple, where the procession parted in neat lines.

"Will you be okay?" Dev asked, low enough so nobody else could hear.

Iravan couldn't afford not to be. The city's ever-changing politics demanded constant vigilance. Just two days ago, the Nohri guards had unexpectedly withdrawn from Tejomaya, a variable that shifted the calculus of their plans. The mystery of *why* plagued him, and his best guess led, unhelpfully, to the woman who had withered like a dry flower under his touch.

Mariam Mariam Mariam.

He couldn't shake her name or the image of her face. It would forever be tied to his loss of control. Despite what people might think, Iravan did not enjoy resorting to force to find answers, not since the Temple had burned down, but he had almost played judge, jury, and executioner with someone who may hold the answer to their plight. After all, he was certain the councilmember he had seen Mariam speaking with was Jezeme Cano of Nohri.

If his gut was right—and it often was—then Mariam had knowledge that had prompted the Nohri to leave, essentially dissolving a third of the Coalition. Years of violence couldn't do what she had accomplished with words in a mere few days. He had gone to her home, but she hadn't been there. He'd tried searching for her in the parts of the Hammer usually occupied by Urjans, but no one recognized her from his description.

A young acolyte stepped to the front, drawing a hush. They always chose the youngest to honor the future, the people who would have to overcome horrific circumstances to make it to the same end as the rest of them.

"We are gathered here today to mark the fiftieth Anniversary of the Carnage, to honor those who came before us and lift up the ones who are still to come."

Iravan noticed them then: two bloodstrippers at the corner of the artery, watching. His blood chilled. No matter their dislike for one another, the bloodstrippers had always stayed out of the

way the week of mourning. With what had happened with the
Nohri, he'd imagined they would be left alone this Anniversary,
but the Gehennese encroached as usual.

More guards appeared at every corner, their weapons at the
ready. The crowd pushed inward as muffled whispers spread.

"If things take a turn, take Yadav and run," Iravan whispered.

Dev smirked. "Cold feet?"

No, only a visceral knowledge that things were about to tip
into something new. They'd set into motion a reckless gambit,
and while he was certain of its payoff, the extent of their sacrifice
would be determined in the following hours. He focused on the
acolyte who cleared her throat, moments before her lovely voice
rang above the din.

> *Come, hear my echoes calling around the*
> *mountainside.*
> *There's a path down to the sea,*
> *Where the forest gulfed in stone will cast*
> *your footprints in disguise*
> *And whisper to you my plea.*

The crowd stirred. Iravan stared at the acolyte in shock. He
knew this song—they all did—but rarely was it performed anymore. Lore said it had started as a secret set of instructions,
passed through rhyme and song by their ancestors before the
protests. It evolved into something more, verses added with every
bard, recording their strength, their fight, their eventual demise.

> *Come feel the winds are changing, the worst*
> *is yet to come.*
> *And there's no shelter to seek.*

Your bones may grind to dust, forgotten like
    the stolen sun.
You're afraid no one will hear you weep.

Guards gathered closer to the perimeter of the crowd, as though they could sense the beating heart of the city roaring back to life. Someone bellowed, and one by one, people joined in, shaking off the rust of old, forgotten shackles.

"It's a shame we don't hear this often," Dev whispered at his side, a slow grin spreading across his face. "We say the last line all the time, but we've forgotten the point of the song."

Come, lay your grave by me, one day you'll
    learn to fly.
And your soul will find a place beyond the
    fallen skies.

Iravan felt every word as the acolyte drew her last notes.

May your soul find a place beyond the fallen
    skies.

It was a song of revolution.

Bloodstripper presence had left everyone uneasy.

The crowd dissipated to their respective places of mourning and worship. The devout would cluster around the rubble of the Temple, seeking solace from the acolytes who would remain there through the evening and well into the night. Others would return home, content with private confrontations of faith, something Iravan never understood.

Now, he asked himself: What else woke someone every day in a world that wept with their blood? If not faith in the Janmiri Souls, the Urjan Gods, or even the Gehennese Holy Altar, then a belief there was something in the universe that fed them purpose.

This was the one day Iravan wished he could leave the city. So he went to the sea.

The harbor was quieter than usual. A handful of bloodstrippers patrolled the port, but the boats transporting passengers to and from the mainland were notably absent. The Gengs had suspended their normal activities. Good. All the more energy for what was to come.

Iravan was about to skip a rock across the water when a flash of green caught his eye.

Concealed behind a defunct lighthouse was Mariam, speaking animatedly with someone. A discreet sidestep revealed who—a uniformed guard.

Iravan's hand flew to his gun, but he kept his distance. Was this to do with the Nohri withdrawal? Her dealings with the Council? When the bloodstripper left, Mariam slumped against the harbor railing. Iravan approached her from behind.

"That looked intense," he said by way of greeting.

Mariam whipped around to face him, her loose glasses sliding down her nose. She was a vision, in an emerald dress with a one-shoulder strap that bared her unblemished neck. He warred between relief he had not left a mark and wishing that he had.

"You should know," she said, gathering her composure. "You're the wanted man."

"What?"

"They've been asking about you," she replied, oblivious or

indifferent to the hint of malice in his voice. "Said you've been seen near my home, asking if I know your plans."

Souls, he'd been careless. Of course he'd been noticed lumbering about the Bow. Iravan fought to keep his temper level. "And what did you tell them?"

"That you came by on behalf of an acolyte to collect Urjan sweets," she answered, absently, studying the island in the distance.

Iravan stared at her in disbelief. "That's imaginative."

She could have told them about the medicine. Bilal and the soul-sickness were no secret.

Mariam hummed. "Some truths are none of their business."

He didn't know what to say to that, so he blurted out, "About the funeral."

The air whipped a thin braid across her cheek.

"Yes?"

He wasn't prepared for this. "I acted inappropriately."

"You did."

"I shouldn't have—" he started. Tried again. "I'm sorry."

He couldn't remember the last time he had apologized to anyone. If Mariam felt the weight of what had occurred, she gave no indication of it, leaning so far over the railing that he wanted to pull her back an inch.

"You said he was family," she said, as if that was answer enough. He joined her in watching the island in silence. "You know, this harbor reminds me of my family. Of Urjan. We have many islands hanging off our coasts, some as close as this one here. As children, we used to see who could count the most islands. You can imagine the quarrels that ensued."

It was her tone and the fond recollections that were more foreign to him than the guttural way she rolled her syllables.

He didn't think there was anything he could speak about in this manner that would not simultaneously shred his insides with loss. What was it like to allow for pain and love to exist in the same space? He wasn't sure he would ever be able to—his pain and love had both been too large to coexist. They had blended into terrifying anger.

"Why stay away?" he asked, brazenly. It was easier to talk to her like this, side by side, without eye contact.

"They are safe where they are. And my work requires me to go where it is unsafe. I hope with time, I'll have fewer places to go."

"Was speaking to Jezeme Cano part of that work?"

"Yes," Mariam said. "I shared with them the work that Urjan has been doing over the years, and how it may benefit their people. How it would be best for them to join us now, since this city doesn't have long left."

He spun toward her. "Is that a threat?" The moment of peace between them passed as quickly as a cool breeze in Tejomaya.

Mariam cocked her head, and the thick beads of her gold necklace caught the murky light. "In some ways, yes. It is the sky's threat, though, not my own."

"What do you mean?"

She let out a small laugh. "Iravan Khotar." The way she said his name sounded rehearsed, like she had tasted each syllable several times before uttering it out loud. "You ask me to give you an answer I have worked my entire life to try to uncover."

Iravan swallowed his exasperation. "What do you want?"

"I don't want anything," she said, quietly. "Only your time. I simply cannot tell you everything you need to know, here and in these circumstances."

"Very well," he said. "Let us find a quiet place to talk."

They headed to Mariam's home.

"I had a friend who was kind enough to share their home with me," Mariam said, the quirk at the corner of her mouth indicating he hadn't hidden his silent questions about her habitation in his city as well as he had thought. She jostled the lock, then let him into a small room that looked as out of place in Tejomaya as Mariam did. The walls were painted a warm taupe, complementing the maroon sofa pushed up against the back wall. Large, plush pillows hung at its edges, depressed in the corner where he imagined she sat, curled up with the book that lay face down on the glass coffee table. A small but well-stocked kitchen gleamed next to a closed door. His look of surprise reflected back at him from the ornate wall mirror. This was firmly Mariam's home: colorful and unapologetic.

"She inherited it from another friend and told me to make the place my own. I imagine it has served each Urjan prophet who has come to the area."

Mariam leaned against the oval table in her living room. Outside the window behind her, the sky swirled, drawing crimson lines above her head. The faint smell of ginger loosened Iravan's muscles. "Well, prophet, tell me what is so important that you have hounded me since your entry into this city."

"Calor is killing your people."

"What do you mean?" Iravan asked, sharply.

"I have been studying calor for a long time, its history and evolution," Mariam said. "Since Tejomaya has been the only city to receive calor in the form of blood rains, it has drawn many of us prophets over the last few decades. We have conducted tests and observations and concluded that calor as a substance has grown more unstable over the years. It's the temperature around the world, but especially here: it has gotten too hot, and shows no signs of slowing down. In some ways, this is a positive feedback cycle. When calor falls, it grows hotter; when it grows hotter, calor falls apart."

Iravan's throat dried. "Falls apart?"

"Calor exists in a different state when it is in the sky relative to its state on the ground. In the sky, calor is liquid, hence its descent upon us in the form of rains. On the ground, when left unprocessed and uncollected, calor turns to gas, building under the surface of the earth. This is an extremely unstable, dangerous form of calor. But up until now, it hasn't been an issue, because there hasn't been enough of it to make a difference. Then the Carnage happened, turning the rains into blood, and everything changed.

"There's something about the metal in blood that has triggered calor. We think calor has built to a lethal point in areas that receive a high concentration of rains and where gas is escaping through the ground in short gasps, killing those who inhale too much of it."

The pieces clicked in Iravan's head. "The sickness. It's the gas."

Mariam nodded, pushing her glasses up the bridge of her nose. "Think about it. Why has calor never been used in people? Our bodies are hot and compact. Within us, it turns gaseous and causes us to combust."

With a jolt, Iravan remembered the injections, the decision he had made. His heart dropped at the implications.

"But then why isn't it killing more people?" he asked, his mind racing.

"Because the quantities escaping are still small, affecting specific areas and the people who spend an inordinate amount of time there. Your victims were likely those who remained at the foothills. The majority of calor runoff accumulates there," she replied.

"Shouldn't this happen at the island too?" Iravan asked, but he knew that once again, fate favored the Gengs. What crimes had his people committed that they were destined to pay for everyone else's?

Mariam shook her head sadly. "The island is all stone. Blood doesn't absorb into the ground the way it does here. The chemical reactions are different, and their collection system is more advanced. Regardless, the issue here is that things are getting worse. Calor in the sky is starting to become a problem, the environment continuing to change as it rots. That's what has been driving the drought."

"The maelstrom," Iravan said, quietly. "Does that have something to do with this?"

"Our first recorded instance of calor gas escaping through the rift," Mariam said. "And look what it did."

Look what it all did.

"What do we do?" he asked.

Mariam chewed on her lip. "I find reasons, you find solutions. But if you want to take my advice on anything, I suggest you get everyone out of this city, as fast as you can."

CHAPTER TWENTY

Anastasia

Anastasia had never been good at waiting.

She smoothed out the round collar of her shirt, toyed with its partly frayed hem, then tucked it into the waistband of her pleated skirt. Unsure what to do with her hands, she clasped them behind her back and stared at the stone trunks in front of her, wondering how so much could change behind such an intractable structure. Any moment now, her father would emerge from the stone forest and declare her the newest councilmember. Then, she could halt his alliance with Dev and put forth her plans for revenge.

She had envisioned how this would feel. As a child, it had been her dream: an opportunity to further a legacy the Drakos family had fought tooth and nail to acquire, until the family name had become synonymous with Tejomaya back in Gehanna. Hamish had never meant to be on top. When the Gehennese first came to Tejomaya in the hopes of harnessing the calor reserves above the Janmiri capital, he had been a mere foot soldier. He'd risen on nothing but incessant efforts at developing a refined extraction process, armed with steely determination.

In her precocious teen years, she'd prepared for her eventual ascension as one would polish a weapon. Her perspective had undergone an unfortunate shift, a rite of passage for those of an age in which they believed they knew everything—finally old enough to establish a history of errors, yet young enough to see the foolhardy ways of the generations earlier. The years that followed had proved her tragically wrong.

Now, she marked this day as what it was: her catharsis. Her steps echoed from her bed to the entrance of the stone forest, where all upper-class Gehennese, Nohri, and Finzish islanders had gathered.

Given it was a private Council, no one but the councilmembers and a handful of guards were allowed entrance. The Gehennese behind her brimmed with anticipation. They knew how momentous this day was, but not for the reasons that mattered. Anastasia felt the Anniversary around her, the land, the air, and the sky pulsing in recollection. Her stomach tightened at the thought of commencing her conquest on a holy day, but she pinched the flame of guilt. She had bided her time—ten years—and she would not step aside out of sentimentality.

"Ana?"

Charvi wrestled her way through the mass of people, ignoring the pointed glares and dragging a frazzled Baruna by the hand. The latter looked solemn, admonished, her hastily tied braids uneven. Anastasia recoiled. The gatherers had been banned from this announcement, sequestered to the extractor quarters, a decision made to maintain peace.

"What are you doing here?" Anastasia asked. Charvi had been

avoiding Anastasia. The years Anastasia had spent drowning in her guilt and sorrow, her rage as vital as oxygen, didn't matter. Charvi would have a difficult time reconciling Anastasia's plan with what would come after—her war against the dons, against the people they used to know. Anastasia had been happy to comply with this rare distance. She wasn't sure how to broach the topic of Hamish's betrayal with her best friend. It was the first secret Anastasia had kept from her.

"Your father summoned me," Charvi said. Sweat studded her forehead, brown cheeks henna-stained from the rapid journey she'd made across the island. When Hamish Drakos called for his gatherers, they appeared.

Anastasia wasn't sure why Charvi would be summoned. True, the Council would be discussing matters beyond her own appointment, but the only thing that would have prompted this would be news of rains. She looked up, unconvinced at the prospect, then eyed her friend. "What does he want with you right now?"

Charvi's hands clasped over her stomach. "I'm not sure," she said. "But I can't bring Baru with me, and I didn't want to leave her there—"

Anastasia was already shaking her head.

"Ana, please!" Charvi hissed. Glacial fingers wrapped around Anastasia's wrist and dragged her from where Baruna stood, still dazed.

Something was wrong.

"I know I'm asking this of you on a day when it's difficult," Charvi pleaded, raking fingers through her hair where it lay matted to her face. Her wild eyes spun from Anastasia to her daughter. "But it will just be for a little bit. I need to report to your father, and I'll be right back. I promise."

Charvi's fingers twitched involuntarily.

Anastasia contended with the notion that her secret wasn't the first between them. "What's wrong?"

Charvi fisted her robes as though willing her body into submission. She couldn't even look at Anastasia anymore, remaining fixated instead on her daughter.

When she answered, Anastasia had to strain to hear. "I did something, Ana."

In the little over a decade Anastasia had known Charvi, she had been nothing but loyal. She'd never strayed a toe out of line unless at Anastasia's request.

"What?" Anastasia asked.

Charvi's lips curled, her shivers replaced by a strangled sob.

"I took some," Charvi whispered. "I think he knows."

Anastasia did not have time to react.

With a belabored "please," Charvi was gone, her lithe body dipping behind the first cluster of tree trunks.

Baruna's hand was so small in her own, smooth, warm skin so foreign that she dropped it immediately, not daring to look at the child as she told her to stay put. They had drawn attention. Islanders glanced between the child and the darkness that had swallowed her mother, no doubt wondering about the cause of the intrusion and why Anastasia hadn't stopped it. She didn't know what to tell them.

I took some. Took what?

She recalled Charvi's disheveled appearance, the fraught nerves maligning her features. An ugly thought reared its head, but this was no time for paranoia. Baruna surveyed the crowd with open curiosity. The child was eerily calm, unperturbed by her mother's strange behavior.

"Baruna," said Anastasia, sharply. "What did your mother tell you?"

In the long moment Baruna didn't respond, Anastasia was mired by fright, one foot poised to chase after her deceitful best friend.

"She said you would take me somewhere safe," Baruna said, so low Anastasia had to bend to hear her. "She said to stay with you, no matter what happens."

No matter what happens.

What had Charvi done?

Anastasia scanned the crowd, a specific absence sending a chill up her spine. Nowhere in sight were the uniformed blood-strippers. Between the planned rebellion on the mainland and the processions taking place, her father had ordered all forces to Tejomaya to make sure things didn't get out of hand. Only a few remained on the island, and they were inside with the Council.

She searched for the next best alternative.

"You," Anastasia barked, pointing two fingers at a messenger who stood close by. He walked over immediately, avoiding eye contact.

"I need you to go to the extractor quarters," she said. "Take someone else with you. I need you to check on the gatherers waiting there." Remembering the extractor from the classroom, she added, "Ask for Ronin and bring him back." She didn't trust anyone on the island, least of all this mouse of a man cowering before her. Hamish had always said, *In the absence of trust, look for differences.*

The messenger gave her a quick nod, angling to rush away, only to be pulled back by Anastasia's hand around his wrist.

"Discreetly," she hissed. Terror appropriately inspired, his subsequent approach to the group of messengers standing to their right was considerably more measured. He relayed her demands to a dark-haired woman, and the two made their way toward the extractor quarters.

"Everyone," she called out, quelling the low swell of murmurs. "Thank you all for your patience today. As you know, the Council is discussing numerous matters of importance and will be with us shortly to deliver a summary of their session. They are running a little behind. After all, it is a momentous day."

She knew then what they saw when they looked at her, as they accepted her command without concern. They saw the girl who had grown from ferocious thorns, just for the years to steep poison in her blood. They saw the woman who walked beneath a bleeding sky as though life were at her beck and call, and death a familiar companion. But most of all, they saw a Drakos, and her name meant something here. Anastasia placed a tremorous hand on Baruna's shoulder. No matter what was happening, she would get to the bottom of it.

When the pair of messengers raced back to the stone entrails, no Ronin in sight, she grew rigid.

"Stay here," she instructed Baruna, meeting the messengers halfway. She couldn't have them near the crowd, not when everyone could feel the unmistakable shift in energy that something was *wrong*. Not when there were no bloodstrippers there for her to command, to mitigate any issues.

"What is it?" she asked, taking in their splotchy flesh, blood vessels bursting under sunken cheeks.

"We could—couldn't find them," the messenger stuttered. "The gatherers or extractors. No one was there. We looked around the quarters, but there's no trace of them."

"How is that possible?" Anastasia demanded, shaking him by the arm. "Where did they go?"

But he had no answer. Then, a sharp cry sliced through the air like a carefully aimed spear.

Someone raced out of the stone forest—a black uniform, a guard, one of the few who were watching over the Council inside. His jaundiced eyes were wide as saucers, and his skin was covered in deep-red hives. They spread across his cheeks and around his temple, where a vein bulged.

"The water," the bloodstripper sputtered. "They poisoned the water."

He dropped to the ground.

It was both a gift and a curse that in moments such as these, time adapted. Everything slowed to a taunting rhythm, each horrifying visual given its own still frame, but there was nothing to be done about it. His swollen tongue lolled. Spittle drooped from the side of his mouth, and the crowd exploded.

Her mind raced to catch up with her body, which was already barreling toward the forest, painfully piecing together that something had gone *wrong wrong wrong.*

When Anastasia halted in the guts of the stone forest, she saw the devastation had already occurred. As she looked at the bodies slumped over in their thrones—Petra, blond hair fringed red, fanning her face; Gohren, neck bent at a gruesome angle; others with their throats slit—she realized there was nothing she could do. Her father stared back at her, his skin a putrid yellow, eyes unseeing. As the crowd swarmed, with aghast cries and anguished screams, the cavities in the frozen trees looked like terrifying smiles.

"What did you do?" A woman's scream tore Anastasia's attention away from the grayed face of Hamish, no more than an old man cradled in death's bosom, to the figures who remained hidden behind the trunks at the back. Charvi walked out of the darkness, Varun by her side, their brown gatherer robes dark as an impenetrable night. They led the other gatherers out of the shadows, their bodies trembling as though possessed. Something wrestled with their souls for space within their too-frail bodies, about to erupt at any moment.

"Mama?"

Baruna appeared next to Anastasia. She wasn't supposed to see this, this monstrous version of her mother, this moment when everything had gone so terribly wrong.

There was never meant to be a rebellion in Tejomaya. The rebellion was here.

The Council chamber was never meant to contain such a horde. One by one, people started dying.

Baruna screamed as a shaking gatherer, eyeballs veined purple and red, struck a man with a dull blade, sprays of blood splattering Anastasia's face. To their left, a woman fell, taking her child down with her in an earsplitting wail. A man turned to Anastasia, face harrowed with hate.

"Varun?" Anastasia whispered, barely recognizing the man in front of her. This was not the mild-mannered gatherer she'd spent time with, whose hair she'd cut, who'd joined her in song.

"Get out of here," Varun said, teeth gritted. Spit flew from his mouth as he clutched his head, a knife pressed against his skull. He let out a blood-curdling howl, like there was something in him he needed to expel. Anastasia stumbled backward, pulling Baruna with her, until she slammed into a hard chest.

"Drakos." Another gatherer, who said her name like a curse. He was the man who'd been with Varun that day at the port, the one who'd made her uncomfortable. He swung his arm up, the tip of a blade shimmering. There was a drop of blood, hanging precariously on its edge. Anastasia's legs were too stiff to move, but she pushed Baruna behind her, prepared to take the blow in a motherly instinct she thought she'd lost.

"No!" someone shouted, and the gatherer's head snapped to the side, the dagger falling from his hands. His body followed, revealing Charvi standing behind. A hilt shone from the back of his neck, blood oozing.

The moment stretched infinitely. Baruna fled to her mother's side, leaving Anastasia bare. And when Charvi's mouth shaped an apology, it was in reality a goodbye.

"Stop!" Anastasia cried, as Charvi scooped her child into her arms. She could not leave like this, Anastasia would not let her leave like this. The distance between them was packed— Anastasia kicked and clawed through the bodies. Charvi was weighed down by Baruna, but she still managed to clear the thick of the crowd, pausing briefly to take in the damage she'd wrought. She looked squarely at Anastasia as she swept an arm in farewell.

The last of Anastasia's delusions caved until she had no choice but to confront the truth.

"Get her!" Anastasia ordered, pointing after the woman she'd called her sister. But as the islanders looked up, searching for a voice of reason, Charvi let out an unearthly scream.

The chamber trembled. Stones grated against one another, branches unknitting from long-set formations. With a chilling groan, the root at the thrones shook itself free, sending bodies sliding off its cracked surface before slamming back into the ground. The trunk corkscrewed, tearing out more of its roots, and the ground rippled and tore from its force, like stitches ripped from a gaping wound.

The forest had only ever been a stoic observer, patient. Anastasia couldn't wrap her head around its sudden burst to vicious life. Cries throttled the air, arms grasping at anything for measure. In one fell swoop, the islanders found themselves bound to the ground by malevolent roots, while the remaining gatherers prowled, temples bulging from unspoken power.

The forest was betrayed, Charvi used to say. Anastasia had sneered at the statement, but around her was evidence of nature's vengeance. The trees may have turned to stone, but Charvi's unholy power had awoken them.

The forest remembered, and feasted upon them all.

Anastasia couldn't look away from the gruesome scene, rock breaking warm flesh. Debris filled the air, brown auroras like spillikins in the purple sky. She coughed blood as her knees gave out. Maybe she would stay there until the trees found her too. Her nails scraped the ground so hard they nearly ripped off. All her dreams turned to dust. She had known from her brief exposures to calor that it had undeniable power, but this restoration to life—or a gruesome imitation of it—this blew past her wildest expectations.

Somewhere, somehow, someone called her name. Who was seeking her so soon after so much death? She wasn't prepared to face her demons just yet, was too weak to don her armor. But she heard it again and again, a softer call, younger, more fragile. Insistent and alive. It couldn't be . . .

"Ana!"

Baruna.

Anastasia stood in a world dark and full of pain. Where had

Charvi gone? The slimmest piece of land opened at her feet, like the Isle was showing her which path to take. Her name grew louder, the cries more strained, and then Anastasia was at the port, where Baruna and Charvi had fallen into a boat.

Charvi was seizing.

"Help!" Baruna cried, leaping off the vessel to hold Anastasia's hands. So much like her mother. Did Baruna know that ten years ago, Charvi had held her hands the same way, cried with the same tears, when it was Baruna who'd needed help?

She wanted to doom them the way she'd been doomed that day, to inflict the kind of pain she had suffered. Maybe then, Charvi would understand, maybe then she'd grasp the depths of what she'd done. But for that to happen, Charvi couldn't die.

The boat was stocked with calor already. This had always been the plan.

Anastasia got inside, turned on the engine, and made the journey she swore she never would.

CHAPTER TWENTY-ONE

Zain

Zain was late.

She tasted blood from chewing out her inner cheek as she walked past the Temple's ashes, fighting the flames that clouded her memory. The screams that echoed in the recesses of her skull. The cries for help that haunted her every night. Horrified faces staring at the monument. Dev's hand around her wrist, snatching her from the crowd, his voice whispering *No one saw you, it's okay,* and for a bleeding moment, she melted into his false comfort.

Just a little farther, a little faster.

Her legs were sludge by the time she reached the slums. The unreasonable impulse to run home was overwhelming. Not for the last time, Zain ached for her younger self, the one that could hide under Kanak's pallu and let her problems fall away. Back then, her fears had been superficial, fanged monsters hiding in the dark. Now, they were shadowed men that followed her wherever she went, and nothing could destroy the sense that they were always at her heels.

She studied the unremarkable hut just a few feet away. It was larger than the other homes in the slums, built of cheap stone with peeling layers of paint that gave away its many reincarnations. First a dark gray, then a funny-looking peach, and finally a faded powder blue. A clothing line stretched outside, shirts and underwear hanging limp on the windless patio. The wooden door boasted corroded hinges and a long crack that ran from the top-right corner to the middle.

How many times had she stood there, replaying the events that had led to this point? That had dictated the course of her life since that one tragic night, a horrifying culmination of a series of misguided decisions. The unfairness of it all was unbearable. Every child made mistakes, but hers had caught her in a rigid grip and wouldn't let go—not unless she chopped off the ringed fingers that wrapped around her throat.

A calmness settled over her like armor. One way or another, it would all end now.

The smell of Anniversary cooking and the sound of chatter blurred, her mind repeating Leander's instructions over and over again.

Just bring him to the Sickle.

That was all she had to do. Leander would make his way to Dev's hut shortly—he was positioned just adjacent to it on the artery. Theron would be . . . wherever he would be. Watching over his brother, she guessed. She would be alone with Dev to rectify an error that should have been untangled a long time ago. If he was home.

When Zain knocked on the door, she found herself wishing he were away.

Dev answered quickly, as though he'd been expecting someone. The muscles in his right arm bulged as he leaned against the doorframe, a hint of surprise shaping his mouth. The sight of him tied a knot in her gut, nearly suffocating her plan.

"You're right on time," he said, teetering off balance as he leaned out to assess the skies. He was already wasted. "Did it rain today?"

She could smell his rank breath. It took every bit of effort not to recoil as he touched her arm with undeserved intimacy.

"No," she replied. "But I was able to acquire some."

Dev froze. Had he wanted her to fail? Maybe he was thinking of ways to make it so she still would.

"How?" he breathed, heavily.

"An inattentive bloodstripper. Out by the harbor this morning." She angled her face down. "I did it for you."

A shadow passed over him, like he saw right through her threadbare plan. She hadn't been as subservient recently, so she was relying on his habit of heavily imbibing on the day of the Anniversary to massage his perspective. Thank the souls he'd retained those proclivities—maybe she was wrong, maybe nothing else would happen today. His fingers dug into her arm.

"Give it to me," he said.

She shook her head, trying to ignore how her blood rushed to her face. They had played this game before. As long as she stuck to the rules, it would proceed as it always had.

"You know I can't, not here," she whispered, glancing around with fear that wasn't pretend.

"Fine," Dev said. "Give me a minute."

And so they began.

Zain toyed with the fake vials in her pocket as she led Dev on their usual route, her mind clinging to actions she had meticulously rehearsed. His hand rested on the small of her back, burning a hole straight through her skin. Could he hear her heart beating? Could he feel how hot her blood ran?

Dev jerked to a stop. "Do you smell that?" he asked.

None of Zain's senses were functioning the way they were supposed to. All she could hear was a muffled roar; all she could see was his face. She sniffed, forcing a straight expression as she smelled what he was referring to. It was putrid, like rotten eggs and sulfur.

"No," she lied. "It's probably all the cooking." A nervous, guttural laugh floated to her throat.

Dev cocked his head, his hand falling from her body. "That's not it. Where is that smell coming from?"

Yellow air snaked around the wooden stilts of a raised hut, just over his shoulder. She blinked and it was gone. She focused harder on the depression in the ground, certain she was hallucinating, only to be pummeled by the foul stench again.

The sound of people flooded the slums. More were returning, and she was running out of time. Without thinking, she grabbed Dev's hand. She never touched him first. It was numbing, and her nerves unraveled.

"Come, before they see us," she urged. "It's probably just the tavern still stuck to your clothes."

Dev looked unconvinced, but she had committed to the act of persuasion. Her window of time was narrowing, and not even another yellow streak shooting from the ground would be enough to stop her from accomplishing what was so, so close. Her gun cooled in reminder. That morning, she had loaded it with two bullets. An extra, in case she missed. Her throat thickened as she remembered Theron's observation, that her gun was never loaded. She had carried an empty weapon for the last ten years, after she'd shed enough blood to punish her for many life-times to come.

For Dev, she had lost herself once; for him, she would lose herself again.

They traversed into the depths of the slums before coming out behind the Temple. They'd planned for it to be empty right then, but she was still overcome by terror. What if Iravan came home early? He was never here the day of the Anniversary—she knew the pain was too much for him—but what if someone else walked by? Worse, what if something went wrong? Leander would be expecting her to be by the Sickle.

"Okay, we're here now," Dev groaned. His recent vices had rendered him more irritable, and she flinched at the rising inflection of each of his words. "Give it to me."

Zain hesitated before fishing out the vials, filled to the brim with thick yellow liquid. Five vials, as requested. Dev performed the briefest examination before grinning from ear to ear. "Well done, Z."

When he looked up, her gun was out.

She hated how the barrel shook. Dev's smile didn't falter, but his gaze darkened.

"Look who grew some balls!" he exclaimed, then let out a low whistle. "I was wondering when this day would come. Got tired of our little deal, did you? I have to confess—it took much longer than I thought it would. Ten years, you've been such a wonderful pet."

Her hands grew sweaty, slippery around the grip. She held on tighter, but it only made the weapon shake more. Her useless finger wobbled on the trigger. Inside her mouth, everything she'd wanted to say formed, then vanished, as insubstantial as air. All that practice crumbled in seconds against the darkness on his face.

Dev raised his hands in mock resignation. He took a step forward, skin rippling with sweat, sinewed arms wide enough to ensnare her if he wished.

"Step back," she said, hating the way her voice quavered. In the distance, children laughed. The smell of eggs still hung around them, mixed with her own terror.

"Why would I do that?" Dev asked, running his tongue over his lower lip. "We both know you won't shoot me."

"I will," Zain whispered, but as hard as she tried to bring her finger down—one single movement that would end this all—she couldn't. Dev advanced and he was too close, much too close to shoot. She'd be covered in him. Zain took an involuntary step back, and her heel clipped stone. She stumbled for half a second.

That was all he needed.

Dev slammed into her. Her finger hit the trigger and the gun went off, shooting to the side. A lost part of her worried it had hit someone accidentally, but the thought evaporated when Dev punched her in the face. Her nose exploded, his rings crushing bone, tears hot as lava across her cheeks as he knocked the gun out of her hands and straddled her.

"You fucking bitch!" he yelled, pressing down. Leander had not put any of his weight on her that day by the turbines, she realized uselessly. He had never meant to harm her. Dev dug into her stomach, fisting her hair to bare her neck.

"Look at me," he said. Spit rained down on her face. His rageful eyes were so comically wide, she nearly laughed. His cold rings pressed into the flesh of her neck, crushing her windpipe.

"I've got a gun, you know." Dev started laughing. The same maniacal, cold laugh that stalked her waking moments. "But I need to feel you under me."

Zain coughed, choking, but he didn't let go. Dev leaned in, lips hovering just above her own.

"You know," he whispered, so calm, even when she was seizing under him. There was *no air, no air, no*—"I have always wanted the smell of a dead lover on my breath." His mouth closed over hers, and the world turned black.

He tasted of ash and horror, sweat and despair. She relinquished, dipping into the darkness that had long called her name. It wasn't tinged with blue anymore. It didn't burn.

Then, the weight lifted, and a cry ripped her from the abyss. She gasped, air slicing her lungs in time to see Theron throw Dev to the ground. The bloodstripper launched on top of the don, landing a punch square in his jaw. A sickening crack sounded. The slumlord wrestled beneath the guard's grip, before his legs bucked, displacing Theron.

Theron may be a guard, but Dev had been a child of the streets.

I've got a gun, you know.

Zain lunged for her gun. Dev kicked out, forcing space between him and Theron, before finding the grip on his own holster. Theron realized his error a second too late, and stared down the slumlord's barrel.

"No!" she cried, pointing hers at Dev in turn.

Dev smiled, his teeth coated red. He stood, his gun still aimed at Theron, as he looked between them. Zain remained on the ground, too afraid to move.

One bullet. She had one bullet to get this right.

"I'll shoot him faster than you'd shoot me," Dev said.

Zain stole a glance at Theron, who was watching Dev intently. The guard spat a wad of blood to his side and wiped his mouth with his sleeve. He meant nothing to her—she should let Dev shoot him, then blow the slumlord's brains out the next second. It would solve both her problems.

Dev stepped back. "It's your lucky day, Z," he said. "Looks like I'll be seeing you later. Might even pay Samiah and Kanak a visit."

Her throat dried. *Shoot him, you idiot,* her brain screamed, but again her attention went to Theron. He still wouldn't look at her, like he didn't want to see her choice when she made it.

Just one click.

Dev inched away, nearly out of range.

Shoot him now.

Zain's mind raced. She conjured the explosive sound of the shot, imagined the red rose blooming from his chest, his head, his arm. The fantasy tasted so sweet. But she couldn't do it. Her arms grew heavy, and her finger cramped on the trigger.

"Good girl," Dev called, and it was painful to see how natural this was for him. The ease with which he ducked behind a building, out of her reach, out of her sight.

Her gun fell.

Theron rushed over, and she didn't know what she'd been expecting. He stared at her, expression unreadable.

"Thank—" she started to say, but he cut her off.

"The slums," he said. "Something is wrong."

CHAPTER TWENTY-TWO

Iravan

Calor seeping through the ground and killing people.

Iravan was a veritable maelstrom as he sprinted through the streets of the Bow. Bloodstrippers and Janmiris alike did a double take, surprised to find the don in this part of the city, but he couldn't feign a purpose if he tried. He was thoroughly rattled, resisting the urge to light the fuse and ring the evacuation bells in the courtyard. They had bled on this soil in honor of their home. How could he ask everyone to abandon their land, their sacrifices, based on a phenomenon he had never seen, let alone understood? A leader he may be, a scientist he was not. He needed Dev.

The cobblestone streets of the slums felt never-ending. His head throbbed in warning as the air shimmered a brighter orange, tinged with sparks of sickly yellow. *Not now,* he pleaded. A stale odor hovered over the outermost houses, overwhelming him entirely. He took a mental fist to his throat, like he could will his nausea into obedience.

The alleyways were congested with pedestrians. He blinked,

clearing his spotted vision. A woman held a scarf to her mouth, gagging as she leaned against the brick walls. The smell. It was not a function of his migraine; he was not imagining the vapor. In a flash, the same yellow dustlike substance varnished the velvet sky.

Iravan spotted one of his men and reached for his arm. "What happened?" he asked, his palms so damp they left a stain on the man's sleeve.

The man shook his head. "I'm not sure, I was at the tavern when people ran in, said the slums were covered in this yellow mist. They said it was coming out of the ground? Seems harmless so far, but I sent some of the leeches to check."

A tinny sound rang in Iravan's eardrums. "Get everyone out of here now."

The man frowned. "Sir? Do you know something about this?"

Iravan grabbed the man's collar. "Listen to me. Take everyone you know inside, order all the merchants in the Hammer to shut their doors, seal the windows. Ring the evacuation bells, we need to move everyone out of the slums."

He released the man, who stumbled once, twice, knocking over other terrified passersby. Then, a cry tore through the air.

It was too late.

"EVERYONE OUT NOW!" Iravan bellowed over the ensuing pandemonium. "GET OUT!"

He peeled off his shirt and tied it around his mouth and nose. How much had he inhaled already? Chaos crackled, and everyone was bespelled by a mad frenzy, as though the sky's rotting pieces were hailing down on them.

It wasn't just his orders that were inciting panic, he realized, as he hurried toward the sound of the first cry. It was the first victims, and people were noticing.

The woman he'd just seen was crouched over an unconscious young boy—her son. His umber hair, which lay splattered on the gray asphalt, looked like old blood. His pale skin was pinched red, like he had been exerting himself, but his cheeks were still plump. He couldn't have been older than sixteen.

For an agonizing second, Iravan was grateful his child hadn't lived to die like this.

"He went in there and I told him not to," the mother wailed, cheeks glistening. "And then he collapsed and won't wake up!"

Iravan could see it then. How that beautiful brown hair would crumble in his mother's hands, how his skin would puddle. Instead of Gayathri, it would be this mother staying until her loved one became unrecognizable—that is, unless she was next.

"You need to go," he said. "Get inside. Take him with you if you can, but keep your nose and mouth covered. This is poisonous."

He hoped he'd reached her through the sorrow, wished he could carry the child for his mother, but as the city squalled around him, he remembered one life was just that. He was needed by everyone else.

Iravan stood tall, biting the fabric deeper as he took stock of the area. It was impossible to identify faces, but people had absorbed the gravity of the situation. More held clothing to their mouths, racing toward the Bow and the Hammer. Doors flung open and closed, and he launched into action, directing people to safety.

His legs cramped as he corralled another stream of people in the direction of open homes and stores, places that would leave their doors open for those who had nowhere else to go. The stench grew worse. He dry-heaved into his shirt, inhaling sweat and grime. He couldn't remain here much longer, or he wouldn't be able to help with what came next.

Iravan ordered the last of the leeches away and raced to the Bow. He was out of his depth and needed Mariam and her expertise, but as he navigated onto the artery, Dev stumbled into sight, hobbling toward the slums.

Iravan broke into a run, calling Dev's name. But something was wrong. A feral rage as sharp as hewn steel speared from his partner's eyes.

"That cunt tried to kill me," Dev said.

"*What?* Who?" His mind raced through potential options, but each one was less likely than the last, and, souls, he didn't have time for this. Dev was impervious to the utter mayhem, had not once questioned what was happening.

"Zain!" Dev yelled, whipping a gun out of thin air. "She tried to *shoot* me. I'm going to find her."

The last thing Iravan needed was an errant gunshot to sow further discord.

"We can discuss that later," he yelled, snatching Dev's weapon. "We need to get indoors. Now."

Dev let out a frustrated cry at being disarmed, but Iravan had at least jolted him out of his stupor. When Iravan marched ahead, Dev followed.

In the distance, bells started ringing.

CHAPTER TWENTY-THREE

Anastasia

It took everything in Anastasia to drown out the sound of Baruna crying.

The sky unspooled in a carpet of crimson leather, wrinkled around the rift they were traveling under. As the fog parted, Tejomaya grew brighter, as though revealing a mystical fairy-tale land. Tiny homes jeweled the city's rugged terraces, tucked around weary, winding roads, and the courtyard walls glowed red. A corrosive sound splintered the air, echoes of the forest's assault. When the boat hit port at last, she realized it wasn't the sickening crunch of stone on bones she was hearing: it was the bells.

Anastasia hadn't thought those bells even worked. Either word of the island disaster had traveled to Tejomaya quicker than Anastasia herself, or something on the mainland had gone awry as well. Given that the only survivors of the island's disaster were on the boat with her, she was inclined to believe the latter.

"Hamish Drakos is dead," she informed a port bloodstripper,

who looked aghast at her climbing out of the boat, a limp woman in her arms and a child at her heel. "Seize the city."

And into Tejomaya she went.

It had been ten years since she'd last been there, yet the streets remembered her. The stone sang a song of welcome as she dipped over the once-familiar crevices and bends. It was there she'd once found her calling; it was there she had lost it all.

But right then, all she could think about was Charvi, hanging heavily over her arm as calor exposure sent her body into shock. She didn't have long left, and there was only one place where Anastasia could find help, where Charvi might walk out alive.

She didn't knock when she arrived at the building with the blue tiles, the ones she and Charvi had tried to add to in their youth. The door lever gave way with practiced efficiency, her shoulder paving the path ahead thereafter. Baruna sobbed, pattering behind, relentlessly reaching for her mother, who was now foaming at the mouth.

The room Anastasia found herself in looked exactly the same as it had before. An old walnut table occupied most of the space, a matching chest loaded with trinkets right by the door that led to a well-loved store. The sky clock ticked on the wall behind, standing vigil over the rug that concealed a trapdoor.

Parchment lay strewn like the feathers of a dead bird. Anastasia swept her arm across the table, clearing space. Something clattered to the floor, a call for help, in case her barging through the back door hadn't done the trick. She laid Charvi down on the table, despair mounting at the foam trickling from her mouth. She had to find him, but where would he be—

A gun clicked behind her.

"You have some nerve coming back here." His voice crackled

the way she remembered it, his accent dropping the ends of his syllables.

Anastasia raised her hands.

"I know you want to kill me, Yadav," she said, her Janmiri a long-abandoned machine whirring back to life. She turned slowly. "But you may want to delay your revenge."

He looked older, with more white around his features, dotting his temple and his mustache. His skin was sallow, probably from the anger that had been stoked over decades. Baruna let out a frightened whimper, drawing the man's attention.

Realization dawned upon him, and the gun swung limply by his side. "Is that—" he started to ask, but Anastasia stepped aside, revealing Charvi's convulsing body.

"Your daughter needs your help," Anastasia said.

For a man in his sixties, Yadav moved remarkably quickly. He barked instructions at Anastasia, who was more than happy to have something to do other than comfort the young girl crying into her mother's bloody robe. She shouldn't have to see this, but there was no one around to take her away. Charvi needed their undivided attention.

It was borderline miraculous how quickly she fell into the smooth direction Yadav laid out, how comfortably she sank into what had once been routine. Of course, it had never been a body on the table back then; it had been chores and strategy, conversation and work. Her fingers reached for ingredients as Yadav called them out, and she realized that even the details of this place had remained the same.

In a buried corner of her mind, laughter resonated: Charvi inducting her into the family, teaching her how to open the nebulous back door before showing her around the store, all while Yadav looked at them disapprovingly. She almost expected the vials to have her fingerprints around their necks. Yadav had preserved the skeleton of his home, perhaps for this reason: he wanted to keep everything intact for the day his daughter returned to him.

"It's too late," Yadav huffed, holding Charvi's mouth open as he tipped a concoction down her throat. She choked, and Anastasia steeled her grip around Charvi's back, holding her up. If Yadav really thought it was too late, he would be praying for his daughter's safe ascent; yet here he was, fastidiously working down to the last second.

"How much did she inject?" he asked.

Anastasia frowned. "Am I supposed to know?"

"I thought you knew everything," Yadav snapped.

She stepped back, and her foot rolled over a tubelike object. She gasped, letting the table catch her as she examined the culprit. A syringe. She shouldn't have been surprised. Who else would have been developing this?

"You can't come home just to leave again," Yadav ordered an unconscious Charvi. His voice cracked, belying his composure. "You can't go like this."

It stirred no empathy in Anastasia. All this was his fault, and he had the audacity to turn it around on her.

She wanted to know, though. How long this had been going on for, how long her only friend had been working to assassinate the Council, knowing Anastasia was soon to be part of it? How easy had it been for Charvi to kill her father?

Hamish's lifeless face flashed before her eyes. *I wish you didn't have to lose everyone else first.* Her lungs grew heavy, but she couldn't stop to think. Her wrath centered on the people in front of her instead.

Her intentions for saving Charvi were not entirely pure. She needed answers, and if walking into the home of a codger who would happily slit her throat gave her them, so be it. He'd do her no harm since she'd brought his daughter and granddaughter home. Yadav was a man of integrity and virtue, all the things she was not, and all the things that would help her now.

A bell tinkled.

"Yadav!"

He groaned, directing a glare at Anastasia.

"You stay here with her," he said. "If anything happens, call me immediately."

The nerve. Anastasia bristled, not wanting to be alone with an unconscious woman and her pitiful child. She wanted to escape, but he pinned her in place with a look that reminded her painfully of her own father. She stayed.

Yadav pried the door open and crept out, greeting his visitors with such cheer that Anastasia knew he would have made an impeccable councilmember. But then their voices rose with a tenor of horror.

Anastasia sidled to the door and pressed her ear against it. There were multiple people talking over each other, so hysterically that she couldn't make out anything.

Yadav said, "I need you both to calm down."

"Don't tell us to calm down," a woman screamed. Someone gentler soothed her in low murmurs.

"Samiah," said Yadav, impatiently, "I was just at the slums this morning, so I don't understand how this could have happened."

She caught only pieces of the conversation: yellow gas, a miasma set upon the slums like a curse, the earth rising to swallow them whole. She thought of the stone forest and its vengeance upon her people. In that moment, it had shocked her, but Tejomaya had always felt alive. The ground sang beneath her feet, the walls in her apartment laughed and cried. Tejomaya raged too. The city did not discriminate when it came to its grudges— Janmiri or Gehennese, merchant or acolyte, adult or child. They were all at its mercy, and the only question was what would come next.

The other visitor said something about a lockdown, and Yadav sternly responded that they couldn't stay there. When they pleaded, he said, "Go back to your home. You have a cellar there. I have to keep my shop open for those who do not have the same luxury."

"We can't walk back in this. Do you not hear the damn bells?" Samiah cried.

Baruna whimpered. She sat next to her mother, fingers plugging her ears, like she could shut everything out if she tried hard enough.

"You have to be quiet," Anastasia whispered, bringing a finger to her lips. She moved her ear to the door again.

"Where are the bloodstrippers?" Yadav demanded.

Samiah replied, "There are rumors of something happening on the island, a riot of sorts by the gatherers. They're saying Hamish Drakos is dead."

Anastasia knew that what had happened on the island was not isolated. It had been orchestrated from the mainland. She hadn't panicked, though. With the manpower the Council had on land, she would be able to assume control.

Anastasia sagged against the door. How wrong she had been, thinking she didn't understand the city because of her time away. Tejomaya had lived inside her all these years, and now it awoke in her chest.

"The bloodstrippers will manage this, I'm sure they're already contacting his next-in-line," Yadav said. Oh, he knew who was next, who he was harboring in his shop. "We need to take care of our own."

Samiah let out a harsh laugh. "The bloodstrippers have staged a coup."

CHAPTER TWENTY-FOUR

Zain

B y the time Zain arrived at the slums, she knew it was too late.
She had seen that yellow vapor before, only wisps of it, nothing like the cloud that was spreading over the slums, curling into corners and foaming at its edges. It didn't seem as though anyone knew what it was, but no one had stuck around to find out.

She coughed into the braided collar of her ivory blouse. A searing pain shot through her nose like a hot poker to the brain, a reminder of the injuries she had sustained.

"Zain, wait!"

Theron caught up to her. She didn't want to hear what she knew he would say. That this was out of their control.

The decades had been merciless in teaching them about the fallibility of humans under a sky that bled like a bruised heart, in the face of a maelstrom that razed lands, when forests turned to stone. Nothing was as effective at showing someone how little power they had as when the world decided it'd had enough, but each time, it was the people she loved who paid the price.

"I did this," she whispered. Theron came around her,

obstructing her view of the rows of homes misted in yellow. "I saw it when it started, I knew it smelled strange. I wanted to go ring the bells and look into it, but I had him right there . . ."

Theron's expression cleared. She didn't know how much he'd seen or heard, but she gathered that he had witnessed enough. She still felt Dev on top of her, his mouth tinged with the putrid smell of sura and salt, the crush of his thighs on her ribs.

His threats were as good as vows. Her life was over, but the matter of when was still up to her. She could turn away a coward, live in fear for the little time she had left while being hunted by the cruelest man she knew. Or she could embrace her fate. Her dignity had long been lost, but she could afford someone else theirs.

She tried going around Theron, but he mirrored her side step. He pulled her chin up gently.

"We need to find Leander," he said, and this time, she noticed amber flecks dancing in his eyes, which reflected the yellow mist around them.

"I have to go," she pleaded. He didn't understand—couldn't understand. It was the Temple burning; it was the slums wreathed in poison. In all her endeavors, there was blood on her hands.

The ground hissed in warning, just enough for her to hesitate.

"I have an idea," Theron said, his hand twining firmly with hers. "And then we'll go together."

Zain had never been good at verbally expressing what she wanted or needed. Her needs and wants were always too much, filling up her throat until she was drowning in all the things she couldn't force herself to say, and all that emerged was a choked quiet. Theron might not have understood what she'd meant, that she intended to go into the slums to make sure her friends and family were okay. She'd heard the bells and seen the sealed doors and windows, the same ones usually left ajar to find reprieve from the suffocating heat. Her heart eased knowing that many had found their way indoors, but Zain was concerned with the ones who hadn't. The people left behind.

Theron led them to Leander while she tried making sense of her despair. Leander sat against the wall of a worn-down chawl, his knees drawn to his chest, clawing at the thin hairs on his head as he heaved. Clumps of hair lay by his side, drifting away.

"I didn't get any," Leander rasped.

The calor. Zain had forgotten the original plan in the midst of all this frenzy. Leander's face was marred with tears and mud.

"And the doors, they're all locked, but I didn't want to leave without you both. I got held up by some of the other bloodstrippers during the shift change, so I was late to Dev's. By the time I could enter, there were too many people, and then this strange fog came out of the ground. It's like what that Urjan told me. The calor underground, it's growing unstable. She invited us to Urjan, where they're going to be independent of calor. We need to go—"

"We need the masks you showed us the other day, the ones that protect against the air," Theron interrupted.

The masks . . . He couldn't possibly mean to—

"You want to go in *there*?" Leander asked, looking between them as if they'd confessed to murder. "I haven't tested them enough. I certainly haven't tested them against *this*. Did you not hear me? It's calor built up, it's—"

"Now," Theron demanded.

"This is a bad idea," said Leander, but he reached for his bag. He ruffled through its contents and pulled out two masks.

"Do you have more?" Theron asked, taking one for himself and handing the other to Zain. When Leander nodded, Theron added, "Put one on and go back to the Sickle. That should be a safe distance away. If you can find a place where you can shelter indoors, that would be best."

He slid the mouthpiece over his head, securing the back with ease. Zain copied his actions, but Theron stepped behind her to help when she grasped clumsily for the catch. The mechanism was instantaneous—as soon as she heard the snap of its closure, the seal suctioned around her nose and mouth. She gingerly ran her fingers along her tender, stinging nose bridge as Theron patted his brother's back in farewell. Souls, she hoped this would work.

There was no visibility when they headed back into the slums. The smog felt thick and heavy, dampening Zain's blouse and trousers within seconds. Despite the pocket of protected air, she could still smell it, the pungent, pulverizing odor that grew worse as they moved deeper, past the peripheral homes.

Theron pointed to himself first, then gestured behind him. *I'll go there.*

Zain shook her head frantically. Everyone she loved lived on that side. She gestured at him, then pointed emphatically in the opposite direction. After a grim moment, he nodded, and they parted ways. She didn't understand why he was there. They had no evidence to suggest people still remained in the slums, just Zain's guilt and a gut instinct that pulled her in the direction of lives she'd destroyed.

Maybe he would abandon her. Maybe this time she would deserve it.

She should have been systematic, diligent, but it was impossible. Zain ran straight to Gayathri's home, knowing the turns through the rows of huts like the scars on her back. Her breath was so hot it fogged up the glasses of her mask as she shouldered open the ajar door.

No one. There was no one there. Just their tattered mattress shoved against the wall, sinking under the yellow mist.

Mahini's home was next. Zain sprinted past open doors, slicing her arm open on the edge of a low-hanging metal roof as she halted outside Laila and Lufi's house. Her fingers hooked on the door where the knob used to be, finding the latch on the other side. She sobbed when it clicked open, revealing the inside of the living space, three blankets rolled neatly and stacked atop each other. Bags of grains and lentils lined the walls, and Zain stumbled inside over a row of sandals, searching, letting out a strangled cry of relief when she found it absent of any life.

They'd gotten out.

On she went, from hut to hut, checking on old friends and leeches, the family that had made her the vase sitting on her bedside table, another who'd woven her a skirt too beautiful for her to ever want to wear. She cringed at how familiar homes had turned barren and flaxen, like old paintings stained with coffee. All empty. Her heart thudded louder. She should have been relieved, but her concern shifted to Theron. They had been there for so long. If the masks were ineffective, then it wouldn't be long before they succumbed to its poison. Only two huts left. She hoped she hadn't risked his life for nothing.

At the last hut, Zain felt the boy's presence, cold and still, before she opened the door.

He was a little younger than Leander, lying flat on his back in the middle of a crammed room. His tongue was so swollen that the corners of his mouth were cut open. Over his linen tunic, the nice one he likely donned for the Anniversary, Zain could see strange bulges. With a nauseating jolt, she realized his intestines had bloated. His hair lay in globs at his side. And his eyes . . . wide open with fear.

Zain retched violently, clasping her mask to her face in a fervent prayer that it stayed on. She felt compelled to go closer, to see what this poisoned air did up close, the fate she may face. To her horror, the boy blinked. Zain stepped back, mind whirring. Had she imagined it?

He blinked again.

Zain screamed.

Despite how swollen his body looked, he was soft, too soft in Zain's arms, as she lifted him up. Her muscles tensed under his weight, but she hauled him out of the house. She relied on her years of wandering and memorizing the slums' streets to navigate past clusters of now-unrecognizable huts. She tripped on an empty bucket, wincing at the sharp pain that lanced between her shoulder blades when she caught their combined weight. The boy's head fell against her shoulder, and the soft exhale of his dying breaths made every hair on her body stand up.

"I won't leave you," Zain whispered through her tears. She didn't know if he could hear her, but she told him anyway. "I'll get you out of here."

He trembled, and she cried, and they both fell apart in different ways as the fog at last thinned. They were on the outskirts, near the alley where she'd left Leander. She wanted to strip off her clothes, burn them in a fire, burn her skin off too. They could not fight this monstrous form of calor. Zain dragged the boy to the locked-up chawl, where Theron was already waiting.

The guard said nothing as she took the gun from her holster, loaded with the single bullet she had left. Her hand shook under its weight. Tears ran down the boy's cheeks in a wordless plea. Souls, she couldn't do this. She couldn't kill another child.

Theron took the gun from her hand. The guard's characteristic intensity had given way to grim understanding. He brought the barrel to the boy's head.

Zain couldn't watch, and she didn't know how to tell him why. He didn't stop her when she left.

Coward.

The gunshot shook the ground beneath her feet.

Zain's legs hung over the wall adjacent to the turbines, the mask discarded by her thigh. The air was parched, the stench dulled.

The bells had stopped ringing, the city quiet at last, the loss of lives measured only by the cries behind closed doors. According to Leander, the bloodstrippers had retreated to their quarters, dubious of the city's safety. She didn't know where most people were, if they had returned to the slums, if anyone was investigating what had occurred. She bit into her tongue, hoping the pain would elicit the tears that should be pouring down her cheeks—but nothing. It was her, the silence, and the ever-pulsating sky above.

Zain flinched as footsteps crunched loose gravel, but it was only Theron. His hands were full with a bottle and wads of fabric, the picture of stoic composure despite having just shot a teenage boy in the head. Meanwhile, every fragment of her was floating in space, and she wasn't sure she'd ever come back together again. She had been dreading this, the uninterrupted time they had to dwell on what had passed.

He laid his supplies next to her before handing her the pack tucked between his elbow and torso. It was cold to the touch. "For your nose."

She murmured her thanks, wincing when the cold pack touched her face. It helped, the pain muting to a throb.

"You should clean those cuts too," Theron remarked, nodding at the rest of his aid kit. The bottle's label had been mostly torn, but it looked like antiseptic.

Zain's knees were bloody gashes that peeked through her ruined trousers. She hadn't yet taken stock of every wound, but slowly and surely, her nerves ignited, overcoming the dull shock. She gingerly extended her right leg, and the fold of her knee burned.

"Later," she rasped, blinking back tears.

Theron reached for her legs but stopped just short of touching her, assessing the tatters of cloth that clung to her lacerated skin. "You've got gravel stuck in here."

Zain hissed as he peeled the fabric away. She rammed the cold pack so hard against her face that her teeth numbed. Theron poured some of the solution onto a clean strip, then brought it to her right knee, a hint of concern disrupting his habitual apathy.

"How are you holding up?" Theron asked.

"With which part?" she said, sucking her teeth as he cleaned her wound. "With the fact that I killed a child?"

"That was not your fault. You gave him mercy," Theron replied, dabbing gently around the edges of her deepest cuts while she tried not to flinch. "Besides, I'm the one who pulled the trigger. And I'm asking about—about what happened before I got there."

Zain's stomach crawled. Sifting through the layers of memories and truths was a harrowing exercise she'd avoided at all costs. But who knew when she'd get this chance again? If Dev killed her, she needed someone to know what he'd done. She needed all this to mean something.

And the rules were different with Theron. Maybe it was because he was the first person she had interacted with outside her community; maybe it was because he drew her fight out in ways she hadn't imagined were possible; maybe it was because he was the only one there to listen. He switched to her other knee, and Zain released her confessions like a dying wish.

"I was always the lucky one," she started, switching to Gehennese. It was easier, more distant. "Orphans have a hard time everywhere, especially ones like me. My skin is too dark, undesirable even for those in Janmir, even though I am one of them. For all that they hate you Gengs, they want to look like you too. But I met Kanak at the Temple, and they were so kind. I followed them everywhere they went, and somehow, they let me follow them out into the real world. I knew I had it all—guardians who cared for me, a home in the Bow, food on the table. But years passed and I was so lonely."

Zain clutched at the wall as Theron touched a particularly deep abrasion. He paused, giving her a second to catch her breath.

"There weren't any other children in the Bow," Zain continued, so softly she wasn't sure he could hear. Theron didn't look up, didn't react, and maybe it didn't matter if he heard her or not. Maybe it just mattered that she said it out loud. "I watched kids playing by the slums, and I found myself wishing I could give up all I had just so they would see me as one of them. And then one day, I decided I *would* be one of them. It took a long time until I truly belonged, but once you become a leech, you are part of the system, and no one can take that away. It was something that was mine.

"Looking back now, I was so young, so stupid," she said. "A child worshipping at Dev's feet. I would have done anything for him, we all would have. He gave us hope that we could become something if we listened to what he said. Did what he asked."

This was where things got too difficult for her. Theron started bandaging her knees, all while Zain's stories slipped on top of one another. She chose the version that hurt the least to tell. "I did things for him that I regret, and one day, I decided enough was enough. But you can't just leave. I had a *quota* to fulfill. And I was so fucking close. I just wanted it to be over."

Tears streamed down her face. Theron tucked in the edge of her wrappings, securing them in place.

"He's still alive," she said. She prayed she was wrong, but she knew.

"I know," Theron replied, stepping back. The air around her felt cold suddenly, like he'd left her on an island and sailed away.

"Is that all?" she asked, as he busied himself with gathering the remaining clean bandages. "Is that all you have to say?"

Theron looked her directly in the eye, expression still cold, still unreadable. "I don't know your life or what you have done, but we all have regrets that haunt us. I have killed too. People who look like me, people who don't. You are content to wallow here, to bathe in your guilt, but I do not indulge in that behavior, or I would have drowned a long time ago."

His nonchalance was like poison. "I wish you would drown," she said, leaning forward until she was an inch from his face, her words poised to hurt. "It's a good thing your mother is dead, or she'd be ashamed of who you've become. A soulless beast."

A sick satisfaction went through her as something shuttered in his expression. She almost immediately regretted her words. He had run into the abyss with her, had bandaged her wounds, and she'd excavated his deepest hurt simply because she wanted someone else to unravel the way she was. She waited for his cruelty to slide through her ribs. A killing blow she knew he was capable of.

Instead, his finger pressed below her collarbone. "You want

a fight, Zain?" he asked, softly. "I can give you one. I've watched you with others, unobtrusive, taking up little space, but you want to fight so bad. Just know you are worth more than you think. Make sure you're fighting something worthy."

He turned his back to her, but she didn't want him to go.

"All those people," Zain said, returning the cold pack harder to her face. Theron paused, and it was under his heavy expectation that she broke. Something crumbled in her chest, leaving her dizzy. Her throat thickened and her vision blurred. "It should have been me."

"But it wasn't."

Theron hoisted himself up on the wall so he was next to her. Her body slackened at the solidity of his thigh pressing into her sore leg.

"I'm not good with words," he continued, gesturing aimlessly. "But the way I see it, the things that matter, this world, what it had to offer us . . . it's all been lost to us for a long time. We are biding our time, trying to relish in the scraps."

Zain let out a laugh. "Are you trying to say people are going to die anyway?"

"No more than you or me," Theron replied, sounding frustrated. "But that's not it. What I'm trying to say is that life has no meaning, hasn't had any meaning for a long while. There is very little that matters, very little that compels us to go on. Power is one thing, yes, legacy is another. And what is legacy when there is no one there to remember it? It is the present. It is the now. It is the decisions we make every second."

"My legacy is death," she said, quietly, tears unstoppable now. "I have ruined this city. I drowned a decade ago, and it never stopped. I'm still drowning."

She waited for him to ask her for more because there were so many holes in her stories, so much sorrow she couldn't explain. But his hand closed over hers, holding her in place, cocooning her as if to usher in an impending metamorphosis.

"You chose to save me today. That counts for something," he said. "And Zain? Just because you're drowning doesn't mean you can't take that bastard down with you."

CHAPTER TWENTY-FIVE

Anastasia

Waiting for Charvi to wake was excruciating.

She lay still, on the cot Yadav had moved from the bedroom to the back room, with a threadbare sheet pulled up to her neck. It was too hot for such measures, but Anastasia didn't dare air her opinions. Yadav already looked as though he regretted not putting a bullet through her head the moment she had entered his shop.

In fact, she was fairly certain the only reason she was still alive was because of Baruna. Despite them never quite warming to one other, Baruna clung to Anastasia's arm. She had forgotten that the child didn't know Tejomaya, spoke worse Janmiri than Anastasia did, and despite the resemblance to the stories her mother had told her, Baruna couldn't recognize her home or her grandfather.

Baruna had been born there, in the very room where her mother was now flirting with death. It had been a day as hot as Tejomaya got. Charvi had lain on the table, padded by blankets and sheets, legs held apart as she pushed, Anastasia by her side.

She'd nearly pulled Anastasia's hand off from the pain. So many people—too many—had been there. Dev had been kicked out by an enraged Yadav for smoking indoors during the delivery, and Anastasia had screamed at everyone else to follow him. Iravan corralled people into the storefront, all while the healer sat intently, watching as Charvi dilated. The sister of one of the don's leeches sat by the healer's side, unperturbed by the sight of bodily fluids, the eviscerating cries.

This is a mess, Anastasia had said. Her fingers had lost circulation, but she refused to let go.

Charvi had smiled as sweat poured over her face. *A mess that will love my child.*

That dream had barely lasted a year. The one place where Baruna was supposed to feel safe had turned monstrous.

Anastasia thought of Hamish until all the fear and adrenaline that had accumulated inside her exploded into scorching rage. How quickly power tilted, like sand in an hourglass. A bloodstripper coup wasn't ideal, but it was better than ceding control to the slumlords.

Charvi mumbled something incoherent, and Yadav flew across the room, bringing a glass of water to her open lips as he held her up. "You're okay, you're okay," he repeated like a prayer.

"Baba?" Charvi said, eyes fluttering open, before widening in frantic realization. "Baru—"

"She's here," Yadav replied, setting down the glass as the little girl let out a strangled cry. Charvi sobbed as Baruna melted into her arms, unwilling to let go despite the evident pain she was in. Anastasia stared at the chest of trinkets, studying each curio with undeserved attention.

"Ana," Charvi croaked. "Thank you. I know how difficult this was for you, to come back here . . ."

The sight of Charvi bundled between Baruna and Yadav, cared for with warmth and love after the destruction she had wrought, was too much to bear.

Charvi read the change in Anastasia's ice-carved features. "I'm—"

"No," Anastasia said, ignoring how Baruna burrowed deeper into Charvi's caved-in chest.

Yadav looked ready to lunge at her, but Charvi extended a hand to stop him.

"You need to start talking," Anastasia said. "And I want to hear the truth."

"Baru," Charvi pleaded, pulling her daughter's chin up. Baruna preemptively shook her head. "Please, baby, I'm not going anywhere. Go outside for a little bit. I promise I'll come get you after."

"Mama, no!" Baruna screamed, and the sound cut through Anastasia like a serrated knife. But she wanted her dues, and she wanted them now. The child would have her mother after this conversation. Anastasia would have no one.

Eventually, the girl relented and disentangled herself from her mother. Yadav escorted her out, as though she would vanish if he didn't serve guard.

"I'm not going anywhere," he clarified, unnecessarily, closing the door after Baruna.

"I don't care," replied Anastasia, focused squarely on Charvi. "You killed my father. I might as well have yours around in case I'm in the mood for revenge."

Charvi's face crumpled.

"Charu," Yadav gasped. "Tell me you didn't—"

"I'm sorry," Charvi cried, sinking her head into her hands. Her words were muffled. "Ana, I'm so sorry. It wasn't supposed to be like this. He told us it would just increase our strength and speed, enough that we could take them hostage, take over the island. I didn't . . . I didn't realize how it would consume our minds . . ."

"What?" Anastasia asked, snatching Charvi's hands from her face. Her friend slumped forward, wailing as though it had been *her* father who'd been brutally murdered.

Yadav's face mutated from confusion to realization.

"Did you not test this?" Anastasia yelled at him. Of course the dons were behind this. The souls knew Charvi hadn't managed this from the Isle, and her damn father was the only one who could have created such a horrifying concoction. But to deploy it without understanding its full potential was beyond his irrational hatred for her and the Gehennese.

For once, he looked flustered, and Anastasia reveled in it.

"You hate me so much, don't you?" she sneered, slamming her hand down on the table in a hollow bang. "I took your daughter away." Bang. "I took your granddaughter away!" Bang. "I put them in danger, in their comfortable home on a safe island. You are no better than I am." Bang bang. Her fist ached, but a sick satisfaction slid through her as he flinched at every strike. Good.

"Ana, stop," Charvi said, but Anastasia was only getting started.

"When did this start?" she asked. How did one measure betrayal? It was grief's close kin. But grief only stole from the future. Treachery was indiscriminate. It mutilated the past, tarnished the present, and left nothing to cherish. "When you offered to come to Tejomaya for me? Pretending to be a good friend to save me from having to come back here? I can't believe I fell for it."

Charvi let out a shaky breath, but at least this time, she didn't hide behind her hands. Despite the shadows that stretched above the hollows of her cheeks, the quake to her jaw, there was a startling lucidity to her. A web of sorrow stretched from their locked gazes, acknowledging that everything had changed.

"I have been in touch with people here for a long time," Charvi said. "I needed parts for my project, things the island didn't import, and once I established that connection, learned about how things were here . . . I missed it, Ana. I was so angry that I had to leave, that I had to stay, that my only choices ended in different shades of pain. But my trip to Tejomaya . . . that really was for you, Ana. I hate that I'm the reason you are back here. I can't imagine how much pain you're in." Charvi reached for Anastasia's face, but she retreated.

Anastasia's throat jammed with regret. She should have known better.

Charvi may have followed her to the island, but there had always been a sea between them, the truth a bridge built to collapse. The day they'd left Tejomaya, it had been easy for Anastasia to tell herself that her best friend had chosen her, that they had fled their horrors hand in hand. When the wounds from that day had begun to heal, that lie became easier to believe.

"You left for me," Anastasia said. "I came back for you. We are even now."

Outside, fists beat on the door.

CHAPTER TWENTY-SIX

Iravan

Iravan had barely stepped inside Yadav's store when a figure blurred past him, knocking Dev into the wall.

Yadav had his hands around Dev's neck, his face filled with poisonous rage. The sight was so unexpected that Iravan could do nothing but watch for a moment. Dev writhed in the man's grip, the tendons around his throat thick as rope. He looked equally dazed.

"How dare you come in here?" Yadav frothed.

"What the hell are you talking about?" Dev demanded. He tried prying Yadav's hands off his body, but the mechanic pulled out his gun and held it to Dev's stomach.

"I'll leave you here to bleed," he threatened, then moved the gun between Dev's legs. "Or I'll leave you alive and let you wish I'd killed you."

That prompted Iravan into action. His head protested the quick movement as he slammed into Yadav's side, disarming him in one motion. The man growled, but Iravan held the gun above his head, praying they wouldn't make him shoot. The sound alone might end him.

Free of his restraint, Dev leaped at Yadav, knocking him to the ground.

"Dev!" Iravan warned, but he was too sluggish to stop his partner from punching Yadav in the face. His knees pinned Yadav's wrists to the ground, and he twisted his weight down so hard that the man let out a sharp cry.

"Stop!" Iravan dropped the gun and tried hauling Dev off Yadav. On a normal day, Iravan and Dev were fairly well matched, but with Iravan's impending migraine, he felt as though he were pulling an immovable rock.

In the background, someone was crying. A door slammed open, and a voice he had long forgotten paused them all in their tracks.

"Get the fuck off him, Dev."

Dev froze. Charvi leaned against the doorframe, her body too thin, too fragile. Her face was hard, and despite the gaunt lines that carved her cheeks from its sunken shell, she looked as though she would throttle Dev with her own brittle fingers. A young child peered from behind Charvi. Her stubborn jaw and bushy hair were so much like Charvi's at that age that the loss of a decade slammed into him. Iravan let out a bark of laughter.

"Charvi," Dev said, standing up slowly, a smile spreading across his face. "What the—"

She ignored him, instead hobbling to Yadav to help him up. "Hey Ravi," she said, an expression of sorrow, guilt, and joy warring for dominance. "Ana just left."

If there had ever been a tear in the fabric of the world, Iravan was looking right through it.

Yadav let out a cry of outrage and darted back into the room from which Charvi came. From the frustration on the mechanic's face when he returned, Iravan knew she was long gone. But she had been there—steps from him. Something fluttered in his stomach.

"Why would you let her go?" Yadav asked, returning to the group. His hands opened and closed as if they could find her and bring her back.

"I owe her my life," Charvi said, nonchalantly, leading the child into the back room.

The conversation muddled as Iravan trailed Dev to the table. Charvi swept the tattered blanket from a cot into a chair and settled into it while the others drew out seats of their own. Her face was much paler in the white light of Yadav's dining room, hair matted with sweat. Yadav told her off while she rested her head in her upturned palms.

The tableau was so familiar, except it had been worn away by time and strife. Dev sat next to him, and he was glad there was a table separating his fellow slumlord and Yadav. At least Charvi's unexpected presence had put pause to their argument. He hadn't seen them fight like that in years.

"We can talk about her later," Iravan said, and the room fell silent. He hated the way they all looked at him, like he was on the verge of a meltdown. As if he'd been the one throwing punches and screaming names. Yadav looked as though he would protest, but Charvi shot him a warning look.

"Fine," Yadav said. "Can we talk about why you were distributing calor injections without telling us?"

The air in the room cooled as Yadav glared at Dev.

"We had to do something," Iravan said, drawing Yadav's ire his way. He knew this moment would come the second he told Dev his plan to use the gatherers for the calor injections.

To strike at the heart of the beast. Dev had already reestablished contact with Charvi and Varun, who'd been eager volunteers. He had known the cost then, and he would pay it now. "How much longer were we supposed to wait? And now, Hamish Drakos is dead. The entire Council is dead. It worked."

Everyone but Anastasia. Something in him hummed.

"You didn't . . . ," Yadav trailed off, and his expression shifted as the pieces fell together in horrifying resolution. Charvi's haggard appearance, the rumors of an island massacre, and a coup that had stunned them all. Yadav pointed at Dev. "Why didn't you tell me this? I told you to hold off!"

The back of Iravan's neck prickled. "What?"

Dev waved him off. "I told the gatherers what they were risking. They agreed."

"You shouldn't have withheld that information," Iravan said, numbly. They were supposed to be on the same page. Had he known Yadav had *any* reservations, he would have reconsidered.

Dev narrowed his eyes. "Two minutes ago, you were defending our plan. What's changed?"

What changed was that his actions had led yet another loved one into danger. And he hadn't even known. He felt betrayed, felt that their partnership had a bitter note he'd never detected before.

"And I'm fine," Charvi snapped. "Dev did not force the needle into my vein. I made a choice for us. What the hell happened *here?*"

Iravan couldn't think about Dev's deceit—the two of them had to hold it together. And Charvi was fine, wasn't she? She was listening with her characteristic attentiveness as he relayed the events of the day. It reminded Iravan of the days spent around this table, Yadav fielding questions from the children about the sky clock he was building, the same one that now hung above the antique chest behind him.

Its persistent ticks drew him back to the present conversation. He left out Dev's interaction with Zain—it ranked low on their list of priorities, and he prayed to the souls above that his friend would forget about the girl. Iravan had listened impatiently as Dev had raged about Zain and her family, but none of the Jatavs mattered now.

"We won't know the extent of the damage until later," Iravan said. "It's too dangerous to return to the slums right now."

"Ana is out there," Charvi said, as though he needed reminding.

"Shouldn't have let her go then," Dev replied at the same time Iravan said, "She won't go to the slums."

An awkward silence strained the air. Yadav cleared his throat.

"But what was the mist?" Charvi's hand wound tightly around her child, who had remained quiet the entire conversation.

He hadn't told anyone what he'd learned from Mariam, and something stayed his hand. If he told them now, he would have to confess that he had kept it a secret, driven by his ego to find an answer himself. All that had happened could have been prevented had he spoken to her sooner or told Dev earlier. He couldn't face his shame. The consequences were already there.

"I don't know," he lied. "But I know someone who does. For today, though, we should all rest. I can sense a migraine. This disaster will still be here tomorrow, and I don't think anyone, including the bloodstrippers, will cause much trouble for the rest of the day."

One by one, they retrieved blankets and sheets from Yadav's storage closet, setting up temporary bedding for the rapidly oncoming night. When Iravan lay down, a part of him wanted the pressure in his head to worsen, to consume him and leave him at the mercy of Tejomaya's maelstrom or mist or whatever accursed trick came next.

He played with his coin under the pillow, wondering if this curse was on the land or on its people. If all their meticulous planning had only delayed an inevitable fate.

CHAPTER TWENTY-SEVEN

Zain

The rag in Zain's hand had gone from blue to violet like the evening sky.

She examined her caked nails, fingers stiff with dry blood. Theron was standing guard at the end of the alley. Leander had ventured out with his mask to gather an update on what had passed. Bilal's death was still a broken rib that hadn't set. She remembered him with every movement, every breath. More loss would shatter her entirely.

Please let them all be okay.

Footsteps rang in the distance, the sound magnifying into a hungry flame. Zain dropped behind the wall, clawing at her head to banish the intrusive image of curling fire. Rapid Gehennese sounded over her head.

". . . unbelievable audacity going on at the island. Matthieu will lose his head," Leander said.

Theron grunted, prompting Zain to emerge from her hiding place.

"What's wrong?" she asked, halfheartedly.

Leander was kneeling on the ground, depositing his mask into his bag. Theron surveyed him, hands on his hips, creases of worry smoothing when he saw Zain.

"Nothing," Leander said, brightly, cheeks stained with red splotches. "We have to go check in at headquarters."

The guards must not have trained him in deceit and manipulation.

Zain swallowed hard. "But what did you see out there?"

For so many hours, she had caged herself. Were people hiding, like her? Or were they dying like the boy she could still feel in her arms, alone and afraid?

"I don't have enough for a full report yet," Leander said, getting to his feet. "The vapor has cleared, and as far as I could see, no one has returned to the slums. There are clusters of people by the harbor, the ones who couldn't find a place to stay. They are setting up there for the night."

Zain's stomach rolled at the image. The slums were much like an intestine, densely populated within its small huts, but once unraveled and spread across the city, it was unfathomably long. Impossible to house all its inhabitants.

Theron's gaze flicked between her face and bandaged knees, where the clean white fabric had turned a muddy red. He'd given her a wide berth after their conversation, watching out for threats instead. But he'd brought her water and bread from his own supply satchel, observed gravely as she hadn't managed more than a bite.

"Stay here," he said, but it sounded like a question. "I think it would be safer for you. We still need to figure out what's happening, with calor and everything else. We'll know more once we report back."

She wanted to laugh, ask him where she would go. All Zain

knew was loneliness. She wanted time, a moment of reprieve from Theron's mercurial whims and Leander's dogged analysis, from the violence only steps away and the web of politics that had ensnared her.

"Fine," she said, sliding down the wall and burrowing her head in her hands. A shuffle of feet near her, a cough of hesitation, but then they left. Zain found herself listening for their footsteps, a morose beat against a city torn apart.

She would find no safety here. If Dev was alive and well—which, knowing his luck, he most certainly was—he would come after her. Iravan too, there was no doubt. And just like that, Zain, the little leech, would be Tejomaya's most wanted. She shuddered to think what Kanak would say, then her spine snapped straight with realization.

Kanak. Samiah. How could she have forgotten? The vapor could have easily spread to the Bow. And if it hadn't, there was Dev. Theron had been watching out for the don, and he hadn't come for her yet, but there were fates worse than death. Dev knew how to ruin her.

She was on her feet without further thought, and it was only as she was halfway out of the Sickle that she realized she had no way to leave Leander and Theron a message.

Stay here, Theron had asked. Pleaded, if she was honest about it. She wanted to stay, but it seemed Zain would remain forever destined to neglect one part of her life in favor of another. She didn't know if things had changed between the three of them or if she was simply vulnerable. Before, she wouldn't have hesitated before leaving, but the sight of Leander curled up in the alley and Theron—Theron holding a rose to her chest, Theron running into the slums by her side, Theron bandaging her knees, asking her to stay, held her back. Just for a moment.

She didn't look back as she ran home.

Zain had expected turmoil, so she took the longer path along the harbor in an effort to hide among the throngs of people gathered there. Some of what she saw was anticipated—blankets unfurled on every inch of the boardwalks; belongings rolled across the planks; people pacing, wearing variations of despair on their faces. But as she dodged an inordinate number of bloodstrippers and an even larger number of Tejomayans who were decidedly not slum-dwellers swarming the boats, she knew something was *wrong*. She didn't dare stop to ask, simply propelled herself forward, faster, faster, faster.

When the door to her house swung open, Kanak all but collapsed in Zain's arms.

"On my soul," they wailed, their hand raking through Zain's undone hair. "Where have you been?"

"I'm sorry," Zain cried, unable to stifle her wrenching gasps. Growing up would never change how quickly she fell apart when Kanak held her, how for a brief second it felt like they would fix everything. But Zain knew better now. No one could save her. "I was hiding out. I came as soon as I thought it was safe, but then I saw all these people down at the boardwalks. What is happening?"

"The bloodstrippers," Kanak said, pulling away to assess Zain. "They have taken over Tejomaya. People are fleeing in droves."

Zain's heart stopped. Did Theron and Leander know? Her mind raced to catch up with the fear coursing through her blood, the last few days replaying through a different lens.

Is that all it takes? Theron had asked her at the market. She'd staunchly denied it then, but the answer had been simple. A few acts of kindness, a listening ear, and she'd lost her well-earned skepticism. Hadn't they acted suspicious when they'd left? What if they'd meant to take her captive, the city theirs at last?

All these years, and she still hadn't learned.

"You have to go too," Zain said, doing her best to ignore the drop in her stomach. This wasn't the time for what-ifs, not when the map had changed, its terrain as unknown as the lands beyond Tejomaya. Her dreams came into alarming focus: her, Samiah, and Kanak somewhere safe. Farther south, where they could join one of the rumored underground communes. Or even North, where the Urjan natives had been rebuilding a home independent of calor.

No calor.

"You have to get out of the city," she said. This was the perfect cover. They could escape, away from the clutches of men like Devraj Basu and Iravan Khotar.

"That's what I have been telling them."

Samiah stood by the bedroom door, arms crossed. Her jaw ticked the way it did when she'd been arguing with Kanak, a rare sight.

"Why won't you go?" Zain asked Kanak, who was already shaking their head.

"I can't leave the Temple behind."

"But everyone is leaving," Zain cried.

"It's not the people they won't leave," said Samiah, toying with the tattered fringes that fell unevenly from her scarf. "Tell her, Kanak."

Kanak nervously rearranged the silk cushions piled atop their blackwood sofa, then gestured for Zain to sit next to them. "I have not told you the truth about why I left the Temple all those years ago."

Zain instantly regretted the few bites she'd taken of Theron's bread.

Kanak continued. "Today, the acolyte service is a wonderfully warm community, and my past exile has hardly mattered when it comes to involvement, but it wasn't always like this. Things then were political and trying and—well, I suppose I'm drifting away from the point, aren't I?"

This was it, the moment Kanak would tell her how she'd ruined their life. Samiah placed a hand on Kanak's shoulder. "I just don't want you to think I didn't love you, that I didn't bring you home because I *wanted* you here with me. But then the book disappeared."

Zain frowned, looking between Samiah and Kanak. "What book?"

"The acolytes' record of Tejomaya," Kanak said.

Zain scoured her memory for this book, and when the realization clicked, her jaw dropped. "The one the slum kids found?" The one responsible for rumors of the reserve, the one Gayathri had read to her and Bilal when they were children. "But that was years after I came home with you."

Kanak averted their gaze. "You found it years later, but the book had already been taken. And I'd been borrowing it, annotating it when I shouldn't have, with secrets no one should have known. I was already in trouble when the book was taken, because I had to tell Inas about everything I'd written in the margins."

No, it couldn't possibly be.

Kanak continued, quicker now. "A few days after the book was stolen, you were playing or maybe hiding, and you ended up where you shouldn't have been. You heard something you should not have heard, and after that . . . well, after that I had to get you out."

Zain remembered that day, all blurred vision and sharp

emotion. She'd been in a closet. She didn't remember where, just the press of fabric against her skin and the pulsing fear as she forced herself to stay quiet. Shortly after, someone pulled her from her sanctuary by her hair, screaming at her to never return. She had never understood what had happened.

I don't understand how we can allow them to stay there! someone said outside. She didn't know who. Scratchy tunics tickled her nose, making her want to sneeze. *The damage they would do if they knew what they had.*

It doesn't matter, another voice replied. *And it's safer this way—they will look everywhere except under their nose. We will deny what's in the book, nobody else knows. Let this secret die with me.*

Kanak took her hands into theirs, as though they could see that day too. Zain crying in their arms, the yelled admonishment incriminating over hushed whispers of a safer future. Then, they said, in the same words they had carelessly written on a page, "The calor reserve is real."

Zain's heart stuttered. She and Gayathri had joked about Kanak being the author, but they hadn't truly entertained the possibility.

"No," she said. With a jolt, she recalled Theron's iciness the day they'd first met, his presumptions about their relationship, the way she had laughed at him. He had even accused her of knowing who'd been responsible for the acolyte's book, must have had an inkling it'd been Kanak.

Zain had never given much thought to the argument between those two acolytes. The options of what it could mean had been endless, given the wealth of private acolyte knowledge, but the reserve . . .

"Before Inas passed," Kanak carried on, "they told me where

the reserve was. I'd already figured out it actually existed, and they didn't trust anyone else in the service. We were going to find the reserve together, until the fire happened. I was supposed to continue our work, but I grew complacent after their death, unsure where to begin. Now, I have to finish what we started."

Beside them, Samiah remained still, yet unsurprised. Betrayal pricked at Zain, but as the streets outside grew louder, her desperate, stubborn hope persisted. They had to keep moving.

"Can you take it with you?" she asked.

Kanak shook their head. "It's not like that, Zain. It's not here in Tejomaya. It's on the island, and I don't know exactly where."

The island.

The damage they would do if they knew what they had . . .

. . . under their nose.

It was all painfully obvious now.

Zain may not be worthy of Tejomaya, not when the city was aching because of decisions she'd made. The face of a child flashed in her mind's eye, shimmering and amorphous behind a yellow veil. Blackened screams. She could hear Inas cry—Inas, a pillar they had lost that night in a vicious fire.

The dream of leaving Tejomaya vanished into thin air, but in its place, Zain swore another oath. One she owed to her guardians, to Inas, to herself.

"Then I will stay and find the reserve," she said.

"I will not leave you," Kanak said, shaking their head rapidly. "That is out of the question."

She'd been expecting this response. What was this but another act they'd rehearsed her whole life? Zain, desperate for independence; Kanak, frightened and reluctant. She'd always lashed out, left anyway, hurting Kanak and Samiah over and over again. It was the louder option, easier to inflict pain and distance. A coward's way out.

For once, Zain told them the truth.

"I tried killing Dev today," she confessed. "The dons will be coming after me, and you as well, if only to hurt me. You must leave, and I cannot come with you."

She'd been selfish, thinking an escape to uncharted lands would grant her safety. But, with Dev, there was no guarantee of such a thing. Clearly, this path of redemption was the one the souls wanted her to take, away from her guardians, setting them free from her blood debts.

Samiah went utterly still. Kanak's jaw hung loose. "You didn't—" they started. "Why would you . . . How . . . ?"

Zain had imagined the last time she would see her guardians quite a few times, constantly anticipating abandonment. But it had never gone anything like this.

She told them everything—about Dev, the Temple, the years she'd spent trying to live up to an impossibly high standard that kept moving further beyond reach. To their credit, Kanak and Samiah didn't interrupt.

"I'm sorry I've kept so much from you," Zain finished, blinking tears away. "And I know you love me, that you want to protect me, but I'm telling you what I need from you."

"After hearing all this, how can we leave you behind?" Kanak asked, reaching for Zain's hand. "After we've failed you all this time."

"You've never failed me," Zain said, squeezing their hand three times. *I'll be okay,* she wanted to say. Kanak stared down at where their hands met, stifling their cries. "I've been capable of making my own decisions for a long time, but I haven't owned them. It's past time that I do. I need you to leave, to be safe, and then I need to see this through." When Kanak looked poised to argue, Zain pleaded, "I need you to trust me. Please."

For a moment, Zain thought they would still say no.

Then, Kanak pulled Zain into their arms, and the last of her fight drained from her body. She was so, so tired, but she needed to muster the dregs of her strength for this last battle.

"Promise me," Kanak said, fiercely. "Promise me you'll come to us after."

Zain held Samiah's gaze over Kanak's shoulder. It was an unfair ask, and everyone in the room knew it.

"I'll do everything I can," Zain said.

She hoped that was enough.

CHAPTER TWENTY-EIGHT

Anastasia

A nastasia had been called cruel, cunning, a cunt, but never a coward.

Never, except by Iravan Khotar.

She remembered how his mouth had looked when he'd said it, syllables blending together like salt and water. She could hear him say it the moment he'd discovered her evasion, the reprimand grating. There was so much left unsaid between them. In her death, she would hear Iravan calling her a coward. Saying her name.

Anastasia leaned against the concrete wall lining the slums, looking down the cross section of the artery. People poured in from all sides: the Bow, the Hammer, the slums. So many faces, none of them his.

Unbidden, her thoughts drifted to the day they'd met.

Anastasia learned one thing quickly: no one walked the streets of Tejomaya during a heat wave.

She surveyed the empty alleys before her. All wide open, ready for her to explore. The bloodstrippers may have heeded her father's wishes, but Anastasia never needed anyone's approval to do what she wanted.

Reckless, *her father said in her head. Hearing his imagined criticism was usually how she knew she was on the right path. Anastasia checked to make sure her gun, strapped to the holster around her thigh, was fully loaded. She smoothed her bright-yellow dress and plunged straight into the Hammer.*

The air vibrated against her skin, a sensation she welcomed as she rounded each corner, memorizing the stores lining the streets, noting the locations that would be useful to know. Perhaps she could use this to compel the impossible-to-impress Matthieu, who had been directed to monitor the Council Head's daughter during her stay on the mainland.

That's when she saw it, just past the narrow intersection and through the slim gap parting two large brick buildings—the slums.

Anastasia's breath hitched. In the few days she'd attempted to wander Tejomaya, she hadn't considered visiting the famed slums. She had heard enough about the area to make her nose wrinkle, but her legs carried her forward without conscious command.

It was quiet, like the rest of the city. The shacks in the front row lined up next to each other in neat order, and despite the open steel doors and gapped bamboo roofs, she could see no movement within any of the paper-thin walls. Her brows furrowed, hand drifting to her gun.

"They're at their afternoon meeting."

Anastasia spun, nearly tripping over her own feet as she spotted a man squatting on the roof of a brick-and-mortar house. His eyes narrowed briefly in surprise, and if it hadn't been for years of reading minute changes in people's expressions, Anastasia would have missed it altogether. In his right hand, he tossed a sharp, glinting dagger into the air, then caught it expertly on its descent.

"Careful," she said. "You might lose your hand trying to impress me."

He laughed. Before she could react, the knife hissed through the air, flying straight at her so close she swore it kissed her skin before impaling itself on the wall behind her. She caught the gasp that begged to burst from her lips, forcing her shoulders back as the man jumped off the roof and onto the pavement in front of her.

"I'm not in the habit of impressing anyone," he said, brushing dirt off his trousers. "I am responsible for diverting intruders who have no business being here."

"Oh?" Anastasia dug her nails into her palms. The only thing about this man that was different from the ones she'd endured her entire life was that he bore different features. Underneath his dark skin and tousled hair was the same arrogance she had long learned to mimic. "I'm on public land, aren't I? I don't see a problem here."

The man looked at her then. Really looked at her. She felt undressed as his gaze traveled from her forehead over her décolletage and stomach, then down to her feet. She reminded herself, Nothing you're not used to. She steeled her spine and raised an eyebrow, as if daring him to do more than just look.

"Problems don't tend to recognize what they are," the man said, quietly. Then, as if coming to a split decision, he added, "Go home. You're clearly too young to know any better, but you don't belong here."

Anastasia bristled. Most things she could handle, but being dismissed as a child was not one of them. It snaked under her skin and wound her up.

"I belong here and everywhere else," she said.

The man folded his arms over his chest, expression inscrutable. He advanced toward her, and Anastasia retreated until she hit the wall. He leaned in and pulled the knife out of the wall with a hollow pop. The point of the blade hung dangerously close to her neck.

"No one belongs out in a heat wave," he said. Moments passed as her mind drew a blank, confused. When it became clear she would say nothing, the man began walking away.

Anastasia exhaled, a wave of frustration rolling over her. She hated being silenced, hated not having the last word.

"I'm a Drakos," she called, throwing caution to the wind as she broke the most important rule her father had set: to never reveal her identity. It was worth it for the satisfaction she felt as the man halted in his tracks. "That means dragon in our tongue. We were built for the heat."

The man turned, a small smile playing on his lips. "You're in Tejomaya, Drakos," he called, raising a hand in farewell. "Your name means nothing here."

The taunt followed her every day.

Nothing here nothing here nothing here.

Around her, people charged across the Hammer, toward the sea. Mumbles faltered in her presence, interrupted by recognition, then fury.

A strange feeling swept her as she crossed the balustrade orbiting the bloodstripper quarters, the determination of the woman she had become overwriting the girl who had first entered the capital in the hopes of impressing her father. The engravings on the giant brass doors evoked a memory of Hamish Drakos, grimacing as he delivered her to the arching stone steps. Some things never changed.

She pushed the doors open. The distinct hum of people

outside the walls rose to a riot of voices. A sea of black uniforms parted, a dazzle of golden emblems glittering.

Anastasia's skin crawled from the bloodstrippers' collective attention. She may have worn the same coat and trousers once, but she had never really been one of them. They'd made no effort to include her when she arrived, and it hadn't been long before she'd crossed paths with Charvi. With a sharp inhale, she recalled another day, when she decided she'd had enough of the armed forces and wanted to return to the island. Charvi had begged her to stay, and she had. The island was her home by obligation, but Tejomaya proper was her home at heart.

"Anastasia."

The cloying smell of pepper accompanied the man she had been dreading to see. Somehow, Matthieu looked different here, changed since she had seen him last. Sickly, with pallid, pitted skin. When Anastasia was first in Tejomaya, Matthieu had been the age she was now, and she shuddered at the thought of looking like him in another fifteen years.

His expression settled into cool reservation.

"Matthieu," she crooned, stiffening when he looked to his side and dipped his head subtly. The back of her neck pricked with awareness.

"I thought you were dead," he said. "Imagine my surprise when I received report that you walked off a boat with a gatherer and a child. Quite the spectacle, as always."

"You underestimate me," she said. She tilted on her good leg, assuming a stance that accentuated her imposing build.

"Clearly," he said. Fifteen years ago, she would have missed the way his hand twitched behind his back, but now it was obvious.

Alarm sent her thoughts into overdrive.

Get out.

"I have come to join you, to help lead the city during this tumultuous time." Sweat beaded her forehead as she felt someone approach from behind.

Too late.

Matthieu smiled, his yellow teeth pointed. Still sharp where it counted. "You assume we need help, and that we would accept it from a traitor."

"Traitor?" She was calculating her options, searching for a way out. "How dare you? I would never betray my father."

"I would have agreed a while back," Matthieu mused. "But when the sole survivor of a massacre is the prodigal daughter who decided to slum it with the scum, you will forgive my need to question your loyalty."

Anastasia wanted to claw at his face, but something he said niggled at the back of her mind. A cold realization. "You said you were surprised to hear that I walked off a boat because you thought I was dead. Why would you think that, when I was the one who brought news about the island?"

Matthieu's smile faltered for just a second before he caught it. That bastard. She had never trusted the man, given his allegiance to Petra, but she hadn't doubted his loyalty to the Council.

"You knew," she said.

Matthieu huffed, inching closer. "My guards hear so much more than they let on. They saw the messengers your father sent to the city, thinking he was communicating with the slums oh so secretly. That old man may have been powerful on the little island of yours, but here?" He lifted Anastasia's chin. "I rule here."

She shook him off, the touch of his bare fingers revolting. Matthieu knew about Hamish's betrayal, about everything he had done. "You didn't tell Petra."

"Why would I tell her?" Matthieu asked. "She would have done something stupid. She never knew how to play the long game. I waited for the right opportunity. It's so delicious watching people try to double-cross one another—they do all the work for you. The slums took care of the Council, and now I can take care of them."

Anastasia leaped at him, but two guards restrained her with so much force, they jolted her arms from their sockets.

"You monster!" she screamed.

Matthieu surveyed her with morbid curiosity. "I may be a monster, but at least I'm someone. You are nothing."

A guard kicked her behind her knee, sending her crashing onto the icy tile. Matthieu stepped closer, his fingers grazing her cheek. She tried to bite them, but he pulled away in time.

Matthieu tutted. "So feisty, aren't you? It's about time someone showed you where you belong."

CHAPTER TWENTY-NINE

Iravan

The entire city was purging.

Just like that, Tejomaya had lost everything. Iravan's men looked chastened as they provided their report, and he knew they were planning on following their people across the waters. Word had spread that Urjan and Nohri were welcoming refugees, and the promise of safety was sweet enough to make people traverse the toxic sea.

Iravan didn't try to convince them otherwise.

"What about the guards?" he asked, massaging his temples.

His men exchanged a look. "They have been occupied with something at the quarters. But we're hearing they will begin raids soon. Some of their men have been sent to look for you."

"One more request," he said, pretending not to see their misty eyes as he made his final ask. He'd bled and fought with these men, yes, but he'd also met their families, visited their homes, celebrated births and mourned deaths with them. He was running out of reasons to stay. People without a city were lost, but the lost could be found. A city without its people was haunting.

After his men left with his orders, Iravan returned to the mechanic's shop.

"We should make a decision as to what we want to do here," he said to Yadav, pacing along the back room of the mechanic's home.

"What decision?" Yadav asked. He had been tending to Charvi all day, whose condition continually ricocheted. "I'm not leaving this city. We need to go back to the slums, find survivors—"

"There are no more slums," Dev snapped.

It had been a hard battle to convince Dev to stay indoors. He'd wanted to hunt for Zain, but with the bloodstrippers taking over the city, it wasn't safe for either of them to be outside. It was a miracle the guards had not yet come to Yadav's.

"All that will happen is we get arrested, and they"—Dev gestured at Charvi and Baruna—"will probably die!"

"Then we fight," Yadav said, stubbornly, trying to feed his daughter a spoonful of medicine.

"No," Charvi said, gagging as she tried to keep the putrid mixture down. "I will keep Baru safe. You lot can do whatever it is you want, but I have had my fill of revolution. It didn't work. Now, we run."

"Still as selfish as ever," Dev scowled, forgetting he had momentarily advocated for the very same choice.

"Takes one to know one."

They glared at each other, and Iravan marveled at how quickly they fell into old patterns.

"The point remains," Iravan insisted. "You are too weak to run right now, Charvi. There is no way you can make the journey on boat. The bloodstrippers have been busy with something, but I anticipate that will change soon. They will start coming door to door, and this will be one of their first stops."

"Where do we go?" Charvi asked.

"We don't go anywhere," he said, then pointed over his shoulder where an unremarkable rug lay. Dev slapped his knee, barking a short laugh.

"We hide underground," Yadav finished.

Iravan nodded. "We make it look like we packed up and left with everyone else. We access the tunnel that was reserved for emergencies, and we stay there or even out by the foothills while they raid this place. Then, we return. They won't expect us to remain behind, especially since they don't know about you, Charvi."

"How will we know when they're done?" Charvi asked.

Iravan let out a measured exhale. "I have someone I will make contact with. She will be helpful to us, in more ways than one." It was well past time he told the others about the reserve, but he wanted Mariam to be there when he did.

"Who?" Dev asked.

"Later," Iravan said, more sharply than he intended. He was sick of Dev's bizarre obsession with Zain and had not forgiven him for endangering Charvi, but he didn't have the energy to hash it out.

One by one, they gathered what was most important: medicine for Charvi, weapons for Dev, papers for Yadav. Iravan reloaded his gun and packed his remaining magazines. The ammo wouldn't last long, but it was enough in case of a shoot-out. They were ready to go within the hour.

Dev was to take Baruna and Yadav through the tunnel while Iravan finished ransacking the place to make it look like they had left Tejomaya. He would have preferred Dev take Charvi first, given her condition, but the two were at each other's throats, and she refused to leave before her kid or her father. So, it was under her watchful stare that Iravan wandered from room to room, checking to make sure nothing important remained.

"So, how have you been?" he asked, ruffling through the piles of paper Yadav kept on his desk. Most were old journal entries he didn't feel comfortable reading, so he stacked them neatly under a stone paperweight.

"I've known you since we were ten, for souls' sake," Charvi said. "You can do better than that."

Iravan hunted through the chest of trinkets—there were some handmade antique ornaments, jewelry, Yadav's coin collection. He lifted a beautiful locket between his fingers, one he'd traced around someone else's neck. He let it fall on top of all the other junk. There was nothing of value there. "I thought you could do better than disappear on us all. So, it turns out we were both wrong."

"Ravi . . ." She tried to stand, knocking over a glass in the process.

"Stop moving," he scolded, rushing to her side. Her face warped with pain as she lay back down. Anger vanquished empathy, and forgiveness was as scarce as calor. She had been family, and she had left. He brought her another glass of water.

"I tried contacting you," Charvi said, taking a meager sip. "I wanted to talk to you so badly."

"I told your messengers they could fuck off," replied Iravan. He remembered the leeches who had carried messages from the ports.

Baruna's so grown up now.

How is Baba? Has he made anything new?

I'm sorry about your loss, Ravi.

I miss you all.

It only made him more wrathful. "You chose her over me."

"I wasn't thinking straight!" Charvi cried. "Baru was so sick, and Ana took her to the bloodstripper quarters. How could I abandon her after that? I owed her my baby's life. I thought Baru would be safer on the island, where I would never have to worry about medical treatment. I thought you of all people would understand."

He did. He hated that he did.

Outside, the din grew louder. They were almost out of time.

"Let's go," he said, assessing the room one last time before taking Charvi into his arms. Her body had withered so extensively, it felt like he was carrying a child. He lowered her through the trapdoor, closed it above their heads, then scooped her up, crouching against the wall for support.

"You came back to the city and didn't see us then," he said into the darkness. He'd known they were expecting a gatherer from the island to pick up the injectables, but he hadn't learned it was Charvi until later.

She nestled into his chest, and despite his frustrations, he pulled her closer. Souls, he'd missed her. They'd all missed her.

"I couldn't risk being seen with any of you, and I didn't want Baba to know," she said. "Besides, that trip wasn't for you."

It was for Anastasia.

"You know you can ask me about her," she said, as they moved down the tunnel.

He grunted.

"She was going to be appointed to the Council," Charvi said, ignoring his nonresponse. "She was going to wage war against you."

Iravan faltered, just for a second. He'd made the first move in their battle across the sea. It didn't matter that he'd been grieving, out of his mind with pain, when he'd told Matthieu what

Anastasia was leaving behind in Tejomaya, the secret they had all sworn to keep from her father. He'd turned his back on her, an unforgivable crime.

It was only reasonable that the daughter of the Head Councilmember had arrived at the same goal as her people had, no matter how she'd once spent time in Tejomaya, seen it in a way no Geng ever had. He wondered how it had been for Charvi, once a friend and then a servant, who'd rebelled in fury and been rescued from death. He understood why Charvi had let Anastasia go, even if Dev and Yadav did not. This way, the slate was clean. All that would unfold thereafter would not weigh on her conscience.

"I didn't think she'd ever come back," Charvi said, when they arrived at the end. "She did it for me."

Nothing was stronger or more deceptive than bonds forged over honeyed wishes and whispered promises. He'd wondered if Anastasia remembered those times like he did, if the memory of his embrace comforted her during lonely evenings, if her fingers recalled the touch of his hair, if she still quoted the words he'd said to her like her personal lullaby.

It had been delusional, that hope, for he knew her better than that. None of what Charvi said should have been a surprise. Still, Iravan felt a pinch in his chest as he said, "I know."

Iravan regretted his plan almost immediately.

The tunnel hadn't been used in years. Every surface was coated with dust and grime, which laid siege on Charvi's lungs. The first hours comprised sweeping cobwebs and clearing areas to make it remotely habitable. And then there was Mariam.

She hadn't said much since her arrival, observing in her intense manner while Yadav made up a place for his daughter to rest and while Baruna took to the concrete floors to draw, lines drifting off the edges of the spare parchment. Mariam had remained infuriatingly calm too when Dev spoke to her in a way that made Iravan bristle.

It wasn't until that night, when everyone else fell into a fitful sleep, that she cocked her head, beckoning him away. They walked through the tunnel, all the way to the end of the foothills, where they had a brief glimpse outside. Iravan never thought he would miss Tejomaya's stiff air, but he relished the perfunctory view of the inky sky.

"I'm sorry for bringing you into this," he said. The last favor he had asked of his men was to deliver her to Yadav's by whatever means necessary. In hindsight, he could have used different language. "She was hurt, and the bloodstrippers were knocking down doors, and we had a child with us . . ."

Mariam let him bluster, and he realized how quickly he seemed to fall apart in front of her. With everyone else, he was Iravan the city leader, and they met him with deference or force. Mariam looked at him like he was just another man she was too tired to deal with. He wasn't sure how that made him feel.

"I don't mind helping you," she said, after a minute or so. "I have been thinking about you since you left my hut the other day. I heard about what happened at the slums. I came looking for you."

Her lips were pressed into a straight line, concern creasing her nose.

"Were you worried about us?" he asked, smiling despite himself.

"I worried it was too late."

Couldn't blame her for being honest.

"I have to believe you now," he admitted. "I need your help."

She quirked an eyebrow, the movement jostling her glasses so they slid down her nose. "You haven't told them."

"No, I have not," he said, feeling the need to justify himself. "At first, I was ashamed, thinking if I'd listened to you sooner, none of this would have happened. And it's been nonstop shit since. Now, I don't know where to begin. The idea that our land has grown inhospitable is not easy to accept, especially when we haven't spent as long studying these matters as you have. I need to understand, though—I *want* to understand if there is any way of salvaging this. I know the Nohri left on your recommendation, but Tejomaya was never their home. It means everything to us, and the fact that we have to give it up because of the actions of others . . . It's not right."

"What's not right?"

Mariam jumped closer to Iravan, clutching at his shirt in fright. Dev was just behind the curve of the tunnel, feline in his silent approach. Iravan cleared his throat, bracing Mariam as his heart rate soared. How much had Dev heard? To anyone else, his brother would look unremarkable, but Iravan recognized the disapproval knotted between his brows. Dev once looked at Anastasia that way.

"Let us go back," Mariam suggested, putting distance between her and Iravan. Reluctantly, he let her go.

Dev scowled. "No, you can tell me—"

"She's right," Iravan said, stepping between them. History's unflinching eyes set upon him, looking to see if he had learned from its lessons.

Yadav and Charvi stirred when they returned to the chamber, sleep thinned from anxiety. Only Baruna remained dormant, head safely in her mother's lap. She snored lightly.

"Restless already? I would have joined you," Charvi jested.

Mariam looked expectantly at Iravan. Right. This came down to him.

"Now that we are all here, there is more I need to tell you," he said. The difficulty was that he would have approached this conversation differently with each person. Dev would need a stiff drink, Yadav would require access to an acolyte. With one, he would employ brute honesty, with the other, something more thoughtful. Charvi looked caught between life and death, and he didn't want to tell her at all. In the end, he pretended he was speaking to himself, and he told them everything.

Mariam interjected at times, politely clarifying details, and he winced whenever she was more enthused than was tactful. He knew how she came across—he had cast the same judgments upon her—but now her zeal held a different meaning. Her work he didn't understand, but her passion he did.

"What *is* it, though?" Yadav asked at last.

"Decades and decades of poisoning," Mariam said, with more care than he would have given her credit for. "All these years, we believed it was only the sky we'd ruined. We have been content with separating the earth from its heavens, when the two are but reflections of one another."

"Sounds like a whole bunch of guesswork to me," Dev interrupted. "You said it yourself, the skies have been inaccessible. What proof do you have?"

"That doesn't matter to me," Yadav said, quietly. "Is it true you know a way out of this? A way to save Janmir?"

Mariam met Iravan's eyes. "The reserve," he said.

Everyone turned to him.

"The lost calor reserve. She asked me about it when we first met, but I dismissed the possibility of its existence," he quickly added, cutting off Yadav's imminent question. Dev's lips were pressed flat, and Charvi looked confused. "I tried investigating on my own, but I couldn't find anything."

"Why would you keep this from me?" Dev asked.

For the same reasons you kept things from me. But Iravan wasn't quite sure that was true. He still wasn't sure what else Dev was keeping to himself.

"It doesn't matter right now," Yadav said. "How would finding the reserve help?"

Iravan was taken aback. He had expected Yadav to sneer at Mariam, but the man seemed genuinely curious.

Mariam smiled. "You would need to destroy it."

Dev burst into ugly laughter. "Do you hear her?" he asked Iravan. "She's wasting our time. Destroy the lost reserve? If it exists, do you not think we would have control over it already?"

"You asked and I answered," Mariam said. Iravan could see her turn circumspect, the same way she had when he'd first met her. "I will leave you here to discuss."

Iravan couldn't stop himself from going after her.

"Wait," he said, catching her elbow when they were out of earshot of the others. She would not meet his eye.

He wanted to beg her to stay, to tell him more about the reserve, but what came out was: "Dev is not normally like this. He's just upset."

"You think I care what he has to say?" she said, looking scornful. "Your partner is as important as the rest of us, which is to say, not important at all. As far as it concerns me, he has never been anything more than a means to an end. A rude and dismissive one, but if you think he is the first disagreeable person I have come across, then you are wrong."

"He's not all that bad," Iravan argued, weakly.

Mariam scoffed. "You're not listening. Whether he is good or bad does not matter to me. Whether he is kind or cruel doesn't matter. This land is changing now, because of *us*, because of what we have done. What the elements have been unable to accomplish, *we* have done. This is a stain on the history of the universe." She pursed her lips, took a step away. "I have watched men rise and fall like leaves on wind. I will not be the air that softens the blow. See the stone forest for the mountains they are, Iravan, and maybe then you will understand."

Shame. That's what he felt, its slippery fingers all over his body. They were talking about Dev, but in truth, Iravan had been mounting his own defense. Souls, he had been worse than Dev, nearly strangling her at Bilal's funeral. He'd thought she'd come back to him out of forgiveness or curiosity, but he wondered if he too had been just a means to an end.

"Where is she?" Charvi asked, when he returned to the group. Iravan shrugged, uncertain with how to proceed. So easily, Mariam could turn them over, and he would lose it all. He could only hope she meant what she'd said, that she was concerned with matters larger than them, than him, no matter how it chafed his dignity.

Dev was pacing.

"What is it?" Iravan asked, clocking the tension in the room.

"Why don't you ask him?" Dev gestured wildly at Yadav. "After all this time, and you *knew* I was looking for it too—"

"Enough," Charvi snapped. Baruna sat up, wiping sleep from her eyes.

Yadav set his jaw. "As you know, I was friendly with Inas when they were Head Acolyte. I spent a lot of time at the Temple and heard several interesting conversations. I wrote plenty down in my journals, but there were far too many to bring down here.

I did bring the important one, so it doesn't fall into bloodstripper hands." He retrieved a creased brown book from his overcoat.

"There were many hints over the years—of course, the annotated history book that was stolen and passed around the city— but also internal arguments at the Temple about the service's friendly relationship with the Gengs. Some wanted to rebel, others were content with salvaging their own safety. I could never understand why Inas was okay with how the Gengs treated us, when I knew how compassionate Inas was."

Iravan's anger at the acolytes had dulled over the years. They didn't interfere with his operations, so he was content to coexist with them. He'd never understood why they'd found themselves on opposite sides of the city: the Bow and the Hammer, prayer and poverty. Dev had worked hard to unite all parties at the Temple ten years earlier, but it had ended so brutally that no other efforts were ever made again.

"Go on," Iravan urged.

"I asked Inas about the reserve once, out of curiosity. I wasn't expecting them to tell me anything at all, but they said, *Yadav, if we could reach it so easily, I would have told you to burn it down already.*"

Dev interrupted, "Oh, just get to the point, would you? He knows where the reserve is."

CHAPTER THIRTY

Anastasia

Someone new was watching her.

Anastasia could assess plenty from their footsteps. They were light, lacking the assertion and accompanying mirth of her previous guard.

"Matthieu has sent me a more well-trained dog this time," she said, scraping the hollow barrel of her strength. "Did I give the others too hard a time?"

"You really are a piece of work," Matthieu said, unexpectedly, and her breathing shallowed. His silhouette spilled around the bars, arms crossed. "I thought a few hours in jail would be enough to check your attitude, but two days later and you've still got that mouth on you."

Anastasia recovered, running her tongue over her teeth, savoring the dried blood that caked her gums after the last guard's visit. She opened her mouth in a gruesome smile. "Come closer, and I'll show you what the rest of me can do."

Matthieu didn't take the bait, calmly lowering himself to the ground. Anastasia wrinkled her nose at the scent of spice that wafted toward her.

"Do you want to know what we did today?" he asked, pulling out a pack of cigarettes and drawing one out with his long fingers. A click as he lit its end, followed by a tired, satisfied exhale. "We raided the Hammer. Every nook and cranny. The mechanic's store was a hoard of treasure. I can see why you liked to spend so much time there."

"You're a grown man, Matthieu," Anastasia replied, trying not to think of the guards swarming Charvi's childhood home. "It does not become you to behave like an overexcited boy."

Matthieu chuckled as he dragged on the end of the cigarette. "Oh, I think what we found would go over the heads of most overexcited boys. That man Yadav kept interesting diaries. It took us a while to crack his code, but when my men brought me their findings today, I had to come down here and share it with you."

Anastasia remembered Yadav scribbling in those worn leather journals with their well-loved spines, cracked open time and time again. She had joked about reading them on more than one occasion, but it was in truth a step too far for her.

"He had a lot of thoughts on you, you know. That you were a terrible influence on Charvi and Iravan. He spent many pages wondering how he could get rid of you. Didn't think he was the violent sort, I have to admit, but then the Temple of Many-Souls burned down and his tune on you changed. He was still angry Charvi had left with you, but he seemed softer. Lots of vague, abstract passages on loss. Very poetic," Matthieu said.

Anastasia's stomach spasmed. "These are not thoughts you needed his diaries to understand."

"Of course," Matthieu said, gaze trained on the smoke

painting swirls along the walls of her cell. "Iravan Khotar told me everything I needed to know about that, didn't he?"

She didn't dare breathe. Ten years, she'd had to come to terms with what Iravan had done, but somehow it hurt more hearing the words come out of Matthieu's mouth, as though each memory of his betrayal was a fresh stab to her back and now she was nothing but carved-up meat.

"He was also very invested in finding the lost Temple reserve."

This, Anastasia realized too slowly, was what Matthieu wanted. "I'm sorry to disappoint, but I know nothing about that."

"I think you know more than you realize," Matthieu replied, blowing his rotten breath directly at her face, smirking as she tried not to retch. "The dons have fled this city with everyone else. Given the disaster on the island, that leaves only you to help us with this matter."

"A disaster you caused," Anastasia said. "And you are a fool if you believe they've left this city. They would rather die. They're in hiding, biding their time."

"Now, Ana," he said, "how could I have been responsible for what happened? You saw the perpetrators yourself. Your father was right—it seems this city has corrupted you past the point of return. I suppose not much else matters after you've fallen in bed with one of them. No matter. We can find the reserve without you, and with its power, Finze will have sole control over this city."

"With you at its helm?" Anastasia sneered.

Matthieu looked thoughtful. "Yes. It should have been me all along. The Council knows nothing about Tejomaya. The Isle is a bubble, and they were ruling over something they didn't understand. But I've been a part of this city. I know what makes its heart beat, what makes it hurt."

Her teeth chattered.

Matthieu continued. "Oh, there is one more thing. We found some interesting apparatus at the mechanic's place as well. Syringes and parchments describing calor injections. Brilliant, don't you think? Of course, given what happened, the technology's not quite at the stage of development where I can safely deploy them across my forces. But I have my people working on it, and I'm sure we can find subjects to test its effects on."

"You're an idiot," Anastasia rasped. She thought of Charvi's gaunt face, the bodies crushed within the silent forest. "I saw what it can do to people, and it was not meant for us."

"Perhaps it was meant for you, the girl who walks under the blood rains," Matthieu mused, getting to his feet.

Three guards entered, bringing a frigid chill with them. Metal shrieked as one guard opened the gate to her cell. It took all the control in Anastasia's body not to recoil. To not shiver at the sight of the needle in the guard's hand.

"Three against one? I'm flattered," she said.

Matthieu dropped his cigarette to the ground and crushed the stub beneath his heel. "Enjoy it. Might be the last time you feel that way."

The guards' emblems glittered on their breasts—not the pillars of Gehanna but the lotus of Finze. One held her down while another ripped the sleeve of her blouse to expose pale, veined flesh. She forced herself not to look. She wouldn't give them the satisfaction. The third guard examined the barrel of the syringe.

"Make it hurt, would you?" Matthieu said, drumming his fingers across his arm.

"Fuck you," said Anastasia.

She barely had time to bite down on her lip when the guard stabbed the needle into her bicep and set every nerve on fire.

CHAPTER THIRTY-ONE

Zain

It was quiet at home.

Zain thought she was used to solitude, to the keen tune of the breeze as it whistled through the casement window, to the feeling of grief, a cold pocket in a warm room, but she had underestimated the insulation Samiah and Kanak had provided. The safety they'd taken with them when they'd left.

Dev hadn't come looking for her either.

It was like he had just . . . forgotten about her. Like in the grand scheme of his life, she was nothing, all while she lived, breathed, and ached in his name. Bile seared her throat, churning her into action.

The bloodstrippers had started their raids, and she needed to gather valuables before they headed to the Bow. Maybe she was destined to be a speck in the lives of everyone she knew, but she would be more to the city she owed. She would make sure the reserve—the last vestiges of her city's ancestors and power—remained out of the wrong hands.

Zain knew Tejomaya intimately, but when it came to the

Isle of Vis, she didn't know where to begin. She had prowled the streets, listening closely for news from the island. The Council had been killed, but no one knew precisely where things stood. Was anyone alive? Were bloodstrippers there right now? Without the knowledge of what she was walking into, Zain was lost.

She hadn't heard anything about Leander or Theron either, but she didn't let herself dwell on that. After everything she had been through, she refused to trust men, particularly those whose voices burrowed comfortably in her head.

You're worth more than you think.

Words were just that—words. Dev had showered her with pretty ones, draining them of any power. She washed her hands of the brothers.

Zain peeked under Samiah and Kanak's bed. The slim box with the revolver was barely visible in the darkness. Samiah had insisted on having it for protection, but Kanak, as averse to violence as Zain was, had never opened the leather case. The gun's gleaming surface was probably the only thing not tainted by their departure. It had never known their presence. Zain felt like she was betraying her guardians all over again as she strapped it to her holster. Unlike her other weapons, this was a fresh start.

The streets hummed with apprehension as she made her way to the harbor. Earlier that day, she had scouted for the perfect boat for her needs, the one she and Theron had loaded that day of their joint mission. It was too small to brave the distance to Urjan or any of the neighboring countries of the Lower Tectonic, but it was perfect for Zain to take to the island. She pushed forward, pulling her scarf around her head.

The harbor was disquietingly busy. Most escaping the city had preferred to do so during the day. No one liked moving through the sullen mist when it was dark. But amid the raids,

fear was rampant, and several boats were still loading new passengers, many carrying nothing but the clothes on their backs.
Zain's pulse rattled as she squatted under one of the boardwalks,
waiting for people to pass.

Above her head, footsteps shook bits of debris free. Zain
pinched the bridge of her nose, stifling a sneeze.

"He'll break that Drakos bitch," someone said in Gehennese.
Bloodstrippers.

"I'm surprised he hasn't already. I'm not sure why we've kept
her around this long. Maybe we should pay her a visit . . ." They
moved out of earshot. Zain lurched forward as if to follow.

Drakos.

The memory of the last time she'd seen Anastasia Drakos
erupted in her mind. Anastasia, screaming as the Temple of
Many-Souls burned down, her friend Charvi by her side. Zain
had never heard a sound so devastating. Sometimes, she heard
Anastasia's screams in her nightmares, but when she woke, she
wondered if it was actually her own voice.

Zain knew the notorious Gehennese woman was back in the
city, but she'd remained out of sight. Zain had kept an eye out for
her tall frame and chestnut hair, half expecting to see her stumbling out of the tavern, arms draped around Iravan and Charvi,
or settled on the harbor, feet nearly skimming the water as she
tossed rocks into the sea. But she had disappeared. If the bloodstrippers' conversation was any indication, it was not by choice.

Zain's decision stretched in front of her like a taut rope, one
end wrapped around the boat for her taking, the other aflame.
The ghosts that had kept her company stirred from where they
lay—Inas, the child, the people who'd burned and burned and
burned.

"You're a fool, Zain," she said to herself. No one would

understand the gravity of her debts. She couldn't walk away, even if she wanted to. She turned, and the wood beneath her shifted to granite, then cobblestone.

It always stunned Zain how close her guardians lived to the home of their invaders. The transitions between the neighborhoods weren't subtle. One moment, she was among the townhouses and bungalows of the Bow; the next, she stepped onto the vast expanse of land encompassing the monstrous bloodstripper quarters. All that time living next door, and this was the first time she was there by choice. Still, she had been a leech long enough to know the area decently. She scaled a large tree that hung over one of the patrol routes.

Despite the burning heat, her skin was cool with sweat, forcing her to strip off Samiah's brown scarf, which clung to her neck like a noose. She had arrived there with no plan, only a goal, a surefire way of ending up dead. Even if she knew where Anastasia was being held, how was she going to get her out? Zain cushioned her head on a branch, sending a prayer up to the souls.

For a few hours, she heard nothing of value. In fact, hardly anyone passed by at all. This alone was enough to chill her nerves. With the dons disarmed and the city evacuating, there was little threat to the bloodstrippers. But what was keeping the entire force preoccupied?

She had a disconcerting sense it was Anastasia. Zain's despair grew urgent, and upon sighting no one through the crammed branches, she climbed down.

Zain was only feet away from the large carved-wood doors leading to the back quarters when the first guards appeared.

They shuffled out of the same exit she had taken after she'd been released from jail. One pulled out cigarettes from their pocket, and the other two leaned forward as he lit the ends for them. Zain swore, hoping the tree she was squatting behind was thick enough to conceal her.

She strained to catch their exchange, but only coarse laughter made its way to her. After a few minutes, the doors opened, followed by the sound of gravel crunching under their departing feet. She stretched her legs out, stiffening as she kicked a stray stone.

"What was that?"

Please don't come here please don't come here please don't come here.

"I'll go check," a guard replied, and his voice knocked the world off its orbit. Zain couldn't move as a figure emerged by her side, walking far beyond her tree. Carefully, Theron turned, his attention passing over her. Relief flooded her. He was okay, he was safe. She hadn't realized how much she'd cared.

Theron called out, "No one here, but I can make a round and meet you inside."

The others grunted in response, and Theron marched toward the perimeter. He made it nearly halfway before he spun and charged in her direction. Zain was on her feet, prepared to bolt.

"What the hell do you think you're doing?" he asked. In his panic, he pushed her against the trunk so hard she had to stopper a scream. Blood tinged her mouth, but when she tried to respond, he pressed his hand against her lips.

"Do you want to get caught?" he whispered, angrily. "There are guards on patrol right now. I don't know how you didn't see them. Stay quiet, Zain, or I swear to the gods I'll—"

The door swung open. "Theron!" someone called. "Matthieu just announced that we have to—Cleirigh? Where did he go?"

Theron swore quietly. Indecision raced across his face, and she traced the way his mouth parted and closed, the way his hands tightened on her.

"Theron?"

Another guard. Theron slumped. Their hearts beat against each other in farewell.

"Yes," he replied, loosening his grip. "I found an intruder."

Everything happened so quickly.

Theron pushed her into the open, pinning her arms behind her back. Two guards faced them, the door to the quarters wide open. Their faces blended together in a terrifying smile.

This was it. It was over. One reached for the gun on his belt and —

Two shots pierced the night.

Zain looked down, half expecting to see blood blossoming on her chest, but the wound wasn't on her. The guards collapsed. Theron held his gun out, a wisp of smoke leaving its eye.

"Theron," she whispered. The gun fell limp at his side.

Footsteps pounded down the stairs. They had heard the gunshots. Zain looked around, but it was too late. They couldn't run now.

The bloodstrippers would kill them both.

"Inside," she said, grabbing his hand. "Inside now!"

Through his shock, he listened, and they darted toward the open door. The stairs were long and winding, stretching endlessly before them. Questions pounded in her head. Were there more guards downstairs? More prisoners? They couldn't be seen down there.

Cries echoed overhead. Theron came to in that moment. "Not this way," he said. She followed him blindly down a narrow corridor. They blazed past empty cells, their footsteps heavy enough that if the guards above stopped to listen, they might've been able to hear them. Theron shoved Zain through an open wooden door, then followed quickly behind. It was a closet, not at all large enough for the two of them, illuminated only by a thin sliver of light that entered through the crack under the door.

His right arm wrapped around her, holding her body flush against his, while his left hand came up to her mouth. Outside, it sounded like multiple guards were down there, setting Zain's teeth on edge.

"Check on Drakos," someone called. "Matthieu wants us guarding her closely. Everyone else, out to the perimeter. They couldn't have gotten far."

Something behind Theron's head caught her attention.

A skull stared down at her.

Had Theron pushed them into a *coffin*?

Zain whimpered a little behind his hand, staring at the gaping hole of the skull's mouth. She imagined fire searing its sockets, before she felt the phantom flames running across the back of the coffin. Her claustrophobia reared its head, the walls converging. She couldn't do this. She would rather face the blood-strippers outside.

Theron tugged the back of her braid.

Look at me, he seemed to say.

She tore her eyes away from the skeleton to see him shaking his head slowly. His hand slid up her face, cautiously. His touch blazed a warm trail over her cheek before brushing her eyelids closed. Her forehead pressed against his chest, the light thud of his heartbeat demanding the attention of all her senses.

The irony that it was Theron who had become her anchor was not lost on her. The man was vicious, unforgiving, and cruel. But he had her back. She had fought so hard to hold on to his

tirades, ignoring the unflinching decisions he'd made on her behalf. Somewhere along the way, her body had grown to trust him,
despite her mind's staunch resistance.

She had realized it when he'd grabbed her outside. That kind
of roughness would once have sent her into a tailspin, but instead
she'd been overwhelmed by concern. Then, he took those shots.
Chose her, when she hadn't known she was even a choice.

It was overwhelming, and she didn't know how to process it.

They stood there for so long that Zain's feet tingled. Theron
tucked her hair behind her ear.

He whispered, "I'm going to go out there and pretend I was
knocked out. I'll say I need to give them a full report of the intruder and draw them outside. That should give you enough time
to get out of here. Meet me by the Temple."

Zain nodded. Theron cocked his head, listening for any
movement outside before jostling the door. "Wait a few minutes,"
he said. And then he was gone.

She hadn't realized how much effort he had put into holding her up. Without his arms bracketing her, Zain dropped to
the ground, wanting to be far away from the bones that dangled
above her head.

One Tejomaya.

Two Tejomaya.

Three Tejomaya.

When she reached one hundred Tejomaya for the fourth
time, she cracked open the door, then slid outside. Blind faith.
Theron was the first person to ever earn it from her. There hadn't
been any sign of a disturbance after he'd left, and so she sidled
through the corridor, praying she didn't run across any guards.
She put one foot in front of the other until she was at the bottom
of the stairs.

Anastasia. She had come here for a reason, but with the way things had played out, she hadn't had the chance to tell Theron. How long would he be able to give her?

Zain continued down the hall, searching, and the souls must have been benevolent that evening, because Anastasia was not far.

The area outside the heiress's cell was colder than Zain had expected. A faint stench of urine wafted through the air, and as she squinted, she made out a body lying in the middle of the enclosure. Zain lunged for the bars, searching for a lock.

But the cell was unlocked.

She felt a cold prick right under her ribs. This was far too easy. Zain didn't need all her wits about her to realize the husk of a woman lying on the floor was debilitated beyond belief. That there was no way she could carry herself out of here on her own.

And the bloodstrippers hadn't thought anyone would come for her.

Anastasia moaned, an injured animal left to die. This was the closest Zain had ever been to the Drakos heir, and she couldn't comprehend the translucent pallor of her skin, the jagged edges of her collarbone. So utterly mortal.

From afar, Anastasia had seemed a mythical creature, dancing through the streets, drawing envy and attention. Zain had often thought to herself that Anastasia Drakos would never have fallen victim to Dev, that she had access to a kind of strength Zain couldn't comprehend. But now, watching blood run in red rivers down her arms, strands of thin hair clinging to chapped lips, Zain wondered if she'd mistaken fortune for strength. Maybe when rotten circumstances came calling, Anastasia Drakos was just like Zain, alone in the dark, wondering if anyone would hear her cry.

Zain clicked open the cell door and slipped inside. Anastasia lifted her head, then dropped it with a violent thud.

"Who are you?"

Souls, what had the guards done? Above, bloodstrippers sprinted across the hallway. She had to move quickly.

"Come," Zain said, wrapping her arm around Anastasia's frail shoulders. They collapsed under her touch.

"You look like her," Anastasia replied, slowly sitting up. It was so dark that there was no way Anastasia could see her face, yet she continued. "You feel like her too. You have her softness."

She had gone mad. She wasn't dead, but the woman Zain remembered didn't seem to exist. More cries above, their approaching volume a lethal countdown.

"Lean on me," Zain instructed, hissing through her teeth as she pulled the woman up on her feet and out of the cell. Anastasia may have been withering away, but she was still much taller than Zain, and her bones felt like they were made of lead. At least she was docile and quiet. The ascent was a nightmare, too slow, Anastasia's atrophied legs unable to function. Zain was cold and hot, her gun branding its impression on her thigh. Fully loaded. With a bitter thought, she realized she might have to use it.

"When we get outside," she said, panting through each step, "you need to run toward the trees. As far as you can get into the Bow. If you can make it to the Temple, that would be best. I will cover you." Anastasia's silence was not comforting.

The door swung open, and three figures emerged to her right.

"Go!" she cried, shoving Anastasia away and drawing her weapon. She stepped forward, blocking Anastasia as she fired into the distance. The sound ripped through her body, tearing at the piece of herself she swore she would never give away. Tears streamed down Zain's face as the men fell one after the other.

Anastasia had barely budged, stumbling over loose rocks. Zain sprinted to her side, slung the woman's arm around her neck, and started dragging her as though she were a bag of grain. The Temple was too far. There was no way they would make it.

"I need you to put one foot in front of the other," Zain commanded, desperately. Her shoulders were on fire, her back strained. Anastasia was trying to move, but she could barely lift her feet to avoid the roots.

"You should leave me," Anastasia heaved, somehow growing heavier. Zain was carrying nearly all her weight at this point.

"Just a little farther," she lied. She could see the beginnings of the Bow through the dark, but the distance was a trick of the night. Footsteps of a pursuer cracked behind them, and Zain nearly screamed. Too fast. They hadn't even had a chance to get out of the bloodstrippers' domain.

She dropped Anastasia and pulled out her empty revolver, prepared to use it to strike if she had to.

Her pursuant appeared from the woods. It was Theron.

"I'm going to kill you," he said, slowing down. He looked like he'd run across the entire city. Relief knifed her lungs.

"Help me," Zain begged, pointing at Anastasia, who rolled onto her back, moaning in pain.

For a moment, it looked like he would refuse. For a moment, he looked as though he would berate her further and Zain would have to pick Anastasia back up herself. But then he huffed and lifted the unconscious woman into his arms.

As the two of them ran, Zain wondered if this was her punishment, relegated to an endless pit of suffering, chasing redemption in the darkest of nights.

CHAPTER THIRTY-TWO

Iravan

The tunnel walls thundered.

"How much more can they destroy?" Yadav groused, setting his shoe down. He'd been teaching Baruna to hide important notes in her socks, and the two had folded her drawings into small squares and filled their shoes with secrets. A silly distraction from Charvi's rapidly deteriorating condition and from the walls shaking like it was storming outside.

They'd surfaced to the store for a few hours, concerned by how quickly the cellar's confinement had made Charvi take a turn for the worse. The place had been ransacked, but at least she could lie on a proper cot. Moisture soaked the sheets while her eyelids shivered with disturbed, fevered dreams. Iravan felt the clock tick above his head like a guillotine. He wanted to move back underground.

"I wonder what they're looking for," Iravan said, staring at the curtained windows. The guards had laid everything to waste, shuffled through Yadav's desk, cabinets, equipment. Yadav's face had fallen at the sight of the damage, but his daughter's health was his priority. At least the bloodstrippers wouldn't return any-time soon. "Mariam said they've been turning over shops across the Hammer. They might be trying to knock off a few more be-fore it rains again."

Iravan didn't have to look outside to know how the sky's vessels appeared, bulbous and ripe. The rains were coming once more, but the idea of rogue calor pooling in hidden spaces filled him with dread.

"I still think we should get out now, find the reserve," Dev grumbled.

"We need to wait it out," Iravan said, reining in his tone. He was tired of this argument. "The whole city will be looking for us."

But there was more holding him back. It was all too odd that there was a calor reserve on the island the Gengs had studded with their marble homes. It was a strange place for the acolytes to keep it, out of character for a group that sought only to pre-serve and honor the memories and sacrifices of their people. He wished he could speak to Kanak, but from the little news Mariam brought, they and the other acolytes had left.

It didn't help that Mariam knew he was hiding something, no matter how reluctantly he had agreed to do so, at Dev's behest.

"She wants to destroy the reserve," Dev had said when Iravan broached the topic. "Are you out of your mind? We can't let her anywhere near it."

But what if she was right, Iravan thought, and with another turn of the mind, he was back on Dev's side. It was clear Mariam had her own priorities, ones that went beyond him and his city. He didn't want to disclose the location of the reserve, given it was their last hope to ensure his people's survival. With a large amount of calor, they could settle elsewhere, fertilize the soil, develop essential medications. He couldn't risk losing that, despite the keen intuition that she was ahead in spades.

People bustled outside. Not an hour passed when someone didn't scream, anguish becoming commonplace. Iravan barely flinched anymore, but his muscles were tightly wound as he waited. Mariam was supposed to be back for an evening report.

After yet another hour of listening to the clamor, the trapdoor creeped open. Mariam climbed up, a jute bag over her shoulder, spilling with bread. She kicked the door shut with her heel. Unlike this morning, there was a gust to her movement, a freneticism that made him uneasy.

"Something has happened," she said, rubbing her hands clumsily along the folds of her maroon skirt. Stains soiled her waistline, incongruous with her typically polished demeanor. "I took a turn around the Hammer, and there are bloodstrippers everywhere. It's not normal raids; they're pulling people out of their homes, and I saw some headed in this direction."

"Were you followed?" Dev asked, leaping to his feet.

"Does it matter?"

Iravan cursed, moving to the windows, tugging just the bottom of the heavy drapes apart. Outside, the line of stores was a black silhouette on a deep-plum sky.

"Are they preparing for the rains?" he asked, hopefully. "Maybe scouting out the rest of our turbines?"

"No, I don't think so," she replied, peering over his shoulder. "They were looking for someone. I heard a guard interrogating a woman, asking for Anastasia Drakos. Isn't that the Head Councilmember's daughter? Do you all know where she would be?"

Iravan rested his hand on the windowsill.

"Ana?" Charvi asked, attempting to sit up while Yadav tried coaxing her back down. "Why would they be looking for her?"

"They said she's escaped and that several guards were dead as a result. Anyone found providing her refuge would be executed along with her," Mariam said, brows furrowed.

"Escaped?" Iravan asked, attempting to clear his throat and mind. He thought Anastasia had been leading the bloodstrippers. Charvi gasped, coming to the same realization he just had.

"They're going to come looking for us," Yadav said. "No one in the city will take her in, they know that. If she's out, they will think we are responsible. We need to move fast."

Yadav was right. Anastasia's only perceived allies were in this room. *Where is she now?* He couldn't imagine her outside, lost and dazed. Couldn't picture her sinking into the current of a crowd. He wondered if he'd still move to her like the tide, their souls drawn together by an invisible force. He slipped on his shoes, prepared to find out.

A muffled voice sounded beyond the wall, and his mouth went dry.

Iravan dropped to the ground and raised a hand. Everyone fell quiet as he peeked through the triangle of space between the curtains. There, right around Harshit's store, someone moved.

"It's too late," Iravan said, realization locking his bones. "They're already here."

Countless bloodstrippers poured around the walls like ants on a rotten piece of fruit.

"You are surrounded!" someone bellowed.

Baruna let out a low whimper, before Charvi slid her hand over her daughter's mouth. "If you hand over Anastasia Drakos, we will leave you in peace."

Liar. Iravan raised a finger to his lips and gestured to the rug. The trapdoor.

Dev nodded. Everyone else was statuesque as he slowly pulled the rug from the entrance and hopped inside.

"There is no Drakos here!" Yadav yelled, ignoring Iravan's furious gestures at him to stop talking. Yadav helped Charvi up, but she winced with each step. Baruna trembled behind them, clutching her mother's dress.

Doors rattled, the one to the back room and the one leading to the storefront. They were out of time.

"Why do you still protect her?" the guard called, his voice so close. "She left all of you. You can leave her to us."

"Go," Iravan whispered to Mariam, who was pressed against him. He drew his weapon and pointed to where Dev had disappeared. "All the way to the end. Dev should have scouted the path. Do not let him out of your sight."

He hoped Dev would be enough. Iravan didn't have enough bullets for every guard, but he would be damned if he didn't take out as many as he could.

Mariam gave him a jerky nod, then leaned in as though to say something else, when cries broke out above their heads. Iravan beat his gun in the air, telling her to *go*, and this time, she obeyed, crawling across the floor and toward the open trapdoor. The absence of her body against his was a shock to his system.

"Surrender!" someone called, their smooth Gehennese accent curling like a snake.

He was alone. This was how it would end.

Iravan took a steadying breath, mustering the courage needed for him to launch to his feet. But through the forest of furniture legs, he caught sight of Charvi's lower body still draped over the side of her cot, Yadav and Baruna by her side.

"What are you doing?" he asked, advancing toward the

family, stealth abandoned. Baruna was curled up on her mother's lap, face buried in Charvi's dress. Yadav stared into the distance, his arms around them both.

"Ravi, listen to me," Charvi said, giving him a watery smile. He'd known Charvi his whole life, and he'd seen that expression only twice. Once, when Yadav had nearly sent her away from Tejomaya, and it had taken both Dev and Iravan at the old man's doorstep, pleading for her to stay. The other time was right before she'd given birth, when the healer looked grave at the prospect of her surviving Baruna.

Iravan shook his head, arrested by a terrible feeling.

Charvi held Baruna's hand out. The girl was crying, snatching her wrist from her mother, clawing at her bosom. "You have to take her. You have to promise me you'll keep her safe. I won't—I won't make it."

"No," Iravan said, numbly, even as Charvi took his hand in a grip stronger than her state should've allowed. Baruna screamed, the sound tearing through the bloodstrippers' commotion.

"Baby," Charvi said, clutching her daughter's cheeks, eyes memorizing her face. "I'm so sorry. You have to go now."

Baruna was crying so hard she could barely breathe, and this was what broke Charvi entirely, tears rolling down her face.

Iravan looked at Yadav for support, but the man stayed quiet. Calm, even.

"They know I'm here, because I called out," Yadav said, level-headed as ever. "And when they find our bodies, they'll think we were the only ones here." He looked at his daughter. "And I'm not leaving her."

"No," Baruna cried, holding on to her mother. "Mama, please!"

This couldn't be happening.

"I can't leave you both." Iravan was a boy standing at Yadav's door, walking around in the merchant's large shoes. He was scouting flowers with Charvi, making fun of her as she plucked petals off the buds and wondered if the boy she loved loved her back. He was drinking with Yadav while Charvi held his daughter in her arms. Janmiris didn't have godparents; they had community, and community was family. Charvi and Yadav were more than blood.

Charvi shook him.

"Look at me," she implored, and he did. He couldn't see past her drooping skin, her bloodshot eyes, her parched lips. "I would have done the same for you."

The world fell into focus. She was right.

Iravan was witnessing a father following his daughter to the end and a mother willing to lose her child to ensure her a better future. The souls knew that if it were his daughter in this room, Charvi and Yadav would have done the same for him.

"Please," she pleaded, and that was his one regret, that he'd wasted so much time in despair that he could barely remember the good: the clever spark in Charvi's gaze, the smile lines around her mouth every time he made her laugh. "Go!"

"No!" Baruna screamed, her fingers knotted with her mother's.

Iravan snatched Baruna up. She kicked against his stomach, but the pain didn't compare to what was happening. His hand clapped over Baruna's mouth. She sobbed helplessly, her body convulsing so violently he wasn't sure she would stay in one piece. He wasn't sure he would.

The last thing he saw as he slid the trapdoor shut was Charvi and Yadav, hand in hand, their foreheads pressed together as one.

CHAPTER THIRTY-THREE

Anastasia

They left her in the meadows.

Strange, Anastasia hadn't known there were any meadows left. Something like grass susurrated beneath her, cool and sharp. And voices—there were so many voices talking over one another, begging, screaming. She wasn't sure what was real and what was a calor hallucination.

"We can't just leave her here, people will see," one of the dark figures said, voice familiar. She remembered the woman from the cell, comforting and warm. She sounded like Charvi. Anastasia wanted to tell her this, but when she tried, someone covered her mouth.

Another person responded, but Anastasia couldn't follow along. Water. She needed water. Her vision was fractured by black webs. Someone pressed a hand to her forehead.

". . . as good as dead," she heard. A man this time, and she wanted to protest his crude assessment. She wasn't dying; she still had desire. Surely, death would not come upon her when she had so much she still wanted. But no matter how much she tried to speak, no sound came out.

"I'm sorry," someone whispered. It was Charvi, but with a more youthful edge.

Stay, Anastasia wanted to say. How long had it been since she'd asked someone to stay with her? Ten years. But her silent plea went unheard. The footsteps padded away, leaving her under a cruel sky, a sliver of which filled the little she could see. It was going to rain.

Anastasia didn't know how long she lay there.

Ghostly arms held her down, pumping calor into her. It burned. She cried a little, forcing her body this way and that so fewer blades sliced her skin, so fewer fingers traced her veins and dug into her flesh.

She managed to crawl to her knees when someone approached.

"Oh." The woman had returned.

"Charvi?" Anastasia asked, knowing full well she was addressing a ghost. This person didn't know Charvi. Her vision remained marbled, but she felt the woman draw closer, heard a soft thump as she knelt next to Anastasia. No, this woman was not Charvi; she was shorter and broader, her grip uncertain. She helped Anastasia stand, and bristly hair tickled Anastasia's chin.

"Where are you taking me?"

"Somewhere safe."

Anastasia didn't have the energy to ask more questions. Maybe this woman was leading her to certain death, but there was something about her quiet reassurances, the long-obliterated feeling of being cared for, that made Anastasia relax.

"We have to climb a little now," the woman warned. A door

creaked open. The air grew heavier on the other side of the threshold, forcing Anastasia to take deep breaths as she was half carried up a staircase. The woman was Janmiri. She sounded so familiar, so much like her friend.

"Why are you helping me?" Anastasia asked.

"We're here," the woman said in response.

Another door swung open, and this time, Anastasia was hit by a wave of realization. There was wood beneath her bare feet, then a stiff carpet that crackled under her weight. She wished more than ever that she could see, confirm what she knew in her bones.

"Do you know what this place is?" Anastasia asked, hands clenching.

"Sit."

Anastasia had much to say about this woman's lack of conversation, but her knees buckled. She let out an embarrassing groan as she hit a rigid cushion.

"I know you from somewhere," Anastasia tried again. Something about her savior niggled at her consciousness. Charvi, but not Charvi. Tejomaya, but not Tejomaya now.

"I used to work for Dev," the woman said, hesitantly, pressing a glass of water into Anastasia's hand. It tasted stale, but she swallowed hungrily, her body a shriveled sponge. "I knew you when you were here. Before."

"Why have you not left with the others?"

"I have unfinished business here," the woman replied. "What did they do to you?"

"What do you think?"

Anastasia didn't care to recount how her flesh cooled when her clothes were stripped off her body. Chose not to recall how she'd bit down on her screams when they injected her with one vial, then another, then another just for fun, because she was a bitch who always wanted more. Refused to remember how hot her tears were while she'd lain there, alone, and realized this was all her life had come to.

"What do they want?" the woman asked.

Anastasia shrugged, fatigue setting over her. "Power, just like the rest," she said. *Like me,* she wanted to add, but if this woman knew her once, she knew this already. "They said they're looking for the calor reserve."

The woman cursed in Janmiri. "Then I must go."

Anastasia tried to sit up, but her elbows gave out. "To the reserve? Have you all gone mad?"

"Probably." More shuffling, the sound of cupboards opening and closing.

"Why?" Anastasia asked, blinking furiously. If only she could see more than a dull meld of colors, maybe she'd understand the insanity driving everyone to their deaths.

The woman stopped her rummaging. "Do you have any regrets, Ana?"

Anastasia had never understood regret. Regret implied the existence of two realities, when Anastasia knew full well the finality of time. It was resolute, immovable, and acceptance of this was the only possible way to live with herself. She shook her head.

"I do," the woman said, quietly. "I guess I'm trying to make it up to myself."

She draped a warm blanket over Anastasia. It smelled worn and old, but there was something familiar about it, like tired muscles stretching across a clean bed.

"Was helping me part of it?" Anastasia hedged, suddenly uneasy. This blanket, this room, this woman. "Am I one of your regrets?"

Silence, and if she'd heard the door open or close, she would have thought the woman had left. But then, she cleared her throat and said, gently, "Maybe we all need help sometimes."

"Wait," Anastasia said, but the quick patter of heels signaled the woman's rapid exit. The door closed her in with mounting realization.

She couldn't believe she was here, in her old apartment.

Very few people knew of its existence; even fewer knew of her relationship with it, what it had meant and held. She knew without looking that the Temple of Many-Souls lay outside, in ruins. This chawl was also on the edge of collapse, charred when the Temple went down. Had it been restored, or had the stranger delivered her to another death?

Anastasia's lungs burned from smoke that should have dissipated over a decade ago, and the memory of all that it had taken pierced her heart. Of all the thoughts that swarmed her mind, one crucial understanding took its place, front and center.

The woman knew far more about her than she'd let on, and Anastasia had let her go.

It took a long time before Anastasia's vision crept back. She should have slept, but the promise of tomorrow was as intangible as the ash that lay trapped between the folds of the past. She needed to see her old home.

The room looked exactly like Anastasia remembered it, slightly too narrow and far too dark, only a glimmer of light from the broken back window falling softly over worn floorboards. Cobwebs hung over corners haunted by memories. She couldn't look at the apartment for too long, or it would become too much to bear.

She had sworn not to return. Even on the day she'd left Tejomaya, she had not come there. She had taken what was on her person and boarded the boat to the island, Charvi and baby Baruna in tow, never looking back.

All she had allowed herself to remember over the years was the pain: her all-consuming grief, Charvi's tear-streaked face, a bawling baby in her arms as they raced toward a roiling sea and a land that hung within foreboding mist. Her father's horrified face as she fell at his feet. His rage as Matthieu relayed her betrayal. The vow she had made for vengeance against the people who had committed the worst crime yet—giving her love and then taking it away.

But that wasn't all that had occurred there. On the seat by the window, she had sat and read, watching passersby make their way toward the market, bags in hand. She had bellowed "Old Vicky" after a night at the tavern until everyone had yelled at her to shut up, faces glistening with rarefied joy. The friends she had embraced, the man she had loved, the child who had devoured her entire heart.

A displaced floorboard caught her eye, and her stomach fluttered. Had no one been there since that night? She swallowed the bitter lump in her throat and kicked the board aside. There, covered in a thick layer of dust and fine webs, was a tattered box.

For you to hold us forever.

The sudden recollection shredded her stupor, sending unexpected tears rolling down her face. This was too painful. She was already conjuring images of small footsteps around the stained mattress, feeling the warmth of a belly that rumbled with laughter. She opened the box, her fingers wet from wiping her cheeks, as she grazed the folded parchments that lay within.

My Ana,

The days when I would bare my soul on parchment are behind us, and while I love nothing more than to have you by my side, sometimes I miss slipping paper from hand to hand, sitting here with the desperate hope that my words reach you. I can tell you and show you and love you every second of the day, but you know me. I like to commemorate us, to leave a mark so that one day, when we are gone, our ashes intermingled for all of eternity, someone may come across our love and find one of the few pure things to still exist in this world. Neither you nor I are pure, nor will we ever be, but what we have created proves that broken people can be whole together.

You often jest that I am incapable of poetry, and I wholeheartedly deny your allegations. I see your challenge, and, my love, you know how much I adore showing you what I can do.

Looking at you lying here now, your hair falling across your cheek, I am more certain than ever that you complete me. Your eyes hold both the softness of the night and the allure of shadows. Your touch is the comfort of candlelight and the thrill of a dark, roiling ocean under the slimmest blade of moonlight. You are love and wrath alike, and I covet every inch of you.

Anastasia gasped, the tears free flowing as she set the parchment down, unable to read further. Her heart threatened to crack in half. She crumpled the paper and tossed it to the corner of the room, then gathered her knees to her chest. She didn't know how long she stayed there, but by the time she unwound from the fetal position, she knew she couldn't remain any longer. This home belonged to an Anastasia that had ceased to exist.

She considered burning the letters, but something stayed her hand. They told only part of a painful story, but the writer had also left in there a vital truth. If anyone found the letters days, years, or decades later, perhaps it would tell them the lie they needed to hear. That, somehow, love persisted through tragedy, even when it burned.

She would grant them that small mercy, Anastasia decided, and hope they never uncovered the truth.

CHAPTER THIRTY-FOUR

Zain

Zain hobbled up the rickety flight of stairs.

She hadn't been up there in years, not since the chawl had shut down following the fire. Only Iravan remained in his lonely hut, a watchman over the graveyard. The building hadn't been badly burned, and people lived in less-stable structures these days, but Tejomayans were all too happy to deem it cursed and leave it to haunt the city with its crushing memories.

As she stepped onto the roof, her heart caught midbeat. Theron paced near the parapet, stopping when she accidentally kicked a piece of shattered glass.

He had levied an impressive array of loathing looks in her direction as he carried Anastasia to her old apartment. The city was decomposing around them. At least everyone else had been too busy plotting their own escape to linger on a bloodstripper lugging an unconscious Gehennese woman through the Bow. After Theron unceremoniously dumped the woman on a strip of grass just before reaching the Temple, he'd disappeared. Zain had heard him stomping across the paper-thin roof. She wasn't sure when she'd learned to recognize the sound of his footsteps, when they'd started to draw her toward him like grief to a prayer.

"What the hell were you thinking?" he asked. He'd shed his bloodstripper jacket, his black shirt hiking up his body as he ran his fingers through his hair in frustration.

Her bones felt so weary, so fragile. "What is it now?"

Theron strode to her, broad hands closing around her shoulders. She prepared for pain where his fingers pushed into her skin, but it didn't come. He held her like she was made of sand, and he looked at her the same way, scanning every inch of her face.

"What is it now?" he repeated, falling into smooth and angry Gehennese. "What it is is that we agreed to *you* escaping the quarters while I created a distraction, and then you decided to play hero and kidnap the bloodstrippers' prisoner!"

"*They* kidnapped *her!*" Zain cried in Janmiri, growing agitated. "Did you see what they were doing to her? No one should be—"

"Do you know what half the people in this city endure every day?" Theron yelled, gesturing around them. "You can't be saving everyone! Did you stop and think for a second? That they might see right through me and now have Leander in their possession?"

Zain's head rang as though he'd taken a bat to it. "I'm sorry," she said. Zain stepped back, the sky groaning like it was sick of their shit too.

The faces in her head grew clearer, more menacing. More accusing. Each time she tried to save one, another appeared. She couldn't add to the endless list. She sped toward the stairs.

"Where are you going?" Theron asked, his hand closing around her wrist. "You can't just run back there and get Leander out. Do you have no sense of self-preservation?"

"I can't let him get hurt," she said. Through her tears, Theron was nothing but a blur, and that was for the best. She didn't want to see the disappointment, the disgust. Her head drooped low, and a tear fell to the ground, staining the soiled cement.

"I told him to get out," Theron said, and Zain snapped her head up as the skies released its first drops onto the city.

"What?" Zain asked in disbelief. Theron pressed her backward, but she didn't budge.

"I knew you would do something stupid," he said. "I told Leander to hide in the Sickle, right before I went to find Matthieu. He left under the pretense of conducting more research about the reserve."

The reality of his words hit her. "You just—" she stammered. "You *lied* to—"

"I lied because you can't seem to see how stupid your actions are when they endanger you!" Theron said. The ground disappeared beneath her feet, and it took a moment for her to realize he had picked her up. He set her against the wall, under the eaves and away from the rain that beat his shoulders.

"By the souls, Zain." His voice broke on her name, her heart twinging at his curse. The fire in his eyes softened, and she could see a shadow of herself in them. His hand grazed her chin. "Do you find yourself so difficult to love?"

She couldn't look at anything but his face. Even in the dim red light, she could make out the blood and the mud that caked his hair, highlighting his scar. He had found his mark, and she couldn't stop the tears. Their breaths filled the space between them.

His hand cupped her face, thumb wiping a tear from her cheek. It left a blazing trail, and she was too hot, but she needed more. Zain tugged his shirt, pulling him in.

"You shouldn't be in the rain either," she said, as he closed the distance between them.

"For once," he murmured, "can you stop telling me what to do?"

Against a violent backdrop, his gaze held hers. He was standing so very still. In the shadows, the scruff on his cheeks looked dark. She reached up on her toes and brushed her lips on his neck, right where his pulse beat, a solid rhythm in a crumbling world.

Theron's breath hitched, an abrupt call to reality. She dropped onto her heels, regret setting in like a shock of calor. The souls damn the wall behind her, because she couldn't run, but how was she supposed to look at him when she'd just *assumed* and . . .

"I'm sorry," she sputtered. "I don't know why I—"

Then his lips were on hers, and it was nothing like she could have expected. Theron was gentle where she thought he'd be rough, ravenous where she'd imagined him unmoving. His touch had been different lately, cautious. But there was nothing careful about it now. His hands wrapped around the back of her neck, holding her face in place as he kissed her deeply.

A siren shrieked in the distance, but Theron drew back only an inch. His lips brushed featherlike across her cheek. Though the earth cracked beneath them and the air threatened to set ablaze, Zain was grateful that in her last moments, she might finally learn to breathe deeply. She wasn't sure when they had reached this point. It may have started when he'd taken the gun from her hand after the mist, or in the coffin earlier that night. It might have started earlier. Maybe how it started didn't matter, but the souls knew she didn't want it to end.

The building jolted beneath them, and this time, Theron stepped back. His hand stayed on her waist, but he looked away, worry creasing his brow. The rain was falling harder now, and puffs of white smoke unfurled where the drops crashed into the ground. As the sky rumbled in earnest, she knew they had run out of time. Anastasia was still below, in what condition she didn't know, but that was no longer her concern. She had done her part, and what mattered most lay ahead.

"We have to go," Theron said, reading her mind. They weaved between the banisters until they arrived at the exit. Her heart raced at the sight of his bloodstained back, but she quelled her fears. There was a chance neither of them would survive long enough to contend with the effects of the calor.

"Leander first?" she asked, looking upon the city from above one last time. The sky's spindles had thickened that evening, enmeshing its dark canvas in a sickly red. The city sprawled below her in clusters of dark structures and empty spaces, with rare floating lights revealing precious signs of life.

"Yes, but what then?" Theron asked.

What then? The question she had been grappling with, the answer she'd known all along. The bloodstrippers knew of the reserve, and she was in a race against the clock.

"I have to end this," she said, searching for the blurred island in the distance, before telling him everything else.

"I'll come with you," Theron said, to her utter dismay. "And this is not up for debate."

"You should get out of here," she argued, halfheartedly.

"We started this together," Theron said. "Do not insult me by leaving me out now."

She swallowed her protest, sinking into his side. He held his hand above her head while they walked through the rain.

Leander was waiting for them at the Sickle, huddled under the narrow awning of the dilapidated chawl. "What are you two doing?" he hissed when he took in their blood-soaked appearance. "The last boats leave the harbor in less than an hour. I thought you'd been caught, I thought—"

He fell into Zain's arms, and she accepted his embrace without thinking. A powerful wave of protectiveness swept through her as he erupted into erratic sobs. She met Theron's eyes over his brother's shoulders and knew he was thinking precisely the same as she was. Leander would not be part of this.

"There is still time," Zain lied, guiding him along the alley and down to the harbor. Already, they could hear the cries of the departing, boats spilling over the edges with people desperate to leave.

"This way," Theron said, directing them toward a boat that was so full, it teetered dangerously on the water. There was no way they would take more than one passenger, if that, from the glare the conductor was sending their way.

"We can't go in that one," Leander said, searching for alternatives, but Theron kept walking. "Theron," Leander protested. "What are you doing?"

"Get on, Leander," Theron said, ignoring the curious passengers watching them, the conductor wisely keeping silent at the sight of Leander's uniform.

Leander looked like he'd been slapped. "No! I'm not going—I don't know what the hell you're thinking, but—"

"Okay, okay," Theron interrupted, pinching the bridge of his nose. "I'm sorry."

A resounding crack splintered as he pistol-whipped his brother on the side of his head, knocking Leander out cold. Zain caught his limp body before he fell. They guided an unconscious Leander onto the boat, the passengers giving them a wide berth.

"He is half Urjan," Zain pleaded, as though it would assuage their concerns about a Gehennese bloodstripper onboard. "Take care of him."

The conductor had the wits to nod.

"Where does this boat go?" Theron asked.

"The coasts of Urjan," the conductor said.

Leander was going home.

CHAPTER THIRTY-FIVE

Iravan

Gunfire echoed through the tunnels.

Iravan kept one foot in front of the other. Baruna bit into his calloused palms, her soft cheeks covered in tears. He wondered if the image of her mother and grandfather was seared into her mind the way it was in his.

He didn't dare let go until they reached the exit. He set Baruna down, unsure what to expect from the girl, too afraid to look. The door clicked open, and he ushered her out to find Mariam and Dev on opposite sides of the hideout, both rising abruptly at his entrance.

"What . . . ," Mariam trailed off.

"Where is Yadav?" Dev asked. He read the answer on Iravan's face.

Baruna didn't cry. She stood still as stone in front of him, her thin arms wrapped around her torso. Iravan gently placed his hands on her shoulder. She flinched.

Mariam knelt in front of the girl, and Iravan took a grateful step back. This was too much. He had torn a child away from her family, and was now responsible for her well-being. No one had trusted Iravan Khotar with a child in the past ten years, and for good reason. He hadn't even been able to take care of his own.

No one had known that better than Charvi, and still she had pressed her daughter to him with such undeserved faith.

Charvi had thought she was doing the best thing for her daughter, but time and time again, Iravan wished he could take the place of the people he'd lost. The real punishment was being the one left behind. Living after the dust settled, when nothing would ever look the same.

"What now?" Dev asked. He had been quietly watching, face grim. Iravan shook his head. He was out of plays, out of answers. He had one purpose now—to make sure the child in front of him found a life worth living.

For the first time, he admitted that maybe the battle for Tejomaya couldn't be won. Maybe the city was begging them to leave. As much as it hurt, they could start anew elsewhere, and the thought loosened the decades-long knots in his chest.

"What's this in your hand?" Mariam asked, holding Baruna's arm up. Clutched in the girl's fist was a scrap of paper, badly scrunched but not torn. No matter how hard she tried, Mariam couldn't get Baruna to open her fist. The child was frozen.

"Here," Iravan said. He plucked his coin out of his pocket and held it to her. "I'll trade you for this."

Baruna's eyes glazed over.

"Do you see this? It has the sun and the mountain on it," Iravan said, shakily, running his finger along the outline. "It's a special coin. I got it the day my daughter was born. We called her Surya, for the sun."

Still nothing.

"This coin reminds me of her, but actually, your mother gave it to me."

A father now, Ravi! Here's a gift, Charvi had said, handing him the rusted coin. She'd pickpocketed some Geng at the underground market, and the beautiful inscription gifted Surya her name.

A boy's name, Yadav had said, but it didn't matter. Iravan had liked the way it sounded, the soft vowels an open-ended question, a name filled with a future.

"You can keep it now," Iravan said, swallowing the lump in his throat.

Dev and Mariam were watching him, but he didn't break eye contact with Baruna, whose expression lit with awareness. She looked between the coin and his face before taking it from him. Her other fist relaxed and dropped the paper to the ground.

Mariam beat him to it, picking up the note. Her eyebrows furrowed, a mirror image of Dev, who looked over her shoulder.

"Who gave this to you?" Mariam asked, this time more insistently.

"Baba," Baruna whispered.

Yadav.

"What does it say?" Iravan asked, and Mariam held the note out to him.

Dev cut in. "Wait, I couldn't read—"

"'Don't go to the island,'" Mariam said. Then, "What is on the island?"

Iravan snatched the note from her, scouring the hastily scribbled lines. Would Yadav have left them anything revolutionary in his last moments?

"Well, that's not going to happen," Dev said, peering at the note over Iravan's shoulder.

"What is on the island, Iravan?" Mariam repeated. She was too smart not to figure it out. Her mouth parted as realization dawned on her. "You should have told me."

"I didn't know what you would do with the information," he said, but it sounded like a bitter lie.

"You fool," Mariam said, getting to her feet. "It's going to be too late now. Far too late. We all have to get away from Tejomaya."

"I thought you wanted to destroy the reserve," Iravan reminded her.

"Not destroy it that way," Mariam said, wringing her hands. "My theory is it's the reserve that's causing all the issues in Tejomaya. It's not just calor underground that is a problem; it's calor in large concentrations, anywhere. It's becoming more and more unstable. I wanted to find a way to release the pressure, but all my research has been focused on the soil composition of the city. I don't know enough about the island."

Dev was unperturbed. "We could siphon the calor, relieve the pressure, and replenish our supplies. Wouldn't that work? We could restore the city's power, get everything back in order, and bring our people back."

"Or help set up a new home," Iravan amended. Dev shot him a warning look.

Mariam hesitated. "In theory, yes. But it is still too risky. We don't know how much calor is in there. All this will depend on the concentration, on where it's trapped. Yadav and I discussed this before, and I think he knew—"

Dev waved her off. "We have what we need. No point changing our plans based on a senile man who couldn't even tell us what he'd learned while he was still kicking around."

"That man just died," Mariam said, coldly. "You would do

well to respect those who have passed, Devraj. And my guess is that if he didn't tell you, it's because he didn't think you would do the right thing."

"Oh really?" Dev asked, a mocking grin carving his face into something monstrous. He stepped toward her, his fingers hooked in his belt loops, and said, "And what is it you think I'll do?"

Mariam pushed Baruna behind her and met Dev's eyes. "You think you are so difficult to read," she said, with a hint of pity that Iravan knew would send Dev spiraling. "You are but a greedy boy who has searched his entire life for power. You—"

It happened quickly. Dev raised his hand to strike her, but Iravan's arm shot out, blocking the blow. His shoulder rammed into Mariam, who stumbled back in shock. Her glasses fell off, clattering against the wall of the tunnel but drowned out by Baruna's cry.

"What the fuck, Dev?" Iravan roared, assessing Mariam. She stared at the ground with a whisper of a smile.

"You men," she said. "Such cowards in the face of truth."

"You fucking bitch," Dev said, but Iravan held him back. He was still reeling from Charvi and Yadav, hadn't yet processed the note, and he couldn't handle this right then.

He elbowed Dev back a step. "Stop it."

Mariam took Baruna's hand in hers. "I will be taking her with me. We are going to find an evening boat to Urjan and leave this godsforsaken city." She looked at Iravan as she added, "I will not wait for you."

It was only after they left that Iravan questioned the certainty with which she'd known what his decision would be, before he had known it himself.

I have watched men rise and fall like leaves on wind. I will not be the air that softens the blow.

He had flouted the sentiment when she'd said that, wondering at the weakness of men unable to stand on their own. But right then, he felt the cold hard ground threatening to crush his knees.

CHAPTER THIRTY-SIX

Anastasia

U nbidden thoughts.

It didn't matter that it was raining, that she was soaked to the bone in poison, not when Anastasia was unreachable within herself.

The letter had only been the beginning. Then came the phantom touches, the faint laughter, the foolish flirting of her past with its rancid underbelly. She couldn't remain in that apartment any longer. She made a hurried exit, her hip slamming into the doorframe, and the remnants of the bloodstrippers' work tore her insides. Outside . . . she just had to get outside . . .

The city had fallen apart.

People jammed the streets, parents dragging their crying children behind them, muscled youth leading the charge through thickening crowds. She had never seen this many people outside before. She recognized slum-dwellers mingling with denizens of the Hammer, merchants and common people alike, with one unified goal: to leave. Anastasia ducked her head when a fight broke out to her right, grateful that her bloody state and the ensuing chaos granted her some semblance of cover.

Bloodstrippers knocked down the door to a ground-level home and pulled out a shrieking woman, her bare legs exposed under torn clothes.

"Please," she cried. "You already looked here earlier. They didn't find anyone, I swear they didn't—"

"Shut up," one of the bloodstrippers said, leering. The woman sobbed uncontrollably, and the man shook her until her teeth rattled. "Our reports say she was here. If we find out even one of you was harboring Anastasia Drakos, we will burn all your homes to the ground."

Anastasia froze in her tracks, wishing for the first time that she was smaller. She slipped away, to the one place she could count on whenever she was in trouble. The door clicked open with suspicious ease, and she was inside Yadav's shop.

Anastasia fumbled in the dark. Low calor meant no power, but she located a spare candle that she knew the man always left by the door, shivering at how strangely cold it was. Matthieu had called it a raid, but the term was too tame for what they'd done to the place. The door to the back room hung from rusted hinges, shattered glass littered the floorboards, and jagged edges of wood stuck up ominously from where furniture had been cracked in half.

She searched helplessly for the few items of value, knowing already that the jade locket she had occasionally worn would be missing from atop the now-crumbled chest, which was smashed on the floor of the storefront. Yadav's meticulously curated coin collection was lost to pillage, tearing something from her even though she never concerned herself with sentimental objects. It wasn't just the material worth but the stories behind them, the memories that would be left to fade until her recollections were stained.

In all the destruction, it took her too long to smell the blood.

The windows had been left open, allowing the sky's most recent curse to fall onto the floorboards. Yadav would be mortified, but it was clear they weren't home. Still, she felt as though she wasn't quite alone, and when she swerved the creaking, broken door to enter the back room with the secret trapdoor, the light nearly fell from her hands.

She did not rush to the bodies. She did not turn them over.

One wrapped around another in an embrace.

She bent to see if there was a third body, a fourth, a fifth, and felt vile at the kernel of relief that emerged. Under her feet and to her back were bullet holes and collecting pools of blood.

Eventually, when the blood had soaked her heels and her fingers had traced the same divots in the wood more times than she could count, she walked over to them.

That looks like Dev with a bad haircut, Charvi had once said, as they lay shoulder to shoulder on the roof of her apartment, drunk from the tavern, tracing pictures in the sky's crude veins.

It does not, Anastasia had replied, snorting, and they'd burst into laughter.

Promise me we'll always be friends, Anastasia had hedged in a moment of rare vulnerability.

Charvi had smiled. *On Amu's ashes, Ana.*

The woman lying in front of her was not the one in Anastasia's memory. Anastasia's mouth flooded with bile, and she wrapped an arm around her aching stomach, floundering for breath.

Should she part them? Bury them? She settled for closing their eyes, first father, then daughter, their bodies already cold and hard. At least Baruna had gotten out.

Anastasia could barely see through her tears as she shuffled through the mess of papers on the floor, dizzy and uncoordinated. She didn't know what she was looking for, but there had to be a reason why things had ended this way. Most of the paper was unreadable, torn or blood-soaked. Worse, she knew anything worthwhile had likely been taken by Matthieu and his men. Heart in her throat, she slid an arm into Charvi's and Yadav's pockets, then remembered Yadav's advice from long before.

Anything of value, you keep in your shoe.

In this one instance, he would not mind. Yadav's ankles were stiff in death, but after some jostling, she pulled off his loafers, held his foot, and felt it. A piece of parchment tucked in the arch of his sock. She slid it off and pulled out a folded paper, one edge serrated as though torn from another half.

Reserve—on the island? Calor there is dangerous.

The world ground to a halt. Of all the times Anastasia had listened to talks of a reserve, she had imagined it in Tejomaya. Never on the island. She hadn't believed such a secret could remain uncovered, not when they'd explored every corner of the isle.

Another moment, another interrupted memory. The woman who had brought her to her apartment.

Calor there is dangerous.

She certainly knew it now. The injections had drained her, and the few stimulative benefits were the only thing keeping her upright. It wouldn't be long before she collapsed.

That woman had gone to find the reserve. She had responded to the news of the bloodstrippers' search with the same keen desperation that Anastasia now felt to find her. No one had ever saved Anastasia. No one but this stranger.

Am I one of your regrets?

This woman was not a stranger, but Anastasia couldn't put a finger on it. What a strange thread of kinship, heavy with debt.

She slumped against the only wall uncoated by blood, her teeth chattering as the assault on her body continued. Her fate was sealed, no matter what. Anastasia had spent years thinking she had nothing left to lose, but there was always one final cost, one last trade-off. Life had a way of taking, but for the first time, she was prepared to give.

Power had only stolen from her. It was stripping her of her body, mind, and soul. She was dwindling, the world was moving on, and everything she had pursued was revealing itself to be superficial at best, lethal at worst. In the absence of power, at least she'd had her father, her friend, her lover, her heart. She would die and leave no trace. There was no one left to remember, except for the stranger who'd saved her. That woman still had a life to live, and maybe Anastasia could repay her.

The bloodstrippers would be watching the harbor, ensuring she didn't leave the city with anyone, but there was one thing they wouldn't be checking for. Anastasia traced the curve of Charvi's face. It felt right somehow that her friend would be the last person she touched before she committed her first and only act of bravery.

She could feel Charvi smiling upon her now.

"Did you find that place?" she asked Charvi, remembering the times they had mocked the place beyond the fallen skies, the mythical existence of peace. She never thought Charvi would get there first, and looking at Yadav, her heart broke for a father who had to see it happen. Still, there was some comfort in knowing they had been together. That he'd held her hand as they walked over the threshold.

Maybe her final act would be enough to earn her a place with the souls of the people she loved. She smiled then, sweeping a strand of hair across Charvi's face and tucking it behind her ear.

I'll see you soon.

CHAPTER THIRTY-SEVEN

Iravan

In the thick Tejomayan heat, Iravan discovered that cold did exist, a deceptive layer coating the rough Soulless Sea.

He stood on one end of the old fisherman's boat while Dev manned the bow. They hadn't spoken much since Mariam had left with Baruna. At the harbor, people had bustled around them in droves, littering into boats and carts to depart somewhere far, far away. Even those like Yadav, the ones who had sworn to never leave the soil on which they had bled, understood that their options were limited.

Iravan wanted to start anew, but Dev wanted to wring the city for all it was worth. And then there was that look in Dev's eye—a flash of fury that had always been there, stoked into something quite mad. Dev needed his friend to stay anchored, and so Iravan had agreed. One last time.

"It's strange, isn't it?" Dev asked, his shoulders rising with deep, steady breaths. "We always said we would find a way to leave, and now that everyone is leaving, we're staying." He let out a cold laugh. "Always the sacrificial lambs."

Iravan stiffened. "You wanted to stay," he said, slowly. "This was your idea, to siphon more power from the island, to relieve the calor pressure and replenish our own supplies. To restore the city. We could have taken the boat with Mariam and Baruna."

"The last place I go is with that cunt," Dev said, indignantly. "But the same can't be said for you. You always did have a thing for the defiant ones, didn't you? The rest of us have never been good enough for you. Even now, when we're on the verge of getting everything we've ever wanted, all the power, you're thinking about her."

Iravan was getting really damn tired of everyone thinking they knew him. "What the fuck are you talking about?"

"You switched on me!" Dev bellowed. The boat rocked under his feet as he strode toward Iravan. The mist between them was soft, damp, and white, and even though Iravan could feel Dev's warmth, they felt miles apart.

Dev continued.

"We were supposed to be in this together, but I practically had to drag you away from that woman and child. The Iravan I knew would have beaten me to the boat, but these last few years . . . You've barely done a thing since Surya died, and I've had to rely on Hamish fucking Drakos."

A hum began in the back of Iravan's head, reverberating through his skull.

Dev read his shock and laughed. "And you hadn't even noticed."

Dev and Hamish Drakos. *Hamish?* All that time Iravan had sat in his room, grateful his brother was taking care of the city when he could barely care for himself, Dev had been dallying with the Council.

"How long?" he asked, feeling the groundwork beneath him

crumble until he was weightless, drifting. The boat teetered under their weight. Beyond Dev's shoulder, the fog-garlanded island crept toward them. Iravan reached in his pocket for the coin out of habit and came up empty.

"Years now," Dev said. "How do you think we kept the bloodstrippers from wiping us out those first few years when you turned into a hermit? I handed over most of our calor. He promised not to wipe us out. Dheera was in on it too, and sometimes she gave me more to make sure her family stayed safe. There was a steep price to our survival, and I'm the one who's had to pay it."

"You could have told me," Iravan said. He knew he had withdrawn, but he never would have expected Dev to turn to the Gengs.

"It was like talking to a ghost," Dev said, holding Iravan's shoulders. "But you're back now. And we have an opportunity here. I'm asking you just to do this with me, Ravi. There is no calor anywhere else. With the reserve, we could build back our city to be more powerful than any on the Upper Tectonic. We would have leverage, influence; they'd have to listen to us for a change. We could take over the world."

And there it was again, that kernel of familiar madness. He had backed Dev through many a dangerous plan, and now the depths of his betrayal were too dark to see through. Over the years, Iravan had faced many terrifying things, but this— this fright, of no longer recognizing the person in front of him— chilled him to the bone.

"There is no world to take over," Iravan said, quietly.

Dev contemplated him, disappointment and rage warring on his face. "And I don't need you to do this with me."

In that moment, Iravan wished he had taken Baruna's other hand and left with her and Mariam. He could knock Dev out, but they were almost to the island.

The boat slowed, the water parting to allow it into the port. The sky rippled above them, as though in acknowledgment, in welcome. They stepped onto soil, true Janmiris reclaiming the Isle of Vis, the lost heart of Tejomaya.

Dev was right about one thing—he had been there for the city when Iravan hadn't. This madness had infected him in Iravan's absence, and he wouldn't abandon his brother now. Maybe the answer didn't lie with Mariam or Dev, but somewhere in between. Maybe this was something only he could see.

For Yadav. For Charvi. For Bilal. For Surya. For the countless people whose blood had led to his very position. For the thousands who had died. He wouldn't condemn everyone else to their fate. He would take the reserve and flee, build a new world. A safe one. There would be no more destruction.

His ghosts swarmed him, urging him forward.

The power of the fallen skies had always belonged to them. It was time to see if the land remembered.

CHAPTER THIRTY-EIGHT

Anastasia

A nastasia had spent many years on the island, but it had never felt the way it did now.

Perhaps it was comparable to the time she'd fled Tejomaya. But truth be told, she didn't remember that night, and she had done everything in her power not to stir those memories. They were a key to the person she had become, a person she no longer wanted to be.

One moment, she was with Charvi and Baruna, rushing to get the little girl help from the bloodstripper quarters, the only place with the medication she needed for her failing lungs. The next second, the city was in commotion, all racing toward a deadly fire that marked the first of many tumultuous evenings.

Unlike that night, Anastasia arrived back on the Isle of Vis with clear eyes and an even clearer head. Her emotions were dulled, no longer obfuscating her intent.

Anastasia steered the boat to a port beyond the closest harbor, away from anyone who might have already been there. She pulled up the hem of her skirt and stepped quickly on the dock.

The waters were eerily still, and the boat remained where she left it, serving as witness while she surveyed the city through the fog. The sounds of people fleeing the mainland floated across the sea, and she wondered if the island wanted to call back to the city. A piece of land that she had, in some ways, played a role in keeping away from its main body.

By the time Anastasia made it to her destination, the abandoned shed where Charvi had worked, she was gasping for air. The calor was still working a systematic assault, long overpowering the little adrenaline she'd mustered on the mainland. Now, she wasn't sure if she could make it back.

Do you ever just stop to think? Charvi's ghost mocked in Hamish's voice.

Something crumpled in her, and she toppled backward, her elbows bearing the brunt of the blow. It was as Anastasia crawled to her knees, assessing her forearms for any damage, that she realized the ground beneath her had swollen.

Janmiris spoke of the land as though it was alive. After all, when the sky possessed a mercurial spirit, why should the earth not have a disposition of its own? While Anastasia had thought of it as a metaphor, a vague gesture of respect to the land they had ravaged, she was less sure now, after all she had seen. After the trees had turned violent.

And the land beneath her *breathed.*

Anastasia lurched to her feet, arms pinwheeling as she sought balance. She forced herself still, measuring the lift of the ground, gentle but discernible. She was standing on the belly of a sleeping beast, and she wasn't sure how much longer it would remain dormant.

The strange woman was nowhere to be found. Anastasia hobbled past the molten forest, toward the houses, searching for movement, sound, any proof that the person for whom she'd taken such a foolhardy risk was there. But the island was a ghost town, and the only hearts that beat were hers and the land.

She had to get out of that place, immediately.

Anastasia raced to the boat, her feet protesting every step. She leaped into the back, cursing as she fumbled for the vial of calor she had packed for the return trip. It was nowhere to be found. Her heart thudded violently. She studied the island, as though a giant would rise to its feet if she looked hard enough

She'd row away herself if she had to.

Gritting her teeth, she leaped off the boat and ran back to the toolshed, winded. There had to be something there, wood or metal, anything narrow and sharp to steer her back. As she shuffled through the hoard of supplies Charvi had accumulated over the years, she tripped over something small and soft. Glass cracked beneath her feet.

Anastasia's palms tore open when she fell, and she hissed as pain shot through her bone. Her ankle was still caught on something, a bag. The opening was loose and parted with ease. She dove in, hungry to assess its contents.

For once, fortune was on her side. Despite the ground gurgling, she smiled at the calor injections in her hands.

She remembered Varun leaving something in the shed and his quick departure when Anastasia had arrived. They must have stored extras there prior to the attack, and it was certainly enough to get her back to Tejomaya. In some cruel, twisted way, her friend's soul was watching out for her.

Exhilarated, Anastasia almost didn't pick up on the voices.

People were there.

Carefully, she stepped outside the shed, then made her way to the rocky knoll, which had a better view of the docks. Two figures climbed out of a boat, engaged in some sort of volatile argument.

"Try and stop me," one yelled, and her heart sank.

Iravan and Dev walked onto the Isle of Vis. She watched as Iravan tipped his head back, remembering with an ache his old declarations.

One day, I will go there, he always said about the Isle of Vis.

You did, Ravi, she thought to herself. Once, she would have savored this reunion, savored watching him fall apart. But they were both losers in this war, and there was nothing left to fight for. All she felt was an overwhelming sadness, a bitter regret that she didn't have more time to do this. To talk to him.

She considered warning them of the island's strange ways, but they were grown men well acquainted with the dangers of Tejomaya. They would find their own path.

Still, her pulse quickened as the conversation between the men violated the sanctimonious quiet, Dev's voice harsh as ever, Iravan's worn and leathered.

They wouldn't be alone much longer.

CHAPTER THIRTY-NINE

Zain

Zain stiffened as a loosely tied boat emerged from the milky fog, bobbing near the port. A floating jeer, a reminder that others shared in their goal. The question was who was roaming the land ahead of them, and whether they were friend or foe.

It had been easier than expected to find a spare boat for their journey, Tejomayan superstition prevailing. Several messenger boats had lain abandoned along the harbor. Ever since the uprising on the island, no one who claimed the city would go anywhere near them. Zain had held Theron's hand the entire way through the mist, grateful for his quiet acceptance. At no point had he dissuaded her from her plan, despite its sheer lunacy. Looking back at the impenetrable fog, she wondered if that was what it looked like when one fell off the edge of the world.

"Have you been here before?" Zain dared whisper.

"No, I am destined to visit the places of my nightmares with you," he deadpanned.

Zain rolled her eyes. "I'm not the one who pulled us into a

coffin. Kanak would clutch their heart and insist I cleanse myself or risk falling soul-sick."

"If soul-sickness were a real matter, I'd imagine we would be bedridden by now," he replied, mouth quirking in a small smile. His bloodstained clothes were wet to the touch. "I was given the opportunity to guard the Council. I said no."

She tried not to look surprised. A position on the island was coveted among bloodstrippers. "Leander?"

"He would have had to stay behind. Besides, I was never interested in this," he said, pointing at his uniform. "I came for Leander, and part of me hoped I'd find meaning here. That maybe we'd find a way to Urjan. It sounds ridiculous, I know."

"It doesn't," Zain said. "Leander is on his way now, so maybe the souls listened. With any luck, you'll join him."

"Did Kanak and Samiah go there as well?" Theron asked, ignoring how she left herself out of the future.

Zain nodded. She missed them so much.

"Tell me about them," Theron said, like he could feel her nerves tearing her up, the unbearable anticipation building as they drew closer to shore.

"All I want is to plant a rose garden with them," Zain said. "Kanak had gotten rose seeds for us to grow together, but we ran out of time. We met that way, you know? In a garden. I had a nasty experience with some bullies, and Kanak found me behind the grove, destroying the Temple's plot. Kicking up soil, tearing down the tender shoots that were fighting for life. What a nightmare."

"Some things don't change," Theron said, morosely.

Zain scowled, lightly elbowing him. "I thought they were going to beat me, so I ran away. But the next thing I knew, they delivered seeds to my door. Night after night. They never said anything to me, and one day, I grew bored and tried planting some outside my dormitory door. Obviously, they didn't grow, and eventually, I went to them for help. Their smile was the widest I had ever seen."

"Not a lot of people like that anymore," Theron said.

Zain shook her head emphatically. "Not even one other person. I wanted to be like them. But I'm not built that way, I've hurt too many people."

Theron considered her words, rubbing a hand along his jaw. "I think you set your emotions and actions on too narrow a path. Violence can heal as much as it can hurt; it can come from a place of love as much as anger. The day Kanak left the Temple with you was a day they'd committed violence. Not the same kind you've endured, but they tore away from tradition. You are more alike than you think."

Zain inhaled sharply. "I thought you said you had a hard time with words."

Theron sputtered, before breaking into a low chuckle. Zain couldn't recall the last time she'd heard laughter. She joined him on instinct, both succumbing to their fits until she was wiping tears. It was bizarre, unearthing joy when everything felt so dire, but she contemplated what he'd said about violence and love and wondered if she'd spent too long drawing meaningless lines in the sand.

He squeezed her waist, and she added, quietly, "Thank you."

Fog swirled as they entered the port, their boat docking next to another one that lay abandoned.

"This won't stay anchored here for long," Theron said. Whoever had abandoned the boat hadn't even tied a knot, instead winding the rope's end around the dock cleat a handful of times. It was quickly loosening, the current pulling the boat from its hold. Zain wondered if all things were meant to come apart, if the owner of the deserted boat even intended to return. Maybe they had the right idea, she thought, as Theron tethered their boat to the dock with a firm, thick loop, then headed into the darkness. False hopes were boats expecting to carry people home; false promises were the anchors unraveling under their own weight.

They walked onto the island in shared silence. Zain waited to see if she would feel different, if there would be a jolt of power or *knowing*. She could have sworn the land below her breathed. She waited to see if it would swell under her feet again, but the ground felt unremarkable, disappointingly normal. They both drank in the island.

The Isle of Vis had been a rich, verdant land that had turned hard and cold, a stone jungle hosting souls as icy as it had become. There was a certain discomfort that came with unveiling something so phantasmagoric, seeing whether it would live up to its legend.

"What happened to the stone forest?" Theron asked, eyeing the central mass of the island as they approached, which looked less like a cluster of trees and more like a deformed mountain. Zain knew for a fact that was not what it was supposed to look like. She had heard Anastasia Drakos describe it one too many times back in the day, when Zain would hang around the slums, hoping to be near Dev, and ended up eavesdropping on the Gehennese woman's conversations.

She approached the edge of the mass, squinting at the mangled edges of rock, and something caught her eye.

"On my soul," Zain whispered. "Is that a *hand*?"

Tatters of cloth were crushed between the ridges, shards of

bone and skin scattered in the pools of its fabric. There were bodies underneath this thing.

Zain had heard about the Council massacre on the island, but this was something else. She stumbled into Theron. The air was fetid with the smell of corpses, the stones crushing their ribs, bodies trapped for an eternity.

Theron's hands came to her shoulders, just as they had in the coffin.

"Breathe," he instructed, his thumb tracing circles on her arms.

Footsteps sounded and his motions stilled. Zain had forgotten about the boat next to theirs. One thing about the Isle of Vis was that without the forest in its original form, there was nowhere to run or hide. A figure marched in their direction. Had someone been spying on them this entire time? At least they had numbers on their side. Theron's hand slipped to his gun, but the person's gait, stilted and worn, struck a chord within Zain.

"Anastasia?" Zain asked, head spinning from the revelation.

The woman she had saved from the bloodstripper quarters, whom she had left moaning and whimpering at her old apartment, was standing in front of them. She had not recovered. Her body slouched, long luscious hair now knotted and wet, skin pale. But there was a clarity to her that Zain had not seen since they'd first met over a decade ago.

Anastasia said, "You need to get off this island now."

CHAPTER FORTY

Anastasia

Anastasia had to warn them.

The woman's face went momentarily blank, but it was her companion who drew Anastasia's attention. Her gaze darted from his bloodstained skin to the bloodstripper trousers to his light eyes. The way he angled himself in front of the woman, a fierce warning in his tense muscles. The woman who, she was fairly certain, had saved her from the bloodstripper quarters. Her face she did not recognize—round with dark, narrow eyes and a nose that was slightly too small for her high-boned cheeks, strands of curly hair fraying from a loose braid. But her voice . . . Anastasia hadn't heard kindness in a long time, and she recognized it from a mile away.

She raised her hands in surrender.

"Listen to the ground," Anastasia repeated, this time in Janmiri. Her accent was slippery, but the choice deliberate. The word for "ground" in their language held a holier connotation, more powerful. The woman frowned at Anastasia's diction. She held a hand to the bloodstripper's arm, steadying him.

They felt the island breathe in unison, and a new terror seized Anastasia, as the woman's eyes bugged. She hadn't been imagining it.

"What the fuck was that?" the bloodstripper said, pulling the woman closer to his side.

"I don't know," Anastasia admitted. "But I don't think any of us should stay here to find out."

For some unfathomable reason, the woman jutted out her lip. "No."

"Zain," the bloodstripper warned, and Anastasia registered her name with a tinge of recognition. "I will come back with you, I promise, but it isn't safe now."

"This was never going to be safe, Theron," Zain argued. She scanned the horizon anxiously, studying the ground the way Anastasia had. "You didn't have to come with me, you can go back right now."

Anastasia couldn't comprehend the extent of their delusion. "What is it you both are doing here?" What could possibly be more important than leaving the island as it came to life beneath them? Had they not seen the bodies crushed in its grip?

The look they exchanged was so heavy she felt as though she was intruding.

"There is a reserve here somewhere," Zain replied, finally. "Do you happen to know where it is? If I can find it, we can leave."

"Not this absurdity again," Anastasia groaned. The ground refused to remain flat, and the smell of death had her stomach churning. "I have lived here all my life, with the exception of the few years I was in Tejomaya. I am the daughter of Hamish Drakos, and the only non-councilmember with as much knowledge of the island. Probably more. Believe me when I tell you that if there was a calor reserve here, I would know about it. Souls, we would have drained it during the drought!"

Zain was evidently terrified, but she shook her head. Were all Janmiris so callous with their lives, so blindly obsessed with their goals, that they were unable to see the bigger picture?

"Has there ever been anything here that was strange? Something that didn't make sense?" Zain asked, the island swelling again.

"Everything here is strange!" Anastasia cried, gasping at a sharp pain stabbing her chest.

"I know," Zain insisted, then frowned as Anastasia clutched her heart. Everything hurt, everything felt wrong. "But let's think about this logically, right? Calor has been used to power things. Whenever it's stored, it's usually causing change or a release of energy or . . . Souls, I never paid enough attention when people explained these things, but you know what I mean. Is there anything like that? Anything like—"

There was a resounding, thunderous crack, followed by a faint ringing, and the ground behind Zain split wide open, a long strip of stone emerging from the rift.

"Like that?" Anastasia asked, numbly. Zain and Theron stumbled backward, clasping each other. She seized the opportunity and grabbed their arms. "Come with me now."

Neither argued as she led them away from the stone forest, back to the toolshed. That stone—she was certain it was a root, long buried and now emerging, in a manner she didn't understand. She had witnessed once what the stone forest could do, and she had no interest in being ensnared in it. But the roots . . . How far did they extend? Were they under their feet right now? She relayed her thoughts to Zain and Theron between short breaths, then continued in silence.

She didn't realize she was humming until Theron asked, incredulously, "Are you singing 'Old Vicky' right now?"

"It helps me relax," Anastasia said, through gritted teeth. "You should try it sometime."

"That song never made sense to me," he said. "Particularly the line about—"

"Drenched in stone," Zain whispered, halting suddenly. "Calor doesn't absorb in stone, unless . . ."

"Unless what?" Anastasia asked, heart hammering against her ribs.

"Trees!" Zain said, gesturing wildly. "Trees have roots. They absorb what is in the ground. Rain used to bring them water, but now it brings them blood and, in that, calor."

Anastasia was about to ask if Zain had lost her mind when her meaning became clear. Anastasia recalled the movements of the city, the island, the way they all came to life. She thought back to the mystery of the catacombs, how they had inexplicably closed on the day of the storm. How the roots of the forest extended into the catacombs, like capillaries under skin.

She remembered the forest devouring the Council.

"On my soul," Anastasia said. "The forest is the reserve."

Everyone knew the trees had turned to rock, though no one had entertained the idea that they still lived. But hadn't the forest always felt alive? Charvi had always described it that way.

The forest remembers.

There had never been a tanker of calor, or if there had been, it'd been absorbed by the trees a long time ago. And with every rainfall, the natural reserve had grown.

"What now?" Theron asked, concerned. "You can't take the forest with you, Zain."

It was the way he said it with such affection, as though

moving a mass of rock were even a remote possibility, that tugged at Anastasia's heart. Zain deflated, and Anastasia could have cried from relief. She hadn't asked Zain about the apartment, about the rescue, about anything that mattered. The words tangled at the tip of her tongue.

"Let us go back to the boats," Anastasia said. Her questions could wait until they were back on the water. The ground shuddered, and they broke into a brisk walk, Theron and Zain slowing so Anastasia could keep up with them. On their way out, Zain caught sight of Charvi's creation, a bulky mass with sharp protrusions, towering and grand.

"That is magnificent," she said, awash with awe.

A hard lump lodged in Anastasia's throat.

"The past is a beautiful thing," she said. "Its resurrection, even more so."

CHAPTER FORTY-ONE

Iravan

I ravan should never have let them come this far.

Greed cast his partner in a cruel light. There had only been a handful of times he'd seen Dev like this: as a starving child, plunging through bloodstripper waste in search of food; before negotiations that led to shattered belongings and broken fists; right before his meeting with Inas those years ago. All endeavors had left him hollow. Hungry. Like if he didn't consume all that was in front of him, he would consume himself.

"Do you feel something?" Iravan asked, uncertain whether he was particularly unstable given the heavy calor-siphoning tools he carried. They had walked a quarter of the island's perimeter, around the back ports toward the front harbor, where most of the Geng turbines were rumored to be—according to Dev, anyway, who was more familiar with the layout of the land by virtue of his spies. Iravan tried not to think about how much Dev had learned from his back dealings with Hamish. He soaked in each inch of the island, wondering instead how the fine, gray silt under his feet had emerged from the gravel of

Tejomaya, if the strange marble homes were too heavy for the island to bear.

"It's an island; it probably moves on water," Dev replied, distractedly. Iravan wasn't convinced. Dev paused over a patch of bare land behind the harbor. "The catacombs should be here somewhere. This has to be it."

They had tested several sections already, probing the land, expecting pale-yellow liquid to fill their vessels. But there had only been the faintest trickle. With each stop, Dev grew increasingly agitated, and Iravan swore to the souls that he would do anything for this to work so they could just get out. There was something about the island that wasn't sitting well with him.

Glass shattered as Dev threw his tool to the ground. "Does this shit even work?"

The island flinched.

Iravan straightened. He had not imagined that. Mariam had warned him of all they didn't understand about calor—about what it could do in large amounts—and he had fended her off in favor of his friend's greed.

Iravan knelt, palms flat on the ground. A rumble reached his fingertips.

"Dev, we have to go," he said. "Something is wrong."

"Are you out of your mind?" Dev said. He was looking at Iravan with an expression he usually reserved for the Gengs: disbelieving and repulsed. "We're not leaving here without calor. We haven't even been inside yet—"

But Iravan could hear the faintest reverberations that weren't just Dev's complaints echoing back at them. He quietened his friend with one sharp gesture. Synchronously, they drew their guns, toward the voices that were a hair louder than the idle hum from the nearest turbines.

Closer, and he was certain the voices were headed toward the harbor. A few more steps, and they would be revealed. But then he heard a name, and he called for Dev, but it was too late.

Too late to block Dev's view.

Too late to calm his fury.

Too late to stop him from spinning out of position, his gun pointed at a leech.

Zain screamed, dropping to the ground. The man next to her, a bloodstripper, swung around wildly. Dev gave the guard a look of warning, and Iravan could do nothing but watch.

A gun clicked, but it wasn't Dev's.

"You shoot them, and I'll blow your brains out."

If a voice were honey, hers was caked hard on the comb, but Iravan could smell the scent of her words, the luscious feel of her intonation, no matter how long it had been left out to dry. Anastasia stepped out from the thicket, gun pointed steadily at Dev, the blood-drenched hem of her skirt clinging to her calves. Frame less willowy, sharper, like a warrior's spear struck into the ground.

"Hey, Ravi," she said, softly, sparing him the slightest glance, but that was all they had ever needed. Over a decade later, and he could still see past her act. Ana, his Ana, was angry and . . . resigned. He ached to reach out to her. He'd desperately tried to stomp out this desire the day she'd left him, but like everything else he'd done since then, he failed.

"Drakos," Dev said. "You just won't die, will you?"

She smirked. "Without you by my side?" she crooned. "I could never make it that easy. Now, put the gun down."

The guard stepped in front of Zain, to the leech's dismay. She elbowed him hard, but any efforts to make him budge were futile. The island creaked, sending stones tumbling. Suddenly, Iravan was aware of just how precarious their position was, that even though they faced one another in a perilous stance, they were ignoring the largest threat.

Mariam's premonitions drummed in his head.

"You really are a greedy bitch," Dev said, oblivious to the way the wind wrapped around them, the ground shuddering at more frequent intervals. Spittle flew from his mouth. "You belong under my feet."

Anastasia tilted her head. "Don't pretend you're here for righteous reasons, Devraj. You are no better than me."

"I am *nothing* like you," Dev seethed, gun still pointed at Zain and the guard. They glanced at Anastasia and gave her the most indiscernible of nods.

What had they been doing here, if not collecting calor themselves? Iravan looked them over, but they had no siphoning tools. Dread clutched his chest as the ground throbbed.

"I know a big boy like you doesn't like to do what he's told, but if you want your balls to stay attached to your body, you'll listen," Anastasia warned. "My aim is still good."

Dev addressed Iravan, the whites of his eyes stained red. "Are you just going to stand there and let her speak to me like that?"

There was something in the way Anastasia spoke, the fear Zain wore, the way the Isle of Vis showed signs of strange and unusual life, that felt *wrong*. For once, Iravan ignored Dev.

"Why are you here?" he asked Anastasia. Of all the times he'd envisioned seeing her again, it never went like this. In some fantasies, he plunged a knife into her throat; in others, he was on his knees, begging for forgiveness. It was funny how people placed so much emphasis on *why*. "Why" demanded reasoning, "why" asked for closure, but he wasn't as concerned with the whys as the hows, the in-betweens of all that had come to be, the gaps in his understanding of pain. *How did we get here? How have you been? Did you miss me at all?*

Do you miss her like I do?

"It doesn't matter," Anastasia replied, exchanging another glance with the leech. "But we need to get off this island." She told him about the stone forest, the way it had eaten her people and craved more. The pressure in Iravan's chest built. Anastasia added, "The forest is the reserve."

"That's not possible," he said, repeating what Mariam explained in her home. "Stone doesn't absorb blood like that."

"Stone trees do," replied Anastasia. "There never was a reserve in the sense we'd thought. The island was the last place with a large system of trees, and when the rains fell, most of the calor went to the roots."

All that calor, stored up in a forest that spread across most of the island. If a little bit of calor buildup had wreaked havoc on his slums, what would it do here? Anastasia studied him, reading his thoughts like she used to.

"She's lying," Dev hissed. "She wants it for herself! She's got another Geng there with her, and that traitorous leech—"

"She's not!" Zain cried, louder and angrier than Iravan thought her capable. "She's telling the truth." The guard held her elbow tightly, holding her back from launching at Dev.

Dev laughed, and it raised Iravan's gooseflesh like the tip of a blade running down one's back.

"Wow," he declared, and dropped the gun. "I have seen a lot of things in my life, but this"—he pointed between Anastasia and Zain with his loose weapon—"this, I did not think I would ever see."

Dev turned to Zain.

"Have you told her yet? The price of your loyalty? What she has had to pay for you to be here, doing her dirty work?"

Zain's face drained of color, her hand wrapping around the guard's in a death grip. Anastasia looked as confused as Iravan felt.

"She killed your child."

CHAPTER FORTY-TWO

Anastasia

he killed your child.

S Somehow, Anastasia got out the question. "What do you mean?"

Iravan trembled like a loose leaf. Maybe that night, he would have crumbled just like she had, but Anastasia hadn't remained to watch it happen. She'd been consumed by rage, blamed him for the loss she felt. If he had been there that night, if he hadn't picked that stupid fight, if she hadn't left their daughter in someone else's care . . . And then he'd gone to Matthieu, told the guard about Surya, their precious secret, the child whose existence they'd sworn to keep from the people on the Isle.

How quickly her love for him had mutated into something ugly and bloodthirsty. Vicious, like her.

For many years, Anastasia had convinced herself that Iravan had remained upright while she'd descended, because it was incomprehensible that the man she'd known would plummet as far into the abyss as she had. Looking at him now—the quiver of his lips, his shattered expression—she knew he would have held her hand in the fall.

Your child.

Our child.

Anastasia gasped, but her barrel remained pointed at Dev. His smug expression flickered, then solidified into angry creases.

"You set the fire that night, didn't you, Z? We were all busy with that meeting, locked in the Temple, and you saw an opportunity."

"No," Iravan said, hoarsely. "No, the fire was an accident."

"I assure you it was not," Dev said, daring to move closer to Anastasia. "It was intentional, an attempt to kill me, and the woman you are trying to save was the one responsible. Your daughter was such a sweet little girl, wasn't she, Drakos? She had none of your cruelty, and she was wiped out just like that."

"I did set it," Zain whispered, her dark-brown skin ashen.

Anastasia could hear nothing but the confession that came from the girl who'd rescued her, torrential.

"Dev set the meeting between Inas and you that day, to facilitate new peace talks between all parties," Zain told Anastasia. "He asked me to accompany him to incite a little fear during the processions, to smoke the place out. I thought I could get rid of him that day. I was so angry with him, for all he had done. To me. The fire was supposed to be contained, but it grew out of control."

For all he had done to her. The past reconstructed itself. She remembered Dev favoring a child, Dev with his arm around a teenage girl, Dev's sinister smile. They'd all ignored it. Across from her, Iravan was statuesque.

Tears ran down Zain's face, but she didn't wipe them away.

"I swear to you, I did not know she was in there. I did not know you left her with Inas . . . I ran in there to save her, I promise, I tried. But I got trapped in one of the outer rooms, and it was too late."

There were angry red lines running down Zain's forearms. Her nails sawed a ruthless path. All these years, Anastasia had created her own prison, punishing Iravan, punishing Baruna, punishing anyone whose life had made her turn away for a lethal moment. Punishing herself. Now, she was face to face with the person who had deserved that wrath all along, but Anastasia found she didn't have any wrath to give.

Do you have regrets, Ana?

We all need help sometimes.

Anastasia fought to breathe.

"Dev . . . ," Iravan said.

Surprise rippled through Dev's face, as Iravan stepped away from him.

"Did you not hear her?" Dev asked. "She set it herself to *kill* me! This little bitch didn't learn her lesson well enough that night—"

Theron might have lunged at Dev first. Or perhaps it was Iravan. No human could beat a bullet, though.

Two piercing gunshots sent Iravan and Theron sprawling. Their heads rose, panicked, assessing their bodies to find no damage. Anastasia stared at her target. Zain met her eye, her own silver pistol emitting the faintest trail of smoke.

A single rose bloomed from Dev's shoulder, right next to his heart. Her own sharp inhale cleaved the world in half.

Then, there was the crack of Iravan's knees as he fell next to his brother.

Then, there was the girl wrestling against the guard's arms, which were locked across her chest.

Then, there was the island, awoken by a man's blood on its massacred body.

Dev was frozen in shock, his gun dropping from his hand. Anastasia had imagined his death would cause a visceral shift in energy or, at the very least, take its time, his life force fading like a wilting tree. But Dev's body fell abruptly, and the only disturbance was to the dirt around his limp frame. Anticlimactic, the demise of a man so many had considered indomitable. Then again, did not all formidable men fall to hubris?

Another tremble, and a series of cracks. Anastasia gasped as roots burst through the earth, and the stray stones around the edge of the thicket rose like raindrops in reverse, melding into the nearest protrusions. Theron tried dragging Zain toward the boat.

Anastasia had forgotten about the boat. She couldn't make out what Theron said, couldn't see past the empty look in Dev's eyes.

"You know something," she said to Iravan. He showed no surprise at her appraisal. They had always worked like this. They recognized each other's depravity, their hunger and fear in a world that rejected both.

"If the forest is the reserve, then there's pressure building up within the stone," he said, thickly. "We came here to siphon calor, to relieve some of it, but I didn't realize it would be in the trees. There's too much, it will take out the entire city. The entire country, if we aren't able to stop it. You should have seen what it did to the slums, Ana. I don't know how to help them all."

The sound of her name from his mouth was the sweetest poison. Almost enough to coat his revelation, the truth it revealed.

They had to break open the forest, let out what had been trapped inside.

"There's too much in here," Anastasia said to him, her hand on her chest. He followed the path of her fingers, and for a moment, she thought he would reach out, press the tips of her hand to his mouth. Reduce the size of this world to a single touch. In some ways, Iravan had started her world, and their life together had ended it.

The calor in her body sang to what lived under the land It dragged her down, down, down, and she never knew how difficult it could be to stand, to exist. It was as she stepped away from Iravan, toward the forest, that he seemed to realize what she intended to do. His eyes cleared. Confusion, anger, defiance. He'd always been so easy to read.

"Ana, what are you doing?" he asked.

She wanted to hold his face, to mourn with him. But nothing would suffice now, not when the earth threatened to swallow them whole. Would one embrace make up for ten years of grief, of love lost? It would be too much and too little. She had a commitment to honor, a decision to make.

Other souls she had to see.

Calor in the body produces a burst of energy, destroying everything in one's surroundings.

Her hands fished in her skirt, drawing the syringes she had taken from the shed. Zain, who was resisting Theron, gave a shout of protest.

"No," Iravan shouted, leaping up. "No, I cannot let you."

"I'm sorry," she said, and before any of them could stop her, she pointed her gun at him and shot him in the leg.

He cried out, and she hated that this would be the last time she would hear him. That this pain would be the last thing he remembered of her. But hadn't that always been the way they'd shared one another?

"What did you do?" Zain screamed, falling beside Iravan. Theron knelt at Iravan's leg too, and they both applied pressure to the wound. Iravan's face was scrunched in pain, and there was blood, so much blood spilling through Zain's fingers that Anastasia worried she'd shot him somewhere he would not recover from.

She stuck the syringe in her arm. A rush of calor swept over her, and this time, she knew it was enough. It sloshed through her veins, expanded her essence. The times she'd walked under the rains were child's play. This was what it actually felt like to live on the edge of death.

"No, you can't, you can't do this," Zain cried, but she didn't move, her attention torn between Iravan and Anastasia. As Anastasia moved toward the swelling stone, she told Zain a final truth. Then, she turned and ran to the forest.

It had transformed again, no longer distinct trees or a molten mass. It was a wall, a cracking mountain, a metamorphosis that showed once and for all what the land was capable of. Anastasia summoned the last dregs of her strength and raced through the nearest opening. The stone surrounding her trembled, closing in on her. The deeper she went, the harder it became to move. It was so dark, so cold.

Behind her, the cries of her companions drowned beneath the shrieking land. Anastasia looked up and reveled at how she could see the sky from within the mountain, a touch of red in the midst of black. The rift rippled. Power rushed through her.

Anastasia felt the beat of every passing moment, shaping the world that was to come. Her end, like her beginning, like her existence, was a glorious contradiction. She would come apart and come together, all at once.

It burned. For the first time, she understood the meaning of rebirth, how a phoenix rose from its ashes, how sometimes things needed to be razed to the ground to be built anew.

The pressure grew blinding, suffocating, and Anastasia let it push her deep. Around her, the souls of all those trapped shifted in recognition. In embrace.

Somewhere, someplace, Iravan called her name.

In the flames, she saw the sun.

CHAPTER FORTY-THREE

Zain

Anastasia had disappeared beyond the rocks. A column of fire shot into the air, followed by a plume of yellow vapor that poured and poured and poured. Zain knew what happened when there was too much calor in a body. She just wasn't sure Anastasia's sacrifice would be enough. The land continued to swell.

"No!" Iravan cried. He crawled, dragging his useless leg behind him. Anastasia had known. She'd known he would follow her into the fire, and her last gift to him was a bullet to the leg. Zain's eyes burned.

There was so much she had wanted to say, to explain to the mother of a child whose life she had stolen. She'd considered coming clean at the apartment, but she'd lost her nerve, thought Anastasia too delirious to receive such a groundbreaking confession. And then they had both taken the shot.

She looked at Dev, eyes unseeing. She didn't know whose bullet had hit his chest, didn't know who she wanted it to be. She had expected relief upon his demise, maybe a twisted sadness.

Not this confusion. For once, she didn't know which path her life would take. It was terrifying, she realized, to have a choice.

Then again, the island might rip that away from her too.

The ground lurched, sending Iravan rolling until he slammed into her, knocking her down. Theron helped her up, frantically scanning their surroundings. The center of the island had inflated, putting them on a rising slope, like a balloon that was about to pop, and not even Anastasia's sacrifice had relieved the pressure needed. The island was about to splinter or erupt, and now that Zain was there and had confronted all the monstrosities of her past, she really did not want to die.

"If we run now, we can take the boat back," Theron yelled, but there was no conviction in his voice. He knew as well as she did: no place would be safe once the permafrost exploded.

It flies.

The last words Anastasia Drakos had said to her. She had seen it, the plane that lay beyond the toolshed, the resurrection of the past, the golden era of aviation.

When they could touch the sky.

Zain relayed her wild plan to Theron. Iravan curled into himself on the ground.

"It doesn't fly!" Theron gaped, throwing his hands up. "If we take the boat *right now—*"

"We won't make it!" Zain screamed. They didn't have time for this. She took another look at Iravan, then at Theron.

"Zain," Theron said, reaching for her. "Whatever you're thinking—"

"Get him and yourself to the boat" was all she said, digging her nails into Theron's arms before pushing him away.

And then she was off, the ground a slippery thing, the mutated trees a hard border. But Zain had lived her life slipping

through spaces too small for her, too much for her, too dangerous and wild. She didn't look to see if Theron obeyed, but even if
he tried, he would not be able to follow her there. For once, this
was something she could do.

The Tejomaya in the island recognized her body; they were
so alike in so many ways. Both had been ripped away from their
homes and forced to conform to a life they had not chosen. Both
regarded death as a cloaked figure that peered over the occasional corner. And Zain wondered if the island called her kin,
someone who feared death in the very bones of her body but was
prepared to face it for a love that superseded all.

She hoped it was true, because she had much to ask of it.

"Where is it?" she yelled, wind shrieking between the trees,
the sky rippling like a freshly torn carcass, prepared for a scaven-
ger's feast. The ground swung up, and she flew over its ridges, and
then she was falling, her breath vacuumed out of her body. Her
teeth rattled, and she searched for anywhere to brace her aching
limbs.

Finally, her knees crashed into gravel. She was on the other
side of the island, farther from Tejomaya, all the way at the bottom. The forest had expanded, and from this angle she realized
how impossible it would be to find her way back to Theron and
Iravan. She had to find the plane.

Dust rose in the air, clouding her vision, but she crawled toward the shore. Surely, she could see it by now, it wouldn't be that
hard to find, and then . . .

Two long wings appeared, and a rotor. For a moment, Zain
could do nothing but stare at this relic of the past, of their connection to the skies.

The island hissed, and she sprinted to the plane.

Souls bless that man in the market. The plane's body was

narrow, holding space for only two people, but its fuselage was long, its flat, thick wings doubly so. Coiled rope sat twined to her side, and she fastened it around her seat, tying its ends into two thick fisherman's knots and hanging them off the edge.

A large bag lay at the foot of the pilot's seat, filled to the brim with even more calor injections. Zain winced, thinking of Anastasia, as she started hooking up the vessels, hot liquid flowing into the jet system. This had been built by a gatherer, and she'd left supplies behind.

Kicking the empty bag out of the way, Zain settled into the seat.

"Okay, you can figure this out."

Her hands flitted over the various controls in the cockpit. This was not the same as watching a stupid model. Haphazardly, she pressed down on the black button that she guessed was the fuel knob and pushed the throttle. Just when she thought the calor was most definitely not enough, the machine creaked and it *moved*.

But it was moving toward the mountain. "No no no," Zain said, pulling so hard at the yoke that she worried it would break, and by the souls' mercy, the plane redirected. Could she use the edge of the island as a runway? There was only one way to find out.

It was bizarre, seeing the waters from one side and a rising mass of rock on the other. The wheels below the plane cracked as it flattened a path near the back of the shore, moving faster and faster until Zain was sure this was a mistake, that there was no way this hurtling body of metal would rise *off* the land, that she would certainly end up in the water and drown, when the nose lifted.

Weightlessness tugged at her gut, and then she was off. Flying.

The sky loomed, the rift a horrific maw as always, but there was something different about it up close, from where the land grew small and the waters appeared more blue than gray.

This was what it felt like to have a choice. To soar above it all, wings no longer clipped.

Then, she spotted them. Boats, dozens, like a swarm of black ants on the edge of the water, coming toward a steaming island. They were too organized to be evacuees, and she knew in her heart it was bloodstrippers, coming for the reserve. Had they seen the explosion? Were they turning away? Maybe this was what it was like to be an ascended soul, to see the future etched out, and to be helpless in its wake.

But there was one thing she wouldn't give up on.

The wind mauled her cheeks as Zain steered the plane back to the other side of the island. "Come on," she swore, her heart tearing as she searched for Iravan and Theron. She spotted them near the harbor and pitched the creaking metal body toward them. Theron waved. Her heart dropped at how he clung to the trees hooked right above the waters. The land had distended so severely that she could touch it if she leaned out.

Zain pulled at the air brake and yoke, hissing as the plane jerked and veered sharply toward the ground. Theron shouted, "Go!"

There was no chance of that.

"Prepare to jump!"

Theron looked like he would kill her, but he and Iravan separated, the latter on one good leg, his other bound in a makeshift tourniquet, as she careened toward them, knowing they would have one chance, a matter of seconds, to get this right. The plane clattered, wheels bouncing off the ground, and she tried slowing without losing momentum. One final prayer and she tossed both ropes, returning to steer. The sea was a still gray, too close for her liking. They needed elevation immediately. Zain maneuvered the yoke as she passed the men, who ducked to avoid the lethal cut of the plane's trembling wings. They grabbed onto the trailing ropes just in time.

"We're too heavy," Theron yelled, heaving himself up the rope before slamming into shuddering metal. Zain ignored him, driving the groaning, unbalanced plane, but they were still too close to land. "Zain!" Theron cried in alarm.

"I know!" she snapped, praying he wasn't right, that they weren't too heavy, that they'd get just another inch of lift.

The yoke strained in her sweaty palms. The island whimpered its last warning, and they skated right above the sea before lifting to the sky.

Zain couldn't breathe. "Hold on tight!"

With that, she set off across the Soulless Sea. Iravan let out a howl, expending every bit of energy he must've had left to topple next to Zain, moaning. Blood pooled onto the seat, warming Zain's thigh.

"Are those . . ." Theron's voice was faint as he clambered in on the other side. Zain was too focused on steering them up, up, up, but she imagined the fleet realizing their error, far too late. In that moment, they were all bound by their fates. Zain refused to go with them.

The island let go, like it had waited just long enough. They'd cut it real close, she thought, as the sheer force of the island's release caught the plane's wings and sent them flying into smoke and darkness.

CHAPTER FORTY-FOUR

Iravan

The world looked like shattered pottery, and for a moment, he couldn't piece it back together. The pain in his thigh devoured him whole, and the impact from the crash had damn near taken him out.

Souls, why hadn't it taken him out?

The guard was on one side, Zain on the other. "We need to move," the bloodstripper said, his jaw clenched as he pointed upward. The air smelled rotten. "As high up as we can go."

Iravan looked over the cliff. They had crashed into one of the hills of Tejomaya, and the island smoked as though it were a burned dish, flaming liquid pouring from its heart and into the sea.

Souls, the sea.

"Oh no," Zain whispered. Iravan watched, stunned, as the water pulled back. He winced, trying to stand. The heat of the bullet was melting his bone. Zain slung his arm over her shoulder, Theron mimicking her, and they raced up the hill, leaving the plane behind. Iravan nearly bit his tongue off trying not to scream because, fuck, his leg wouldn't matter if they didn't get high enough in time. They stumbled, and he hated how he was slowing them down. Zain panted hard as they arrived at the top. He collapsed, knowing there was nowhere higher they could go.

"We might be okay," the guard said, quietly, and Iravan turned away, unwilling to address the lie there. They might survive, but nothing was okay about watching the waters swallow their city. Fire and water met in a fierce show of strength, a gruesome maelstrom, as the earth bowed down.

The searing pain in Iravan's chest threatened to split him in half.

Someone said his name. The woman who had taken his family from him. Zain's face crumpled, her silhouette stark against a backdrop of smoke and ash and salt. Behind her, his city was underwater, and he wished it would rush up the hills and pull him under too. But the froth ended far too low, and all he could see was the way the guard's fingers draped across Zain's collarbones. In a flash, those were his fingers around Anastasia's neck, snaking through her hair and tracing her lips.

Gone.

"Iravan," Zain repeated, touching his shoulder.

He pulled away, a blistering pain shooting through his leg at the sudden movement. The bullet was still lodged in there. He should remove it, but he didn't want to let go of the pain. If it was all he would have left of her, then that would have to be enough. Grief tore through him in a way he had not thought possible since the night of the fire.

Zain's confession echoed, a surreal memory. Maybe if he bashed his skull against stone, it would all cease to exist. Maybe if he threw his body off the edge of the cliff, he would wake up from this nightmare.

For many years, Iravan had tried to string together an alternate course of action that might have resulted in a different outcome. He had begun with what he knew to be true, that a meeting aimed toward peace had made it so he would never know peace himself. He hadn't been there, because he and Anastasia had fought earlier, and Dev's presence had been sufficient. Ana hadn't been there, because Baruna had taken ill suddenly and Charvi needed her to ask the bloodstrippers for medications they didn't have access to. Ana had left their child in the Head Acolyte's care, and he knew they had done everything in their power to save their baby. Inas's charred remains had been found wrapped around a tiny skeleton. Anastasia had left, heartbroken, blaming him for their loss, and he'd lashed out in turn, telling the bloodstrippers about her true involvement with the dons.

All these decisions had led to the brutal fissure in Iravan's life. Before Ana, and after Ana. Before love, and after the void that followed.

It was then that Samiah's words returned. *You light the fire in all of us, but you're never there to watch us burn.* It was worse than that. Zain was yet another piece of collateral damage. She had burned for his decisions too, and he had watched it happen.

He'd watched a boisterous girl turn inward, watched his friend become cruel, watched the world tip beyond the point of return, and he had done nothing. His hands were covered in as much blood as theirs. This was a shared sin, this inability to look beyond one's own life. To not see how others hurt and how they inflicted pain.

No more, he told himself.

"You were a child," Iravan said. It was all he could offer and maybe all that needed to be said.

Quiet settled between them, punctured by the waves crashing over the city below.

"What now?" Zain asked, after a while. The wind whistled in response. Theron shrugged, settling next to her, pulling her close.

Iravan exhaled. "Now we find a way to move on."

EPILOGUE

Baruna looked over the stretched salt plains and the ethereal reflection of the sprawling gray skies. Some days, she wondered how the horizon could ever be torn in half, and though she had seen the rift herself, cried until her tears blended with crimson raindrops, it still felt a distant memory.

She spun a silver coin between her fingers. No sun yet, but maybe someday. Despite the years, the inscription of the coin's rays remained clear on the metal. One day, light would break through.

Today was an important day in Urjan. In the fifteen years she'd spent learning the corners of a country not surrounded by torched waters, she liked to spend this day alone. It was a strange tradition, given that the Returning was born from the volatile destruction of Tejomaya, but they had made it out. Still, solitary celebration was something her mother had enjoyed as well, and while there was little she could recover from her own memories of her family, she reserved this one day in honor of the stories she'd been told. At least, for as long as her duties allowed.

"Baru?" Mariam climbed over the sand barristers that bordered the plains. Few people came this far out, but Mariam enjoyed living on the horizons. Coming home had brightened her like nothing else had, eyes sparkling despite the gray in her hair and the creak of her joints. "It's getting late," she said, smiling at the sight of Baruna with her feet dangling over the plains. "The children will be waiting."

Baruna sighed. It was one of Mariam's greatest talents to know when to stay silent, and it was in that quiet that she walked Baruna back to town.

The city of Mahala was bustling with people. She couldn't help but smile at the children squealing in the square, playing games reminiscent of her childhood. Except here, there was laughter, as they leaped between empty spaces, and a cool breeze to brush their cheeks. They'd spent ten years building a home underground, and then five years earlier, they'd been able to ascend, to see a sky more gray than red, breathe air a little clearer, a little sweeter. She inhaled the sounds and smells, hungrily bottling up the joy.

"How is he today?" she asked, when they arrived outside the squat brick building they had created as a school.

Mariam smiled weakly. "As good as can be. But he is looking forward to this. I think you'll have a good session."

Baruna rolled her eyes but reined in her expression as she walked into the classroom, finding Iravan glaring at the gathered children. They whispered about him and he knew it, but if he minded, she didn't know. He walked with a cane now, his leg never fully healed from that bullet many years back. Some said a piece of it stayed there, embedded in his bone.

His expression softened considerably at Mariam's arrival. Baruna still wasn't certain what had passed between them. When he'd first arrived, they had been cold, distant, but the years had brought them closer together. She had gathered there had been someone else, a shadow that hung between them, but as he wrapped an arm around Mariam and pressed a kiss to her cheek, she wondered if their light would have been possible without the dark.

The children giggled at the display of affection, and Baruna clapped to demand their attention. Dozens of brown and black heads turned in her direction, such a stark contrast to the classrooms she used to know. They hushed, as more people slid through the door. Nerves knotted in Baruna's gut, and she grinned at Zain. She should have been teaching this; after all, the legends of Mahala were centered on the woman who stood quietly at the back of the room. But Zain had refused, content with her rose garden, no matter how much Baruna had insisted. As always, Theron could be found to her right, observing.

"Okay," she started, walking over to the giant cloth-covered structure that took up over half the room. How Leander and Laila had transported this here, she didn't know, but they'd been working on it all year. "Everyone, meet *Surya*."

Behind the crowd, Iravan's face gave nothing away. Mariam beamed. Baruna rubbed her hands together, then gripped the edges of the frayed cloth, pulling it down to reveal a plane. She grinned wickedly at the children.

"Today, we are going to learn the principles of flight."

ACKNOWLEDGMENTS

I'd long accepted that this book would never see the light of day. I started writing it during a difficult time, and in many ways, I clawed myself into a place of hope right alongside these characters. After all, if they could go through all *that* and land on their feet, then so could I! They couldn't have done it without their community, and now it's time to thank mine.

My first thank-you will always be to my wonderful agent, Allegra Martschenko. Very few people understand the depths of what you have done for me, and I must have been a saint in a past life to have met you in this one. Thank you for being a genius critique partner, the fiercest advocate, and the kindest friend. Also, the funniest person I know. ☺

Thank you to Zoranne Host for making my dreams come true! It was one thing for you to champion this book, but it was an entirely unexpected bonus to connect with you the way we have. I can't wait to keep blowing up your phone with all my thoughts on our favorite books.

Thank you to all the Fantasy & Frens subscribers for your support! It's been such a pleasure getting to know you all—this would literally not be possible without you.

To my editor, Zhui Ning Chang, you are so brilliant. Your

incisive feedback breathed life into this book, and I can't believe some of my favorite moments (and characters!) didn't exist before you. You have left me a better writer.

The entire team at Bindery—it's an honor to be a part of your first season. Meghan Harvey and Matt Kaye, you are bright lights in this industry, and I cannot wait to see what you accomplish. Thank you to CJ Alberts for your marketing wizardry and Charlotte Strick for your impeccable design eye.

Cat O'Neil, I will never get over the beauty of this cover. My jaw is still on the floor. Thank you for bringing this world to life with such care and detail.

Thank you to the entire Girl Friday team. Sara Addicott, you kept this process running smoothly from start to finish. Thank you to Tiffany Taing for the kind and meticulous copyedit and Jenna Justice for the careful proofread.

My endless thanks to Brittani Hilles and Lavender PR for all your efforts in getting this book into readers' hands.

Sana Z. Ahmed and Emily Charlotte, you are my rocks!!! Not only would Iravan's POV be so much worse without your feedback, but so would my mental health. Thank you for reminding me to pursue joy above all. Valo Wing, your unwavering faith in this book kept me going on the hardest days. I treasure you dearly!

To everyone in There or Square: K. A. Cobell, Megan Davidhizar, Aimee Davis, Christine Arnold, Channelle Desamours, Lally Hunter-Innis, P. H. Low, and Laurie Lascos. You've held me up through tears, manuscript swaps, and plank-offs. I would not be the writer I am without you.

To the Raft: A. M. Kvita, Casey Colaine, Samantha Bansil, Amanda Helms, O. O. Sangoyomi, and Shay Kauwe, I'm forever grateful to sail with you!

Esmie Jikiemi-Pearson, thank you for being the first person to believe I could do this.

Pitch Wars Class of 2021, I would throw all the waffles for you, and Avengers of Color Class of 2021, I couldn't have asked for a better welcome to the writing community. I'm rooting for each and every one of you!

Tammy Kung, all of this started because you told me if I wrote a book, you'd read it. Thank you for being my first reader and for readily whipping out your guitar when I needed a song for this book. Also, happy birthday. ♡

Thank you to Kamayani Gaur for holding me down despite brutal time-zone differences, and to Sanja Knezevic, Achsa Rothe, Maddie Cruciano, Vaqar Syed, Gigi Yu, Shaan Asif, Rowan Curry, Alison Jeng, and everyone in QTT for tending to my sanity. I would never have started (let alone finished) this book without you.

Thank you to Kathy for the brain-altering conversations on shame and compassion.

Last but never least, to my parents, who have given me everything. Thank you for pulling me out of the darkest of places, lifting me up with countless adventures, and always putting a book in my hand, even at the dining table.

THANK YOU

This book would not have been possible without the support from the Fantasy & Frens community, with a special thank-you to the Dragon Fren members:

Adlitam
Alina Dennis
Ashslibrary23
Ava Gaughen
Becca Langewicz
Braeden Weir
Brett Foster
Calista Wielgos
Caralee Stover
Celi
Christian Bellman
Courtney Wyant
Cristina Rowe
David B. Kranenburg
Fairiedancr
Faze
Fowzi Abdulle

GabbyVegaa
Goodestmich
Hannah Hawes
Haylee Slocum
Hhegwood
Ian Beck
Janine Chambers
Jessica McFarland
Jordan Peterson
Kaitlin Long
KristineAalby
Lilacfairy16
Lillie McAdams
Lindsay Chung
Liam Crowley
midnight91princess
Michelle Campbell
Mtreiber

Natasha Renee
Nicholas Houser
ReadingWuv
Russell Boone
Sadie Doucet
Sammie Gillam
Savaira
Shyla Northup
Stevie N. Slawson
Taylor Throneberry
V.J. Hugaux
Whitney Massey

ABOUT THE AUTHOR

S. HATI is a speculative fiction writer, currently residing in the Bay Area. She holds a bachelor's degree in microbiology from UCLA and a master's degree in biotechnology from Johns Hopkins University and pretends to use them both while working in health tech. She writes about brown girls in strange worlds that straddle the line between magic and science.

Fantasy & Frens is an imprint of Bindery, a book publisher powered by community.

We're inspired by the way book tastemakers have reinvigorated the publishing industry. With strong taste and direct connections with readers, book tastemakers have illuminated self-published, backlisted, and overlooked authors, rocketing many to bestseller lists and the big screen.

This book was chosen by Zoranne Host in close collaboration with the Fantasy & Frens community on Bindery. By inviting tastemakers and their reading communities to participate in publishing, Bindery creates opportunities for deserving authors to reach readers who will love them.

Visit Fantasy & Frens for a thriving
bookish community and bonus content:

fantasyandfrens.binderybooks.com

ZORANNE HOST is a book reviewer from Cleveland, Ohio, who shares her love for fantasy with over 150,000 followers across TikTok, Instagram, and YouTube. Zoranne has a highly engaged audience and is the founder of the online fantasy book club Fantasy & Frens, one of the largest groups on Fable with over 13,000 members.

TIKTOK.COM/@ZORANNE_

INSTAGRAM.COM/ZORANNE_

TWITTER.COM/ZORANNE_